TWICE THE GUNS! TWICE THE GALS!

GIANT SPECIAL EDITION

BUCKSKIN

FIGHT TO THE FINISH

About ten feet away from Morgan, Hoff was groaning and trying to get up. Morgan couldn't see, but he knew he was between Hoff and Dowd.

Suddenly, Dowd cried out, "I've got you now!" A gun went off and Hoff screamed and a body fell. In the dark Dowd was yelling and the gun fired four times, the bullets ricocheting off the brick walls. Something hit Morgan in the head and he fell on his face. There wasn't a sound except for Dowd coming closer, his feet scraping through the rubbish. Morgan tried to move, but his muscles wouldn't work. He could hear all right, though. Dowd was bending over him. He heard the hammer being cocked for the killing shot....

There was a sudden scuffle in the dark and Dowd cried out. Morgan smelled perfume, and he felt Dowd being lifted away and something like a small-caliber-pistol shot cracked in the dark. But it wasn't a pistol shot; the sound was different. Like a neck being snapped.

Morgan didn't hear anything else.

D0711593

GIANT SPECIAL EDITION

BUCKSKIN

BAWDY HOUSE
Kit Dalton

LEISURE BOOKS **NEW YORK CITY**

A LEISURE BOOK®

September 1994

Published by

Dorchester Publishing Co., Inc.
276 Fifth Avenue
New York, NY 10001

Printed in the United States of America.

BUCKSKIN

BAWDY HOUSE

GIANT SPECIAL EDITION

Chapter One

"Finding my wife may not be easy," Derwent Bullock said. "I didn't tell Chief Bender everything."

Morgan waited for Bullock to continue. It was a late September evening and the heavy curtains were drawn in the library of the mansion on Nob Hill. The San Francisco wet season had started early and rain swept the windowpanes. A huge fire gave off the scent of cedar and the light of the gasolier overhead was reflected brightly by polished tables, dully by the leather bindings of many books.

Morgan held a stein of beer, Bullock a snifter of brandy. Deep in his chair, Bullock was saying, "Chief Bender speaks very highly of you. You've known him for a long time, I take it."

"Not that long," Morgan said. "A few years, since Kansas City. An old friend was in jail for something he didn't do. Bender helped me to clear him, get him out. Haven't seen Bender since then, not till today."

Morgan didn't like being questioned, didn't like having his story checked against Bender's. If Bullock didn't trust him on Bender's say-so, the hell with him.

"I see." Bullock inhaled the brandy fumes. "How much did Bender tell you?"

"Not a lot. That your wife was missing and you wanted somebody to find her. Not the police, not the detective agencies—somebody who wouldn't talk, wouldn't sneak the story to the newspapers."

Bullock fiddled with his glass. "Yes. That's the nuts and bolts of it, but of course there's more."

Morgan took a good look at him. A feisty little bugger in his sixties, he still had a Yankee twang after forty years in California. A very wealthy man, Bender said, owner of the biggest department store in San Francisco.

"Mr. Bullock," Morgan said. "It would save time if you just told me the whole story straight out. Then we can decide if we can do business. You may not want me."

"That's sensible, but you see Chief Bender wasn't very forthcoming about you. Of course, he's very busy with this police chiefs' convention at the Palace. He did say you might be the right man—at least I should keep you in mind—after I explained my problem. I know the chief from my visits to Kansas City. My brother has a department store there, as I have here." Bullock smiled with well-made false teeth. "The chief is rather a close-mouthed man. 'Talk to Morgan,' he said."

That sounded like Bender all right. "I don't know if he told you I raise horses in Idaho, mostly. I'm still rebuilding the place after a bad loss—and doing pretty well at it, too—but now and then I have to be away, looking to make extra money."

"No," Bullock said. "What you really mean is, you have to get away from the grind. Get off on your own, be free for a while."

Shrewd little bastard. "I guess you're right. This time I was helping an Englishman set up a horse ranch near Eureka, northern part of this state, owned some land there. Rich man, but worked as a ranch hand at my place in Idaho to learn the business, then asked me to help him set up in California. No great distance from Idaho, money was good, so I did it. The work done, I came down here to see the sights."

"Ah yes, the sights." Bullock caressed the side of the big balloon glass with one hand, like it was a woman's ass.

Horny old devil, Morgan thought. "I figured to go home tomorrow then I ran into Bender."

"But now you'd like to make a little more money, eh?"

Morgan didn't like the sound of that 'little.' "As much as I can," he said. "But I have to tell you: I have only a rough idea of the city, from years back. I don't know anybody."

"And nobody knows you, that's what I like." Bullock had a butler, but he got up himself to get more brandy. The butler was gone and the door was locked. Half uncorked beer bottles were in an ice bucket, but Morgan said he didn't want any more. Bullock got back in his chair.

"But I'm no detective," Morgan said.

"Please—" Bullock took a sip, rolled it around, swallowed it. "If I wanted a regular detective, the city is full of them, police and private. Smart and dumb, honest and crooked. Now, sir, will *you* take the job?"

"You haven't told me enough, Mr. Bullock."

"Ah, yes. Of course I haven't. It's always embarrassing when a wife runs away, especially a young wife. Lily is only twenty-six and I'm . . . soon I'll be sixty, no getting away from that. Yet in spite of the difference in our ages, I thought we were happy. I was, certainly I was, and I thought Lily felt the same way. Oh, well, she was a bit restless, but what young bride is not?"

Morgan said nothing to that.

"We've been married less than six months," Bullock went on, looking into his glass like it was a guide to the past. He belted back what was left in it and his bright, darting eyes became brighter. "Before I married Lily, she was queen of the finest parlor house in San Francisco. I didn't tell that to Mr. Bender. Surprised, eh?"

"Yes, sir," Morgan said. What else could he say?

"Well, I couldn't let her get away from me, could I? I met her right after she came to work at Madame De Mornay's, and I tell you I couldn't get out of my trousers fast enough that first night. And mind you, Madame D has some mighty fine young ladies—real beauties—in her stable, and I'd enjoyed all of them, but Lily was in a class by herself. I was so smitten with the lady, soon I was her only gentleman caller, so to speak. That cost me a bundle, but it was worth it. I couldn't stand the thought of any other man being with her. . . ."

The old boy was getting worked up, Morgan thought. Bullock wasn't close to sixty, as he said, but well past it, and still as randy as a billygoat.

"That arrangement worked all right for a while. Ah, yes," Bullock said, thinking about it. "But then she got restless and started talking about moving to New York. Well, I didn't like that one bit, and told her so. Sure, I said, you're the queen here, but what about there, all that competition? That got her mad, and she said she'd be queen wherever she went. You ever hear such nerve?"

"I guess I have," Morgan said, thinking of a few women.

Bullock said, "The long and the short of it, I asked her to be my wife and she consented. Of course I knew that's what she was angling for all along. Fine and dandy, the way I looked at it, a good bargain for all concerned. I got a wife I couldn't bear to lose, and she got respectability, a place in society, this fine house, anything else she wanted. Within reason, that is. . . ."

Morgan knew the old man was talking to himself, trying to reshape the past so he'd like it better. Still, it did no harm to listen. Now, after a long pause, he was talking again.

"But I must admit I was a little worried at first. No need for it, not then. We got along fine. It would have been different, I guess, if I didn't have all my *powers*, but I did and I do, you bet. That of course she knew from Madame D's, but even so she had her little jokes, like the one about my name. A bullock, as you know, is a castrated bull, which by the way is why my store is called Derwent's instead of Bullock's— a silly notion, I guess. Anyway, it sure as hell doesn't apply to me. I still got my balls, of that you can be sure."

Morgan hoped Bullock wasn't going to display evidence of this. Rich men were known to do anything that came into their heads.

"Bender said she's been gone for a week," Morgan said, hoping to get the old man back on the rails.

"Six days. There must have been some warning signs, but I missed them. Maybe she was a bit more temperamental than usual. It's hard to say. As far as I can recall, our life was on an even keel. I left early for the store, but was always home in time for dinner. Then one evening I came home and she wasn't there. Hammond—that's the butler— said she left about noon, carrying two bags. Told Hammond she didn't want a cab, she was going to walk. Didn't want anyone to know where she was going, I guess."

"Looks that way," Morgan said.

"Didn't even leave a note," Bullock said. "Just up and left. Took all her jewels, the household money, plus the money from my drawer, about six hundred dollars in all. "And—" Bullock took a deep breath "—one hundred thousand dollars in negotiable securities, as good as cash, as you may know, and completely untraceable."

Things were getting sticky, as Morgan once

heard his English client say. Bender might have some advice.

"She walked out into the streets of a city teeming with criminals." Bullock's tone was almost admiring. "Carrying one hundred thousand dollars in a leather bag, no guards, no protection. Anyone could have taken it from her."

"Unless there was somebody waiting close by. Or she got a cab a few streets away."

"One or the other, I guess. But you can see, can't you, why I don't want this made public?"

"I can see some of it."

"You should be able to see all of it," Bullock said, suddenly snappish. "I'd be the laughingstock of the city if the story got out. Serves him right, the old goat, I can hear them saying. But there's more to it than that. I have other interests besides the store. I have stockholders to think of. If a man can't control his own wife, how can he be trusted to run a big business? I'm not an old man, but they'd say I was losing my grip. I can't let that happen. In business a loss of confidence can mean disaster. Is that plain enough for you?"

"Yes, sir," Morgan said. It sounded plain enough, but was it? A shrewd brain was clicking away inside that bony skull. Did any wealthy businessman ever tell the entire truth? Did anybody?

"It's not generally known that I married a *whore*." In a sudden turnaround, Bullock seemed to savor the word. A few minutes before she had been his beautiful, queenlike Lily. "I kept our marriage out of the newspapers; it would have been bad for business. Derwent's is a family store, after all.

13

Thirty years ago it wouldn't have mattered much. A lot of rich men married whores and nobody cared. Today is different."

Bullock got up to pour brandy. "This is good German beer," he said, holding up a dripping bottle. Morgan said all right.

Easing himself into his chair, Bullock said, "Keeping it out of the papers wasn't difficult, never is if you have money. Only one editor balked but changed his tune quick enough after I asked how his other wife was, the one he was hiding over in Sausalito. Wouldn't it be terrible, I said, if news of the second wife got into a rival paper. That settled his hash. You're not married, are you?"

Morgan thought he detected a warning in the editor story. "Never have been," he said.

"My first marriage was in all the papers. Big doings. My first wife was an awful bitch. Cold as a Vermont winter, but a lady. I thought Lily would resent not being in the papers but she didn't mind a bit. Said it was best not to be tied in to her past life, so it was easy. Lily's real name is Sears, but at Madame D's she was known as Lily Dalton or just Lily. I never heard her called anything but Lily. I used the name Brewster when I came calling. I guess Madame D knew who I was, but it never came up. Discretion is Madame D's watchword. Wouldn't be in business long if she talked out of church."

"You haven't been back there since your marriage?"

Bullock liked the question. "I don't say I have

14

no fond memories, but no, sir, I haven't been back. Lily was more than enough for me, you bet. After our marriage, Madame D's became a thing of the past."

"That's where I'd have to start," Morgan said.

Bullock seemed to be listening to the rain drumming on the windows. "Talk to nobody but Madame D. She's the soul of discretion, but tell her as little as possible. About the securities—nothing."

"I wouldn't go at it head-on, Mr. Bullock. I'd go in asking for Lily, because . . ."

"Go on, say it. Doesn't bother me. Because you heard she was the greatest fucking whore that ever lived. Would fuck a man till he didn't know which end was up. And still a lady for all that, worth the price of admission and everything you could beg, borrow, or steal."

"Something like that," Morgan said. He was glad Bullock said it; he didn't want to say it himself. "But there's nothing to say she's there. Why would she be, with the jewels and what else she has? She could be on a train, a ship headed for Europe, anywhere. But if she wants to stay here and hide, it doesn't have to be in a whorehouse."

Bullock did some thinking. "What you say is true, but I'm almost certain that she's gone back to The Life, as she calls it. Yes, we talked about it. I found it interesting. Lily was sixteen when she started, twenty-six when she married me—ten years. Lily said she was always treated well, in spite of all the stories you hear, and I don't doubt it. Her beauty, intelligence, so on. But what I'm getting at is, she

15

more or less grew up in The Life, hardly knew any other world. She made friends—good friends, she said—and still has them, I don't doubt. So you see what I mean?"

"You mean she'd feel safe, protected. Mr. Bullock, you're making it sound like she's run off to a convent."

Bullock got snappish again. "You're not listening. She may have been as young as fourteen when she started. Yes, I know I said sixteen. That's what she told me, but I think fourteen is closer to the truth. What was I saying? Yes. She grew up in The Life and has gone back there to hide, for how long I have no idea."

"She has no family?"

"None that I know of. West Virginia is where she comes from. Her father was killed—mine explosion—then her mother died and they put her in an orphanage. An only child, nobody to claim her. She escaped when she was thirteen, worked as a servant girl till she entered her first house."

It could be true, Morgan thought, yet it had the smell of one of those pink paper books that candy butchers hawked on trains. With titles like *An Orphan-Girl's Story* or *Betrayed by Beauty*. He wondered how she got to be such a lady. The word had a different meaning for different people. In some circles a lady was a woman who didn't come to bed chewing onions. Still, there had to be something.

"She was always in demand," Bullock was saying.

Morgan was thinking of Lily's ten or twelve years as a whore. Maybe longer than that. She could be older than twenty-six. How would Bullock know if she'd shaved a few years?

"How long has she been in San Francisco?" he asked. Then he added, "Where did she work before Madame D's?"

Bullock held up his hand. "Hold on there, Mr. Morgan. Before you ask any more questions, you want the job or not? Here's the money side of it. A thousand dollars for the job, half in advance, half when it's done, plus two hundred and fifty dollars for expenses. Additional expenses to be provided if you can show the need. All right?"

"All right," Morgan said. However it went he'd give the old boy a fair shake for his money. But before he started he wanted to talk to Bender, maybe get answers to questions he couldn't ask here.

"Good man. You'll get your money right now." Bullock went to a book-lined wall beside the fireplace and swung back a square of shelves, revealing a small safe. "Damned if I know how Lily got the combination to this. Sure as hell's fire didn't get it from me. She could have watched me, I guess. I've had it changed since she left."

He closed the safe and gave Morgan the money. "Seven hundred and fifty dollars. Count it," he said.

"You want a receipt?" Morgan said after he did.

"Not necessary." Bullock was back in his chair with a fresh drink. "Lily," he said after a sip. He took another sip. "Lily's been in San Francisco

17

about five years, and that's right enough because I made a few inquiries. Eighteen months at Madame D's, three years or so in two other places. The second one hired her away from the first, promised her more money. You want me to write down the names and addresses?"

Morgan said yes.

Bullock took a notebook from his inside pocket and scribbled in it with a gold propelling pencil. "Both are pretty fancy," he said, handing Morgan the torn-out page. "Nowhere as fancy as Madame D's, but fancy enough."

Morgan looked at the sheet of paper and put it in his pocket.

"You'll need a picture of Lily. I have it right here." Bullock picked up a shiny white card from the table beside his chair. Morgan had to get up to take it. "As you see, it's a visiting card with her photograph on it. The other pictures of her are too big to carry around. Will it do?"

"It'll do fine," Morgan said, looking at the card. He knew the old man was waiting for him to say something. "Mighty attractive woman," was what he finally came out with. All he could see was her head and shoulders, but she was a lot more than attractive. An arrogant beauty if ever he saw one was what she was. It was hard to put her together with the wrinkled old man sitting across from him.

"It's a good likeness. Ah, Lord, yes, how I'd like to have her back." Bullock snuffled into his glass and Morgan hoped he wasn't going to cry. Not that tears meant anything: some of the worst fuckers would wipe out a family and cry over a dead pet cat. "Bring her back to me, Mr. Morgan."

"I thought my job was to find her," Morgan said.

"A thousand dollar bonus if you can persuade her to come home. And with the securities too, of course. With the securities, yes."

Morgan didn't like the stress Bullock put on persuade. It sounded to his Idaho ear as if Bullock was yearning for negotiables. He could use the thousand extra, but he wasn't about to bind and gag the woman and put her in a sack.

"What if she's cashed in the securities?" he said.

Bullock gave that a sour face. "Let me worry about the securities. Your job is to find her, get her back if you can. But I must warn you before you start, some of Lily's friends are pretty tough customers, and you'd better be prepared to use that gun in your pocket, if only to defend yourself. Get my meaning?"

The gun in Morgan's pocket was a stubby five-shot Webley Bulldog .45, a going-away present from his English client. It was heavy but compact and could knock down a big man or a small buffalo. His regular gun was in the hotel safe.

Morgan said nothing and that got a laugh from the old man. "Don't miss much, do I?"

"Not much," Morgan said. "Now, sir, do you have an idea where your wife worked before she came to San Francisco?"

"Great scot!" Bullock exclaimed. "Surely you won't have to go that far back. The only answer

I can give you is: I can't be sure. Now and then, Lily did talk a bit after too much champagne. How much of it was true I can't say. One night it came out that her first house was in Fort Smith, Arkansas. I think you can forget that, too far back. Two other places she mentioned were Galveston and Denver—both fancy, she said. Who can tell? Everything was fancy with Lily. I'm still betting on San Francisco, at least for a while. Don't dawdle, Mr. Morgan, this is not a vacation."

"I'll get right to work," Morgan said. The old weasel was worried that he was going to roll around with the women and forget about business. "How do I report to you? You'll want to know how I'm doing."

"Indeed I will. There's a private telephone line to my office. 867 is the number. You can ring me from the Exchange Building if you don't want to be overheard. I'm at the store twelve hours a day, seven to seven. After that you can talk to me here. The number is 1120. Where are you stopping?"

"I have a room at the Pacific Hotel."

"The Pacific, eh? Powell and Pacific Streets, am I right? Right next to the Coast ladies, you dirty dog, not that I blame you a bit." Bullock yawned. "I think that about does it, Mr. Morgan. I'll be expecting to hear from you. Say noon, day after tomorrow." Bullock started to get up.

Morgan did too. "One more question, Mr. Bullock. You happen to know if your wife was ever married before?" He'd been saving this for last.

The old man took it calmly enough. "Not that I

20

know of," he said. "The truth is, I never asked her. Good night, Mr. Morgan."

Bullock showed Morgan out of the house. Rain swept the streets, blurring the streetlights, and it was cold. Morgan turned up his coat collar and started back to his hotel. It was close to midnight, too late to go calling on Bender at his hotel. Bender said he ate breakfast between six-thirty and seven in the dining room. After that he'd be busy with the convention; they were nominating him for something. The big final night was three days away and a lot was happening. But his wife slept late and he had breakfast by himself, so talking to him for part of half an hour would have to do.

Chapter Two

"My best advice for you is buy an umbrella," Nathan Bender said. "You look like a drowned rat. Where's your manners, you Idaho hick, coming in here dripping on the people?"

It was six-forty and they were digging into a big breakfast of ham and eggs, hashbrowns and sausages, toast and coffee. They had a table by a window and rain was beating on the glass.

"At least buy yourself a waterproof coat," Bender went on.

The dining room was filling up with police chiefs. Morgan knew they were police chiefs by their convention buttons. Some of them looked like they had hangovers.

"You can still back out," Bender said. "I was just putting you in the way of making a buck."

"I'm for that."

"Then what is it? Nothing you've told me is that unusual, at least not to me. Smart whore slicks a rich geezer into marrying her, then she decides she doesn't like old age creeping up on her and does a waltz with everything she can lay her hands on, in this case a lot. But not a lot—listen—not such a lot when you consider how much these boobies get milked for every day of the week."

"Bullock is no booby. He's a smart old man and plenty mean, I would say."

"Every man is some kind of a booby when it comes to women. Bullock wouldn't be in this fix if he wasn't. Now he's been suckered and he's hired you to find the wife and the securities and not go mouthing off to the newspapers while you're doing it. What is so strange about that? If he doesn't trust the law, regular or private investigators—well, all I can tell you is, some of the police chiefs here ought to be in jail instead of feeding their faces."

The dining room was getting loud. Some of the feeders were getting brandy in their coffee, Morgan figured.

"What is eating you?" Bender asked. "If you don't like how this smells, give the money back. Don't go on with it on my account. I just know Bullock through his brother in Kansas City. I know him because he's a big law-and-order man, contributes to the support of our magazine. That doesn't mean you can't back out."

"Would losing a hundred thousand mean such a lot to Bullock?" Morgan asked. "To a man as rich as him, I mean."

Bender waved to a man at the far end of the dining room. "You're asking something I can't answer. What you're really asking is, does he want you to find the wife because if you find

23

her you'll find the securities at the same time. You say he says he wants them both home safe and sound, and what's wrong with that? Maybe he wants to spread the securities out on the bed and do whatever he does to lovely Lily on top of them. Love takes strange forms, my boy. But you don't like that answer, am I right?"

"There's something wrong with it," Morgan said. But he knew Bender was right. No way to figure human nature. Get in or get out. "I just don't want to be caught with my pants down."

Bender laughed. "I thought pants-down was your favorite position. All right, no more jokes."

"These securities, why can't they be traced? They don't write or stamp something on them when they're sold?"

"Not that I ever heard of. In their way they're just like paper money. They don't write or stamp on money, do they?"

"But the buyer could do it if he liked?"

"The buyer could wipe his ass with them if he liked. Of course, I don't know how negotiable they'd be if he did that. Yes, the answer is he could stamp or write his name or the name of his company on them. If the original buyer did that, or some other buyer did it, they could be traced back in that way. That's obvious enough, for Christ's sake. Why didn't you ask Bullock all this?"

"I didn't think of it," Morgan said.

"It hardly matters," Bender said. "People don't deface valuable securities. I take it they're not connected to some scheme to grow bananas in Massachusetts. Of course they're not."

"Then Bullock's wife could get rid of them with no trouble?"

Bender waved to somebody else he knew. "The answer to that is yes and no. Look at it this way: a bum walks into a saloon and tries to pay for a drink with a thousand dollar bill. Right away any number of questions come up. How did he get it? Steal it? Is it any good? So they call the police, rob the bum, or throw him and the thousand dollar bill in the street."

"Then Bullock's wife would need a go-between?"

"Probably she would. Somebody to make the introductions. There is always the question: where did she get them? Like the make believe bum, her securities are as good as his thousand dollar bill, but she'll have to offer a reasonable explanation if she goes the legal road. If she doesn't, she can still cash them in but she'll have to take a loss."

Morgan's clothes were drying out, but he thought he'd break down and buy a slicker or a waterproof coat. "Then she'd need somebody crooked?"

"Somebody who wouldn't ask too many questions. It depends. A lawyer, a friendly banker. A bad lad who knows a lawyer or an accommodating banker. Look here, Morgan me boy, you're asking me questions you should have asked Bullock. You don't trust him, do you?"

"Not altogether."

"You'd be a fool if you did. But if it'll make you feel any better, I made a few inquiries about the old fart, discreet as hell like he wants you to be. He's in the latest edition of *Business Leaders of California*, got a copy right here in the reading room. Started out a Vermont grocery clerk like his brother. In 1847, the Bullock brothers arrived in Independence, Missouri, to join a wagon train going west. The brother got stuck on a local girl or her money and decided to go no further. Your Bullock went on to California, opened a tent store at the diggings during the gold rush, sold eggs at three dollars per, made a small fortune. He then moved on here to San Francisco, got richer with another store, started the first real department store. Some years later he built the store he has now, which takes in a whole city block. A very rich man, solid in a business way, which probably means you'll get the rest of your money."

"I'll get it," Morgan said.

"Don't be so grim about it," Bender replied. "So far you haven't earned a nickel of that fine old merchant's money. Why didn't you ask for more expenses? That last place his wife worked in—De Mornay's—sounds like real carriage trade. Milk baths at fifty dollars a quart, suck jobs with crème de menthe, warm the cockles of your cock. Your two hundred and fifty won't go far there."

Morgan smiled. Bender was a joker but always a friend. He didn't really know the man. Behind the chief's desk he'd put on some pounds. He had more gray in his hair and was past fifty by now. Morgan thought he was a sad man at heart.

"Bullock says he's not paying for a vacation," he said.

"No milk baths then. Just as well," Bender said. "You'd probably drown in dirty milk. But you ought to be able to get better than blue plate with that kind of money. What a yob, as Swenson said. I'd envy you if I wasn't a happily married man."

Morgan hoped Bender was as happily married as he said he was. Sometimes he wasn't so sure.

"All in a day's work," he said.

"That's the main thing," Bender said. "And, by golly, Madame's is just the first place you have to percolate. What do you know about the other two?"

"Fancy," Morgan said. "That's all."

"You ought to know more than that, Detective Morgan. Wait a minute, there's Duckie O'Connor over there behind the palm tree. If he doesn't know, nobody does."

Bender waved to a stone-faced man eating by himself. O'Connor saw the wave and lifted his plate off the table and started across the room. A young waiter tried to stop him. An older waiter hissed him away and bowed O'Connor through the aisle of closely placed tables. Morgan didn't see O'Connor's clergyman's collar until he got close. What the fuck is this? he thought.

Bender pulled out a chair and O'Connor sat down with his stack of steak and eggs nearly sliding off the plate. The senior waiter came along behind him and set down a nickeled teapot and a cup.

"Here's your tea, Reverend, piping hot," the waiter said. "The kid didn't realize who you was."

O'Connor scowled at him. A lot of people were looking at this get-together. No wonder, Morgan thought. Reverend O'Connor had the most brutal face he'd ever seen on a man, clergy or not. He was on the far side of fifty, red as a brick, nobody to fool with.

"How are things in the mission business, Duckie?" Bender asked.

That was twice Bender had called him Duckie, Morgan thought. You called a whore duckie if you were so inclined; surely not this bird.

"Bender scoffs at the Lord's work," O'Connor said to Morgan.

"This is my friend Buck Blaney from up north," Bender said. "In the lumber business. Duckie is the fallen woman's friend, runs a big mission and hostel here, right in the middle of town—no back street stuff for Duckie."

O'Connor filled out a large well-tailored black suit with velvet lapels. Neat for such a brute of a man. No cigar ash or soup stains on his vest. His wide face was barber shaved and hot toweled to a smooth red.

"I can tell you're no lawman, chief or Indian," he said to Morgan. "That's a compliment if you want to take it that way." It looked as if he never smiled, or had forgotten how, or never learned.

"Thanks, Reverend," Morgan said.

Bender said, "Duckie used to be the biggest pimp on the Barbary Coast, and the richest. The last of the Sydney Ducks, escaped convicts from Australia, practically ran this city in the old days. Ducky was smart enough to reform before the Vigilance Committee started hanging them from second floor windows."

"Don't listen to this scoffer," O'Connor said to

Morgan. "He'd have you believe I reformed to save my neck."

"No such thing," Bender said. "Everybody knows you do good work. What do you know about a house called Madame De Mornay's? I'm not asking for myself but for my friend here. Buck here—doing very well in the lumber business—is on the verge of matrimony, but wants to dip his wick in style before he settles down to the fireside bright, if you get my meaning."

O'Connor turned his attention to Morgan. "What's the matter with the bride-to-be?"

"Not a thing, Reverend, a fine woman." Fuck Bender and his stories! "It's just that . . ."

O'Connor nodded his huge head. "That's the trouble with these respectable women. If they spread their legs when it's needed, you wouldn't have men looking for a paid poke."

Nice language for a clergyman, Morgan thought, wanting to laugh.

"Please, Duckie, no sermons," Bender cut in. "What about this Madame D's?"

O'Connor lurched around in his chair, threatening to break it. "They got the creamiest cunts in there," he said to Morgan. "Not a woman there over thirty, all good looking, not a prune face in the lot, and believe me, you have to pay extra if you want something real old. They keep one or two on tap. You're not like that, I hope."

"Lord no," Morgan said hastily.

"About Madame De Mornay herself," O'Connor continued. "Madame De Mornay, my 'Stralian arse! I knew her when she was Maggie Moran from

29

over on Grant Avenue. But I'll give the old bat this much: forget the phony French bullshit, she treats her girls right, doesn't cheat them on the money, allows no dope or booze, and has a real doctor check their assets twice a month. You never get a dose there—guaranteed. You want whips and chains, you want to piss on the women—take your business elsewhere. No roughhouse, no blackmail—perish the thought. All that refinement costs money, but you can sin in safety. You get a square deal and good eating at Maggie's."

O'Connor was about to explain what good eating was. Bender headed him off by saying, "Sounds good but what about Burke's and Mendoza's?"

O'Connor swallowed a small piece of steak. "Fancy enough places, but don't have the same class. How could they, run by two jailbirds?"

"Duckie never served a day in his life," Bender explained. "Not in this country, that is."

O'Connor said, "Burke is Liverpool-Irish so he tries to work the English game, calls his place Burke's Peerage, puts out that he's the son of some lord, remittance man, bloody Oxford College and all that. Claims the title will fall to him someday."

O'Connor turned to flag down the nearest waiter. "This fucking tea is fucking cold, mate."

The waiter hurried away with the teapot.

"Burke is a very bad lad," O'Connor went on. "A burglar in New York before he came here, the kind of burglar that kills instead of running if he's disturbed. Not a professional, you might say. They say it was Burke who killed the two watchmen when Jimmy Hope's gang robbed that Wall Street company."

The waiter brought O'Connor's tea. "Berling hot," he said.

"Leave it lie," O'Connor told him. "Mendoza," he said to Bender, "is a greasy, dark-faced bastard who started out a phony gypsy fortune teller conning rich old biddies with good news for the future. 'Naw, I don' see no cancer in de years ahead, señora.' That kind of malarkey!"

O'Connor took a chance on some fresh tea. Morgan and Bender looked on while he put three heaping teaspoons of sugar in the cup, tasted it, added another. He made a face, but it turned out that he was thinking of Mendoza.

"Mendoza is as bad as Burke," he said. "If that's possible. A fine pair they are, the mick and the spic. The both of them would like to be gentlemen, work at it, don't know how. How could they?"

The early breakfast crowd was starting to thin out. O'Connor got up, dabbing at his meaty mouth with a napkin. "Got to push off, gents. Nice talking to you, Mr. Blaney. If you do go to Burke's or Mendoza'a, don't go in drunk carrying a lot of cash. You're not a regular, see, and what could you do if you got rolled? Blow the whistle? You'd be lucky if their hip pocket coppers didn't frame you up as a child raper."

People were listening to this, but O'Connor didn't seem to care. "A well-fixed feller like you might be wanting to make a donation to my mission. Mail it to the Magdalene Mission, this city. God bless you. You too, Bender."

O'Connor didn't stop at the cashier's desk as he went out.

"What is he?" Morgan said, looking after him. "A con man?"

Bender was looking at his watch. "A con man for Christ, is what he is. Takes in plenty, but spends a lot of it on his magdalenes. Keeps a lot for himself, too. Provides food, clothing, and shelter. Protects them from the pimps and the police, helps them find jobs if they want to quit selling it. Gives them train fare home, the ones he believes. Pays for medical treatment or a decent funeral if it comes to that."

"The man is a saint," Morgan said.

"Don't scoff," Bender said. "He does a lot of good in his way. The whores like him because he doesn't preach at them. But he talks tougher—is tougher—than any pimp. Don't let your fucking life go down the fucking sewer, is his prayer."

"But where does he get his money? Surely not in the mail?"

"Yes, that and street collections. Bigtime gamblers are an easy mark. But you're right. Most of it comes from the mealy-mouths—the whited sepulchers, he calls them—who own the meat markets or the buildings they're in. Bankers, bishops, real estate men, rich old ladies. Duckie knows and doesn't let them forget it. Hush-hush money, sure, but they pay, makes them feel virtuous.

"Duckie attends all the police conventions," Bender went on. "Is an honorary chief. Duckie thinks they're shitholes, they think he's a character."

"That's his insurance?"

"Sort of," Bender said. "But don't let that clerical collar fool you. Back in the pimp war days Duckie killed many a competitor. And his mission staff, so-called, are all reformed thugs like himself."

Bender took another look at his watch. "What's all this interest in the Duck? I've got things to do."

"One last question," Morgan said. "O'Connor said Burke, the English Irishman, used to be a bank burglar."

"No, he didn't. You heard Wall Street and right off you thought of bonds and securities. Burke and securities and Bullock's wife. You're making too much out of this, is my answer. Bullock hired you to find his wife, or try to. So I say to you, don't not try. But if you can't find her after a reasonable amount of effort, admit defeat, collect the other five hundred and go back to Idaho. I'm sorry, soldier, but I must be going. You know where you can find me."

The rain had stopped when Morgan got outside. Watery sunshine was trying to break through. It wouldn't be long before it started raining again. Market Street was thick with traffic, cable cars clanging impatiently, pedestrians crowding the intersections. Morgan thought San Francisco would be a fine place if it didn't rain so much. Here it fogged and rained more than it did in Idaho. But he liked it anyway. They called it a go-to-hell town, and that's what it was.

All the waterproofs and umbrellas reminded him that he had to do something about keeping dry.

Down the street, in the first clothing store he came to, he bought a waterproof and put it on. No galoshes, no umbrella, he told the clerk. Tall as he was, the coat hung well below his knees. You could hide a shotgun or a saber under it. The short, chunky five-shot Bulldog would do for now. The damn coat was ungainly, but he was glad to have it when he walked out into a fresh downpour.

Madame De Mornay's was in the Russian Hill section, on Larkin Street between Green and Union. Bullock said he couldn't miss it: a big five-story rose-brick building, no sign, just a small brass plate with De Mornay in fancy script. The clerk in the store told him it was a mile or so from where he was, the corner of Market and Montgomery. He could take the Montgomery Street car to Union, then walk the few blocks from there.

It felt strange to be heading for a whorehouse so early in the morning. Usually he'd be coming out of one at that hour; all the same, he might as well get started. The cable car was jammed with men and women going to work; it smelled of wet clothes and his new coat was too warm. It was a short ride and he was quick to get off when his stop was called. No more cable cars if he could help it.

He walked down Union to Larkin, breathing in damp fresh air, trying to get the streets straight in his head. Russian Hill, where he was going now, was just north of Nob Hill, where Bullock lived. His hotel was at Powell and Pacific, on the edge of the Barbary Coast, no more than a shout from the quality folks. San Francisco was like that: rough districts shoved up close to the rich. He smiled when he thought of the name Bender had given him. Buck Blaney would do well enough if anybody wanted to know.

He turned onto Larkin. Madame De Mornay's was the showboat of the short block. All the houses were elegant, but this one stood out, the rose-brick damp with rain but still glowing in spite of it. Nothing in San Francisco was much more than thirty years old. This house looked as if it was much older than that. It stood by itself, with a spiked iron fence all around it. A small sign for carriages had an arrow pointing to the rear of the building.

It was the fanciest whorehouse that Morgan had ever seen. No roughneck in a doorman's uniform. No class to that, Morgan decided, thinking like a real city gent. A man who looked like a prizefighter who had retired early opened the door when he pulled the bell below the polished brass plate. He had a good black suit on and his face wasn't marked up too bad. In his late thirties, like Morgan, he looked like he could still throw a punch in spite of the soft life he led now.

"Good morning, sir," he said, giving Morgan a quick look with hard, experienced eyes.

Morgan nodded to that. "Not too early I hope. Buck Blaney is the name."

"Never too early, sir," the house bully said, well spoken for a brothel bruiser. Morgan must have passed inspection because the houseman opened the door to let him into the entrance hallway. The carpet was thick and rich looking. Wallpaper was decorated with what Morgan took to be French castles, windmills, and such. Because it was a dark, rainy morning, gaslights glowed behind flowered shades. But for all that it still smelled like a whorehouse, however elegant it might be. It was a subdued smell, nothing raunchy about it, but it was there. No good reminding himself that this was business; Morgan felt a stirring in his pants.

The houseman took Morgan's raincoat and passed it to a woman in a checkroom. "You'll be wanting to check your gun, sir," he said. Morgan gave him a look and he added, "House rule, sir. Applies to everybody."

Morgan gave him the chunky Webley and the checkroom woman put it in a drawer. "Madame De Mornay will want to welcome you, sir. This way, sir."

Morgan had never been sirred so much in his life. Madame De Mornay's office was down the hall. The door was half open and the houseman knocked on it. "A new guest, Madame," he said. "Mr. Buck Blaney."

"How dee-light-full," a woman's voice said in a phony French accent. "Show him in, Pierre. Show *heem* in."

The houseman opened the door for Morgan, but didn't go away.

Chapter Three

The woman who turned in her chair to greet him was in her sixties, hard-faced and brisk, skinny in a stylish black dress, and trying hard for a winning smile. Morgan had seen warmer smiles in open coffins at the undertaker's. This was Madame De Mornay, formerly Maggie Moran from over on Grant Avenue, according to the Reverend Duckie O'Connor.

"Ah, you are Mr. Blaney," she said. Her accent was as fake as her jet-black, piled-up hair. The Old Sod kept breaking through: corned beef and cabbage on French bread. She waved him to a chair beside her ornate desk. It had business ledgers on it, an inkstand, and a cup and saucer. "This is your first visit, no? I would 'ave remember you, yes."

"A friend sent me," Morgan said. "Cyrus—Cy Stagg, from my neck of the woods. Cy was down here maybe a year ago, said he had a better time than he ever had in Boise, where us Idaho boys usually go. Cy said I should ask for a sweet young lady named Lily. Nothing like her in Boise, he said."

Madame De Mornay smirked her contempt for Boise. She didn't have to think before she said, "I am sorry, but no Lily ever work 'ere, no one wit' that name."

Morgan reached into his pocket for the visiting card that Bullock had given him. He had trimmed the card so that only the photograph of Lily remained. He showed it to her, but she waved it away after no more than a glance. "A pretty girl, but she 'ave never work here. Sorry, Mr. Blaney. some other young lady per'aps? We have ze cream of de crop."

Morgan peristed. "It's possible old Cy got the name wrong. Maybe it was Claudette or Fifi."

"No Fifis here," Madame D said with dignity. "My young ladies do not 'ave names like that. We have a Claudette, yes, but she is not the young lady in the picture."

Morgan still had the photograph in his hand. He looked at it again. "Too bad. A girl in a million is what Cy said."

Madame D gave another smirk. "This friend of yours is varry fanciful, no? I would like to 'elp you with this Lily, but she is not 'ere an' nevair 'ave been. Could it be your friend was thinking of the wrong 'ouse?"

"Could be. He does drink a bit."

Madame D pounced on that. "There! You see! We do not allow dronks in 'ere, no matter how much money they 'ave. Forgive me, Mr. Blaney, your friend may be a fine gentleman, but if he came 'ere dronk he would not 'ave been admitted. We will forget about that, a mistake, no? For you I 'ave a young lady who will make you forget about this Lily. You will not believe your eyes when you see her. I would not lie to you."

Sure you would, Morgan thought, you already have. "Lead me to it," he said in his role of a lusty lumberman from the north woods.

Madame De Mornay was not offended. She was well used to well-heeled vulgarians like Mr. Buck Blaney. "But of course," she said. And—but of course, you bet—he had to pay in advance before she gave him the room number and the key. Room No. 1. Second floor. "It is better this way"—when she had the money in her hand—"later it will be different when you become a regular patron, and, I am sure, a friend of our little family."

What Morgan had to pay would have kept him fucking for a week back in Idaho, but all he did was nod. He might be wasting time and money. Still and all, he had to start somewhere, and here he was sure to get a good fuck.

Madame D was a little put out when he said it was a little early in the day to be ordering champagne. "There is no early or late for champagne, Mr. Blaney. It is the drink of lovers." He got a naughty smile. "How-evair, if you should wish it later, please to push the electric bell, or the young lady will do it. Her name is Angelique and she is truly an angel."

Morgan wanted to get up to the room before she had any more suggestions: like some greaser plucking love songs from a mandolin at the foot of the bed. He'd heard about that. Sometimes it was a Hungarian with a fiddle.

He found the room, the first door on the second floor. He went in and the girl on the big brass bed was wearing a thin silk nightgown with a shine to it that made it look wet. It clung to her body and showed her nipples and the darkness at her crotch. She was reading, propped up by pillows, and she put aside the book when he came in without making much noise.

Even lying down she looked tall—at least five-nine or ten—and her figure just stopped short of being boyish, but no boy ever looked like that. Her face was young and pretty, with a lot of mischief in her eyes. She couldn't have been more than seventeen or eighteen. Some whores were worn out by that age, fucked and sucked and buggered until there was no more life left in them. This one was different: she was full of mischief and looked like she had a secret.

Morgan caught a whiff of brandy, but there was no bottle in sight.

"I am Angelique," she said gravely, then grinned at the phony name.

"I'm Buck Blaney," Morgan said.

"You want to fuck, Buck?" She was a little tight, no more than that. Morgan thought she was unusually merry for a whore. But why couldn't a whore be merry? Whoring was probably better than milking twenty-seven pesky she-goats on a country-Sunday winter morning.

"That's what I'm here for. But with love and affection and the fullest appreciation of that there."

Angelique reached down and squeezed her cunt lips through the flimsy nightgown. "You must mean this." She giggled.

Morgan's cock was getting hard when he came in the door. Now it got harder. "That's what I mean." He sat on a chair and started to pull off his boots. The girl didn't offer to help him off with his clothes, and that was just as well. He wanted to get at what she was squeezing and stroking. Madame D might be an old bitch, but she hadn't lied about this one.

It was a nice big room, with none of the usual scarred and battered furniture. Real lace curtains hung from a brass rod at the double window. No dingy oiled-paper shades here. Behind a screen was a sink for washing after the deed was done. Lots of towels. Even a wardrobe to hang his clothes.

Morgan was thinking: This room probably belonged to Lily before she made the climb to Nob Hill. Room No. 1, the best cathouse in the city. It figured: Lily, Queen of the Whores. Well, sir, if Lily was a queen, this one he was looking at, his cock in his hand, was at least a princess.

The brass bed was magnificent, polished bright, no sag in the middle, and maybe it was solid brass, none of that peeling plate. Angelique rolled up close to him and gave his cock a few strokes, causing it to lean out like a flagpole. He got her nightgown off and was about to board her when she said, "Would you like a drink of brandy? It's all I have, but it's good. I'm celebrating. Going to marry a rich young doctor."

"Does Madame D know it?"

"No, she doesn't know. Another thing she doesn't know. I'm leaving tomorrow, bright and early, before she has her teeth in."

"That's why you're celebrating?"

"Why else? I'm going home to Idaho to get married. Hey, Buckie, you sound like you could be from there."

"Right you are."

"I knew it. I'm from Pocatello, next door to it. And you?"

"Ever hear of a place called Vernon?" Vernon was as far away from Pocatello as Morgan could think of.

"Can't say I have." Angelique had to crawl across Morgan to get off the bed. It was a right good feeling, all that nice young flesh, and he gave her sort-of boyish ass a pat. His cock was longing for the honey-hole. She reached into the bottom of the wardrobe and took out a quart of Martell brandy and a glass and put them on the table beside the bed.

"Only one glass," she said, "but we'll make do. Home folks like us, is what I'm thinking, aren't fussy. I'd like to talk to you, Buckie, home-staters that we are, get your opinion on this and that, but so you won't get anxious I'm going to suck you off, all right? Don't worry, you hear. You paid for me and you're getting the best, and that's my personal guarantee. We have all the time in the world, and when you leave here they'll have to carry you on a door. What do you say to that?"

"I won't say no," Morgan said, thinking that a suck-off from a pretty seventeen-year-old girl, a nice girl and friendly, was something most men only dream about. What a yob, as Bender's imaginary jolly Swede would say. God bless Bullock for making it possible. . . .

His cock was in Angelique's sweet mouth and she was sucking it, murmuring as she did, and the vibration of her voice made the sucking all the sweeter. His cock was big, but she knew how to get her small mouth around it. A snug fit and all the nicer because of that. Cold fall rain was sheeting at the window, and that made it nice too, provided you weren't out in it. It was no time to be thinking of business, and he didn't even try.

Angelique circled the shaft of his cock with thumb and forefinger as she sucked him. Her head moved up and down and he helped her with his hands, holding the sides of her head, guiding her mouth. There was devilment in her—this was no tired out whore—and she tickled the head of his cock with her tongue. What he liked best: she didn't suck him roughly, wanting to get it over with, the way so many whores did. Angelique was very young, but in spite of that she was a real artist, a truly expert cocksucker. If this greedy young doctor didn't do something to make her hate him, he was going to get one fine, loving wife.

Now she was taking more of his cock into her mouth, still murmuring; none of what she said was understandable—how could it be—but it felt good. There was a sudden wild urge to shove it down her throat, but he knew he wasn't going to do that. She must have sensed it too because she took in no more cock than she could handle. He wanted to come so bad his balls ached, longing for relief from the almost unbearable tension that was building up in him, and at the same time not wanting it to end. That's how it was with fucking or sucking, any way you did it. There was only so much you could take before you had to let go.

He felt himself starting to come, but managed to hold back. "Um, um," Angelique mumbled, sucking harder, her chin, the corners of her mouth glistening wet. Her tongue probed the eye of his cock, her teeth nibbled gently in a pretend threat, and still he managed not to shoot his load. Crazily he thought he was like a kid with one of the big sourballs they called an all-day sucker. He just didn't want to come to the end of the delicious sucking. That's what it was, absolutely delicious, and there was nothing sour about it at all.

Their heads were so close, with Angelique's hair falling in his face, sweat beading her forehead, her eyes closed in concentration. There were lots of things he liked about her and her enthusiasm was high on the list. For the moment all he had of her was her mouth, but he was greedy and he wanted to get into her cunt, into her ass. Damn right he was greedy: he was a regular fucking hog when it came to this lovely kid. Her body had the smooth softness of youth: not a mark or blemish on it from head to toe, and even as she sucked him he wanted to lick her, taste her. His cock seemed to get bigger as he thought of the things still to come. It got so large, the head of it, and suddenly she began to suck so hard he couldn't hold back any longer and the hot sperm began to shoot up from his balls. . . .

And she sucked and sucked, drinking it down.

"That was a real mouthful," Angelique giggled after she swallowed it. She sat up, wiped her mouth on a corner of the sheet, reached over for the bottle and glass, still a bit tight. Morgan lay there, not tight, but still quivering from his spectacular come. He didn't mind the drinking as long as she didn't pass out, and there seemed to be no danger of that. He'd fucked drunken women, had been drunk himself, but it was better the other way, sober or fairly sober. And even as the effects of her sucking wore off, he began to think of what he would do to her next. So far he hadn't done any of the doing; it had been all her own work.

The good part over with, he knew he should get started on Lily. It was hard to heed the call of duty while a sweet young girl was gobbling your goose. But he wasn't sure how to start off. Asking straight out about Lily might get him cold-shouldered or worse. Like asking the most famous actor in the world about the other most famous actor in the world. Just the same, he had to think of something.

Angelique took a good sip of brandy, then handed the glass to Morgan. He didn't want it, but he took a small drink before he gave it back. Angelique drank a little more. "James is surely not rich, not yet anyway, but he's going to be," she said, nudging Morgan, who was still a bit weak. "You're not even listening."

"I'm listening." He was thinking about Lily.

"James is the reason I've been doing this for two years, helping to get him through his medical

45

schooling in Chicago. A real medical school. I wanted my man to have a real medical diploma. He has it now and we're going to some big city to get rich, with James treating rich old ladies for make-believe complaints. Where's the harm in that, may I ask?"

She asked it like a prosecuting attorney. "Not a bit of harm," Morgan said, then added, "It'll make these rich old ladies feel better, I would say."

"Exactly what James says. What's wrong with going for the main chance, James says. What's wrong with that?"

Morgan was glad that she didn't seem to need an answer. This James of hers sounded like a real schemer. Whatever happened to dedicated young doctors who doctored Skid Row bums or tried to persuade the Navahos not to shit in the waterholes? As if they ever would.

"I know what you're thinking," Angelique went on, putting on a face. "You're thinking James will dump me now that he's got his medical diploma. What can I do, take him to court?"

Morgan thought he was going to lose his mind with this story.

"I'd kill him," Angelique said fiercely. "I'd cut off his balls with one of his own knives. I'd blow up his office."

Morgan felt like sticking his cock back in her mouth to shut her up. "Don't be like that, young lady."

"At least I'm not like Lily, the fucking cold-hearted bitch that had this room before me."

Morgan opened his eyes when she said that.

Angelique was going good now. "At least I'm marrying a normal young man, not like that creepy old pervert she did. The walking dead. Some catch even if he is rich. I had one session with him—Lady Lily was down with the flu—and that was enough for me. Took half an hour to get it up, then had to put on a rubber thing—a wampus, they call it—to keep it up. And his bleary old eyes closed the whole time he was doing it, or trying to, calling me Lily—I could have killed him."

This was more like it. "I guess she got what she wanted."

"And welcome to it. Never liked her, nobody did except maybe Madame D, who thought she was so cool and ladylike, like butter wouldn't melt in her cunt."

"Guess she never came back to visit?"

Angelique took another small drink. "That's what's so crazy about this whole thing. Three nights ago—slow night, middle of the week, wet and windy out—I was sitting in the parlor with three of the other girls when this big huge drunken lug starts beating and kicking on the front door, yelling like he was crazy. Everybody got scared, not knowing what it was. Madame D is out of her office, yelling for Pierre to do something, so Pierre went to the door to see what was going on. Pierre is a pretty hard man, used to be a prizefighter, but this big lug slammed him with the door when he opened it and down he went. This lug stomped all over him and came charging into the parlor yelling where's his wife, Lily? Where were they keeping her, where was she hiding . . . ?"

47

Angelique paused to catch her breath; Morgan said nothing.

"A real madhouse," Angelique said. "The girls screaming, Madame D wringing her hands, this big lug threatening to tear up the place. He was trying to get at Madame D, making like to choke her, when Pierre crept up behind him and laid him low with a sap. Had to hit him three times before he went down. . . ."

Morgan knew he didn't have to fill in the next pause.

Angelique giggled, feeling good with brandy and a wild story. "It would have been funny if not so scary, guests looking down from the stairs thinking it's robbers or the police, or maybe their wifes were behind it. Madame D was so rattled she forgot to put on the French accent and ordered us all to our rooms, all the time trying to calm down the guests."

Morgan laughed. "Was Lily even there, after all this commotion?"

"Not a sign of her. I'll get to that in a minute. In the meantime, Pierre was kicking this big lug lying in the parlor. I tried to see more, but Madame D shoved me up the stairs. Last I saw, looking over the banisters, was Pierre and Sebastian—that's the black porter—dragging the big lug out of there. Sebastian is my friend, does me favors, like bringing in this brandy. Sebastian doesn't like Madame D—probably hates her—because she treats him like a nigger, which of course he is, but he can't help that, can he? Later on, after they came back, he told me they dragged the big lug and dumped him in an alley five blocks away. Pierre was still mad and warned the big lug when he came to that he'd go in the Bay if he made anymore trouble. Isn't that some story?"

"Sure is," Morgan said. "Did they find out who he was?"

"Yes, they did. Pierre went through his pockets and found papers. Clem Hargis is who he is, just out of the Colorado state penitentiary this past July; that's what the prison paper said. The other thing was just a rent receipt from the Fremont Hotel here in San Francisco. Pierre can't read so good, so Sebastian had to read for him. The prison paper, a release form, said something like he had served seven years for attempted murder and was hereby discharged, meaning he hadn't escaped and shouldn't be arrested, I guess."

"Bad bastard," Morgan said. "Let's hope he doesn't catch up with Lily."

Angelique narrowed her eyes. "What do you care? I hope he does." She drank a little more, drained the glass. "But he won't find her here. About an hour after the ruckus in the parlor, Sebastian told me, Madame D sent him out to fetch a cab for Lily. She left as soon as it got there."

"And you didn't even know she was in the house?" Morgan thought it was safe enough to say that. There wasn't much more to be learned—what he'd learned was pretty good—but he wanted to go easy. Angelique was a hot-tempered little brat, and the liquor was getting to her now; anything could set her off, especially too much interest in Lily.

But she went on as before. After all, it was her story. "That's something I'm a little bit mad at Sebastian for, not telling me she was here. The tips I give that old coot, he should tell me everything. Guess he was scared of Madame D. Anyway, when I pressed him he told me that Lily was upstairs in Madame D's flat for most of three days before the wild husband showed up. Came in Madame D's private entrance, went right upstairs and didn't go out again till she left that night. What's going on, I would like to know."

Morgan had to find out what Clem Hargis looked like. Angelique kept saying how big he was, but that didn't mean much in a big city. "This husband must be a real ugly bastard, the way you describe him."

Angelique scolded him a little for the remark. "I didn't say he was ugly. Has a real ugly temper, is what I said. Maybe he isn't like that when he's sober. I'd have to say he's kind of good looking in a country way, maybe not so bright. I can see how a woman could like him if she got him cleaned and sobered up. Got thick black hair with a white streak in it." Angelique giggled. "You'd think seven years in jail would give you more than a white streak. Not much more than thirty, I would say. Well, maybe a few years. Hey, if this is her legal husband, that makes her a bigamist. What kind of a sentence can you get for bigamy?"

"It's against the law, I'd say." Morgan wasn't giving Lily's bigamy much thought. "I don't know what she'd get, if anything." It was time to give this girl a good pumping and go looking for Clem

Hargis. Too bad he couldn't fuck the day away, but he had to tell Bullock something. He'd fuck an hour's worth, then head for the Fremont Hotel. Hargis, he hoped, would still be there.

Morgan jerked his attention back to Angelique. What was she going on about now? Lily and the crime of bigamy, what else? Of course it was against the law, and only a country fool would doubt it. Lily was going to get plenty.

Morgan grabbed her to keep her quiet. "I don't care what she gets. I want to get into you." She laughed at that, spread her legs obediently, and he got between them, shushing her when she started to explain that she meant to call him a country fool in the nicest way, like she was talking to her kid brother. The kind of loving he had in mind was far from brotherly.

Some whores used petroleum jelly as lubrication; no need for that here. She was wet and ready and he drove his cock in all the way. She giggled and said, "Oh my goodness, sir!" A good thing he mounted up before she got any more brandy.

But she was a professional, young though she was—no more giggling—and she settled down to give him a really good fuck. It wouldn't have mattered what she did: she was going to get the long and strong of his cock. He shafted her like a piston and soon there was the good familiar smell of two hot bodies straining on a bed. A fuck was good anyplace you got it, but there was no place like a big soft bed. Morgan didn't feel like rolling around yet—the bed was big and flat enough for that—but for the moment he was content to hold her firmly in place and larrup it into her. His big hands were clasped around her small rounded ass, kneading it like he was readying a loaf for the oven. Morgan was a big man, but she was strong enough to bump her crotch upward to meet his thrusts. She locked her long legs around the small of his back, trying to hold him as tight as he was holding her. Lord but she was strong, and the brandy was making her stronger. Nothing like health and strength! Nothing like a tight young pussy, hot and greasy and smelling like a pussy ought to smell. His balls tightened up even more as her forefinger poked into his ass. Her finger was greasy with the juice that was oozing out of her and she poked it in and out in a finger fuck that made him groan. . . .

He felt her slim body shake with silent laughter and he thought, she's teasing me, is she? It felt good to be teased by a lovely brat half his age, and maybe she was daring him to fuck her in the ass. Maybe she thought he was the kind of cardboard citizen who wouldn't even think of doing that. If so, she was dead wrong. There was no ill humor in any of his thinking. It was just that he liked a challenge. If this was going to be her last butt fuck as a professional, it was going to be a good one. One she could tell her grandchildren about. Morgan found himself laughing out loud. Angelique joined in as he turned her over and spread them. "Not too rough," she said, still laughing. "Do it right and I'll come crazier than the other way."

He was glad to see he wouldn't be going in dry. Vaseline glistened when he spread her cheeks and he felt like a wildcatter drilling for the big one.

She was young and tight, but she loosened up so he could guide the head of his cock in. In it went, long and strong, and she was able to take most of it. But it wasn't like cunt fucking and you couldn't just go at it like a pile driver. It was different with every woman: you had to get used to them, and them to you. This one liked long sliding strokes and that's what he gave her. He slid his hand under her and tickled her clit. Sometimes she tightened up so much that his cock was trapped for an instant. Then she relaxed her muscles and his cock was moving again, not in a ramming motion, but sliding smoothly. As his finger quickened on her clit she began to buck under him and he rode her like a young filly. Her soft but firm ass was like a cushion and he bounced a little on it. It wasn't that warm in the room—just right—but suddenly he was sweating buckets and his cock was moving faster. Suddenly she buried her face in the mattress and began to scream, the sound muffled but still loud enough. Morgan was sweating buckets and it felt like he came in buckets. It was a long come and his body quivered toward the end of it and he lay on top of her after every drop drained out. Slowly, slowly, when he was strong enough to do it, he started to pull out his cock. It was only when it was all the way out that he realized she was asleep. Not faking it, really asleep.

He washed and dressed and left a good-sized tip on the dresser. Angelique didn't stir. "Good luck with Dr. James," Morgan said, and then he left.

Madame D's door was closed when he got downstairs. Pierre gave him back his gun and helped him on with his raincoat. "Everything satisfactory, sir?" the thug said smoothly.

"Better than Boise." Morgan went out thinking how much he'd like to punch Pierre in the mouth.

Chapter Four

A streetsweeper told Morgan where he could find the Fremont Hotel: Jones and Clay Streets—not a long walk, right down from the corner—he couldn't miss it. It was drizzling again and he buttoned his raincoat and turned up the collar. If he ever quit the horse business he decided he'd move here and open a store that sold nothing but raincoats, umbrellas, galoshes. He'd make a mint.

The hotel where Morgan was staying was all right, but the Fremont had more class to it. Just looking at it you knew it had to cost a lot more—hardly the kind of place you'd expect to find an ex-convict country pimp. New but small, only five stories high, everything about it was well kept. Looked like ol' Clem had come into some money, and if he hadn't pulled any recent jobs, it must have come from Lily. No way to be sure of that, but it was one explanation. Maybe he traced her to Bullock's and she bought time with a few hundred dollars, with the promise of thousands to come, then flew the coop with everything she could lay her hands on. You're just guessing, he told himself. Save it for later.

The desk clerk gave him what he thought was a funny look when he asked for Hargis. Yes, he said, the funny look still on his face, Mr. Hargis was in his room. Room 310, third floor, end of the hall. The clerk looked like he was going to say something else, then changed his mind and started fussing with some papers on the desk. Morgan knew he was being watched as he turned away. He wondered what was bothering the man. It wasn't likely that Hargis had been breaking up his room or pissing out the window; no decent hotel would stand for that.

The elevator was up at the fifth floor, so he took the stairs. It was a nice hotel all right, clean and quiet and smelling of furniture polish. A man he met coming down looked like an alderman or a prosperous salesman. He got to the third floor and walked down to Room 310, his boots making no sound on the thick carpet. No sounds of revelry or anything else came from inside the room, but he unbuttoned his coat and put his gun in the waistband of his pants before he knocked.

He knocked once and waited, then he knocked again. "Mr. Hargis," he said, not too loud. Nobody answered and when he turned the doorknob, the door opened and he found himself looking at the Reverend Duckie O'Connor, who was standing by the bed. A very big man Morgan took to be Hargis was sprawled across the bed, his bare feet sticking out over the edge. There was no light in the room except what came from the curtained window. O'Connor said nothing, just looked deadpan.

"Small world," Morgan said, closing the door.

"Ain't it though," O'Connor said, showing no surprise. "But then San Francisco is a small city for all its brag. You're wanting to see Mr. Hargis, are you? I've just been seeing to the lad. Took a terrible beating from some jackrollers. Was blind drunk or they couldn't have done it. As you can see, he's a slave to drink, poor man." O'Connor tapped an empty whiskey bottle with his toe; the floor was littered with empty bottles. "Came right over when I heard about his plight, the least I could do for a stranger in our city."

"That's very charitable of you."

O'Connor didn't move, didn't change his flat-faced expression. "What brings you here, if I may ask? When last seen you were heading for the fleshpots."

The room smelled pretty bad: whiskey, half-eaten food, sweat, piss. It was a nice but not very large room and none of the furniture had been broken yet. Hargis, lying on his back, was a mess, half a week's stubble on his battered face, wearing nothing but his pissed in pants. The window was closed and the room was overheated.

"I have private business with Hargis," Morgan said, wondering how this was going to go.

"Private, how?" O'Connor said. "Forgive my tone of voice, Mr. Blaney, but you see in a manner of speaking I've taken this unfortunate lad under my wing. I want to help in my humble way." Morgan thought O'Connor looked about as humble as J.P.

Morgan. "No reflection on you, Mr. Blaney, but I'd like to know what you're doing here. You see, I already regard the poor lad as one of my flock."

"I thought your flock was whores."

"Ah yes, Bender has been telling you things. Don't believe everything you hear about me, Mr. Blaney. Bender and his Kelly and Kline music hall jokes. What can he know about my ministry, the Kansas City scoffer?"

"Bender said you do a lot of good. Be that as it may, I'd still like to talk to Hargis."

On the bed Hargis mumbled in his sleep, but O'Connor didn't look at him. "I don't know if that's possible right now, Mr. Blaney. What with the beating he took and a disappointment of a personal nature, he bedded down with a bottle—a lot of bottles—and now he's got the DTs." O'Connor clucked his tongue. "A shame. Had to give him some chloral hydrate—a medicinal Mickey Finn— to send him into a peaceful sleep."

"Looks like he's getting it all right. Guess I'll hang around till he wakes up." Morgan thought he detected a glint of anger in O'Connor's dull eyes. It was gone in an instant, but he was sure he'd seen it. "Was that what you planned to do?"

"Sure thing."

"Then I'll wait with you." Morgan didn't want to tangle with O'Connor, but it had to be said. "I mean to do it."

O'Connor said it just as plain. "I'm afraid I can't allow that, Mr. Blaney. Let me know where you're staying and I'll send word when poor Hargis is able to talk. That's the sensible way to do it."

Morgan stood his ground. Somehow he got the feeling that once Hargis was out of his sight he wouldn't see him again. He'd worked hard to get this far and wasn't about to walk out on it just because O'Connor warned him off. He didn't know what O'Connor's game was, but it wasn't Christian charity. He'd take on the brutal so-called clergyman if he had to, but it would be no cakewalk.

"I mean to stay," he repeated. "Don't try to stop me, Reverend. It's been a long time since you busted skulls and sure as hell you won't bust mine. Besides, you don't want a fight that would bring the coppers."

O'Connor gave Morgan the ghost of a smile. "It wouldn't be a noisy fight, Mr. Blaney. I doubt you'd last ten seconds." He didn't get to say anything else because Hargis came snarling up off the bed swinging an empty quart bottle. The attack was so sudden and fierce that O'Connor could do nothing to avoid the heavy bottle that caved in the top of his derby hat. There was a clunking sound as the bottle hit his skull through the hat and he dropped like a stone. The bottle didn't break and Hargis threw himself on the unconscious man and tried to smash him in the face. Morgan jumped forward and hit Hargis over the head with a cane chair, knocking him forward without knocking him out. He jumped to his feet, quick for his size, and came at Morgan, howling like a madman. Morgan threw the chair at him and he blocked the throw with the bottle. Somehow Hargis caught the flying chair with the other hand and whipped it behind him, shattering the window. Blood was running down his face and the unbroken bottle was still in his hand. He stopped before he got close to Morgan, rubbed blood from his eyes, then broke the bottle expertly on the dresser like a saloon fighter breaking it on the edge of a bar. He shook his head and stared at Morgan for an instant, as if seeing him for the first time. He came at Morgan holding the broken bottle out in front of him, the jagged edges glinting in the dull light of the room. Whiskey crazed or not, he knew what he was doing. Morgan drew the heavy Webley and backed away, thinking, I can shoot the fucker and finish this. But he held his fire, thinking at the same time: I want this fucker alive so he can talk. But the bottle was still swinging at him like a multi-bladed knife. Morgan didn't think it would do any good to shout a warning. He shouted anyway and Hargis jumped at him, slashing at his throat. Morgan jumped to one side and the jagged glass points scraped the door. Hargis was turning when Morgan hit him squarely between the eyes with the muzzle of the chunky pistol. It stopped him but it didn't drop him. He looked more like a dazed bull than a man, eyes bewildered, spit dribbling from his mouth. Morgan swung the Webley and hit him full force on top of the head. Even then he took a few steps before his legs gave way and he fell on his face. Morgan was glad he didn't have to hit him again. He might be dying right now, but he was still breathing. His scalp was split and maybe his skull; no way to be sure, so much blood. The whole thing hadn't taken more than a minute or so, but it was noisy while it lasted. Morgan heard voices in the hall and knew the police would be there pretty soon. The chair going through the window was enough to guarantee that.

O'Connor was muttering and his eyes were open. An odd thing was that his derby was still on his head, rammed down hard by the blow from the bottle. Morgan tried to lift him and felt the gun under O'Connor's arm. A gun-toting sky pilot. Didn't surprise him, not when the padre was Duckie O'Connor.

"Leave me be," O'Connor growled, getting up by holding onto the bottle-scarred dresser. "I can take care of myself."

"You weren't so spry a minute ago."

"Caught me by surprise." O'Connor wrenched the hat from his head and punched out the dented crown. A good-sized lump was coming up on his bald head. He touched the lump and winced, then put on his hat so it just perched there.

"Guess I owe you," he said, looking at Hargis and the broken bottle. "Didn't give him enough chloral, I guess. If not for the hat . . ." He still looked a bit dazed.

Morgan grabbed him by the arm. "I saved your life, don't forget that. Right now we have to get out of here. Coppers must be on their way." And he heard them coming to the door even as he said it.

Knuckles hit the door and a loud voice said, "Open up in there! This is the police!"

"That's Dowd," O'Connor said. "Open it. Let me do the talking."

The door was flung open before Morgan got to

it and two plainclothes policemen were looking at him. Dowd, as O'Connor called him, was an angry looking man about forty with mottled red skin and ginger eyebrows. The man behind him was younger, about twenty-five, and taller by four or five inches, which allowed him to look over Dowd's shoulder. Both wore dark suits and derbies.

"Move back in there and don't try anything," Dowd told Morgan. "What's going on here? There's been a complaint."

Morgan moved back and out of the way. O'Connor said, "Lieutenant Dowd, just the man I want to see. Come in. Come in."

"What else would we do?" Dowd said irritably at the door. The two policemen came in followed by a third man dressed in a swallowtail coat and gray trousers. He had a waxed mustache and a pearl pin in his necktie. His mustache quivered with indignation as he looked at Hargis on the floor, the empty bottles, the broken window.

"This is disgraceful," he said. "Lieutenant, I insist—"

Dowd held up a pink hand with ginger hairs on the back of it. "I'll handle this if you don't mind, Mr. Sloan. What's been happening here?" he said to O'Connor. Then, without waiting for an answer, he said to Morgan, "Who are you?"

"Mr. Buck Blaney," O'Connor said. "From Ludwig, Oregon."

"Let him talk for himself, O'Connor." It was plain that Dowd didn't like O'Connor.

"*Reverend* O'Connor—please."

Dowd ignored him. Morgan said, "My name is

Blaney, like he said. I'm in business up north."
Well that part was true, Morgan thought, he
was in business up north. But he didn't have to
say anything else because Dowd turned back to
O'Connor.

"Well?" he said.

It seemed to Morgan that this man jumped
around a lot. The police chiefs might think
O'Connor a character; clearly Dowd wasn't of
that opinion.

Slow talking though he was, O'Connor told his
lying story fast enough. Minister to the unfortunate
that he was, he had come to see what he could
do for Hargis once he learned of his plight. The
poor man, a slave to demon rum, had been beaten
and robbed by strongarms. What else could he
do but help him? Mr. Buck Blaney, a well-to-do
lumberman from up north—a good man interested in his missionary work—had accompanied
him. . . .

"Wait a minute," Dowd said. "This man can't be
a bum if he's staying here."

O'Connor said patiently, "He soon will be if he
keeps on the way he's going. Next stop: Skid Row.
Just last night he came to my mission seeking
help spiritual and otherwise. Unfortunately, he
ran off when he was only partway through his
story. Overcome by guilt and embarrassment, you
might say. However, he did let it drop that he was
staying here. I came here today with Mr. Blaney."

Dowd sniffed the air and bent down beside
Hargis. "Smells like he's been drinking more than
whiskey. Chloral. I don't see an empty bottle."

63

O'Connor looked doleful. "Who can say what he did with it? They drink it to head off the DTs, or so they hope."

"Didn't work this time, did it?" Dowd was looking at Hargis. "Anyway he's still breathing. Did you do that to him?" he said to Morgan.

Morgan didn't like being back in Dowd's sights. "No other way to stop him. He was asleep, so we decided to wait till he came to—"

"Sleep is the great healer," O'Connor put in.

Dowd ignored that, waited for Morgan to go on. "We were talking quietly about doing something about the mess here when suddenly he jumped off the bed and hit Reverend O'Connor with a bottle. Only his hat saved him from serious injury. See for yourself."

Coming in on his cue, O'Connor lifted his damaged hat from his head and displayed the big lump on the crown. "Poor demented bloke nearly killed me," he said mildly. "Knocked me cold."

Dowd looked back at Morgan. "He was fixing to hit him again," Morgan said. "I grabbed a chair and hit him, but it was like hitting him with a pillow. He grabbed the chair away from me and threw it through the window. He still had the bottle in the other hand and he broke it on the dresser there"—Morgan pointed and they all looked—"and came after me. I drew my gun and warned him off, but it was no use. See the gouges on the door there?" They all looked. "That's when he nearly got me. I hit him over the head and knocked him unconscious."

"Ah, the poor man didn't know what he was

doing," O'Connor said. "He can't be held respon-sible."

Dowd didn't think much of that. "We'll see about that. Let's see the gun."

Morgan showed him the five-shot Webley. Dowd broke it open, checked the loads, snapped it shut, and sniffed at the muzzle. Morgan had no idea why he was doing all that; no shots had been fired. For a moment he thought Dowd was going to keep the gun, and what he could do about that he wasn't sure. It was his experience that the police could do pretty much as they pleased.

Dowd was still hesitating when O'Connor said, "There is no concealed weapons law in San Francisco, Lieutenant."

Dowd didn't like having the law quoted to him. "There ought to be. However, there are laws against assault and attempted murder. This man may be dying."

As if to dispute that, Hargis started to groan and then to curse, and his fingernails scratched at the carpet. Dowd told the other plainclothesman to put a pillow under his head. "Go down and call an ambulance," he said.

O'Connor didn't want that. "If you'll just leave him to my care. What Mr. Blaney did was in self-defense—"

"So you say."

"So I do, Lieutenant. It was self-defense and you know it. Or do you want me to telephone Mr. Seligman? Or the Commissioner? I was talking to him just last evening at the Palace. The Police Chiefs' get-together."

Dowd glared at him, Morgan's gun still in his hand. Morgan didn't know what was between Dowd and O'Connor, but there was something. "Nobody said anything about charging Blaney," Dowd said angrily.

"Then give him back his gun."

Dowd gave Morgan the gun and he put it away. "If this man assaulted you—"

"Mr. Blaney doesn't want to sign a complaint and neither do I. It would be like kicking a man when he's down," O'Connor said. "No complaint. It wouldn't be right."

This was too much for the manager. "Well, I certainly will sign a complaint. Who's going to pay for the damage to this room, not to mention the damage to this hotel's reputation?"

"I'll pay for the damage." O'Connor took out his wallet, but instead of money he gave the manager his business card. "As soon as you have arrived at a figure, send me a bill. You're guaranteed prompt payment. I'm sure you don't want to sign a complaint."

Dowd's temper had been simmering. Now it boiled over again. "Mr. Sloan has every right to sign a complaint."

"I just want this ruffian out of here," Mr. Sloan said. "Right this instant I want him removed from my hotel."

By now Hargis was fully awake and trying to get up off the floor. But every time he did he fell back again and lay there cursing. Dowd turned his anger on the young policeman. "Didn't I tell you to go down and call an ambulance? This man is going to the hospital under guard."

"I'm telling you I'll look after him," O'Connor said. "He'll have the best of care. What's all this under guard business? If nobody signs a complaint, where's the charge?"

Dowd gave O'Connor a mean smile. "He can be charged without a complaint. You didn't know that? It's for the district attorney to decide—not you, not me."

O'Connor's laugh was mirthless, but he tried. "You'd be the joke of the department, trying to bring a pissant case like this to the district attorney. All's well that ends well. No real damage has been done. Leave the poor man to me."

"I'd be shirking my responsibility if I did," Dowd said piously. Morgan could see Dowd didn't give a shit about Hargis. He just wanted to get at O'Connor. "What this man needs is a hospital and I'm going to see that he gets it. Whether he's charged or not remains to be seen. But first, a doctor. Sorry, *Duckie*."

Suddenly O'Connor's dead face was like a thundercloud. "Listen to me, you Irish cock-sucker—"

The pot calling the kettle mick, Morgan thought. Why couldn't O'Connor just let it go? He'd already pushed Dowd pretty hard, threatening him with the Commissioner and Mr. Seligman, whoever he was—probably some high-powered lawyer. But maybe the dangerous old bastard knew what he was doing.

Dowd didn't seem to think so. He gave another mean grin, as if finally, at long last, he had

O'Connor over that barrel. And he began to tick off the charges he had in mind. "Abusive language to a police officer," he started off. "Threatening a police officer, even more serious. Number three—"

O'Connor didn't blink an eye. "Why don't you kiss my 'Stralian arse? Wait while I take down my trousers. You've got no witnesses, you miserable little git."

Dowd looked around for the hotel manager, but he'd gone downstairs with the other plainclothesman. Morgan almost felt sorry for the angry, red-faced copper, but not quite. Life had taught him not to give anything away to lawmen of any stripe. But he wished to hell he was somewhere else, like maybe back in Idaho.

"One of these days," Dowd started to say, but he was so choked up with rage he had to stop. "You," he said to Morgan when he got himself under some kind of control. "Blaney, Buck is your name, what's your address in the city? This is not the end of this."

"He's staying with me at the mission," O'Connor said before Morgan could answer. "You know where that is."

The young plainclothesman came into the room. "The ambulance is on its way, Lieutenant. Anything else you want me to do?"

"No, that's fine," Dowd said quietly. "We'll just wait for the ambulance. You two *gentlemen* can leave. One last thing, Blaney: if this man takes a bad turn and dies, something like that, I don't want to have to hunt all over for you. Is that clear?"

Morgan nodded. "I'll be at the mission till further

68

notice." That's what he said, but he wasn't sure where he'd be. This whole thing was getting too complicated; the money from Bullock wasn't enough to pay for real trouble with the San Francisco police. And Dowd would be wanting to make serious trouble if only to spite O'Connor.

Hargis was trying to sit up and the young plainclothesman was trying to make him lie down. "Keep him still," Dowd ordered. "Try to keep him from moving. He may have a fractured skull."

Dowd wants him to have a fractured skull, Morgan thought. Dowd wants him to die. He wondered if Dowd might not give him a few kicks in the head to help him on his way. He knew he'd probably get off on self-defense, but he didn't want to go to all that trouble.

The ambulance men were coming up the stairs as they went down. Morgan didn't see the blood on his shirt and pants until he was out in the daylight. He buttoned his raincoat to hide it.

Chapter Five

Two patrolmen were watching the ambulance at the side entrance to the hotel. O'Connor waved to them, called their names, and they waved back. Morgan, who had seen enough law for one day, wanted to be gone.

"Take it easy, Mr. Blaney," O'Connor said after they moved off. "You're in no trouble, at least no trouble that I can't set right with a word or two in the right ear. Let's go and get ourselves a glass of beer and have a talk. You agree it's time we had a little talk?"

"You're right." Morgan had no idea where they were going. It was O'Connor's town and he let him lead the way. "What's this about me staying at your mission?" he asked when they were at an intersection waiting for a string of wagons to go by.

"You're better off there for now." They started across the street, then turned down another, narrower street. "Dowd could take a notion to call at your hotel."

"I can handle Dowd."

O'Connor flipped a nickel to some snotnose kid who started dogging them. "Don't be deceived by Dowd's size. He's a rough bugger when there's nobody to see him do it, nobody that counts. Did you see that tall young bloke that follows him around? Dumb and friendly but roughhouse all the way if that's what Dowd wants. No, sir, Mr. Blaney, you couldn't handle the two of them unless you shot them, and then where would you be?"

"You think they'll come looking for me?"

"I don't know what Dowd will do. After I talk to the right people he won't do anything. That's one reason he hates me: I have friends in high places and he has none at all. Other reasons I'll tell you about later. Right now you'd better stay with me."

They had to stop again, this time for a water wagon that was creeping along, wetting down the street. "Look at that," O'Connor said in disgust, "it's raining and they're wetting down the dust. Pity the poor taxpayer."

"I have money in the hotel safe," Morgan said. "A good bit of money and my gun. I'm paying by the day. If I don't show up—"

"I'll take care of it. Come on. I've got a sour taste in my mouth after talking to Dowd. A cold beer will be good."

They were passing a saloon. To Morgan it looked as good as any. "What's the matter with this place?"

"Nothing. But we're going to the Brian Boru, right down the street. We can talk in private."

They walked along and Morgan started to say something about Dowd. "Wait. Wait," O'Connor said. "Let's not be discussing business in the street. Did you know Brian Boru was the highest king of all the high kings of Ireland?"

Morgan didn't answer. O'Connor was a crafty, dangerous bullshitter, no one to be trusted as far as he could see. The smart thing would be to turn about and go the other way. But what the hell, he might as well hear him out.

"Here we are," O'Connor said, as if Morgan didn't realize that they had finally arrived at the Brian Boru. The front of the four-story building was painted bright green and above the door was a plaster statue of some long-bearded old geezer with a sword that Morgan took to be Brian himself. He knew it wasn't Stonewall Jackson, though there was some resemblance; the name of the place was about two feet high.

"Nobody's going to bother us here," O'Connor said as they went in. "Man who owns it used to be a bigtime copper till they kicked him out for cheating on the graft. Not a copper on the force he doesn't know and if he's in doubt all he has to do is ask one of his barkeeps, all cashiered coppers like himself. A gumshoe comes in here they treat him like a leper."

"You think Dowd—"

"Not so loud, not that you have to be careful in here. They know me and I know them."

Whatever that means, Morgan thought, deciding he'd have to take O'Connor as he found him. Until it was time to walk away, that is.

72

Whatever the Brian Boru might be—probably a hangout for crooks—it was doing land office business. Big as a small barn, with drinkers three-deep at the bar, several bartenders were working their asses off trying to keep up with the demand for beer and whiskey. With O'Connor clearing a path through the crowd—waving, handshaking, backslapping—Morgan followed along slowly all the way to the back, where a man with a black suit and a squint showed them into a private room. He closed the door and asked what they were drinking.

"Two schooners, right," he said after O'Connor told him. Then he lowered his voice though there was no one else there. "Thanks for taking care of that. I mean it."

"Anything for a friend, Packy. Think nothing of it."

"I'll never forget you," Packy said fervently, then rushed out to get the beer.

"Poor man," O'Connor said while they were waiting. "Pimp got hold of his sister, who had taken to strong drink and finally the streets. I should say the docks—anywhere she could sell it for the price of a cheap bottle. Poor Packy came to me for help. I said I'd take care of it."

"I guess you did."

"Always do what I say. In this case I bet the pimp he couldn't swim to Oakland with both hands tied behind his back. Not only did he not take the bet, he skipped town and hasn't been seen since."

"Is there a lesson in that for me?" Morgan asked.

If O'Connor gave a flat-out yes, that would be the end of it.

Packy knocked and came in with the beer. O'Connor made a pretense of reaching for his wallet, but Packy wouldn't hear of it. "I wish you'd have something better than beer. We have Bushmill's, no finer Irish whiskey than that."

O'Connor said beer was fine. "Packy owes me now," he said after the squint-eyed man went out, "and I don't want him repaying me piecemeal with costly whiskcy. In answer to your question, I meant no lesson for you. I just wanted to point out that I never go back on my word, that's all."

"Glad to hear it. Neither do I." Morgan picked up the schooner and drank from it. It was real San Francisco steam beer, as good a beer as they made. "What happened to the sister?"

"She's at the mission. I don't know if she can be helped, but at least she's off the streets. No use scaring off one pimp with another one just around the corner. That's a manner of speaking, of course. Jesus pity the pimp that hangs around my mission."

O'Connor swallowed a lot of beer, then sat back in his chair. "Before we get started I'd like to set your mind at rest about Dowd. All right, here it is: The bastard would like to use you to make trouble for me. In his present set-up—the Hotel Squad, so-called—there isn't much he can do. And I mean to have him put in his place. It was different when he had the Morals Squad. Yes, there is a Santa Claus and there is a Morals Squad in the San Francisco Police Department, the Barbary Coast, all the whorehouses notwithstanding—"

There was a knock and Packy stuck his head in. "You gentlemen ready for more beer?"

O'Connor sighed. "Bring a real big pitcher, then go away and stay away," he said with mild exasperation.

"Coming right up." Packy closed the door.

"When Dowd was with Morals he couldn't get it out of his head that my mission was a front for something." O'Connor's blank face darkened at the thought. "I don't know what he thought I was doing with those poor women. Sending them south to Mexican whorehouses? Selling them to the Los Angeles Chinamen, who are mighty hard up for women of any color? Whatever it was—and I never knew for sure—he gave me a lot of bother. Raiding the mission, the cocksucker, coming in with warrants, that kind of shit. Anyway—"

Packy arrived with the pitcher of beer. "I'm going. I'm going." He left.

"Anyway," O'Connor went on, "it took some doing to get him transferred from Morals, but I did it. Wasn't easy, like I said, because he had the backing of the reform crowd. In fact, one reform candidate keeps saying he'll make Dowd Commissioner of Police if he's ever elected, which of course is not going to happen. So getting him fired was out of the question. I had to settle for shunting him off to the Hotel Squad. It's a dead-end job, responding to calls from good hotels and dumps—mostly dumps—and he hates it. It's what brought him to the Fremont today. I hadn't seen him for months—

why should I?—till he showed up with that clown of his."

O'Connor paused to pour beer for both of them. Morgan said, "You said you were going to put him in his place?"

"Nothing else but. Of course there's nothing I can do to alter the events of today. That would be asking too much—Dowd is very careful with his reports—but what I can do is to see that he doesn't overstep his authority. In short, he'll be told to stick to sneaking around hotel corridors, something he's well suited for, and to let the Hargis case, so-called, die a natural death."

Morgan helped himself to beer. "Then he won't be coming after me?"

"Not unless he decides to do it on his own, which I very much doubt."

"But supposing he does? Suppose he tries to press a charge against Hargis?"

"He'll be warned off Hargis, didn't I just tell you?"

"Yes. But what if he doesn't listen? What if Hargis denies everything you told Dowd?"

"Not too likely. Anyway, who'd listen to the ravings of a drunk? I'll say it again: don't worry about Dowd. I'll block whatever he tries—if he tries it—and this time I'll get him fired. Now drink up before it gets warm. We didn't come here to talk about Aloysius Dowd."

Morgan smiled at him. "What did we come here to talk about?

O'Connor tried to smile back. "I thought you knew. Don't you?"

"Why don't you lead off? You called the meeting."

"Why don't you drop the country boy act? You may be country, but at your age you're surely not a boy, no offense intended. What you're not, I'm pretty sure, is a lumberman. You don't have the broken hands most of them do. I spotted that at breakfast when Bender introduced you as such."

"This is good beer," Morgan said, and he took a drink to show how good it was.

"Your name probably isn't Blaney, but I don't mind that. What's in a name and so forth. What I do mind is somebody thinking I can be fooled. All those questions about the classy whorehouses. Bender thinks he's so fucking sly. I knew right off you weren't the kind of a man who would need a guide to get fucked."

O'Connor held up his hand. "Spare me any more comments on the beer. Hear me out, if you're so inclined, and then you can talk. I get around and I hear things. I make it my business to know what's going on. People tell me the damnedest things. Coppers, whores, bellboys, morgue attendants, scrubwomen. Sometimes I pay for information if I think it's worth it. Sometimes this information is sold not directly to me but to another party, who then sells it to me. Very often this information has to do with large sums of money or what can be turned into money: where it can be found, or who's stolen it, or where it's hidden. Sometimes the person who has this information can be approached. Say a certain butler in a Nob Hill mansion knows something—"

"A certain butler," Morgan said. What did Bullock call his butler, the elderly Englishman who had ushered him into the library, the old boy who had brought in the iced beer and then disappeared? Hammond, that was it.

"We'll get back to the butler," O'Connor continued. "It came to my attention that a drunken ruffian who called himself Clem Hargis was making a nuisance of himself, trying to track down his wife Lily, a professional prostitute, a house worker, he kept telling people. Very good looking, very classy. Now if there is one thing San Francisco has, it's whorehouses, so he had his work cut out for him. But finally, I was told, he learned that she no longer worked in a house but had married well. Are you with me, Mr. Blaney?"

"I think so," Morgan said.

"As well you might, sir. Lily Bullock, to give her her married name. What happened next is unclear, but there is no doubt that Hargis confronted her somehow or somewhere, the drunken blackguard and the lady of the manor, so to speak. Hargis, by the way, is an ex-convict, as you may know, so it isn't hard to picture the scene. Here is this thug without a pot to piss in, and suddenly there is the pot of gold, all for him at the end of the rainbow, with old man Bullock as the leprechaun. Except in this case the one who can deliver the gold is his lovely wife. Now this Hargis is certainly not too bright, but he's crafty. Bullock, through Lily, is the golden goose, the money cow, and as long as she stays married to Bullock the money flow will never dry up. Hargis sees a life of ease ahead of him, the best of everything, and he doesn't want to hear that Bullock is a tightwad. The money is there so Lily can get it, and there is always blackmail as a last resort. Are you still with me, sir?"

"I'm listening with great interest," Morgan said, wondering if there wasn't anything this fucker didn't know.

"Lily knows Hargis is going to fuck up everything she's worked for: respectability, social position, a fine house. And when Bullock dies, which can't be far in the future, everything will come to her in the natural way of things. So she has to make a decision. And what she decides is to buy off Hargis, tell him he has to wait, and then clean out Bullock's safe and make a run for it. I know she cleaned out the safe because Bullock changed the combination after she left. How much she got nobody knows except Bullock and Lily and, I think, you."

"I might only know what I was told."

"That's true. There could have been much more. But let me go on. You see I'm laying all my cards on the table. Well, sir, you can imagine poor Clem's rage and disappointment when he learned that his lawfully wedded wife had done him dirt. Once again she disappeared, as she did after he was sent to prison. That part is obvious—he had no idea where to find her when he got out. But this time the crafty fellow had a clue: the last house she worked in before she married Bullock was Madame De Mornay's, and so there he goes after getting drunk. He threatens to tear the house down if they don't give her up. But instead of getting his wife back he gets laid out by the bully and dumped in an alley."

"And you just happened to hear about it?"

"Not exactly. I had been making my own inquiries. And Madame D's black porter feeds me the odd morsel of information. As I told you, I know all sorts of people and they tell me things. The exception, of course, is you. You haven't told me anything."

"In a minute, maybe. What were you going to do with Hargis when I walked in? You'd already doped him, you said. Were you fixing to take him to the mission? The door wasn't locked."

O'Connor nodded. "That was the plan. Telephone the mission and get my people to come over with a cab. My mistake was not giving him enough chloral and unlocking the door too soon. But I'm not complaining. Likely Hargis would have attacked me anyway. I guess you saved my life."

"No guess about it."

O'Connor thought for a while, his two huge hands folded across his belly. It was quiet in spite of the racket outside in the saloon. Morgan was thinking too, trying to decide which way to go. Trust came hard to him, yet he had to make up his mind whether to throw in with O'Connor or cut loose from him. The man was in this for the money, but how much did he want? Some of it? All of it? They would have to talk about that. What he couldn't understand, when you got right down to it, was why O'Connor wanted him to come in with him. There wasn't much he didn't know, so why—

At last O'Connor said, "You want a guarantee that I won't turn on you. That's what this saving-your-life talk is about, isn't it? A man whose life you saved ought not to turn on you. That's as it ought to be, but it isn't always that way. All I can say is, I've never doublecrossed anybody in my life."

Morgan waited and O'Connor said, "Not unless they tried to doublecross me first. Fairer than that I can't say."

Morgan looked at him, but there was nothing to read in that impassive face. "It's fair enough as far as it goes, but why do you need me? Why don't you go after Bullock's wife on your own?"

"Hargis's wife. No matter. You're right though. I could go searching for her, but I don't know what she's got or how much. Jewels? Money? Securities? Bullock is a tightwad with a great love for money, so I can't see a lot of cash lying about. Another thing: he can't be stealing from his partners because he has none."

"Wait a minute. You still haven't answered my question. Why do you think you need me?"

"To tell me what Lily has, but that's just part of it. You have the inside track with Bullock. I doubt if he's told you everything—men like that never do—and there may be more information forthcoming if you press him for it. He hired you to find Lily—don't waste time by denying it—so he must have some trust in you. As much trust as he places in anybody, that is. Or—and I don't like to say this—he may be trying to play you for a fool."

"Like how?"

"I don't know. But hasn't that thought occurred to you?"

"It's crossed my mind," Morgan said. "But the reasons he gave for hiring me seemed reasonable enough. He says he'd become a joke if it got into the papers, the old goat who couldn't hold onto a young wife. Bad for business and so forth. He doesn't trust the police and says private detectives are just as untrustworthy. So he hired me, on the recommendation of a friend, because I'm a stranger here and have no connections with the newspapers or the law."

"How much is he paying you, if I may ask?"

"A thousand dollars to find his wife." Morgan had made his decision. O'Connor knew most of it, and maybe he knew more than he said, so it didn't make much difference.

"A thousand dollars," O'Connor repeated. "That's lunch money, considering how rich he's supposed to be. You ought to be able to do better than that."

"I made a deal and I'm going to stick to it. The deal is: a thousand to get back what Lily stole, another thousand for Lily herself. I don't see that as lunch money."

O'Connor waited without saying anything. "What she took was a hundred thousand in negotiable securities," Morgan said, thinking, well it's out in the open now, not that it mattered a whole lot. O'Connor already knew Lily had stolen big.

O'Connor nodded in his solemn way. "A sizable amount. I wonder why he didn't keep the securities in the bank. Very strange, given the man's reputation for closeness in money matters. You say Lily took no cash?"

"A few hundred dollars, is what Bullock said."

O'Connor did some more thinking. "That sounds about right. Only a few hundred dollars household money, yet at the same time he kept a hundred thousand dollars worth of securities, as good as money, where any safecracker could break in and take it. I wonder why."

Morgan had no answer for that, though the same question had been in the back of his mind. It hadn't seemed all that important—what Bullock did with his securities was his business—and maybe it wasn't. He wasn't being paid to pry into Bullock's affairs, just to find the missing paper and return it to its rightful owner. For which he would be paid the second five hundred dollars. Just the same . . .

O'Connor said, "It's your firm intention to return the securities to Bullock if you find them?"

"That's the deal."

"You wouldn't be tempted to take the whole kaboodle? Let Bullock go fly a kite?"

"No, sir." They were finally getting down to cases, Morgan thought.

"What could he do if you did? If he's so scared of publicity, how could he come after you? Just asking."

"Sure you are. Well here's a question for you. How much do you expect to get out of this? A generous reward?"

O'Connor allowed himself one of his rare, thin

smiles. "I have to be honest. I'd like to split it fifty-fifty with you. Think of all the good I could do with fifty thousand dollars. Believe me, I could steal, if that's the right word, every cent Bullock possesses with a perfectly clear conscience. It takes money to do the Lord's work."

O'Connor sounded sincere, but Morgan was too old a hand to be taken in by appearances. "You don't seem to be hurting for money."

That brought a windy sigh. "You mean just because I wear good clothes and eat in good restaurants. What would you have me do, go about in rags carrying a beggar's bowl? Good restaurants, the race track—this is where you meet men with money. You'd be surprised how little good restaurants and good clothes cost me."

Morgan didn't say it wouldn't surprise him at all.

O'Connor got off the subject of good works. "You've been asking why I need you and I think I've answered some of it. Now as to why you need me, I don't think you have much chance of finding Lily without my help. Getting onto Hargis was sheer luck, I would say. How did you do it?"

Morgan told him about Angelique, keeping it short: the porter telling her about the trouble Hargis made and what happened afterwards. The hotel receipt, the prison discharge papers.

That got an approving nod. "And you got a good fuck besides." O'Connor reached into his pocket and took out two folded papers wrapped in oiled paper. "This first one is Hargis's discharge from the Colorado state pen dated last July. Served seven years of a seven year sentence for attempted muder. No time off so he must have been a bad lad inside the walls."

Morgan looked at and pushed it back across the table.

"And this is a marriage license made out in Fort Smith, Arkansas, ten years ago. See the names: Lily Newell Sears and Clement C. Hargis. So it's bigamy all right, not that it matters a hell of a lot in California. Half the state is running away from sour marriages. Still, it would be embarrassing for old man Bullock if it came out. It's one way to put pressure on him, if necessary."

O'Connor put the papers away. "The discharge was in his coat pocket. I found the marriage license under the bottom drawer of the dresser. That and three hundred dollars that I took for safekeeping. So, in or out of the hospital, Hargis is flat broke."

"So he'll be desperate," Morgan said.

"Meaning he'll look all the harder for Lily. Somehow or other he found her the first time, tracked her all the way from Colorado after a seven year gap in time. I don't know how he did it, but he did it and I'm hoping he'll do it again. You see, he has one advantage over us: he knows Lily better than we do—"

Packy knocked and came in looking mad. "Excuse me. Excuse me," he said before O'Connor could start in on him. "George just spotted Dutch Hoff hanging around outside. 'Cross the street, down a bit, looking in a window, tying his shoelaces and such. Thought you'd want to know."

"You did right to tell me," O'Connor said calmly. "Tell George to keep an eye on the fucker. We'll be leaving in a few minutes."

The door closed and O'Connor said, "Dutch Hoff is one of Dowd's clowns. The nerve of that cocksucker, sending that kraut after me. Can't be some hotel thief he's after. They don't get them in here. Goddamn and fuck it, I'm going to nail Dowd to the fucking cross."

Morgan thought of his horse ranch in the green hills of Idaho where everything was so simple.

Chapter Six

They left in a cab because O'Connor said he had a real bitch of a headache and wanted to get home and lie down. Packy wanted to know if the cab should come to the side entrance, which opened onto an alley, and O'Connor said why the fuck should they do a sneak act? They weren't breaking any laws. Packy then asked how about dropping a brick on the plainclothesman's head and when O'Connor said no, he made one last offer: "How about a bucket of shit?"

"Don't do a thing, but thanks for the thought." O'Connor greeted the cab driver by name; no need to give him the address. The cab moved away from the curb into heavy traffic. Most of the wagons tying up the street belonged to some brewery. O'Connor sank back on the padded seat and closed his eyes; he was no longer hopping mad at Dowd, just sore as hell.

Eyes still closed, O'Connor said, "I'm going to sic Joe Seligman on that sneaking cunt." By now

Morgan knew that when O'Connor said 'cunt' he meant Lieutenant Dowd; he never spoke of women as cunts. It was strange to hear a man described as a cunt. Morgan guessed it was something they said in Australia. "Joe is the mayor's personal attorney and a good friend of Billy O'Brien. I guess you've heard of Billy O'Brien?"

"I know three Billy O'Briens," Morgan said.

O'Connor was massaging his eyeballs. "This O'Brien is one of the Comstock Four. Silver kings. Nevada. Billy's got a house on Nob Hill that makes Bullock's place look like a shanty. Dowd's going to shit his pants when Joe puts on the squeeze. Joe owes me a favor. It's better Joe does it than going straight to the Commissioner, you understand?"

Morgan didn't know what the fuck he was talking about, but no matter. Just as long as somebody shoved Dowd out of the picture.

"I wonder if Joe could get rid of the cocksucker once and for all. Wouldn't that be something? Can't push it too hard though." Just thinking about burying Dowd had put O'Connor in a better humor and he opened his eyes and rubbed his big hands together. "I'll teach him to fuck around with me.'

The wagon traffic petered out and the cab picked up speed. They were on Sacramento Street, a sign said. "Forget Dowd," O'Connor said, as if Morgan still wanted to talk about it. "We've got to see what we can do to get Hargis out of that hospital. At least keep an eye on him while he's in there, be ready for him when he gets out. Then we'll see how the wind blows."

Up ahead the street was blocked by a bunch o

women carrying placards and banners. Morgan thought a few of them weren't bad looking; the rest were crows, young and old. "We want the vote! Equal rights! Equal rights!" was some of what they were chanting. A bugle was blaring, a bass drum thumping; bluecoats were trying to block their march.

"Crazy women," O'Connor said mildly. "They're all over the city. Last week they pelted the Mayor with rotten eggs, God bless 'em."

"How are you going to keep an eye on Hargis?" Morgan asked. "You know somebody in the hospital?"

Some of the women the police had dispersed were back in the middle of the street. The cab slowed again and up on the box the driver was cursing, yelling down at them: "Why don't you go home and clean your houses, you dirty bitches!"

The cab started to move again, but not before a wild-eyed young woman spat in the window. "Jesus Christ, sister, I'm on your side," O'Connor said.

"Fuck you, Father," she screamed before she was grabbed and hustled away.

The riot dropped away behind them and O'Connor settled back again. "Some of those ladies are going to end up in the hospital . . . the hospital, yeah—Hargis. I have a woman at the mission that will keep an eye on Hargis, check on him every day, more than once a day. Pose as his worried wife, will look just right. A good woman, a tough woman, used to work for the Bannerman Detective Agency in Chicago. Name of Harriet Streeter. Fell for a con man she was

after for the agency, got conned herself. Good
looking guy, I guess. Got knocked up, got fired
and followed him out here, but he'd disappeared.
Started drinking and doping, in some ways like
Packy's sister, only brighter, more education. I
found her half-dead in a hospital and took her
in. I don't know what happened to the kid. She
never talks about it and I don't ask."

"Sounds all right." Morgan couldn't think of
anything else to say. O'Connor had so many grim
stories. Maybe he did a lot of good. Maybe it wasn't
all bullshit.

"You'll meet her when we get there," O'Connor
said. "Don't be put off by her manner. She's been
abandoned by her family, cheated by johns, beaten
by pimps, rousted by the coppers. She's as hard
as nails. Women don't have an easy time in this
world."

"How long has she been at the mission?" Morgan
wondered how many more people were going to get
into this.

"You mean can I trust her? Probably I can trust
her. Anyway, all she'll be asked to do is check on
Hargis—at first, that is. But she was a private
detective—a pretty good one, I guess. She could
come in useful. She's been at the mission three
months and shows no signs of moving on. That's all
right. I put her in charge of the girls and the place
has been running smoother since she came."

They passed a big church with a tall spire. Looking at it O'Connor stroked his jutting chin and grew
meditative. "How about that crazy woman taking
me for a priest? She called me 'Father,' and me not

even a Catholic. But it's no secret I studied for the priesthood back in Sydney. An old mate of mine let the cat out of the bag, God rest his soul—the mouthy bastard."

Morgan didn't ask how the student priest got to be a convict and later, according to Bender, the biggest pimp on the Barbary Coast. The cab turned onto Kearny Street and drove down to Washington. At the intersection was a beat-up looking park with ratty trees and rattier people.

"That's the Plaza," O'Connor said. "Where the bums and beggars and low class thieves rest between their labors. Streetwalkers, too, when the coppers let them. Very hard on the feet, streetwalking."

The mission was on Front Street, not far from the Bay; steam whistles and foghorns sounded so there must have been fog on the water. The mission was a four-story building that looked like a cross between a warehouse and a temperance hotel. Grim as a hellfire sermon, it had a dirty brick face and clean windows. Well scrubbed stone steps went up to the entrance where a hard-faced man of about fifty stood with folded arms. Above the door was a sign: MAGDALENE MISSION, with black lettering on a white background. Morgan thought the door—thick nail-studded oak with a small barred window at eye level—was as formidable as the tough bird guarding it.

"How's everything, Wilfred?" O'Connor asked.

"Dead as granddad's nuts, Duckie," Wilfred said, opening the door.

"Carry on," O'Connor said, ushering Morgan in

ahead of him. "This place used to be a sailor's hostel," O'Connor told Morgan when they were both inside. "They couldn't make a go of it because most of the sailors, as you can imagine, balked at all the rules, preferred to lay up in the Coast. Oh, they got a few old religious nondrinking misers off the ships, not enough to fill a corner of the place. So it fell empty—stayed empty for a year—before I put in my bid for it."

Another man, middle-aged like the door guard, was behind a counter built into a plastered wall with patches of brick showing through. The counter had a metal grill running along the top, with a space in the middle. The clerk, or whatever he was, got up off his stool when they came in. He was small and mean-faced, with thinning gray hair and no teeth. O'Connor greeted him as Mikey.

"Where can we find Harriet?" O'Connor asked. To Morgan he remarked, "She's all over the place."

"I think in the typewriting room," Mikey said. "Or the laundry or the kitchen. You know Harriet."

They went down a long hallway tiled to the height of a man. It smelled of strong soap and the tiles reminded Morgan of the entrance to a morgue. No wonder the sailors hadn't liked it. But it sure was clean—a lot better than the streets and the woman-beating pimps.

O'Connor stopped to look at a blackboard with messages chalked on it. "You know, I had to fight to get this place. Good thinking real estate men held back their bids, knowing I wanted it so bad. Some I had to put a little pressure on—to make them bow out, I mean. All but our friend Bullock."

"Bullock—"

"A company he owns wanted it. Man named Dyer owns it on paper, but Bullock is the real boss. Dyer is just a front. City owned the building by then. Bullock tried to get it condemned so he could buy it cheap. Nearly succeeded too. Bullock wouldn't even talk to me. It took Joe Seligman, pulling every string he had, to block the greedy Yankee bastard. I still have it in for the fucker. You blame me?"

Morgan shrugged. This thing was like a jigsaw, one piece after the other fitting into place. Or were they? It might well be O'Connor was bending and trimming the pieces to get them into place. But Morgan was here and he might as well go the extra mile. He hoped he wouldn't find himself at the edge of a cliff.

Midway down the hall was the door to the typewriting room. O'Connor opened it and they walked into the noise of six machines clattering at the same time. The six women seated at two long low tables were young; some looked to be doing better than others. Behind a desk in the front of the room was a woman in her early thirties, good looking but hard-faced. It looked like she had been giving them hell.

All the machines fell silent as soon as O'Connor showed himself. "Carry on, ladies, didn't mean to disturb you. Can you spare a minute, Harriet?"

Harriet Streeter followed O'Connor and Morgan into the hall. O'Connor made the introductions and Morgan got an unsmiling nod, no offer of a handshake. Morgan's raincoat was unbuttoned and Harriet Streeter said, "You've got blood all over you."

"I know." Morgan decided she was tough all right. O'Connor said, "We'll get him cleaned up. Something I want to talk to you about. We'll be upstairs."

Harriet Streeter nodded. "I'll be up in a few minutes."

Climbing the stairs with Morgan behind him, O'Connor said, "Some of those ladies will never learn to typewrite. Some are too lazy, others too stupid. The smart ones, if they stick to it, which isn't always the case—the lazy habits of whoring are hard to break—can hope for jobs in offices. We've had some success there."

They got to the top floor and O'Connor unlocked a sturdy door with three locks. "Tempt not and ye shall not be stolen from," he said. "Most of our ladies, smart or dumb, are all right, but there is always the hardened sinner who refuses to change—or can't change—her wayward way of life."

O'Connor closed the door and put his hat on a chair. "This is where I live, and if it seems a bit on the fancy side, you must remember that it's also a place of business, so to speak. Now and then a wealthy man, a potential benefactor, drops by to see the mission, and it's only fitting that I receive him in comfortable surroundings. It's been my experience that wealthy men are more at ease with a chap who looks like he's doing all right than with somebody who puts on a poor mouth. You have to meet them on more or less equal terms, don't you see?"

O'Connor was doing better than all right, Morgan thought, and at a quick glance it looked as if his quarters took up the entire top floor. Once upon a time, the long, wide living room must have been taken up by any number of sailors' cubicles. Now, in their place, was a comfortably furnished room that wouldn't have looked out of place in a luxury hotel or a mansion on Nob Hill.

"If the truth be known," O'Connor said, feeling the lump on his head, "I myself can make do with very little. A cot and a few sticks of furniture, three squares a day, a place to wash up—what more could a sensible man ask? Unfortunately, my fund-raising activities do not permit me to live like that. Sit down, Mr. Blaney. Would you like a bottle of beer? Coffee? Something to eat?"

Morgan sat down on a leather covered couch. Everything here cost money, from the couch to the rich Turkish carpet to the teak bookshelves that lined the walls. A marble bust stood above the enormous fireplace. To one side of it was a polished sideboard with a row of liquor bottles on top.

O'Connor was waiting. "I'd like a beer," Morgan said. He expected O'Connor to go for it himself; instead he took off his coat and sat in a deep armchair facing the couch. "John!" he bellowed. "Where the hell is that Chinaman? John! John, you rascal!"

A young Chinese appeared in a doorway. He was dressed in some kind of white pajamas with decorations on them and even had a pigtail. "Yes, boss," he said.

"Two beers, chop-chop, and a headache powder." O'Connor lay back in his chair. "My fucking head is killing me. I hope Hargis's head is hurting just as bad, or worse."

The young Chinese brought in the beer—two bottles, two glasses on a silver tray. He set it down beside O'Connor's chair and handed him a packet of headache powder and water to chase it. O'Connor spilled the powder into the glass of water, stirred it with a spoon, and drank the mixture. It made him burp.

"I'd take a stiff drink, but it doesn't agree with me," he said. "Good for some men, bad for me, makes me mean. Drink got me sent to prison— ten years for killing a man in a pub. Haven't had any liquor since then."

The Chinese was hovering in the doorway. "Anytin else, boss?" he asked when O'Connor looked around at him.

"Beat it." The Chinese disappeared. O'Connor said to Morgan, "I don't trust that bloke. Claims to be a Christian, calls himself John Smith, and I still don't trust him. He's always sneaking around. I'd like to make him wear hobnailed boots so I'd know where he was. You notice how I mixed that powder myself, didn't trust him to do it."

Morgan stared at him. Maybe he was crazy— it would explain some of the things he did and said. "Why do you keep him?" He wished he hadn't asked.

A knock on the door stopped O'Connor from

explaining. Harriet Streeter came in and sat stiffly on the edge of a chair. No, she didn't want beer or anything else. Morgan couldn't decide what her feelings toward O'Connor were. Going by her face it was hard to tell how she felt about anything. Her face was as somber as her black dress. Just the same though, it was a good looking face in spite of the downturned mouth, the lined forehead, the smudges under her eyes. And she still had a good body on her, yes sir.

She sat and listened while O'Connor told her what he wanted her to do. "Go to St. Bonaventure's Hospital, the O'Farrell and Leavenworth block—take a cab—and inquire about Clement C. Hargis, your husband, brought in today. You came to San Francisco to meet him at the Fremont Hotel—that's at Jones and Clay—and were told he'd been injured and taken to the hospital. You don't know what happened. You're a worried wife and all you care about is your husband. He's probably under some kind of guard, so you can act surprised if you like. If detectives are there, which is doubtful, stick to your story and keep it simple. Find out how badly he's injured and how long they intend to keep him. Any questions?"

"What's my first name?" was all Harriet Streeter said.

"It's Lily. Your maiden name was Lily Newell Sears. You married Hargis—call him Clem—in Fort Smith, Arkansas." O'Connor thought for a moment. "You're a schoolteacher. But listen now. I doubt you'll be asked for any of that, so don't volunteer information."

97

"You're forgetting I used to be a private detective." Harriet Streeter's voice was sharp.

"Good. Get back as quick as you can. Now if you folks don't mind, I'm going in my room to lie down. My head. Mr. Blaney, you have the freedom of the house. If you want to take a nap there's a room next to mine. Anything you need—a bath, something to eat—ask John. I'll be waiting to hear from you, Harriet."

Morgan was left with Harriet Streeter, who was standing up but hadn't left. No doubt about it: she had a right good figure, and that hard good-looking face could be softened, he felt pretty sure, by tender loving care. Also a big cock. But he wondered if her bitter experience with the con-man might not have turned her into a woman-licker. As boss of the girls she'd have plenty of opportunities.

"You look like hell with all that blood on you. You better peel off and let me have your clothes cleaned." Her voice was as severe and bossy as her black dress. "Don't worry about your nice new pants getting ruined. They'll be cleaned with naphtha, the shirt laundered."

Morgan looked at her, standing there like the schoolteacher she was supposed to be. Giving up his pants was like giving up his gun. "It's not that bad," he said.

"It's worse. Don't be such a fool. Give me the shirt and pants and"—she sniffed the air, sniffing Angelique— "your drawers while you're at it. Your things will be ready in an hour or two. You can undress in the bathroom. Come on, I've got to be off."

Morgan never argued with women when it didn't matter; there was no point to it. Anyway his clothes were messed up with Hargis's blood and he couldn't go around with his raincoat buttoned all the time. Harriet Streeter showed him where the bathroom was and waited outside while he stripped off and handed out his shirt, pants, and drawers. It was a great big fancy bathroom with a marble tub and he thought he'd take a bath after she left.

He was knotting a big towel around his waist when she stuck her head in the door. "I'd like a word with you." Morgan nodded and gave her a tight shitkicker's smile. She didn't smile back. "Not in here, for Christ's sake. In the other room." She was one irritable woman.

Morgan followed her back to the living room. She didn't sit down and neither did he. "Just so you'll know it and won't forget, Mr. Blaney, Duckie O'Connor's the only man's ever been decent to me. People say this and that about him. I don't give a fuck. Try any tricks and you'll have me to deal with."

Morgan didn't like to be pushed. As far as he could tell, he hadn't done anything to antagonize this bitch. "Is that it? Are you finished now? Because if you are, I'm going to take a fuck-ing bath."

Of course she flared up. She probably did it all the time, taking out her misery on the women downstairs. "No, I'm not finished and you'll hear me out!"

"I will if I like." Morgan knew he was going

99

about this all wrong. He should listen to what she had to say, maybe learn something. "All right. I'm listening, Miss Streeter."

For some reason, that was the wrong thing to say. "Fuck that Miss Streeter shit!" Morgan waited for her to control herself; it took some effort. "Look, Blaney," she said. "I don't know you and I don't want to know you. I'm just warning you: no tricks."

"Why would I want to play tricks?"

"I don't know. For money, I suppose."

"Playing tricks on O'Connor wouldn't be so easy."

"Don't bullshit me, Blaney. I can tell Duckie likes you. Somebody who likes you is the easiest to fool. I'm warning you."

Morgan was getting tired of this, hearing the same thing over and over. "All right, I'm warned. I hear you. I'm warned."

"See that you are. I mean it." Harriet Streeter stalked out carrying Morgan's dirty clothes. Morgan looked after her thinking, is there no peace for a poor hard-working horse rancher from Idaho? He guessed he was tired from tussling with Hargis and Angelique. Lord, but wasn't that a fine fuck? Just thinking about it cheered him up. Angelique would be gone tomorrow, but what the hell: the world was full of willing women, for hire and for free. Fact was, he liked one kind as well as the other. To get into Harriet Streeter's drawers—now *that* would be something. It could happen in spite of all the odds.

He found a bottle of beer in the kitchen ice-chest

and drank it while he took a long hot bath. It sure was a fine bathroom. Shiny tiled walls and a wooly rug to stand on when you got out of the tub. A fancy shitter and wash basin, both made of marble like the tub. Towels galore, and a radiator to ward off the chill of the San Francisco rainy season.

Morgan drank the beer from the bottle and wished he had another one to see him through his bath. But he wasn't about to drip water all over the place going for another bottle. Soaking away his fatigue in the hot, soapy water he thought, if only the boys back at Spade Bit could see me now—especially his foreman and friend, Sid Sefton, a man who followed politics in the newspapers and took life seriously.

It must have been an hour or more later when he heaved himself out of the tub and dried off. With a towel wrapped around his middle, he went into the living room to wait for his clothes. O'Connor was still in his room and there was no sign of the Chinaman. Something odd there, he thought without much interest. As a rule, people got rid of employees they didn't trust unless there was some reason for keeping them around. Usually they didn't talk about it.

Morgan walked around sipping beer, looking at O'Connor's odd collection of books. Among many were *The Lives of the Saints, Complete Plays of William Shakespeare, Autobiography of an Australian Convict, Ten Nights in a Barroom, San Francisco City Directory,* a set of *California Statutes,* and *Business Leaders of California.*

Somebody knocked on the door and Morgan

went to answer it. "Who is it?"

A woman's voice answered. "I have the clean clothes, sir."

Morgan opened the door and the sauciest-looking laundress he ever saw came in.

Chapter Seven

"I brought them right up directly when they was ready," she said, coming into the room and looking around to see who else might be there. All she saw was Morgan in his towel and she beamed a great big smile at him and came closer than she had to. "I did a real nice job, did everything myself, wouldn't let nobody else touch them. Smell them. Don't they smell nice and clean and fresh?"

She came even closer and held up the clothes draped over her arm. Morgan nodded and backed off a bit, but she crowded in after him. The only word he could think of to describe her was 'saucy.' She was like a saucy servant girl in a private dirty show for businessmen on their big night out, the kind of buxom lass that wears a maid's cap and nothing else. This one was short and strongly built, but with country good looks, a farm girl come to the sinful city. The loose high-collared plain gray dress hung to her heels, but you'd have to be blind not to see what was under it.

"Thanks. You did a fine job," Morgan said again. A shame he couldn't take advantage of this, but it wasn't the time or place. "I'll tell Reverend O'Connor what a fine job you did. He's right down the hall in his room."

No good. She tossed the clothes over the back of a chair and reached for his cock. "I'll give you a nice quick blow job for two dollars. Come on, be a sport, they never give us any money. Duckie's sleeping. I can hear him snoring from here. Please, mister, you'll enjoy it. I need the two dollars."

Morgan felt like a shy virgin as he continued to back away. "A dollar then," she pleaded, making another grab for his cock. "One lousy dollar, mister." Her next grab pulled the towel loose and it dropped to the floor and Morgan's hard-on was in full sight. No, no, a thousand times no! He felt like a fool. He was trying to grab up the towel when Harriet Streeter walked in. Morgan half-expected her to say "Aha!" like they did in a melodrama, but she didn't. Her hard eyes took in everything at a glance and all she said was, "Out. Get out of here, you slut." The girl gaped at her, then bolted for the door.

Morgan had the towel back in place. Harriet Streeter stared at him, saying nothing. Morgan said, "Nothing happened, if that's what you're thinking. I was just telling her what a nice job she did."

She continued to stare at him, then she said, "You're a fucking liar. She'd be sucking your cock right this minute if I hadn't walked in."

Morgan didn't know what to do; anything he said

would be sneered at. But he gave it a try. "I didn't encourage her, honest. What are you going to do? She's just a kid."

It didn't work. Harriet Streeter was determined to ream his ass. "Like hell you didn't encourage her. You've got a hard-on like a poker. And what're you doing prancing around naked?"

Aw, God! "I wasn't prancing, for Christ's sake. *Prancing!* I'm wearing a towel because my clothes were being washed. As you well know. You insisted on it."

That didn't work either. "You weren't wearing any towel a minute ago, *Mister* Blaney. You didn't have to let her in. You could have reached out for the clothes and closed the door."

Morgan was tired of this. "Believe what you like. I'm going to get dressed."

Something made her relent a little. "You don't understand how closely I have to watch these girls. Duckie thinks he knows them, but I know them better. I was a whore myself, remember. She offered to suck you off, didn't she?"

Morgan started to pull on his pants. Goddamn! She just couldn't let go. "No, she did not," he said.

"Then it had to be a quick poke. They're always trying to get hold of a few dollars, some of them. Trying to smuggle in liquor or dope or saving a little so they can go back on the streets." Harriet Streeter sighed. "Sometimes I think it's a hopeless cause. You should know better, Blaney. Where's Duckie?"

Morgan was fastening his belt. "Still sleeping, I

guess. He's still in his room."

"Tell him I'll be back later. Or I'll be down-stairs."

"Wait a minute. What'll you do to the kid? Kick her out?"

"Not for me to kick her out. I would if I could. Kicking out is up to Duckie and he hates to do it. You have to do something really bad. But one way or another, that girl will be back on the streets."

"You going to tell O'Connor?"

"No, I'm not going to tell him. What good would it do? But I'm asking you—please. Keep your cock in your pants as long as you're in here."

Harriet Streeter was at the door when O'Connor came in rubbing his eyes. "Hold up there, young lady. I thought I heard your voice. Brought up Mr. Blaney's clothes I see. What news from the hospital? You get to see Hargis?"

Still standing, Harriet Streeter said, "I saw him. They let me up after visiting hours when I said I was his wife, sniveled into my handkerchief. I talked to a doctor when he came by. Hargis started acting up when they brought him in, so this doctor had to give him an injection. A sedative. Morphia, I suppose. This doctor said his skull isn't fractured, but he's suffering from concussion. Not serious, but he'll need rest. He's as strong as an ox, the doctor said, so he'll make a complete recovery. The doctor says he'll be there four or five days."

Morgan was back on the couch, O'Connor on the chair facing it. "Sit down, Harriet," O'Connor said. "Is he guarded?"

Harriet Streeter sat down. "He isn't in a locked ward—"

O'Connor said to Morgan, "That's where they keep men under arrest. Men shot and wounded during robberies, wanted men shot by the police."

"Hargis is in with more or less violent cases. Men with DTs, suicides who didn't make a good job of it—wrist cutters, poison drinkers, high jumpers. A policeman sits outside the ward to keep an eye on them. I didn't stay more than a minute or two. No point. Hargis was still knocked out by the dope when I left. That's it," Harriet Streeter said at the end of her report.

O'Connor was pleased and said so. "And no detectives, I take it. Nobody questioned you?"

Harriet Streeter shook her head. "No detectives. I just had to explain who I was. That's all it took."

"Good. You'll be going back every day till Hargis is ready for discharge. Except you'll just inquire at the information desk. Don't go up to see him. He could be fully awake next time you go."

Harriet Streeter gave Morgan a hard look before she left and for a moment he thought she had changed her mind about dropping the issue of the laundry girl. But the worst she did was give him the hard look. It was as if to say, you got away with it this time, don't press your luck.

"That's a right smart woman." O'Connor had changed his suit, clerical bib, round collar and all; the other suit had been messed up a bit when Hargis knocked him down. "I'm feeling much better. Put an ice bag on my head, got some sleep."

The lump on O'Connor's head was now a reddish purple, but the swelling had gone down some and his face was no longer furrowed with pain. "We have to be ready for Hargis," he said.

"Why are you concentrating so much on Hargis? He doesn't know where his wife is any more than we do."

"Hargis found her before. I'm hoping he'll find her again. I told you that already. Call it a hunch if you like. You don't believe in following your hunches?"

"Sometimes I do and sometimes I don't."

O'Connor cranked out a laugh like a rusty hinge, so he was feeling better. "That's no kind of answer, Mr. Blaney. Hunches can be wrong, of course, but in this instance what else do we have to go on?"

"What about all your tipsters and informers? Bender says you have a lot of old reformed hard cases that work for you. What about them? They could be watching the railroad station and the piers ships leave from."

"That's already been done," O'Connor said. "I got them started on it as soon as I heard about Lily. I also got word out to my tipsters, as you call them. Cab drivers, hotel clerks, anybody a woman in flight might be seen by. So far, nothing."

Morgan was beginning to think they might never find her. "Maybe she's already left town."

"You sound like you're ready to quit. Why don't you?"

"I can't do that. I haven't even earned the first five hundred."

O'Connor came up with one of his bloodless

smiles. "My, my, aren't we righteous? Don't take that the wrong way, Mr. Blaney. If that's how you are, far be it from me to try to change you. But I'll tell you something. I want more than a thousand dollars out of this. We never got around to that, did we?"

They were back to that, the most important part of all. In the end, Morgan thought, everything has to take a back seat to money. "How much do you have in mind?"

"Twenty-five percent," O'Connor said. "That is, if we recover the securities together, the two of us working together, with me doing my full share of the work. I told you before. I don't think you have a prayer of finding them without me. What are you going to do without me? Go up and down the city, a mighty big place, buttonholing strangers? Excuse me, sir, excuse me, ma'am, there's this lady I'm trying to find. Foolishness!"

Morgan had to say, "But suppose I do find her on my own."

"You mean we aren't working together anymore, Mr. Blaney?" O'Connor clucked his tongue and put on a disapproving face. "And I thought we had reached a meeting of the minds, as they say."

Getting through this was harder than putting shoes on a mule. "We *are* working together, but just for the sake of argument—"

"For the sake of argument, if you find the securities without my help, I won't claim a cent. You can return the hundred thousand to Bullock, and may God forgive you. I give you my word on that."

109

Morgan didn't quite know what to say. "Bullock will have to agree to your end of it. I'm supposed to telephone him tomorrow, tell him how I'm doing."

"And what are you going to tell him, Mr. Blaney?"

The "Mr. Blaney" business was getting tiresome. "My name is Morgan, Reverend. You might as well know it."

"I already do. But I wanted it to come from you. I telephoned the Pacific about your money and your gun, et cetera—described you to the desk clerk and he told me. I told the clerk you'd settle up when you're ready. So your valuables are quite safe, Mr. Morgan."

"Morgan will do. I hate to be mistered."

A weary smile. "Then you must call me Duckie. A ridiculous name, to be sure, but I'm used to it and I wear it with honor. Now back to Bullock if you don't mind. I repeat: what are you going to tell him?"

It was no easy question and Morgan had to think about it. He had been thinking about it and getting more expense money was only part of it. "I'll have to tell him about Hargis, how I traced him. That ought to shake him up if he's holding something back."

O'Connor nodded his great solemn head. "He won't welcome being told she's a bigamist. It will be interesting to see how he takes it. Unless he knows it already."

"What?"

"I'm not saying he does. It's just that I have

110

a naturally suspicious nature. And as I said before, there is something suspicious—at least something unexplained—about these securities. That, I am sure, will come out in the course of our investigation."

Morgan hadn't thought of it as an investigation. After all, he was no kind of detective, just a man trying to earn a buck by looking for a missing wife.

O'Connor said, "I wouldn't tell him where Hargis is."

"Why not?"

"Because something might happen to him. He could die in there and nobody would care. His doctor might be puzzled, but that would be from a professional standpoint, nothing to lose sleep over. Doctors lose patients all the time and if a patient is a penniless nobody like Hargis, who'd give a damn?"

It was hard to think of Bullock that way. Or maybe it wasn't: there was an ingrained meanness in the little Yankee that he hadn't missed. But meanness was one thing, hiring a killer was another. "You're going pretty far afield . . . Duckie, or am I wrong?" Morgan wondered if he'd ever get used to calling this strange brute Duckie. "Hiring a killer—"

"Not a killer, not in the sense you mean. Not a professional assassin hired in the back room of a saloon. Somebody in the hospital could do it. An orderly, a patient in his ward, even the policeman who's standing guard at the door. A pillow over the face in the dead of night. Now I'm not saying that's going to happen, but it might. Don't tell Bullock where Hargis is, is my advice."

"What do I tell him?"

"That you got a good lead on Hargis—learned about the Arkansas marriage, his time in jail—but haven't been able to find him. But you will. You're confident that you will. You don't want Bullock to think his money is being wasted. Of course you won't bring me up tomorrow. Too soon."

Far too soon. Morgan wasn't sure that Bullock would ever agree to pay O'Connor twenty-five percent of the securities. But that was jumping the gun. "It will take some arm twisting to get him to pay much more than he's paying me."

"He'll pay," O'Connor said, all confidence. "After it's explained to him. There's a rotten fish in there somewhere and I mean to hold it under his nose."

Morgan didn't like the sound of that, but he let it go. A lot of things he was letting go—they'd talk about it later—and maybe some of them would come back to haunt him. "You know," he said. "All Bullock has to do is talk to Madame D and he'll know as much about Hargis as we do. The Fremont Hotel, who was there, what happened to Hargis to put him in the hospital."

O'Connor wasn't too worried about that. "What you say is possible, but I'm thinking Bullock will want to keep out of it for now. After all, why did he hire you if not so he could keep out of it? If too much time drags by, if he thinks you're not getting results, he may want to get involved. He may even tell you to drop it altogether. But unless I'm wrong, that won't happen just yet."

Suddenly Morgan was restless. All this talk, he wanted to do something. It was getting dark outside and he didn't want to stay cooped up here, listening to O'Connor. He thought of the saucy laundry girl that Harriet Streeter had chased out. Now if he could take a crack at that, the night wouldn't seem so long.

"I'm going to Burke's place, wherever it is," he said. "Maybe I can turn up something."

"I doubt it. You got lucky at Madame D's. That's not to say you'll find another nugget on the same day. Lily would be a fool to go to Burke's, trust a cunt like him. Back when Madame D heard about Lily—how good she was in the bed line— and thought she'd like to sign her on, Burke tried to keep her by force. It took a couple of Madame D's pet detectives to get her out of there. Burke was as sore as hell, no doubt still is. Burke is the last man Lily would want to trust."

"Burke would know how to cash in the securities. Get rid of them without attracting attention."

The look on O'Connor's face said that was a foolish idea. "Burke would get rid of the securities *and* Lily. The minute he got them in his hands, she'd never be seen again."

Morgan got up and walked to the window and looked at the lights of the city. He was restless and wanted to get out there if only to walk around. "Nothing to be lost by going to Burke's. I'm just going to poke around."

O'Connor stayed in his chair. "You could lose your life, that's what you could lose. But I see you're determined to go, no way to stop you. Poke

113

around, poke the whores if you like, just don't start asking questions about Lily. If Burke has heard rumors—he might have, he just might—you could find yourself in the basement hanging from a pipe by your thumbs. My best advice is don't go. You know where it is?"

Morgan said he had the address.

"I'll tell you how to get there." O'Connor looked at his watch, a fine gold timepiece. "It's five to nine now. If you're not back by twelve, one at the latest, I'll come looking for you and I'll bring some of the boys."

Morgan put on his raincoat. "You don't have to wet-nurse me, Duckie. This isn't my first time away from home."

O'Connor was unmoved. "One at the latest," he repeated. "Then I'll call out the Marines. For Christ's sake, three or four hours should be enough time for any man. How much fucking can you do?"

Morgan turned at the door. "Will I have trouble getting back in here?"

O'Connor stood up. "No trouble. I'll go down with you and tell the night men. Burke's is not that far from here, in a nice little square back of California Street, off Kearny. Ask the cab driver. . . ."

Morgan walked out into cold, drizzling rain, but felt no need to hail a cab even if one had been available. Front Street was close to the docks, not the kind of street that got much cab traffic. Anyway, he was in no hurry and wanted to walk. The chilly night air felt good and he didn't mind the light rain. He liked San Francisco best of all the big cities he'd been in, not that he'd been in that many. Back east the cities were old, too set in their ways, while here the wild life was still going full blast on the Barbary Coast and laws were made to be broken.

He turned onto Kearny Street and suddenly knew he was being followed. The feeling was so strong that he didn't doubt it for an instant. He'd relied on his instincts too often—and been proven right—not to trust them. Somebody was dogging him, but he didn't turn as another man might have done. Doing that would tip off whoever was back there. Instead, he kept walking as before, neither fast nor slow, looking for a place where he could check the street behind him.

Up ahead a narrow street, more like an alley, ran back between two commercial buildings and he turned into it. It wasn't dark, but there were few lights and no people. Down from the corner was a big stack of bricks and he ducked down behind it. He was still close enough to the corner to be able to see anybody who stopped to look into the alley. He was still waiting, less than a minute later, when a short slender man—maybe a boy—with a pasty face and a cloth cap stopped at the mouth of the alley, took a few steps into it, then turned and went back the way he had come. Morgan got up and went back to Kearny, but there was no sign of the man—or boy—or whatever he was.

Morgan walked back a block, thinking maybe the sneak had ducked into a doorway. The son of a bitch had disappeared. Saloons and a few stores were open and he could have ducked into any one of them. Trying to check all of them would be a waste of time. Besides, the sneaking fucker could have jumped onto a moving cable car—one had just gone by on Kearny—or been picked up by a cab tailing along behind him. There were a lot of cabs on Kearny, going in both directions. Morgan gave up and kept going in the direction of Burke's place. Now and then he stopped to check, but the runt—as he thought of the short man—was nowhere to be seen. The part of Kearny he was on now had more people than down toward the mission end, so the runt could still be on his tail, dodging along behind the nighttime strollers. Somehow he didn't think so, but he couldn't be sure about that. His instincts didn't tell him everything.

He didn't think the runt was a killer. A killer would have gone into the alley to look for him. A killer had to have nerve, had to take chances. But the runt just stopped to look and then, not seeing him, had skipped out before he could be grabbed. No killer worked like that, no killer that Morgan had known or heard of. So, unless he had it wrong, he was being followed for some other reason. What that reason was he could only guess at, and for the moment he was tired of guessing. Maybe O'Connor would have some idea of what was going on. It could be that the runt was one of the 'boys' on the mission staff. But the two men he'd seen were middle-aged Australians, reformed thugs, and Bender said the rest of them were, too. Which didn't mean that O'Connor might not have somebody else on tap.

Give it a rest, he told himself. Concentrate on what you're doing. He had to smile when he considered this good advice. Concentrate on what? Unless he found, in O'Connor's words, another nugget on the same day, all he was going to get at Burke's was a costly fuck. Nothing wrong with that. He looked forward to it. But O'Connor was right. He couldn't go in there asking questions that would find him swimming in a cesspool. And it wasn't at all likely that he'd draw another Angelique. That would be hoping for too much. Angelique was an accomplished cocksucker and a regular information bureau, all wrapped up in one bratty woman-child. The girl he'd get at Burke's would be nothing like that. If she ran true to form, she'd be no different from most other whores, but she'd be good. She'd have to be good if she worked at a money place like Burke's. Thinking of how good she'd be, whoever she was, Morgan walked a little faster.

A short, narrow street led into the small square that O'Connor had described. The square itself was about half the size of a city block, maybe smaller than that. Houses were on all four sides of it, and another narrow street went out at the other end. There were trees and carriage lights outside some of the houses. No business buildings, no garish signs. This was not the classy end of town, no Nob Hill—honky-tonk California Street was close by—yet the little square had its own air of gentility. Morgan stood in the shadow of a tree, making one last check on the runt before he went looking for Burke's whorehouse.

Nobody showed, but he gave it a little more time, trying to get a clear picture of the runt as he'd seen him in the entrance to the alley. A cloth cap with the peak pulled low over a pasty face, a short man with a slender build. That much was for sure. Trouble was, he hadn't been able to get a clear look at the face. The lights of Kearny Street were behind him, the alley was only half-lit, and his face was in shadow. But even in the bad light the face showed up as pasty, no mistaking that, and Morgan felt sure he'd know the little sneak if he saw him again. And that, he felt just as sure, was bound to happen.

He found the house and it was nowhere as fancy as Madame D's. It didn't stand on its own grounds, but was one of a row of houses on the north side of the square. It was brick like the others, four stories high, and better kept than the house next door. A miniature British flag, the Union Jack, hung from a pole above the door. A brass plate beside the door read BURKE'S PEERAGE. O'Connor had explained that *Burke's Peerage* was a book that listed all the British nobility. O'Connor said only a dyed-in-the wool blackguard would have the gall to name a whorehouse after such a noble book. Morgan thought it was funny.

The square was quiet and so was the whorehouse. No mechanical piano rattling away, no whoops and hollers coming from the windows. Sports might be drinking champagne out of ladies' slippers, and other ladies might be under the lash, but you'd never know it standing outside.

Morgan went up the steps and rang the bell.

Chapter Eight

The man who opened the door was dressed as a Beefeater, one of those sturdy Englishmen who guarded the Tower of London. Morgan knew what the uniform looked like because he'd seen it on a dummy in a traveling wax museum that came through Idaho when he was a kid. And there was a famous brand of gin with a Beefeater on the label. High-class women liked it a lot.

This Beefeater was sturdy enough, an Englishman or trying to sound like one, a hoodlum to the roots of his dyed red beard. "You've not been here before, sir," he said in that peculiar accent. Morgan decided he wasn't English after all. He gave Morgan the usual quick once-over. "You're most welcome, sir."

Another Beefeater took charge of Morgan and showed him into the parlor, where four scantily dressed women sat around, watched over by a middle-aged woman in a blue silk dress. There was no sign of Burke. Morgan didn't know what he looked like, but thought he'd know him when he saw him. The four women were reading, knitting, yawning, or just sitting. They all smiled at Morgan.

The woman in charge had plenty of lard on her and she had to struggle to get out of her chair. Once she must have been pretty; her face was still dolllike cute in spite of all the fat. A whore in her time, like the women she bossed now, she had been promoted to a higher rank and didn't want you to forget it. With her blue silk dress and small, mincing feet, she was as cheap-fancy as the rest of the place. She minced over to Morgan, saying, "Yes, indeedy, sir. Cast your eyes over these young beauties. Aren't they lovely? If you're out for a bit of fun, you've come to the right place."

This one's English accent was real, Morgan decided. But what happened to good old American whorehouses? Madame D's was fake French, Burke's was fake English. Fake was exactly the right word. The walls here were crowded with cheap oil paintings of English kings, knights in armor, pinch-faced ladies with ruffs. Morgan was no expert on art, but he knew cheap shit when it was staring him right in the face.

"Anything strike your fancy, sir?" the fat lady asked coquettishly. "I'd be surprised if it didn't."

Morgan had already decided on a young auburn-haired girl sitting in a corner by herself, a suit of tin armor behind her. She was well built, but not overbuilt like so many whores who sat around too much, gobbled too much chocolate, and got no exercise except fucking. Though some of the other girls there were prettier, she was the one he liked, and maybe it was because she didn't look like much of a talker. If she had no information to give—and he was sure she didn't—he didn't want to listen to a lot of irritating chatter.

The fat lady, who introduced herself as Mrs. Windsor—surely not her real name—followed his glance and approved of his choice. "Anne is a lovely girl," she told Morgan in a whisper that you'd have to be wearing ear plugs not to have heard forty feet away. "I'll break a rule and tell you her full name. Anne Boleyn, a famous name in English history, the second wife of Henry the Eighth and the mother of Good Queen Bess. Let me take your raincoat."

Taking off his coat, Morgan wondered who had primed her with all this history bullshit. Surely not Burke, who was pig-ignorant, according to O'Connor. Probably some poorly paid school-teacher did it for a few dollars.

The fat lady looked him over after he gave her the coat. But this time there was no gun bulge to be spotted. The stubby Webley .45 was stuffed into the top of his boot and covered by his pants. He didn't expect any trouble at Burke's, but he wanted to be ready for it if it came up.

They settled the money part in the fat lady's cramped little office. Twenty-five dollars wasn't too bad, a lot less than Madame D charged. Here he got no key, but the fat lady told him he could find Anne in Room No. 4 on the second floor. Her tone said he was in for an experience that he ought to have bronzed like baby shoes.

Still no sign of Burke, no easy way to ask about Lily as he headed for the stairs. So far it was quiet enough here, but somehow the atmosphere was meaner than it was at Madame D's. The man who let him in was a real hoodlum, menacing behind the red beard and the insolent politeness, not a retired prizefighter like Madame D's hard man. And the fat lady was a bad old bitch—you could see the meanness in her artificial looking blue eyes, like a doll's, staring out from between rolls of fat. If somebody like Hargis started throwing his weight around here he'd be squashed like a bug, not just roughed up and dumped in an alley.

No Angelique this time, but you couldn't have everything. The so-called Anne Boleyn lay naked on the double bed, her legs wide open. "It was too hot in here," she said in a drawling voice," so I opened the window a bit. You can close it if you like."

French windows that led out to an iron balcony were open a few inches. "Doesn't matter," Morgan said. "If it gets cold we can close it."

"Cold! Don't make me laugh. You'll be burning up in no time. I'm going to give you the time of your life." All this was said without too much enthusiasm. A tired professional, Morgan thought, but he knew she'd do her best. One complaint to the fat lady downstairs and she'd be in trouble. In a place like Burke's, trouble could mean anything from a reprimand to a slap in the face. "You're going to remember me for the rest of your life," she added for good measure.

Morgan got his clothes off and got his cock into her. "Oh, it feels so wonderful," she said, putting her tongue in his ear. "Has anyone ever told you what a wonderful lover you are?" Morgan didn't know about that. So far, all he was doing was pumping in and out of her, getting his stride. He didn't mind her phony bullshit, and sometimes it was a nice change of pace to fuck a real professional, even though this one was troweling it on a little too thick. With a working whore who knew her business, you got what you paid for and you could hardly expect her to fall in love.

He quickened his stroke and she cried out, "Oh, you're such a passionate man! I love a passionate man! You're getting me all excited!" Morgan was getting excited himself. He had his cock in there and he was getting it. There was plenty of her to hold onto—not that she was heavy, just well built— and he was making the most of it. She had a big cunt, but she knew how to control it. She could make it so tight he had to use his cock like a ram. Wham! He'd drive it all the way in and she'd trap his cock like it was in a sticky vice, then she'd laugh and let him draw it back for another long, penetrating stroke.

"Oh, my God! I'm coming!" was the next thing she tried on. Her heels drummed on the bed and she clawed at his hair without hurting him. "I'm coming! I'm coming! Fuck me! Fuck me! Don't ever stop fucking me!" Some men liked their women to talk dirty. "Come with me! Please come with me!"

Morgan shot his wad, and you'd think he'd shot a string of pearls the way she carried on. If he hadn't known she was faking, he would have tried to pull her back from death's door, at least called for a doctor. It was all bullcrap but he enjoyed her performance.

"Oh, it was so wonderful for me," she said, still gasping. "Was it as wonderful for you?"

"It was wonderful," Morgan said. "You bring out the best in a man, you know that?"

She simpered. "Oh, it makes me feel so good to hear you say that." She fluttered her eyelids. "You have such a big one, you know." All men liked to hear that. "I don't know when I've seen one so big." Morgan lay beside her and tickled her clit. "It's all for you," she said.

Morgan got back to it after he'd rested for a while. Getting it up again in so short a time was a tall order, but she helped him. "Oh my, you're so virile," she said. "You can't get enough of me, can you?"

Morgan didn't say there was enough of her to go around. What he said was, "I can't help myself," and he fucked her again. This time he took it slower, enjoying the way she worked every trick she'd ever learned. She wasn't much over twenty so she must have started early or learned fast. There was nothing she didn't know how to do, from putting her heel between the crack in his ass to sucking on his nipples. She didn't kiss him—most whores would kiss your cock but not your mouth—but that was all right too.

Her second bogus come was just as wonderful, and she said that maybe it was even more wonderful than the first. "You're such a gentleman. You always hold back until you know I'm coming. I like

124

that in a man. It shows real consideration."

She talked but she wasn't a talker, meaning that you didn't have to listen to anything she said. You didn't have to answer, you could grunt if you liked. To her it made no difference what you said or didn't say. But Morgan always liked to play the game and it was just as easy to be pleasant as it was to be surly. Even the most case-hardened whore had some feelings and it did no harm to respect them.

"Would you like me to suck your cock?" she asked demurely.

"I'd like that very much," Morgan said, ever the Idaho gentleman. And he lay back and let her suck his cock. He hoped Bullock wasn't tossing in his sleep, having bad dreams about how his money was being spent. Little Angelique, now reunited with Dr. James, no doubt, had been an inspired cocksucker. Anne Boleyn, not so slender, was doing it by the book but he had no complaints. It must have been a pretty good book she'd learned from, and what she lacked in girlish enthusiasm she made up for in knowhow. She wanted to get it over with, but she was able to hide how she felt. She was going faster, really applying the old suction. Morgan wasn't having the time of his life, but he was having a good time. He shot his load into her mouth and she turned her head aside to let it dribble out on the sheet. It was skillfully done, no gagging or spitting. Some men objected to that. Morgan patted her head.

"I nearly came myself, I got so excited," she said.

"I could feel it," Morgan said, thinking maybe he'd done enough for one night. He wanted to save some energy for the next day. He was about to get out of bed when he heard what sounded like shouting and screaming some distance away. It started suddenly and got louder by the minute. It sounded familiar.

"Bloody feminists," Anne Boleyn said. "They've been making trouble at some of the other houses. I wondered when they'd get here."

Morgan got up and put on his shirt and underpants. Feminists! All he needed. By the time he had buttoned his fly and pulled on his boots and went out on the balcony, the square was starting to fill up with marching, chanting women. Some of them carried flaming torches, others banners and placards, and they moved with a mighty, determined, righteous fury that was not to be stopped by any mere man. It was just like the demonstration he'd seen earlier in the day on Sacramento Street except that there were more of them now, and instead of chanting about the right to vote they were chanting, "Prostitution! Prostitution! Is an evil institution! Strike a blow! Strike a blow! Pimps must go! Pimps must go!" To Morgan it sounded a little like eeny-meeny-miney-mo, but these women down there weren't fooling around. They were in a deadly serious mood, as only women who are all fired up can be. They marched and they chanted and some of them screamed. There must have been a hundred of them, all marching on Burke's whorehouse, and they filled the small square with noise and commotion. This time, instead of just a bugle and a drum, they had a sort of marching band that had trouble keeping together but played loud enough to wake the dead.

Morgan looked along the front of the building and saw that he was the only one who had ventured out onto a balcony. One man did stick his head out, but pulled it back and closed the window. Morgan moved back, not wanting to make a target of himself, but not fast enough. Some of the women spotted him, started pointing and jeering, and all the others joined in. "Whoremaster! Whoremaster! Dirty Bastard! Dirty Bastard!" It didn't quite rhyme, but the meaning was not to be missed. The crazy chant reached up to him, wanting to kill him, and along with it came pulpy tomatoes, rotten eggs, stones, and broken bricks. The balcony had a waist-high front wall and he ducked down behind it when the barrage from below became too heavy. Morgan cowered there like the craven fool he was, grinning to himself, waiting for them to lose interest. No more rocks or bricks came his way and he thought it was safe enough to stick up his head. Something was going on down below. A man was yelling at the women and they were yelling back. There was only one of him and about a hundred of them, so he didn't have much of a chance to make himself heard. But Morgan, standing up now, heard some of what he yelled. It came in snatches through the steady drone of the chanting, the high notes of the screams. The man, in a gray suit and gray derby— it had to be Burke—kept shouting over and over, "You have no right to be here. You are breaking the law. This is a lawful business." But he might have been shouting into a storm at sea, for all the good it did. The chanting went on louder than before and by now some of the chanters were just plain screaming.

Morgan moved to the end of the balcony to get a better look at Burke. The demonstration was turning into a riot, a lot more violent than the one on Sacramento Street, but Burke stood his ground like the tough whoremaster he was. Three thugs stood behind him to back him up, but Morgan didn't think they had much of a chance against a small army of raving bitches. Morgan couldn't get a clear look at Burke—the angle was wrong—but he made him out to be short and barrel-bodied. The three back-up thugs were bigger and younger, and a fourth was dragging a firehose out through the door. A rotten egg hit Burke in the chest and his reasonable protests suddenly became a torrent of obscenities. He grabbed the brass nozzled firehose away from the thug who held it. "I'll wash out your dirty cunts, you bitches. You dirty interfering shit-assed ugly-faced cocksuckers, you couldn't get a man to fuck you on Devil's Island." Morgan smiled, enjoying this. That last was a nice touch. Burke had the gift of the gab. He was Irish all right, even if he was Liverpool-Irish. But he didn't get to say much more. Another barrage opened up and he raised one hand to shield his face, holding on to the hose nozzle with the other. As soon as the barrage eased up—maybe they were running out of ammunition—he used both hands to push down the lever on the nozzle, but instead of a powerful

128

jet of water he got nothing. "Turn the fucking thing on," he yelled at the thug in the doorway. "Get the fuck back there and turn it on."

It was better than the clowns at the circus, Morgan thought. The thug Burke yelled at stumbled back into the house. Burke was cursing again and the women were screaming. A magnesium flare flashed whitebright somewhere in the mob of women and Morgan knew there was a photographer out there. Suddenly the hose nozzle jerked in Burke's hands and he had to fight to keep his hold on it as the water came on full force. Five women at the foot of the steps were knocked down by the first fierce blast of water. One large woman, the loudest shouter—she had a megaphone—was sent rolling in the gutter. The megaphone clattered beside her and she grabbed for it, still shouting. Her clawing hands got a grip on the tin noisemaker and she was halfway to her feet when another blast of water knocked her flat on her back. Burke kept hosing her and she kept on shouting. Burke was the man with the big gun, so now all the feminist artillery was aimed at him. But for the moment, like the small boy carrying the flag in all the Civil War battle-charge stories, he seemed to lead a charmed life. The thug standing next to him got a brick in the head and went down. The fanlight over the door was shattered, and then a window, and then another. A bottle broke on the door frame, showering the back of Burke's head with bits of glass. One of the other thugs was hit by a bottle that dented his forehead but didn't break, and he stumbled into the hallway followed by the others.

One of them came back to the door and tried to pull Burke inside, but he knocked the man aside with his shoulder and kept on hosing the enemy. Another magnesium flash turned a patch of the square whitebright for a split second and Morgan caught a glimpse of a young woman with a big camera on a tripod, another woman holding up a flash tray beside her. He couldn't tell how old the other woman was. War photographers, they were making a record of this. They had balls on them all right. A photographer made a real target, but for now they were too far back for Burke to get them with the hose. Down below, Burke whooped and did a little jig when a sudden downpour started. All day it had been drizzling, but this was a cloudburst, and some of the women screamed as if boiling water was raining down on them. It was just heavy rain, but Morgan knew how they felt: they were getting another dirty deal. Even the weather was against them, and it wasn't fair.

Dry or fairly dry under the canvas canopy of the balcony, Morgan wondered how long this could go on. Where were the police? Maybe the police had been called, but were slow in responding to Burke's distress. There was no letup in the rain and the attack was beginning to falter. The mob was thinning out as the more faint of heart dragged themselves toward the streets that ran off the square. The fiercest of their comrades screamed after them, cursing them for gutless cowards. But no one came back to rejoin the battle. Another flash went off, this time far back in the melting crowd, and it looked like the photographer and her assistant were taking off, themselves. But even as the retreat went on, enough hard-core women were left to continue the attack. Morgan couldn't understand why they didn't run all over Burke and take possession of the house. There were enough of them to do it, but they didn't. Instead, they kept on screaming, kept on pelting Burke and the house with everything they could lay their hands on. Most of the windows were broken by now, and the front of the building was stained yellow and red by rotten eggs and dripping, pulpy tomatoes. Burke had a big cleanup job ahead of him; maybe he could use his trusty firehose. Morgan stopped looking down at Burke when a match flared in the middle of the moving crowd. The light was bad, but he was able to make out what looked like a big, tall woman, all in black, shielding the flaring match from the rain. Something started to burn and there was a shine of glass as she raised her arm high and back, as if to throw something. Christ! It couldn't be anything else but a firebomb. There were screams and a quick scuffle as the women closest to her tried to stop her. Then the bottle with the trailing, burning wick sailed up high into the air and there was the sound of breaking glass as it crashed through one of the windows on the upper floors. Just then, paddywagon bells began to clang from far off and the remainder of the women started to run. There was real panic now and many of them fell on the wet cobblestones. The police wagons were coming fast and it sounded as if they were coming down California Street. The women were screaming and running and falling.

Morgan looked up at the smoke billowing from the fourth floor windows. Whores were screaming up above, frightened men were shouting. Jesus Christ! Morgan thought. It was no longer a joke.

Some women were still in the square when the first of the police wagons came rattling in. Policemen were jumping down, swinging their nightsticks. Two more paddywagons came in behind the first one. The doors of the wagons were open and policemen were everywhere. The women not quick enough to escape were screaming at them. Morgan looked down as Burke threw away the hose and started into the house. Men and women running out nearly knocked him over. The photographer's flash went off again and Morgan froze as he got a split-second look at the runt, clearer than day in the blinding light. It was him, it couldn't be anyone else, the pasty face made whiter by the camera flash, the small size, even the cloth cap. Morgan couldn't see much of anything after the flash died. The runt was gone when he could see again. So were the women with the camera. Down in the square, screaming women were being dragged to police wagons. A few whores and clients were still coming out of the house. A fire engine pulled by huge horses came thundering in followed by two more.

Morgan went back into the room. The door was open and the whore was gone. Dresser drawers were pulled open, clothes scattered on the floor, as if she had tried to save what she could. Smoke was drifting in the door and was thicker in the hall when he went out there. Most of the clients and whores were out by now. An elderly man with a game leg was having a terrible time trying to gimp his way down the stairs. At least you could say this for the mean fat lady: she hadn't panicked and run out as fast as her little feet would take her. Morgan heard her yelling up on the third floor landing. The smoke was thicker there and she was coughing as well as cursing. No sign of Burke. He had to be up on the top floor. His living quarters would be up there and probably his money.

Morgan knew this would be his last chance to look for Lily. If Burke had been hiding her on the fourth floor, surely she'd be down by now. Maybe she was. Maybe she was out there in the rain, running for a new hidey-hole. The hell with that. He had to look. He didn't think she'd still be in the house, but he had to check what rooms he could. All the doors were open on the second floor. Nobody was in any of them. He had to fight his way past the fat lady and a fainting whore to get up to the third floor. The whore was naked and the fat lady was half-carrying her. "You're going the wrong fucking way," she shouted at Morgan. Morgan struggled past her and got to the landing. The smoke was so bad he could barely see. Up above on the top floor the fire was raging out of control, eating its way down through the house. If Burke was up there he was a goner. If Lily was with him, she was gone too.

Morgan looked in two third floor rooms before he had to give up. The ceiling was splitting, flames licking through the cracks. He was running down the stairs to the first floor when he heard the roof caving in. In the doorway, two firemen were carrying out the thug who had been felled by the brick. Morgan ran down the steps and away from the house before the whole thing collapsed. He sucked in cold wet air until his lungs stopped heaving. None of the policemen took any heed of him. Loaded with screaming women, the doors locked, the paddywagons started to pull away. One of the women clawing at the bars on the paddywagon door spotted Morgan and screamed, "Whoremonger! Whoremonger! Dirty bastard! Dirty bastard!" Her voice faded.

Morgan turned to look at the house. Burke's Peerage was burning to the ground. There was nothing the fireman could do to stop it and the houses on either side of it were starting to catch fire. Within a few hours, the whorehouse with all the fake English class would be nothing but a pile of wet, steaming ashes.

Morgan thought it was time to go. He didn't think the runt followed him back to the mission. If he did—and Morgan checked a number of times—he didn't see him.

Chapter Nine

O'Connor was delighted. "Think of it," he said, rubbing his big hands together. "Frank Burke dead. From what you say, he has to be. At least, I hope he is. No greater blackguard ever lived. It's nice to think he got a taste of hellfire before he found himself roasting in the real thing."

Sitting on the couch, drinking a beer, Morgan had no feelings about Burke. He wasn't sorry, he wasn't glad—the man meant nothing to him. "I lost my raincoat," he said. "I didn't think to look for it."

"Small wonder," O'Connor said absently. "You can buy another. There was no sign of Lily, you say. Of course there wasn't. She wasn't there. I told you that before you left. Now about this runt you keep harping about—"

Morgan's lungs still burned from the smoke. "I'm not harping. I wasn't seeing things. He was there. First on Kearny Street, later in the square. Do I have to tell you again?"

135

"You saw something. I don't doubt that for a minute. Just don't jump to conclusions. This runt, as you call him, may have nothing to do with Lily. Somebody follows you, so you think it has to be that."

Morgan wiped his face with the wet washcloth O'Connor had given him. It was covered with dirt when he got through. The beer felt good going down his parched throat. "Why couldn't he be working for somebody who wants to find Lily?"

"He could be," O'Connor admitted. "But we don't know that. I've already sent men out to look for him. If he's watching the building—if he comes here to do it—they'll grab him and he'll tell everything. He will."

"I doubt they'll catch him. He's pretty slick."

"So are my men, some of them. They'll catch him, bring him up here. You can question him yourself. If sweet reason doesn't work, I'll see what I can get out of him. Hold a man out the window by his heels, there's nothing he won't tell you."

Morgan picked up the second bottle of beer. One wasn't enough to get rid of the bitter, smoky taste in his mouth. "You think he could be one of Dowd's men?"

The mere mention of Dowd's name put a sour look on O'Connor's face. "If he's the runt you say he is, the answer is no. Dowd has the big clown that works with him most of the time. He has another, Dutch Hoff, also very big. He can call for help if he needs it. Doesn't always get it because his superiors don't like him. But he has no runts. I can tell you that for a fact."

"Could he be working for Madame D?"

That got a grimace of annoyance. "He could be working for the Pope if it comes to that. Madame D is too well-fixed to go in for shady stuff. In her younger years maybe, but not now. She's worked too hard to get where she is, to risk it for crooked shit. She owns her own building and it's worth a bundle. She has a bundle in the bank. Forget about Madame D."

Morgan pulled on his beer for a while.

"What the runt could be," O'Connor said, "is part of a strongarm team, a spotter and a choker. The spotter spots a likely looking mark and follows him. For instance, your hat, your boots, the way you walk mark you as an out-of-towner. Maybe you're out for a night on the town, the spotter thinks, maybe have a nice wad of money. The way they work, the spotter follows along, thinking to get you on a side street or even a quiet part of a main street. Then the choker moves in. The choker chokes you or saps you and holds you up while the spotter goes through your pockets. Over in seconds and they're gone."

"For Christ's sake, do I look like I have money?"

"You look like you could have fifty dollars on you, at least that, maybe a hundred. Enough for a night on the town. To these cocksuckers fifty dollars is a good score, especially if they pull a couple more jobs before the night is over. If they got a hundred off you, they'd come in their pants."

Morgan still wasn't buying it. "You mean they'd tackle somebody as big as me?"

"They'd tackle somebody as big as *me* when I was twenty years younger. How big and strong doesn't count. Surprise is the thing. They get you from behind. Choker—always a big mug—comes up behind you in gumshoes and whack! You're seeing stars. Happens every night of the week."

Morgan knew O'Connor could be right. This was a man who knew the worst side of the city. "But what was the runt doing outside Burke's, across the square from it? I could have been in there all night."

"Same idea," O'Connor said. "Obviously you missed him and he followed you a second time. If he saw you going into Burke's, he knew you had a sizable amount on you. Well worth waiting for if it didn't take the whole night. He wouldn't wait that long, but he'd give it some time."

Morgan was still thinking about the runt, not what he was, or the people he worked for, but how he looked. O'Connor didn't say anything for a while, then he said, "This runt with the slight build and the pasty face: sounds like a regular city rat, a thieving guttersnipe. They don't have to be big, you know."

Morgan was only half-listening. "That flash pan lit him up like a flash of lightning. He was half-turned toward the flash pan when it went off, so the camera must have caught him."

O'Connor was skeptical. More than that. "For heaven's sake, you said yourself it was raining cats and dogs. It was night, women running all over the place, a house on fire, Burke watering the flowers." Thinking of Burke and his firehose,

O'Connor grated out a laugh. "You think they made a clear picture—any picture—with all that going on? Not a chance. It's hard enough to make a picture when the person is standing still."

"The runt was standing still."

"Maybe he was, but you're forgetting these women you saw can't be any kind of professional photographers. I mean, female photographers with a regular studio. I've never seen any in my travels."

"A lot of women are interested in photography," Morgan said. "So I've heard. If they're interested enough, they could be pretty good at it."

O'Connor conceded the point. "Well yes, there are women's camera clubs around. It's a female kind of thing. I guess they could have taken a picture of this little rat. But even if it does exist, where are you going to find it? And to what purpose, if the little fucker is just a strongarm? You're not going to take it to the police?"

"Nothing like that. I'd like to show it to you. Maybe I didn't describe him right. Maybe you'll know who he is."

"The way you describe him, he could be any one of a thousand gutter rats in this city. Even if you showed me a good clear picture, I might not know him. You can hardly expect me to know every petty criminal in San Francisco. He could be from out of town. Every city has a floating population of smalltime crooks and ex-convicts. But I'll look at his picture if you can find it. That will be the main trouble, finding it."

"I'm going to try," Morgan said, setting down the second empty bottle.

O'Connor called for the Chinaman and told him to fetch another beer. Morgan looked after him as he went out to the kitchen. His face wasn't yellow— Morgan had yet to see a *yellow* Chinaman—and it wasn't pasty white either. It was pale more than anything else. Just the same, in artificial light, in the bright flash of a magnesium pan, it might show as pasty.

The Chinese brought in the bottle of beer and left. "Was he here all evening?" Morgan asked O'Connor.

At first O'Connor didn't get it, or pretended not to. "Who are you—"

"The Chinaman," Morgan cut in. "Did he go out after I left?"

O'Connor's big body began to shake with silent laughter. "You mean my Chinaman? That's the most ridiculous thing I ever heard. You think I set him to following you. Why in hell would I do that?"

"Maybe you thought I needed protection. Maybe you wanted to be sure I was going to Burke's and nowhere else."

O'Connor took out his watch and looked at it. "I'll let this nonsense pass because it's two o'clock in the morning and we're both tired. You've been through a fire and your nerves are still kind of rattled. All right. All right. I take that back. You're an iron man. But you're also like an old maid looking for rapists under the bed."

Morgan had to smile at that. "I guess I am kind of rattled."

O'Connor put his watch away. "Believe me, I

sent no one to follow you. If I thought you needed protection, do you think I'd send somebody like John? You'd get two of the toughest blokes on my payroll. John, my alabaster ass! What could that nervous nelly do in a pinch? As for tailing you, that Asiatic nincompoop couldn't spot an elephant in the middle of Market Street at high noon."

"I apologize," Morgan said.

O'Connor yawned but made no move to head for bed. "Accepted. If all it took was sneakiness, he'd be way ahead of everybody. But he was here every minute you were gone. He's free to go out if he gets his work done first. He seldom does. I know he didn't go out tonight." O'Connor yawned again. "I don't know what you're going to do. I'm going to bed. You ought to do the same. You must be worn out with the women."

"You don't approve?" Morgan wanted to hear what O'Connor had to say about that. It might clear up a few things.

O'Connor got his bulk out of the chair and talked standing up. "Lord no. I don't approve or disapprove. As long as there are horny men and women can sell it, that's what they'll do. Whores we'll always have with us. I just wish they'd get a better shake, not be so cheated and bullied and beaten down. If they want to quit, I try to help them. More than that I can't say. . . ."

Morgan looked after him as he left the living room. Strange man. Hard to decide what he was really like underneath all the blather. Morgan was in no mind to trust him completely. Wait and see was the way to do it. It had worked pretty well in the past. He took the third empty bottle out to the kitchen, thought about drinking a fourth and decided against it. And when he found himself yawning like O'Connor, he went to bed.

It was a nice room and its best feature was the big double bed. He stripped off and stretched out on the crisp sheets. The bed was soft and he was tired, but he didn't drop off to sleep right away. A lot had happened in a single day and he found himself going over it. It wasn't his way to chew on things he couldn't do anything about right at the moment, but when he was ready to sleep, he did just that.

He didn't see that he'd done anything he shouldn't have. Not that he was going to worry about it if he had. If he'd done anything wrong at all, it was getting mixed up in this in the first place. But he couldn't say that he regretted that either. At least he'd gotten one memorable fuck out of it. The whore at Burke's was all right—she tried hard to give him his money's worth—but she was no Angelique. If he'd learned anything new at Burke's, it was that Lily hadn't been there—probably hadn't—and wouldn't be there in the future.

That there might be a picture of the runt somewhere nagged at him a bit. He knew he had to find out who the woman photographer was. That could turn out to be a tall order because he had no idea how to find her. No matter what O'Connor said, she could be a professional photographer hired to do work for the feminists. She could be a feminist herself, and probably was. The place to start looking was where these wild women had their headquarters. There had to be a place where they planned their demonstrations, painted their slogans, collected their rotten eggs and soggy tomatoes. Of course, the police would have pulled the place apart by now. A house had been burned, maybe more than one, and a man had been killed, which was a far cry from just yelling in the streets and blocking traffic. The police hated these women—most men did—and would make it hard for them. Morgan couldn't say he hated them—it was hard to hate women, now that he thought about it—he just thought they were crazy. Yes sir, crazy they might be, but even while the riot was going on he'd spotted a few hysterical good lookers that it would be a pleasure to pacify. . . .

Back in Idaho, Morgan always woke up at five o'clock in the morning. But when he was away from home and there was nothing important that had to be done, he could sleep well past his get-up time. This morning he slept till nine and could have slept another hour if hunger hadn't driven him out of bed. The day before, with this and that going on, there hadn't been time to eat—always a mistake. After he shaved and took a shower and came out looking for O'Connor, the Chinaman told him he could find him in the dining room. A dining room! It seemed like poor old humble Duckie had everything. The place was so big, the Chinaman had to show him where it was.

O'Connor looked fresh as a daisy for a man who said he'd been up for hours. "I don't seem to need much sleep." Morgan remembered having read somewhere—maybe in the *Police Gazette*, maybe some preacher told him—that saints got by on very little sleep or none at all. It was hard to think of O'Connor as a saint. He was digging into a big platter of steak and eggs—was it his second breakfast?—enough food to keep an ordinary man going for a day and a half.

"You can have anything you like," he told Morgan. "You don't have to eat what I eat. When I'm away from the fancy places, I prefer humble but nourishing fare."

It didn't look so humble to Morgan, and that's what he said he wanted when O'Connor yelled for the Chinaman. "Coffee for Mr. Morgan," O'Connor yelled after him. "Americans don't like tea." To Morgan he said, "God help me, I love the fucking stuff, couldn't get through the day without it."

Morgan didn't ask about the feminist headquarters until he got a cup of coffee down. It was good strong coffee, just what he needed.

O'Connor refilled Morgan's cup, poured tea for himself. "Well of course I know where it is," he said, spooning in sugar. "I'm just not sure you should go there today. The police may be watching the place, and you can be sure they've been in there already. You don't want to run afoul of those bastards. They won't be grieving for Burke, the rotten fuck, but he was a source of graft and will be missed in that way."

The steak was as good as the coffee and Morgan went at it. "I'll be careful. Where is it?"

"Sacramento Street, not far from where we ran into that riot. Sacramento, near the corner of

144

.

Taylor. A good location they couldn't afford if Henry Dunaway's flighty daughter wasn't paying the rent. They couldn't do half the things they do without her. She's over twenty-one, has her own money, and can do as she pleases. Her father doesn't much care, if he cares at all, spends most of his time in Europe collecting statues and such. Pots and pots of money in that family."

"You think she might be there?"

"You mean is she good looking? Why not? A fella like you. I'm joking, of course. I don't know that much about her, I'm afraid. I work a dirtier side of the street. It's doubtful if you'll find her there today after what happened last night. My experience of rich people is that they talk a good cause but hide when the shit starts to fly. If this woman is different, I'll be very much surprised."

O'Connor poured another cup of his ever-loving tea. "I was thinking last night just before I went to sleep, and this idea of finding the runt's picture isn't a bad idea. I could show it around at the Palace, the convention. Could be one of those friendly police chiefs would recognize the little bastard. A long shot, but worth a try. You could show it to Bender."

Morgan had been thinking about that. Trouble was, if the runt wasn't known in San Francisco, was new to the city, then he could be from anywhere. Going by Morgan's description O'Connor called him a city rat, but that covered a lot of territory. And could he reasonably expect somebody as high up as the chief of some city police force to recognize a lousy little strongarm? A patrolman might, a sergeant might, and on up through the lower ranks. But a police chief, usually a man long gone from the streets? Not too likely.

Morgan went on eating his steak and eggs. "I have to telephone Bullock at noon."

"Well I'll leave that to you. We've been over it enough. Make sure you ask for that extra expense money. Bullock won't offer it if you don't ask."

"I'll ask for it all right. These whorehouses are leaving me flat."

"You have my deepest sympathy. But when duty calls we must obey." O'Connor indulged himself in one of his three smiles for the day.

"I'm going to tell him what you suggested," Morgan said. "The Fort Smith marriage. About how I got a good scent on Hargis and then lost it."

"Temporarily, of course. You're confident that you'll catch up to him and Lily—especially Lily— right soon. I'll be interested to hear how he takes it. How he takes it should tell us a lot. Shake him gently and see if he rattles."

"He might not rattle at all. He's a tight, tough little man."

"Tight he certainly is. You know, you could telephone him from here, but it's better you do it from the Exchange Building. I wouldn't want him tracing you here. But there's a problem that has to be faced before you go over there. What will you do if he tells you to keep the first five hundred and forget the whole thing? Telling him about the marriage might make him want you out of it. If you know about the marriage, then maybe you know too much and should be long gone from this city. No more money, he'd expect you to go home. Would you?"

"What else could I do?"

"You could continue to work with me. I have no intention of quitting, no matter what Bullock says to you. Once you're no longer working for Bullock you'll be a free agent. We can find the securities and split them fifty-fifty like I said. No need to let your conscience bother you. Bullock is a rotten, gouging little miser and deserves to lose everything he has. All we'd be taking is a measly hundred thousand. Fifty thousand, you could built the finest horse ranch in the State of Idaho."

Morgan poured out the last of the coffee. "Getting fired hasn't happened yet. Let me think about it." That was what he said, but he had no hankering to rob Bullock no matter what happened. If Bullock told him to call it a day, that's what he'd do, unless he decided to see this through to the end for his own satisfaction. No matter how he found the securities, working for Bullock or on his own time, he wasn't about to rob him of one red cent. And he wouldn't stay honest because it was the best policy or any of that shit. He just didn't rob or cheat.

"Don't think too long," O'Connor said. "An opportunity like this doesn't knock too often. If Bullock says he has no further need of your services and you simply go home, you may regret it in the years to come. You're in vigorous health now and think there's always a dollar to be made, but who knows what's waiting down the road?"

"I said I'd think about it. Turning to crime is no

small step." Morgan wanted to see what O'Connor had to say to that.

O'Connor took it the way he took things he didn't want to be pinned down by. "Crime, did you say? You make it sound as if you'd have to follow this up by living like a desperado. Robbing trains and all manner of dastardly deeds. Nonsense. All you'd be doing is seeing your chance and taking it. You'd be independent. That's what having money means. Once and for all, you'd be through with working for other men, a man like you, trying to make ends meet. . . ."

O'Connor was laying it on thick, as only he could. He could be trying to lead him into temptation or testing him or, when you thought about it, he could be attempting to do both. Nothing to wonder at if you knew O'Connor. Trouble was, the longer you knew him, the harder he was to figure.

"All you'd be doing is taking money from a tricky little miser, a man who got his start cheating honest miners back in the gold rush days. Now I ask you, how is it a crime to take money from a wretch like that?"

"Duckie," Morgan said, "if I decide to go partners with you in robbing Bullock, I won't feel the need to work up a lot of hate for him. I'll just do it."

"There you go again, talking like a desperado." It was plain that O'Connor didn't like to hear the words 'rob' and 'cheat'. "There's a moral question involved here, but we need not go into that right at this moment. "All I'm saying to you is this: in the end, the only reason to have money is to tell any son of a bitch who bothers you to kiss your arse."

"I do that anyway, Duckie," Morgan said.

"That may be," O'Connor said, "but with money you can make it stick. Now I have never have used money to get back at those who have wronged me in the past. But, may God forgive me, the urge is still there. I'll carry my grudges to the grave, I'm afraid. It's some consolation to remind myself that in the Old Testament the most upright people went around seeking to exact justice for old wrongs. Doing dirt is what I call it in simpler language, but however you phrase it, it comes to the same thing. Now wouldn't it be nice to have enough money to settle a few old scores?"

"Maybe I'd like to settle a few scores, but I don't lie awake nights thinking about it. Anyway, my kind of score settling wouldn't be done with money."

O'Connor pressed on. "Well yes, I can see that. But if you did shoot a few blokes, you'd like to have a good attorney to represent you. Good attorneys don't come cheap. That's where money comes in. How many rich men, I ask you, have been sent to the gallows? I know I'm tempting you, yet—"

"Get thee behind me, Satan," Morgan said, smiling at this amiable villain.

"Sometimes I think that lad isn't as bad as he's painted," Reverend Duckie O'Connor said.

Chapter Ten

Morgan started for the Telephone Exchange Building at eleven o'clock. O'Connor said he could get there in twenty minutes. All he had to do to find it was stay on Front Street all the way to Market, then walk down a block and make a left turn onto First.

On his way out O'Connor asked him, "You've used the telephone a lot?"

"Sure have," Morgan said, lying and grinning about it. "Back in Idaho I'm on it all the time. Hello, Central, put me through to the line shack."

"That's the ticket. Just remember, you don't have to shout."

Downstairs he met Harriet Streeter in the hall and she gave him a baleful look, but passed without speaking. "And a merry Christmas to you, too" he said to himself. But he had to admit she looked pretty good, for all her sourness. This morning, instead of the severe black dress of yesterday, she was wearing a more stylish skirt and shirtwaist that showed more of her. Now if she'd only stand in front of a mirror and practice smiling for a bit, try to relearn how it was done, he'd be more than willing to put his boots under her bed. Hell, he was ready to do that whether she smiled or not.

He took his time getting to Market Street. Earlier it was raining but it wasn't raining now, which was just a fluke, and he had to remember to buy another raincoat. Front Street was close to the docks and wasn't what they called fashionable—far from it. It was lined with warehouses and ship chandler's stores stocked with all kinds of seagoing equipment. No clothing stores here unless you wanted to buy a pea jacket or a sailor cap. He'd have to wait till he got to Market.

Market was where the Palace was, where Bender was, but there wasn't time to go looking for him now. Besides, he might be up to his ears with the convention. Morgan figured it was better to wait till maybe he had the runt's picture to show. But even if he came up empty, he still wanted to talk to Bender. There were questions.

He checked his back trail twice without spotting the runt. Maybe the little rat's ass was up so late he needed his sleep. Maybe O'Connor was right and he was at the other end of the city, looking for a mark or thinking about it. Just the same, Morgan couldn't altogether lose the feeling that there was more to the runt than just a strongarm on the prowl. He checked again before he turned onto Market. The street behind him was empty. Nothing there but a cat stalking a pigeon.

He had to walk two blocks down Market to buy a

raincoat in the store where he bought the first one. The same clerk recognized him and said cheerfully, "I see you like our coats so much you want to buy another one. This time, sir, may I show you our fine line of umbrellas?"

To get back to First Street he had to walk past the Palace Hotel a second time. It sure was a great big monument of a hotel, even had a special entrance where you could drive your carriage right into the building and register without stepping down. It was twelve-fifteen when he found the Telephone Building. Looking for the room where the public booths were, he opened the wrong door and found himself looking at a long line of women, mostly young, seated on high stools, busy as one-armed paper hangers with wires and switches. They all wore shirtwaists and skirts and laced boots and some of them looked pretty good, especially a redheaded lassie not far from the door who threw him a quick smile and was severely reprimanded by a stern old biddy standing behind her. The same dragon told him how to find the right room and showed him the door. He didn't think she had to slam it so hard behind him.

There were ten booths and four were in use; men who looked like salesmen were jawing away as if they did it all the time. Morgan had talked on the telephone a few times when he had to. It had been around for some years, but to him it was still a new-fangled invention. He didn't have to wait long after the operator rang him through. Bullock answered right away. "Is that you, Morgan?" he asked before Morgan had a chance to talk. His

cranky voice sounded crankier than when Morgan
first heard it.

"That's right," Morgan said. At their meeting in
the library he had been "Mr. Morgan." Since then
he had been demoted to just plain Morgan.

"Well, get on with it." Bullock was cranky all
right, or nervous, or something.

Morgan stuck to the story, as planned. How he'd
gone to Madame D's, where a talkative whore told
him about Hargis busting in and what the Negro
porter told her later. How the house bully and the
porter turned up the Arkansas marriage license, the
prison discharge paper. Morgan thought Bullock
would interrupt him at this point. He didn't. All
that was left to say was that Lily had been hiding
upstairs for three days, had sent for a cab after
Hargis left, and was still on the loose.

"But I'm sure I'll find her," Morgan said.

"How can you be sure of anything when you
don't know where she is?"

"This man Hargis—" Morgan started to say.

Bullock didn't allow him to finish. "That marriage document he has must be a fake. You say
he served a prison sentence for attempted murder.
Well for my money he's a blackmailer to boot. Let
him try it, by God. If what he has isn't a fake, Lily
must be in this with him and I want no more to
do with her, is that clear? I just want my securities.
She can go to hell. She can go back to whoring."

Morgan started to say something about Lily and
Bullock jumped on it just as quick. "It's not your
place to defend her, Morgan. You're not being paid
to argue. Find her and take the securities away

from her and that will be the end of it."

Well now, Morgan thought, the old bastard was really flying off the handle. Just a few words and Lily was banished from his bed and board forever. No doubt it would rattle any husband to find another undivorced husband in the woodpile. Even so, Bullock didn't even want to talk about it.

"Did you hear what I said?" Bullock had gone from cranky to downright nasty. "Find her and bring the securities to me, then you'll get your second five hundred. And you'd better hurry up about it."

Morgan thought he heard something besides old man's crankiness in Bullock's voice. Something was making him nervous and he wasn't saying what it was. "I'll find her," Morgan said.

"See that you do and make it quick. You're getting good money for just wandering about asking questions."

"I'm not wandering around, Mr. Bullock. I'm leaving no stone unturned." Morgan smiled when he said it.

"Well, you needn't bother with Burke's. It burned down last night. Do your job and you'll get your money, that's all I have to say. I want you to ring me the same time tomorrow, before then if you find anything new. In fact, call me any time—here or at home—if you have new information."

This time it was Morgan's turn to jump in. "I'm going to need more expense money, Mr. Bullock." He started to explain, but Bullock cut him off.

"I don't want to hear it. Go to the Merchants' Bank on Market Street right now and the manager will give you five hundred dollars in cash. It's a few blocks from where you are. Give me a few minutes to telephone the manager. And I might add, that's all the expense money you're going to get."

The line went dead and Morgan was glad of it. It had been easier than he'd expected, no need for any more lying about Hargis. All Bullock wanted to talk about was his securities; his bigamous wife was in the dog house. That was peculiar in itself, after all the weepy bullshit about his lovely Lily. "Please try to persuade her to come home, Mr. Morgan," the old man had said that night, words like that, with a crack in his voice. Now he had written her off like a bad investment. No man, even a flinty old man like Bullock, had such a sudden change of heart. Naturally the bigamy shit would come as a shock, but you'd expect him to ask for more information before Lily was condemned so abruptly. It would all come out in the wash, he thought, or as he knew goddamn well, it might not.

He went to the desk to pay for the call, then out to the cigar stand in the lobby to buy a newspaper. There were a lot of newspapers there, some of them scandal sheets, but he wanted the *Examiner*, the most reputable paper in town. The feminist riot, the firebombing, Burke's death glared at him from the front pages of the yellow journals. RIOT! ARSON! MURDER! was one headline. IS THE RIGHT TO VOTE THE RIGHT TO MURDER? the other headline demanded. The yellow journals were good for a laugh, but played too fast and loose with the truth. Facts never got in the way of a good story. The *Examiner* made for dull reading, but they'd get it right.

He sat on a fake marble bench and skimmed through the story. The riot and what followed were front page news, even in the *Examiner*, but the headline wasn't so loud, the story sober and factual except when it came to describing Burke and his whorehouse. Burke was described as "a sporting man," his whorehouse as a "club." No good telling the citizens what they already knew. The rest of the story was to the point. After a diligent search by firemen, only one body was recovered from the ruins of the house, that of Francis X. Burke.

Morgan left the paper on the bench and headed for the bank. It was certain then that Lily hadn't been there, was still on the loose. That made Morgan feel better—and worse. If Lily had been in there, that would be the end of her, the securities and this so-called investigation. And, he thought, the end of the money. Maybe that wouldn't have been so bad. He could go home to Idaho and forget about it. With Lily alive he could stay in the game, play what cards he held and hope to get lucky. At the moment his hand didn't look too promising, but it might get better. It might.

He got the five hundred without any difficulty. Didn't even have to show any identification, and that was good because he had none. All he had to do was sign a receipt and the manager handed him five crisp hundreds in an envelope. He changed one of the hundreds to tens and fives before he left the bank. It was nice to fatten his bankroll a bit, but he wondered again why Bullock had turned so much money loose without arguing about it first. That first night, all he was ready to part with was two hundred and fifty dollars in expense money, and you'd think it was breaking his heart, the way he went on about it. Now he was tossing big bills around like Diamond Jim Brady. Morgan smiled at the idea of Bullock doing anything even close to that. But something had happened to make him unsnap his purse. One explanation might be that he had suddenly become more anxious about his missing securities, and that was reasonable enough on the face of it, but why had it happened in less than forty-eight hours? If he wasn't so hard-talking and jittery two nights before, why was he like that now? The hell with Bullock and his bad nerves. There was a full day before he had to talk to him again. Time to look for the place where the wild women hung out.

He headed for Sacramento, glad that he had the new raincoat—it was raining again. According to the *Examiner* story, a number of feminists were being held on various charges, among them unlawful assembly, rioting, destruction of property, arson, assault on police officers, and manslaughter. There was even something about charging the leaders under the new anarchy law. Morgan figured they'd try to nail the leaders and let the rank and file down easier. That was usually how it worked. There was no mention of a woman named Dunaway, and that could mean she hadn't been there, or hadn't been arrested if she was there, or had bought her way out of jail.

Anybody rich enough could do that, especially in San Francisco.

He stood in the rain and looked up at the big plate glass window on the second floor. EQUALITY FOR WOMEN, INC. was painted on it in big gold letters. That was fair enough, he thought, not sure what the INC. meant. Were they in business? Did they make and sell things like straw baskets and samplers saying GOD BLESS OUR HAPPY HOME to hang on the wall? After having been pelted with rotten eggs by these ladies, he hardly thought so. He saw no uniformed policemen watching the place, unless they were in the German restaurant on the first floor, and no detectives disguised as organ grinders or knife sharpeners. There was a uniformed copper at the end of the block, but he was busy trying to get a drunk up off the sidewalk. Morgan decided it was safe enough to go upstairs, and if he found a police padlock on the door, well, then he'd have to try to find the woman photographer some other way.

But there was no police lock and he opened the door just by turning the knob. The police had been there all right, the place was a shambles. Overturned office furniture, pulled out filing cabinet drawers, scattered papers, tipped over potted plants. And sitting at a desk in the middle of all this mess was a young woman wearing a white fedora hat and smoking a cigar. Standing beside the desk was a well-dressed middle-aged man who looked like a lawyer. They were arguing when Morgan came in. He stood there unnoticed and had to clear his throat and say, "Excuse me" before the woman looked up and the lawyer turned to glare at him.

"Yes. Yes, what is it?" the lawyer said impatiently. "Can't you see we're busy? Whatever it is you want, you'll have to come back another time."

The woman waved her cigar, a great big fat one. "Hold on there, Rex. No need to bust your britches. Let's see what the gentleman wants. What *do* you want?" This was said in a very precise voice, with the words clipped off, the way they taught them to talk in finishing school. Morgan liked the voice and the heart-shaped face under the hatbrim.

"I'm looking for Miss Dunaway," he said, still just inside the door.

"Come closer," she said. "We don't want to shout like train callers, do we?" Morgan walked to the desk, the lawyer still glaring at him. "And what do you want with Miss Dunaway?"

The lawyer let loose with, "I refuse to let you talk to this man. You don't know who he is or what he is. He could be from the police, trying to entrap you. Miss Dunaway has nothing to say to you, absolutely nothing," he said to Morgan.

The woman knocked cigar ash to the littered floor. "Oh, do stop it, Rex. Such fucking rot you talk."

"As your attorney—" Rex was furious.

Miss Dunaway gave him a sweet smile. "As my attorney you can go down and get me a pot of coffee and a sandwich—I'm starved. Brisket of beef on pumpernickel, not too much mustard. Tell Otto to make it himself. He knows how I like it, sliced thin and lean. Get along now, my belly thinks my mouth's gone on strike."

Working men said that. Morgan wanted to smile at the way she said it. Like the way she said "fucking." With her voice it came out as "fakking." If she said "Cunt," it would sound like "kant." She hadn't said it yet.

"This is outrageous." Rex's long pale face had spots of red in it. And he still hadn't moved. "I refuse to leave you alone with this man. He could be an *agent provocateur.*"

Miss Dunaway laughed, a nice musical sound. "That's French for police spy," she said to Morgan. "You're not a police spy, are you?"

"No, ma'am." Morgan wished the fucking lawyer would go and get the sandwich. "I'd like to talk to you if you're Miss Dunaway."

She waved the cigar and Morgan was reminded of a brass band leader waving his baton. "Just a moment." The lawyer was still there. "Rex, will you please go down and place my order? You don't have to come back with it. Otto can send one of the waiters. Scat now."

Rex went out with as much dignity as he could muster. Morgan thought it must be a bitch to be ordered around like that, even if you were getting well paid for it. "Are you Miss Dunaway?" he said to the woman.

"Yes, I'm George Dunaway," she said.

"Nice meeting you, George," Morgan said. No skin off his ass what she called herself. "My name is Blaney."

She raised her dark eyebrows. No way to tell

what color her hair was. It was stuffed up into her hat, the hat pulled low. "You're not surprised by my name?" She seemed surprised that he wasn't surprised, but she tried to hide it.

"No, I'm not surprised." Morgan wanted to get this name business over with. "If that's what you want to go by, why not?"

"I don't go by anything but my real name, which is George. It's on my birth certificate, so it must be real." Her sharp response softened into a smile. Everything about her was sweet—the heart-shaped face, the slightly olive skin, the violet eyes. "My mother was a great admirer of George Sand, the famous French writer, perhaps the first feminist. Have you heard of her?"

Morgan could honestly say he hadn't. "Was George her *real* name?" He didn't know why he said that. After all, it was O'Connor who got hit on the head.

"Her real name was Amandine Aurore Lucie," George Dunaway said, savoring the sound of the words. "She changed it to George Sand, unofficially of course, because it was even more a man's world then than it is now. To get in the spirit of the thing, she wore male clothing and smoked cigars." George Dunaway waved her own cigar. "And so do I."

"So I see." Morgan wanted to make some progress before sundown. "Nothing like a good cigar, I'm told. Now if you can spare the time, there's something I'm trying to find out."

But George Dunaway was not to be rushed. "I know what you're thinking." As if Morgan hadn't spoken. "George Sand liked men, but not all the time. Now and then she liked a change, like me. Does that shock you?"

Why the hell did she keep on trying to shock him? He was long past being shocked by what people did in bed or out of it. Did she think him such a rube? "Not shocked at all, George. Calamity Jane is like that, or so they say. Wears men's clothes, smokes stogies, swears like a trooper, has her lady friends. Of course, she's as ugly as sin."

George Dunaway wasn't sure she liked that. "All that doesn't make a feminist. It's what's in the heart and the mind. Why don't you find a chair and we'll talk about it. There's one over there."

Morgan found the chair and sat on it in front of the desk. All this talk was very educational, but it wasn't what he had come for. It would be a relief if she came back down from the clouds. Looked like she wasn't ready to do that just yet. An enameled cigar box was pushed toward him. "Thanks but I don't smoke," he said.

"And you don't chew tobacco."

"No. And I don't dip snuff."

"I started by smoking cigarettes," George Dunaway went on. "But now I prefer cigars. Cigarettes are such skinny little things, so unsatisfying. I like something I can get my mouth around."

Was she joking? If she wasn't, he had just the thing for her to put in her pretty mouth. And it was bigger than the biggest cigar they ever made. He watched while she stubbed out the cigar she'd been smoking, took another one from the box and sucked on the end of it, turning it in her mouth before she struck a match on the top of the desk.

Lucky cigar, Morgan thought lewdly, not a bit ashamed of himself. Watching her sucking on the smoldering cigar gave him a hard-on. It would be embarrassing if he had to stand up. He didn't have to. She stood up, why he didn't know; maybe she wanted to show herself off. Whatever the reason, she got up and walked around for a bit, and what he thought was a dark green velvet jacket turned out to be a complete suit, not a man's suit, but definitely mannish. Her shirtwaist was fine white silk, her tie matched the suit, her soft leather boots looked Spanish and had high heels. The bootheels clicked on the bare wooden floor. Everything about her brought to mind General Phil Sheridan: short, dramatic, always in command of the situation. Of course that was just the overall impression. Nothing at all like homely little Phil when you considered her features one by one. For a start, her small heart-shaped face was very beautiful, the violet eyes gave you a shock, and that compact body made a nice package. . . .

His eyes followed her as she walked about talking, waving the cigar, stopping now and then to look at him. "Sometimes I think George Sand walks with me, Blaney. I can feel her presence. She talks to me, you know. Do you know what she says?"

"What?" Morgan wondered if George Sand talked French to George Dunaway.

"What she says is, keep up the good fight, don't ever stop fighting, cherie. That's what she calls me—cherie. I confess I blush when she says it. Men, she says, beware of men. Love them with all your heart, but always be aware of their treachery, for they are weak and cannot help themselves. And she says you must be careful, too, of the women you love. Crush them to your breast, accept them, make love to them, but do not be deceived by their womanly wiles. You yourself are a woman—a strong, vibrant, *throbbing* woman—you must give the gift of yourself to the world. Never hesitate, never hold back, when the powerful urge to love—be it man or woman—is upon you. Fight for women and love them, love men and fight for them in their weakness and helplessness, fight, cherie, for everything. . . ."

Now she was pacing the floor behind him, still talking. She sure was doing a lot of fighting. All that money wearing out the floorboards, talking war. He wished she'd sit down where he could see her, get started on photography business. But that was not to be, not for the moment anyway. Coming up close behind him, she placed her hands on his shoulders and he could smell her perfume. No twenty-five cent fragrance, this stuff—it was light and heady at the same time, doing not a thing to distract his hard-on.

"Blaney," she said, kneading his shoulders through the raincoat. Too bad he had the fucking thing on, too bad he wasn't ready to go. "Blaney, George Sand is telling me you did not come here by accident."

"Tell her she's right," Morgan said. No wonder this one's father spent most of his time in Europe. But he wasn't complaining. He wasn't her father, and thank God for that. How old was she? About twenty-four, maybe twenty-three, a sweet age. He tried to keep his mind on why he was there. "No accident, George. I came to talk to you. Can we do that?"

She gave his shoulders one final squeeze. "Yes, cherie, we can do that." She let go of him and went back and sat behind the desk. It was good to see her again, and he liked the way she called him cherie. "What do you want to talk about? You won't try to sell me insurance, I hope?" That was a joke and she laughed at it. Like fairy bells, he thought. He was turning into a fucking poet, a male George Sand with a hard-on.

George Dunaway was waiting, one hand holding the cigar, the other playing with the buttons on her shirt. That hand drew his attention to her breasts, small but surely lovely. It was hard to get started, but he managed to do it. "I hope you won't throw me out of here, won't think I was spying, but I was at Burke's when the riot started last night. I watched the whole thing from beginning to end."

"It wasn't a riot, Blaney, it was a demonstration." Her voice was kindly, as if explaining something he ought to understand. "Burke started the riot. But please continue."

Morgan got going again. "I was on a second floor balcony—"

"I might have seen you."

"Did you?"

"I might have . . . if I'd been there."

"Were you?" The moment Morgan asked the question, he wanted to take it back.

Her marvelous eyes narrowed, but her voice

stayed relaxed. "Why are you asking these questions if you're not from the police?"

"I'm sorry. I didn't mean to sound like a policeman. I don't even much like the police. Believe me, I'm no kind of detective."

"But I don't know that, do I? On such short acquaintance, how can I?" She shoved the chair back and put her boots on the desk, not a ladylike thing to do, but this spoiled lady wasn't concerned with appearances. "Go on with it, I'll decide how much I want to listen to. Rex is a fussbudget but he's right. I have to be careful."

No more questions for now. This rich lady was spoiled and affected, but she was smart. She'd throw him out in a minute, maybe holler for a bluecoat. Rich people treated the police like servants. He stuck to his original story. He was a lumberman from up north, in San Francisco to have a good time. He didn't say where he was registered, no need for that unless she asked. He was on his way to Burke's when he noticed that he was being followed by a short, slender, white-faced man wearing a cloth cap. As a man who'd been around a bit, he knew immediately that he was being stalked by a strongarm robber working with an accomplice, usually a much bigger man. He doubled back on the little man, but he ran away.

"I thought I'd seen the last of him," Morgan said. "But then I spotted him again, right at the end of the demonstration. He was standing there when a photographer's flash pan went off and I saw him as plain as day, half-turned toward the camera, which must have taken his picture. I saw two women earlier with a camera and a flash pan. I thought they must be part of your group—"

"And you hoped to find the plate or the developed photograph here." George Dunaway gave him a lovely smile. "The question here is, why are you going to all this trouble?"

Chapter Eleven

"You're not working for my father, are you?" she asked when he gave no ready answer. He had an answer prepared, but that was before he met George Dunaway. Now it seemed kind of lame. "Daddy pretends not to care what I do, he's very busy with his art collecting and his women, but I know he does care, the old darling. I must say you're not my idea of what a private detective looks like, which I suppose is very clever. If I didn't know better, I'd almost be willing to believe that you're really in the lumber business. Well, not lumber exactly. You have more the look of a rancher or someone who raises horses. Which is it, Blaney?"

By God, she'd hit it right on the head. "Sorry to disappoint you, but I'm in lumber, like I say. As for this robber—"

She laughed. "Yes. Yes. This robber! Get on with your tall tale, but don't take all day. It's bound to be amusing."

It was hard to explain in the face of that and

what he said had a hollow sound even as he said it. "I'm very strong for law and order. My father was a county sheriff"—that part made her laugh—"and I'd like to find a picture of this blackguard" blackguard! where did that come from? "So I can take it to the police, have him put away. So you see why it's so important to me."

She laughed so hard he thought she was going to fall off her chair. Laughed so hard that she dabbed at her eyes with her necktie, though there was a handkerchief in the breast pocket of her jacket. "By gum and by golly," she said, still laughing. "It certainly sounds important. For heaven's sake, Blaney, you're the worst liar and the worst actor I've ever laid eyes on. Law and order, my alabaster ass. You never obeyed a law you didn't like in your life. One look at you is all it takes to know that."

"I'm a respectable businessman, that's the truth."

"You may be in some business, but you're not respectable. Don't think you'll win my trust with that kind of malarkey. I *hate* respectable businessmen. *Hate* them. I've seen enough of the fuckers when I was growing up, always coming to the house, sucking up to my father. I'll say this for my father, he never was a respectable businessman and now he's an old rake."

The door opened and an aproned waiter came in carrying a tray covered with a napkin. Morgan took him to be a waiter until George Dunaway said, "For heaven's sake, Otto, you didn't have to bring it up yourself."

Otto did a German heel-click. "To a nice lady I

169

bring it myself. A nice piece of strudel for dessert, a gift from me, no charge."

George Dunaway uncovered the tray and said, "You're the devil himself, Otto, always tempting me with sweet things."

Otto was a big, rough looking man, but he simpered like a schoolboy with a pretty, new teacher. "Ach, it is nothing." Morgan received a suspicious look. "The police have not been back, such a mess they make. I would have help you, but they are so many of them, and I am a foreigner. Gott damn them, they are like the Prussians." Otto left, closing the door behind him.

Morgan thought Otto looked like a Prussian himself. George Dunaway thought he was sweet and he was—sweet on her. "Otto is so rough he can afford to be gentle. One of the nice men of this world. He'd tear your head off if he thought you were lying to me."

"I'm not lying."

"Yes you are, and there's no point going on with this unless you tell the truth." George Dunaway poured coffee for herself, then remembered Morgan had no cup. "There must be a cup around here somewhere." She looked around before she found one behind an overturned table, blew dust from it, and brought it back to the desk. "You'll have to drink it black," she said, filling the cup.

"I'm willing to pay for the picture," Morgan said, thinking of the five hundred in his pocket.

"Bullshit! You think that means anything to me?" She didn't mention her money—that would be too crude—but that's what she meant. "The only price is the truth. Tell the truth or get out. I'll drink your coffee myself. Another thing, don't think you can walk all over me and look for it yourself. I'll scream and Otto will come bounding up the stairs to tear your head off."

Jesus Christ, would she never shut up about Otto? Morgan hadn't the faintest notion of over-powering her and searching the place. Anyway, where the hell would he look? There was no camera lying around in the litter. A tripod camera was big, not something you could hide that handily. He wondered if the police had taken it.

"I'd like to believe you have the picture," he said.

"First, tell me the truth. What the hell is the matter with you?" George Dunaway was getting mad—not too mad; it wasn't her way to get too mad. "If you're not working for my father or the police, what is there to hide?"

Morgan took a chance and told some of the truth. It was the only way he had a chance of seeing the goddamned picture. He didn't give Bullock's name, simply referring to him as "a wealthy businessmen" who didn't want to be laughed at or injured by bad publicity. O'Connor was kept out of it altogether. She didn't press him for details, so he thought maybe it was all right.

But it wasn't. "Why should I help you to find this woman? Good luck to her is all I can say. If he's a wealthy businessman, then he must be old. Not very young, anyway. I can imagine what he's like. Awful. If she can find freedom and one hundred thousand dollars to enjoy it, I think she should be commended. I'm afraid you'll have to find her without my help. I'm sorry. No, I'm not."

"If I don't find her, he'll send somebody worse than me after her. A lot worse. I talked to him on the telephone today and he's getting impatient, made it clear that I don't have much time before he hires somebody else. Some tough mug from the Barbary Coast, I guess. She's in for some rough treatment if he does."

George Dunaway pushed her hat back, like somebody in a poker game. Her hair was shiny dark-brown, almost black. "Yes, they might do that, knowing what she's been."

"They would, and maybe worse. My client doesn't want her back, just the securities. She'd be on her own, but she'd only have me to deal with."

"And you're not so bad?"

"That's right. I wouldn't force her back into a whorehouse."

"Very noble of you, I'm sure. Let me think while I eat my sandwich. You want the strudel?"

Morgan didn't want the pastry, but he drank the coffee.

"If you find her, bring her here to me," George Dunaway said with her mouth full of bread and beef. Getting back at the finishing school, Morgan thought. Next she'd be picking her teeth. "I'll take care of her if nobody else will. In a way I'm ashamed of you, Blaney, doing this sort of thing for money."

Morgan liked the way she dismissed money as

something of absolutely no importance. "I needed it," he said.

"Oh fudge! Is your ranch doing as badly as that?"

"Not that bad. I still needed the money. Now George, I've told you the truth. What about the picture?"

She swallowed the last of the man-sized sandwich. Otto hadn't stinted on the meat. "Supposing I have it, what does this little man have to do with finding this woman?"

"I don't know," Morgan said. "All I know is he's mixed up in it somewhere. I think he is. He could be working for somebody who thinks I'll lead them to the securities."

George Dunaway ate the strudel in a few bites. "It's like a Chinese puzzle box, one inside the other. It's like an Edgar Allen Poe mystery tale, or one of Mr. Doyle's over in England. Is there such a thing as a woman detective? I would dearly like to be the first."

Morgan thought of Harriet Streeter, but said nothing.

"All right," George Dunaway said. "I have the picture, meaning I have the undeveloped plate. But it's at my flat. You don't think I'd leave my camera here for the police to damage or confiscate."

This was more like it. "Can we go get it?"

"Yes. You'll have to wait while it's being developed. I have a completely equipped darkroom in my flat. I do all my own work. Let's go."

They talked in the cab on the way to her flat. Lord, she smelled nice in the confined space of the cab. It was a lot more enjoyable than riding with O'Connor, who was a clean man but gave off a powerful odor of Witch Hazel. "It will be good to get home," George Dunaway said. "I had to sleep on the floor last night—none of my comrades are strong on cleaning and dusting—and I'm a bit grubby. But I felt I should be there when the police arrived. I might as well have gone home after the demonstation broke up. The police didn't get there until morning."

"Did they bother you much?"

"Not very much. But they did have a search warrant and they did make a mess of the place, looking for what I can't imagine. Captain Clancy, who isn't as mean as he looks, tried to get me to leave, but I refused. Instead, I telephoned Rex and he came right over. The police had left by then, taking with them several cardboard boxes full of our pamphlets and handbills."

"Then you're not in any trouble?" Morgan wondered where they were going; the streets were completely unfamiliar.

"Heavens, no. What could they charge me with, taking photographs? I'm quite well-known as a photographer, by the way. No, I'm in the clear, but I feel a little guilty that I'm not in jail with the others."

"Never feel guilty about not being in jail."

"Oh, I've been in jail a few times, not for very long, and I hated it. Have you ever been in jail?"

"A few times, if by jail you mean the lockup.

Never anything serious enough for prison. Fighting, talking back to mean marshals, that sort of thing."

George Dunaway laughed a few notes of her musical laugh. "Just as long as it wasn't for beating women. Here we are. Chez Dunaway."

Morgan dug out some money, but George Dunaway insisted on paying half the fare. "Equality in everything," she said to him. The fare wasn't very much, but it took some time to straighten it out, the way she fiddled with small coins. "Are you sure you can spare it?" the driver growled after she gave him what must have been a miserly tip. Morgan thought about giving the driver something decent, but didn't want to start an argument with this arrogant woman. The photograph came first.

"It looks like a hotel," he said, looking up at the building she lived in.

"It's supposed to look like a French chateau. It's the first apartment house in San Francisco and I love it. This is Telegraph Hill. Isn't the view wonderful? You can see the Bay. Come on."

They went up in a birdcage elevator to the top floor. The elevator boy must have started that day and could hardly keep his eyes off her, sneaking looks in the mirror angled above his head. Morgan didn't blame him one bit. With her white fedora hat and elegant velvet suit and necktie, she must have been the fanciest and most unusual lady he'd ever seen. The whole place was fancy and she was completely at home in it, taking it all as her due—the fountain playing in the lobby, the marble floors and polished brass, the statues of ladies holding

175

their hands over their thing.

After they got off the elevator, heels clicking on marble, she said, "I have only half the floor, but they're trying to get the other tenant out so I can have it all. He has a long lease, but they think they can break it. Rex is lending a hand." She unlocked the door—no triple locks here—turned a switch and electric lamps came on in a living room so elegant that it made O'Connor's pretty fancy living room look like a cow barn in comparison.

"Hello the house!" George Dunaway called, sailing her hat away from her. It landed on a red leather couch. "Perfect aim. I always say hello the house when I come in. I like the sound of it, so country and old-fashioned. Do you say that in Idaho when you come home?"

"Would be no point. Nobody lives in the main house but me."

"What, no woman you can call your own?" She winked. "No man?"

Morgan didn't take her up on it. She liked to tease people. "Nobody." He wondered if he'd get more from her than the photograph if he hung around long enough. But maybe this was her week for women.

"I thought my assistant Effie would be here. Maybe she'll be here later. She's very sweet, you'll love her." George Dunaway took Morgan's coat and hat and threw them on the red couch. "She's sweet but she's moody, which is why she doesn't live here all the time. I throw her out when she gets too moody and she goes back to her rooming house until she's in a more cheerful frame of mind. Make yourself as comfortable as you can. I'll be in the darkroom, but don't come in. No one is allowed in there but Effie."

"How long will you be?"

"Not long, just wait."

"What's that clicking sound?" Morgan asked. He'd been listening to it since they came in. It stopped and started and now it was going again.

"That's a stock ticker," George Dunaway said. "Haven't you ever heard one before? It provides stock quotations and important financial news. Prints automatically by telegraph, on a paper ribbon. Really quite simple."

The clicking had stopped again. "I thought you hated business."

She gave him an apologetic smile; any way she smiled was aces with him. "I do hate it, but at the same time I like to know how my stocks are doing. It would be foolish not to, don't you agree?"

"I certainly do." Morgan thought of the few hundred dollars he had in the bank. The money he got from the Englishman in Eureka was already earmarked to pay off some old and pressing bills.

"Well, I must get to work. If Effie comes in, you can keep her company until I'm finished." That got another wink—what a beautiful winker, so full of contradictions. He heard her going down a hall, a door opened and a strong smell of chemicals came to him; then the door closed and he was left to himself.

He sat on the red couch and picked up a magazine from a table with a reading lamp on it. *The Financial Times*. There had to be something better than that to pass the time. He picked up the rest of the magazines and shuffled through them, not one that wasn't about money, not a *Police Gazette* in the lot. Looked like George Dunaway had money on her mind when she wasn't talking to George Sand. Nothing so very unusual in that, he supposed. The Englishman he helped to set up liked to play at being one of the boys, and he was, some of the time. He was also a rich man with a keen knack for making money.

A key turned in the lock and Effie came in. It had to be Effie, who else would it be? If she was surprised to see him, she didn't show it. What she did show was hostility, and she showed it plain. "You're the new one, I suppose. I'm Effie. What's your name, if it isn't a secret?"

Morgan told her Blaney. "George is in the darkroom."

"You're waiting for dirty pictures, is that it?" She threw her raincoat and rainhat on the red couch. Morgan felt like he was sitting in a cloakroom.

"I'm waiting for one picture. It's not dirty." This abrupt-talking Effie was easy on the eyes, nothing at all like George. Taller and fuller in the body, she had yellow hair and blue eyes, either a German, a Swede, or a Polack. She wore a skirt and a blouse and had a Dutch Boy haircut. She was good looking in a manly sort of way. Morgan liked her even if she didn't like him.

But she opened up a bit after she threw herself into an armchair and stretched out her legs. "I'm worn out," she said, "I've been making the rounds all day."

"The rounds of what?" Morgan asked politely.

"Photographic studios, looking for a job. I'd like to get a job so I can be independent of you know who. But there are no openings right now—the same old story—and my rent is due, so I'm back. I think I'll smoke a pipe. Would you care to join me?"

"No thank you, I don't smoke."

That got him a look. "I don't mean smoke, I mean *smoke*."

Morgan got it, hick that he was. "I don't smoke that either."

"Have you ever?"

"One time in Seattle, a lot of Chinese there. Woman I knew urged me to try, so I did. It didn't agree with me. Made me sick and dizzy and I threw up. But you go ahead."

She went to a lacquered table and got out a pipe and opium fixings from the drawer. "It doesn't agree with everybody the first time, especially if they've been drinking. Had you been?"

"Yes, I had."

"Then you should try it again." Effie was shaping a pill to put in the pipe. "It will relax you. You look nervous."

"I'm not nervous. Go ahead and smoke."

"You'll have to move off the couch. You have to stretch out when you smoke. I know there's another couch, but I like the red one. After a few pulls I think I'm in China."

They swapped places. Effie stretched out and put a match to her pipe. The sweet smoke brought back that bad night in Seattle and Morgan felt slightly sick. Already, Effie was talking drowsily to herself. Morgan wished he had a drink of whiskey, but made no move to get it. Just as well, he heard the darkroom door opening and closing. George Dunaway came in holding the picture between two fingers. She was saying, "It isn't quite dry yet" before she sniffed and saw Effie lying on the couch. "I see the party's started without me."

On the couch, her eyes closed, Effie was mumbling something about a great swooping bird with red wings.

"She's always talking about that fucking bird," George Dunaway said to Morgan. "A pain in the ass. Here's the picture but be careful with it, don't mess it up with your fingers. Later it can be set down to dry. I think it came out as well as can be expected."

Morgan took the photograph, a large one, and held it under the reading lamp. By God, there was the runt, not full face but close to it, turned a little to one side, startled as hell. There was the thin pasty face, with even the checks in the cloth cap showing. The nose was little, the mouth small and pinched, the eyes half shut. The odd thing was, the face could have belonged to either a man or a woman. It was a young face, so maybe that was it.

"Well?" George Dunaway said.

"It's him," Morgan said. "You did a fine job."

"Thank you, kind sir. Now I'll just put it in a safe place so it won't be damaged if things get a bit wild."

Morgan looked at Effie in an opium stupor or

the couch. "Why should things get wild? She looks pretty peaceful to me. They always do."

George Dunaway gave him one of her loveliest smiles. "Oh, but you see, I don't smoke opium. I smoke cocaine. You know what it is?"

"More or less, made from the coca leaf. I saw them sniffing it in Central America. I never saw them smoke it."

"Well, I smoke it and I hope you'll join me. You have to wait for the picture to dry, that's going to take a while, so take off your corset and relax. Come on, Blaney, get gay, yore sich a gloomy cuss. Got two pretty gals willin' ta participate in the revels an' thar yew stand, a face like a funeral."

Morgan looked at Effie on the couch, talking to herself again. Two pretty gals willing to participate? Didn't look as if Effie even knew where she was. Two at the same time? By God, there was a thought that got your attention. "I'm not a bit gloomy," he said.

"Then show it." George Dunaway danced around. "I'm going to get gay right now." And she went to the lacquered table and got out an ordinary briar pipe and a can with a lid on it. "This is my special mixture, powdered cocaine mixed with flake tobacco, gummed together with a dab of honey. Take a sniff, you old sourpuss. Doesn't it have a lovely smell?"

She screwed the top off the can and held it under his nose. He didn't know what it smelled like except peculiar. The stuff in the can looked like brown putty, though not as smooth a texture. "You can eat it, does you no harm, does you much good." George Dunaway danced up and down in front of him, getting gay. "Real dope fiends inject it, a solution of cocaine and distilled water, but I'm afraid of the needle. I prefer to smoke it. I'm a smoker, so come on, Blaney, let's smoke."

There was a thick, soft rug on the floor and she sat down on it, crossed her legs, put the pipe in her mouth, held a match to it. All it took was a couple of puffs to get her gay. She jumped up and handed the pipe to Morgan, who was just standing there. "I've got to get out of these clothes, can't get in the mood with clothes on. Come on, you old fuddyduddy, smoke up, get gay, get naked."

She danced around, her clothes flying all over the place. Morgan got a playful slap with a pair of silk drawers. What the hell? He took a pull on the pipe and it made him cough. Smoking was something he'd never got started on, no special reason. "Take it easy, take it slow." George Dunaway danced around, slapping her bare ass with both hands. "The pipe! The pipe! Let's have the pipe. I'll show you, watch me." She took a pull on it, inhaled the smoke, held it, let it come trickling out. "It shouldn't gag you, Blaney, that's what the honey is for, makes it smooth. Try it again."

Morgan took another draw and held the smoke without gagging. He took another and another while she watched, impatient to get the pipe back. Morgan gave it to her, thinking that this was a lot of shit, that most of it was in her head. Then it hit him like a rubber mallet, a blow on the head that jolted him without hurting, and it seemed the most natural thing in the world to start taking off his

182

clothes. He didn't just take them off—he sent them flying the way George Dunaway had, something he never did except when he came home drunk. Was he drunk now? He didn't think so. What he felt was a lot different from being drunk. Drunk, you had no real control over what was happening and sometimes you knew it, sometimes you didn't. But this was a different feeling altogether. It was like you were in total control of everything and knew it, didn't doubt it for a minute. He sat down on the floor and crossed his legs, his hard-on sticking up. Like this lovely naked woman sitting up real close—he was in control of her, could do with her what he liked, anything at all, and he could do the same to the other one stretched naked on the couch.

"You're getting there, Blaney." Her voice was excited, her laughter sweet music. He took back the pipe, sucked on it, felt—didn't see—bright lights in his head. He felt like jumping up to do a dance, didn't do it. Controlling himself was as important as controlling these two women. He wished he had a couple of dozen to control. He looked down from his lofty thoughts when he felt George Dunaway uncrossing his legs to get at his cock. "My favorite cigar, a White Owl," she said, taking hold of it, raising her head, putting it in her mouth, sucking on it. Morgan went on smoking while she sucked his cock, a nice feeling, getting a blow job while you enjoyed a pleasant pipe. Too bad he didn't have a newspaper so he could scan the day's events. He found himself laughing, stopped it, became serious, very serious about how she was sucking his cock. Oh Lord, didn't it feel good, better than good, better than all the other times he'd had it sucked in the past, better even than than the blow-job Angelique gave him? Here there was a faint twinge of guilt at his disloyalty, but he dismissed it. Suck, suck, sucking was good wherever you got it, but this blow job was made in heaven. . . .

There was a thump as Effie rolled off the couch and started crawling toward them.

Chapter Twelve

Her eyes were glazed and she was growling like a tiger.

By gum and by golly, she was going to mix into this, and the more the merrier. "Welcome, little darlin'," Morgan said, feeling very generous, ready to share. "But you got to shuck your clothes, get gay, you darlin' little gal."

Effie was a big little darlin' and she growled again. George Dunaway, preoccupied with sucking, took no notice or wasn't aware of what was going on. When Morgan got serious, he had laid the pipe aside in a a shallow brass bowl the size of a barrel lid. Still growling, Effie crawled to the bowl and picked up the pipe and took a long deep draw. "That's the spirit, darlin'," Morgan said indulgently. "Now get up, peel off, get gay."

That's what Effie did after a few more pulls on the pipe. Not only did she do the getting-gay dance, she sent her clothes flying as she did it. She was a fine big broth of a girl, lots of saddle room there, you'd have to ride her like a bronc buster, strong as strong could be, could be broke just the same. Oh Lord, he was getting his cock sucked faster and faster, a lot of suction there. The come started to volley up from his balls and he held her head tight as he filled her mouth with the hot, sticky stuff. He unloaded so much into her mouth that she gagged and would have spit it out if he hadn't held her head in place with both hands. "Swallow it, darlin', it's good for you." She gulped it down, but when she came up for air, she was so mad she gave his cock a whack that didn't hurt and made him laugh. "You call everybody darlin', you laughing hyena?" But she laughed before she turned serious, nervous, frantic. "Where's the pipe? Where's my pipe?" Her hands clawed the pipe off the big bowl and she sucked on it and cursed when she found it empty and cold.

Morgan scrambled to his feet, saying, "Stay where you are, I'll fix another one." He wanted her to know that he believed in complete equality between men and women. He found the tin in the drawer and started to shape a load for the pipe. He wasn't as handy as she was and settled for cramming the bowl of the pipe with the brown putty and pushing it down with his thumb. He found a match and lit the pipe and turned to hand it to her.

But she wasn't where she had been half a minute before. She had her head between Effie's thighs and was sucking her cunt, making some noise as she worked, getting a lot of deep groaning from

186

Effie. Effie's eyes were rolled back in her head and her hands were tearing at George Dunaway's short-cut hair. Morgan smoked the pipe and looked down at them. The more he smoked, the lighter his head became, and it felt like his head had no more weight than a balloon and would soon float away if he didn't hold onto it. He raised a hand to make sure it was still attached to his body, and it was. His head was all right, but his cock, sticking out hard again, seemed to be pointing him toward the two women. Like it was telling him, hey pardner, all that good stuff there's going to waste.

The pipe hit the bowl with a clang and he dived right in. George Dunaway was flat on her belly, sucking like crazy, and he had to get into her cunt from behind. It slid in like a greased rod and he was pleased by the thought that she was getting the best. Her face stuck into Effie's bush, giving out sucking sounds; she sort of gurgled when she felt it going in and her toenails scraped at the carpet. Morgan was glad she was feeling as good as he was and he reached up to stroke her hair, having to compete with Effie for even a patch of it. But then Effie stopped fighting and held his hands with both of hers and suddenly he felt a great love for both these women and it was like they were one tight little loving family, with Effie holding his hands while she was being sucked by the other woman and him shafting George Dunaway from behind. He could hardly believe it when they all started to come together. Bewildered by the goodness of it all, he lay on top of George Dunaway while his cock drained out but stayed hard.

But the women weren't as happy as he was. After they stopped trembling from their comes, they wanted to get back at the pipe. George Dunaway rolled him off and went crawling for it with Effie crawling behind her. There was a brief struggle for the pipe and George Dunaway won, and she sucked on it before she gave it to Effie. Morgan lay where he'd rolled, on his side, propped up on his elbow. It made him smile to see the women fighting—it wasn't a real fight or he would have stopped it. Yes sir, he was in control of these lovely creatures and he wasn't about to let them hurt each other. That would be a shame; they were meant for better things than hurting. He wondered what they were going to do next, hoped they were thinking the same thing. There were so many ways three people could do it, and he seriously considered this and that. If he sucked George Dunaway, that would leave Effie free to suck his cock. Or, if he sucked George Dunaway, he could fuck Effie at the same time.

And that's what they did, not right away because the women were passing the pipe, smoking it right down to the dottle. Only then did they turn their full attention toward him, and for an instant he felt like a not very large pork chop that had to be shared between two hungry track-layers. "Don't fight over me, ladies," he said, meaning it, not joking at all. George Dunaway laughed, but Effie became so enraged that she came up off the floor as if she had springs in her heels. Morgan seemed to know what was making her so mad. In Central America one time he heard a story about a

Bawdy House

cocaine crazed cane-cutter who had to be shot ten or twelve times before he stopped hacking people with a machete.

Effie had no machete, but she came at him, screaming in his face. "Ladies! Ladies!" she screamed at him. "We're women, women, not fucking ladies! I'm not a lady, George is not a lady!" George Dunaway jumped to her feet and started screaming herself. "What do you mean I'm not a lady? I'm a woman and a lady and you're just a fucking horse. Get the fuck out of here before I have you thrown out."

"Women, women!" Morgan shouted. It was up to him to get this thing under control.

No one heard him, no one listened. Effie was screaming, "I'll get out, you bet I'll get out, but not before I tear the eyes out of that fucker's head. Get out of my way, you phony little bitch." Morgan thought it was very nice for George Dunaway to try to protect him, but he knew he didn't need it. But right after he had that thought, Effie dodged around the other woman and punched him in the jaw and tried to kick him in the balls. He staggered back and Effie crowded in after him. George Dunaway kicked Effie in the back of the knee and her leg buckled under her. She went down with a crash. George Dunaway aimed a stiff-toed kick at her face, but she dodged it and got back on her feet. They circled, the two of them, Effie big and awkward, George Dunaway small and quick. "Women, women," Morgan protested and was ignored. It was all between the two women; he might as well not have been there. He moved

189

around them and sat on the red couch and watched with great interest. Effie swung at George Dunaway and got a sharp kick in the leg that made her howl. George Dunaway was so fast with her feet, Morgan thought. Not just fast, she knew how to aim her kicks, could kick high. My Lord, she sure could kick high. Effie tried to back away from her, but before she could, both of George Dunaway's feet left the floor and knocked her down with a vicious double-kick in the belly. Effie lay on her back, gasping, and George Dunaway could have finished her off with a flurry of kicks. As it was, George Dunaway stood over her, swinging one leg back and forth, getting ready to deliver more kicks if Effie tried to get up. Morgan watched the way she kept the toes of the swinging foot stiff. Goddamn, the pint-sized little darlin' knew French foot-fighting. Morgan had heard of it, had never seen in it action. He wanted to applaud, but didn't. It wouldn't be sporting with Effie flat on her back.

"You had enough?" George Dunaway's voice had real menace in it. "Sing out or I'll break your bones."

Effie didn't sing out, she didn't have that kind of voice. What came out was a strained whisper. "I've had enough, I've had enough."

George Dunaway said, "I should think so." She turned to Morgan. "Fuck her, Blaney, horse-fuck her. I'm going to have a smoke."

Morgan didn't feel bad about fucking Effie on command. What he was about to do would please George Dunaway, please Effie too when he really got going. The wonderful thing was, he was stiff and willing and eager to do it. What a party this was turning out to be, beat the usual Saturday night shindig back in Idaho by a mile. Effie glared up at him, but remained silent as he spread her legs and guided his cock into her with his hand. And what was even more wonderful, she began to respond to the first long, sliding strokes. After that terrible kick in the belly, the poor woman deserved some consideration. Smoking in an armchair, George Dunaway said sharply, "I told you to horse-fuck her, Blaney."

Morgan was beginning to feel tired. Why he should feel tired, he couldn't understand and it made him irritable. "Listen here," he shot back, "who's doing the fucking here, you or me?" Before George Dunaway could say anything, Effie began to cry out, "Horse-fuck me, Blaney, fuck me like a stallion. Rough, Blaney, whang it into me, drive it right in."

He had to fight the encroaching fatigue and at first he succeeded. His manhood was at stake here and he'd be damned if he'd quit. Gathering all his strength, he rammed it into her, slammed it in and out until she was screaming with pain or pleasure or both and the sweat rolled off him and wet the carpet. Then she was coming like a mad woman having a fit. He started to come himself, and when he did it nearly killed him. Darkness was dropping down and as it got closer and closer he felt movement, and just before his eyes started to close he smelled George Dunaway's cunt pushing into his face. He licked at it, but his tongue felt

191

numb and so did all the rest of him, and then the darkness swallowed him up.

Morgan went to sleep with his face in George Dunaway's crotch, but he didn't wake up that way. When he did wake up, the windows were dark, it was night outside, and he was on his back on the floor, covered by a blanket, a pillow under his head. His head felt awful and his mouth had a foul taste in it. George Dunaway, fully dressed in another mannish suit, this time a different shade of green, sat on the red couch looking at him. Her smile was as sweet as ever. She looked calm and rested, as if all the fucking and sucking and kicking had never happened. Her smile offered him sympathy, but he was in no mood for it. There was no sign of Effie.

George Dunaway picked up a glass of wine from the table beside her chair. Looking at her, Morgan thought it was odd, peculiar, the way he thought of her as George Dunaway, the two names together. He called her George when he spoke to her, but in his head he always added the second name and he didn't know why. She was saying, "Do you want some ice-water, cold wine, or some of Effie's beer?"

"Beer." The place had been set in order while he slept. The windows were open and chilly damp air blew in. It felt good. His eyes were gritty and he had a dull headache. Jesus Christ, had all that happened? How the hell did he get into such shit? But he had to smile in spite of how bad he felt. With his eyes wide open, that's how. What the hell, it would be an afternoon to remember. A memorable afternoon and now it was eleven-fifteen at night by the sunburst clock on the wall. He tried to get the time straight. He'd telephoned Bullock at noon, come here about three o'clock; after that first smoke, time was a blur.

George Dunaway came in with a bottle of beer and a glass, another glass of wine for herself. Morgan took a swig from the bottle before he put on the rest of his clothes. Water to a dying man in the desert wouldn't have tasted better. He sat on the red couch and filled the glass with the rest of the beer and drank it in two long swallows.

"Poor darling," George Dunaway said, "you'll feel better after a while. I have some headache powder—"

"Nothing, thanks. I'll be all right." He didn't want to take any powders or potions she might give him. Lord knows what would be in them.

She drank some of her wine. "Perhaps you'd like a smoke—hair of the dog?"

That was vicious. "I'm done with smoking. Never again."

She laughed. "Have you ever awakened with a hangover and said that? Of course you have, but that didn't stop you from drinking again. It's the same with cocaine. Once you stop feeling guilty and confused, you'll want to try it again."

"I'm just confused, but I'll get over it," Morgan said, thinking it was time to get out of there. The runt's picture was still on top of a piano and he wanted to take it back to show O'Connor.

She must have read his mind because she said, "I was hoping you'd spend the night with me.

We'd be quite alone. I gave Effie money to pay her rent and she's back at her rooming house. Of course she'll return, but not tonight. I made that perfectly clear."

Morgan stood up, feeling better now, no longer wanting to leave. But he had to make the effort. It would be easy to let things slide, with this woman, this place. "Thanks for everything—I mean everything—but I should push off." He picked up his raincoat and started to put it on.

George Dunaway didn't get up to show him out. "Goodbye then. Give my regards to Lily and Mr. Bullock."

That stopped him cold and when he turned she was smiling. "Don't be angry with me, please. As soon as you started your story, I knew the people you were talking about. Mr. Bullock is certainly no friend—we don't move in the same circles, my father despises him—but San Francisco really is a small city after all. I know who Mr. Bullock is—after all he's one of our leading businessmen, owns the biggest department store we have—and I also know some other things. At the time it wasn't generally known that he'd married a whore. A few business people knew it—some were scandalized, some amused—and I heard it from my broker, who was one of the people who found it funny."

"I didn't lie to you," Morgan said.

"That's true. You wouldn't be here if you had. A word of advice from one who keeps her ear close to the stock ticker and knows people who know things." Morgan thought she sounded like

O'Connor. "Work for Bullock if you must, but make sure you get paid."

Morgan was surprised, didn't try to hide it. "Surely he's good for it?"

George Dunaway shrugged. "Well, I'm sure he's good for five hundred dollars. But his business is shaky, very shaky, that's the most I can tell you at the moment. For you—what's your name anyway? Morgan, that's a nice plain American name, better than Blaney. Blaney sounds like a ward heeler. For you, Morgan—" she smiled "—I'll make further inquiries. My broker is sure to know something."

"I'd be obliged." Morgan was thinking about how cranky and jittery Bullock was on the telephone. Had some big creditor suddenly appeared with a demand for a lot of money? It could be that. "I wouldn't know where to start. It's hard to think of Bullock so close to the skids."

"I didn't say that, for goodness sake. I said his business was shaky; there's a difference. That old wretch won't end up in the poorhouse, though it's happened to a few. You see, Mr. Bullock, for all his so-called Yankee-trader shrewdness, is not much of a businessman. If his first wife hadn't been rich, he would have gone under long ago. He was scared to death of her, but she kept him going. To people who don't know, the department store is doing fine. Mr. Bullock has that mausoleum on Nob Hill, so he appears as sound as the Bank of England, except he isn't. If I had to guess, I'd say he's been draining off money from the store, making investments that haven't turned out too well. Smart investors don't pour good money after bad—they get out. Apparently—I'm guessing, of course—Mr. Bullock hasn't done that. One way or another, it may be too late."

"The securities ought to help if he can get them back."

"Perhaps not. A hundred thousand may be a drop in the bucket. He may want them so desperately because he plans to run away before everything collapses."

"Hard to think of an old man on the dodge." Morgan got a picture of Bullock riding hell for leather, a small man on a big horse, with a posse of creditors whooping along behind him with a rope.

"In some states, he wouldn't have to dodge at all. Or he could go to Canada or England. Age—listen, age doesn't mean that you're ready to lie down and die. I intend to be getting gay—and making money—when I'm ninety. How about getting gay in bed, Blaney, the kind of gay where you don't have to smoke? Come on, it's after twelve and you don't want to be out in the dark, wet streets."

"All right," Morgan said.

"But first you're going to get a bath. Even with your clothes on, you smell of women. Tonight, I want the only woman smell in my bed to be me."

"All right," Morgan said again. Damn these women, always trying to get him in the bathtub. But this time was different; he knew she was going to join him, with the bath salts and the back brush, and especially herself.

Later, in her big canopied bed, she was like a sweet young wife to him. No crazy stuff—anyway not too crazy. Fucking her, or just lying beside her, he didn't know what to make of her. So many contradictions in her nature, laying out her own money to keep EQUALITY FOR WOMEN, INC. afloat, but scotching on the tip for the poor cab driver. She was generous and greedy, kind and mean, talked to George Sand and listened to the stock ticker, all at the same time. There was no use trying to figure her, not that he hadn't tried, a mistake he kept on making with other women down through the years.

"Goodnight, Morgan" she said when it was close to morning, and gave him a chaste kiss on the forehead.

When he woke up after a dreamless sleep, she wasn't in the bed or anywhere else in the apartment. Taped to the big enameled ice-chest, where the beer was, was a note.

HAVE GONE TO MY BROKER'S TO MAKE INQUIRIES. WILL GO LATER TO STOCK EX-CHANGE. TELEPHONE ME FROM WHEREVER YOU ARE HIDING. DON'T THINK I MISSED THAT. IF YOU DO NOT RING ME, I WILL START LOOKING FOR YOU.
DETECTIVE DUNAWAY
P.S. MY TELEPHONE NUMBER IS 1658.

Morgan smiled as he reheated a pot of coffee on the gas stove. Rich girl playing detective. He didn't think there was a lot more that she could tell him. Bullock was in a bad fix, what else did he have to know? He wanted to see her again—Bullock or no

Bullock—but that would have to wait. He had the runt's picture and he had to show it to O'Connor, then try to get a hold of Bender.

The apartment door had a spring lock and it locked when he closed it. He took a cab back to the mission and gave the driver a good tip. O'Connor was still eating breakfast when he went up. Morgan was glad to see him.

"The prodigal returns," O'Connor said, shaking his head, the teapot poised to pour. "Last night it got late and I got worried, took two of my people and started looking at the ladies' dugout. Place was dark and locked. That German, doing his books or something, said you'd left with a lady earlier in the day. Afternoon. Wouldn't say who the lady was, didn't know where she lived, got tough about it when I tried to press him. Wherever you were, you look kind of strained, to say the least."

Morgan wanted to shake O'Connor up a little, see if he could get a rise out of him. "I was with Henry Dunaway's daughter. She took the runt's picture. It's in the envelope. Take a look."

O'Connor opened the envelope and studied the runt, taking his time. "Nope," he said, putting the photograph back in the envelope. "Don't know him. Has the mark of the gutter on him, like ten hundred thousand others of his kind. Go down the coast, and you'll see a face like that on every block."

"Too bad. I'll show it to Bender; then you can have it." Morgan asked for scrambled eggs, toast and coffee when the Chinese came in. That was all he could handle, his stomach still queasy from the dope.

"Put you off your feed, did she?" O'Connor's face showed one of his anemic smiles. "Henry Dunaway's daughter, eh? Keeping pretty high-toned company."

"George is her name, no joke. She's very smart, knows all about business, even has a stock ticker in her flat. She says Bullock's business is shaky, he's hurting for money, may go under. I'd say she knows what she's talking about, knows some big men in the Stock Exchange. So Bullock isn't what we think he is."

O'Connor opened the envelope and took another long look at the runt. "Nope, don't know him." He put the photograph back in the envelope and fastened it. "I guess she's right about Bullock. She would be. Daughter of one of the richest men in the city, she'd hear things. Damn, I hate to be surprised like this. I should have thought to make some discreet inquiries about Bullock, but I didn't. Must be slipping."

Morgan got his breakfast. "What's the difference? We know it now."

"So we do. A nice girl, is she?"

"Sweet as pie. Just don't you let her hear you calling her a girl. Would make her go on the warpath. By the way, I didn't tell her I was putting up here, thought you wouldn't like it."

"You're wrong there. I'd like it fine, a nice girl like that." O'Connor buttered another blueberry muffin, his fifth since Morgan came in. "Maybe she'd like to visit the mission, see how we do things here. Invite her over, why don't you? We can have an early lunch, say eleven."

"I have to tell you, she can be tight with money. Sometimes, it depends. Don't expect her to whip out her checkbook if she does come. She may not want to."

"Don't you ever think of anything but money?" O'Connor was having trouble pouring tea from the teapot. He took off the lid and looked into it. "Strainer is clogged. Why wouldn't she want to see my mission, if she's a feminist? Even if she doesn't contribute financially, it wouldn't hurt to have her name on our stationery, our list of sponsors. Did you fuck her?"

"Hey, Duckie, that's not nice. A gentleman never tells."

"That's quite true. But you're not a gentleman so it's all right. My interest isn't salacious, merely general. But you don't have to tell me if you don't want to."

"We did get together," was all Morgan was ready to admit.

"Good man. There's a lot of men in this town would like to be in your shoes. Henry Dunaway's daughter, eh?"

Morgan didn't want the rest of his eggs, but O'Connor's lip-smacking had nothing to do with it. He yawned, still feeling the effects of the getting-gay party. What he needed was more coffee.

O'Connor was looking at him. "This new information about Bullock, we're going to have to think about what it means. I didn't ask you how he was on the telephone."

"Cranky, mostly nervous." Morgan told the rest of it.

"Doesn't want Lily back, eh. That's a sudden turnaround. Just the securities. And he didn't balk when you asked him for more money." O'Connor shook his head slowly, as if Morgan had just told him that he hated women. "A cause for wonder in itself."

"It surprised me. Just go to the bank and get the money, he said. But he made it plain that I wouldn't get any more."

"He would say that, the nature of the beast. It'll be interesting to see what your rich lady friend turns up. Why don't you telephone her? She can't ring you here, not knowing where you are. Invite her over. John will fix us a nice lunch."

Morgan was thinking about George Dunaway and Duckie O'Connor, what an odd meeting it was going to be if she came. "She may not be home yet, but I'll try to get hold of her."

O'Connor gave him a sly look. "Try to do that. Harriet's already left for the hospital to ask after Hargis. Ought to have something to tell us."

"No word from any of your people?"

"They're still out there," O'Connor said. "One man thought he had something good when he got a tip about a woman holed up at the Southern Pacific, hotel near the station. In her room most of a week, never goes out. Turned out to be just a drinker. Lily is still out there somewhere."

Out there somewhere, Morgan thought. He wondered if she might not be dead.

Chapter Thirteen

"Why do you think that?" O'Connor said, not liking the idea. "There's no evidence of that at all."

"There's no evidence that she isn't." Morgan was stretching out his last cup of coffee, wanting to give it a little more time before he tried to get George Dunaway on the telephone. "She's a real target, a woman alone with all that money."

"Anybody with a hundred thousand, carrying it around in a bag, is a target. But who's to say she's alone? She may be hiding out with somebody she knows, somebody she trusts or trusts enough not to kill her and take the swag. Trusts because she's promised them a share of the cash-in. Of course, if Lily is as smart as they say she is, and I haven't heard different, she won't trust anybody more than she has to. Which means no trust at all, if you're always watching out for betrayal."

Morgan listened to the sound of the Chinaman's carpet sweeper in the hall. It stopped and he wondered if the Chinaman was trying to get an earful. O'Connor said he was just a fool, but O'Connor wasn't the know-it-all he thought he was. He hadn't known about Bullock and his money trouble. Shit, Morgan thought, he wasn't all that smart himself. Anything he had learned so far had come from other people. Angelique, O'Connor, George Dunaway. But that was the way it was done, wasn't it?

"There's no real reason to think Lily is dead." O'Connor wanted to believe that, Morgan thought, didn't want to accept the possibility that all that money might be in the hands of some killer, or at least some thief. "A woman as smart as Lily knows how to take care of herself."

"Maybe she does."

"Well, she's done all right so far. She tricked a trickster like Bullock, outfoxed a sneaky-smart country fox like Hargis. We haven't found her, all my people haven't found her. I'd say she's doing all right, wouldn't you?"

"On the face of it, yes." Morgan got up from the table. "I'd better call Miss Dunaway. It may be too early."

"Keep trying," O'Connor said. "Ask her what she'd like for lunch."

George Dunaway answered the telephone after just a few rings. "Dunaway speaking," she said like a no-nonsense businessman. "How are you feeling, Morgan? Where are you?"

"Duckie O'Connor's mission on Front Street. You know who he is? You're invited for lunch."

"Of course I know who he is, doesn't everyone? You're not joking, are you?"

"No. Duckie wants to know what you want for lunch. Will you come? He has a Chinese cook."

George Dunaway laughed. A nice sound even coming over the noisy telephone wires. "In that case, I'd like chop suey. You know what that is?"

One time, Morgan had eaten what they said was chop suey in a miserable mining camp in Utah. He had to take their word for it, hadn't liked it, and wouldn't have eaten it if he hadn't been wolf-hungry. "I know what it is." They were getting sidetracked by Chinese food. "Anything new on Bullock?"

"Wait till I get there. I'm leaving right this instant."

"Wait a minute. Are you sure you want chop suey? It's pretty bad."

"You don't know what you're talking about. It's delicious if it's done properly, so seldom is. Yes, I want chop suey. You can eat belly and beans if you like. I'll be there as fast as I can lash the cabby."

Morgan took the chop suey news to O'Connor. "Good Lord!" O'Connor said. "Of all the things in the world. Poor people eat it because it's cheap and filling. But we mustn't deny the lady."

"Have you eaten it?"

"Of course I have, when I was poor."

"When were you ever poor?"

"Very seldom." O'Connor called the Chinese and told him chop suey for three for lunch. Morgan thought he looked disappointed. It was like asking the finest French chef on Nob Hill to make a fried egg sandwich. But he took it in stride. "Okay, boss," was all he said.

O'Connor insisted on going downstairs to greet George Dunaway when she arrived. They waited on the steps and her cab got there about ten minutes later. Morgan had told O'Connor not to try to pay the cab fare. So they waited while she paid the cabby and added her usual miserly tip. The cabby, a burly man with a boozer's face, muttered something under his breath and O'Connor picked up on it. "What was that you said, mate?"

The cabby stuck out his bristly jaw. "I said I hoped she wouldn't go broke."

O'Connor was ready to pull the cabby down from the box. "You called the lady *she*, you miserable cunt." Turning to George Dunaway, he touched his hatbrim and said, "Pardon my French, Miss Dunaway." Then back to the cabby. "Take your self off pronto, you ignorant man. Begone or I'll throw you in the fucking Bay and I'll throw rocks at you every time you come up."

"Nuts to you, duckass," the cabby shot back, but he was already starting his horse.

O'Connor just laughed sourly, enjoying it. "The nerve of that mug. My apologies once again, Miss Dunaway, but you can't let these blackguards get away with too much." He waved his hand toward the sign above the door. "This is my mission, or I should say, *our* mission—the ladies, you know. Would you like to take a look around now, or would you like to do it later?"

"Well, I'm rather hungry, Reverend."

"Call me Duckie, please. We'll go up now. I'm sorry there's no elevator, Miss Dunaway."

"Call me George. I'm impressed with the way

205

you put that rude cab driver in his place. You're so gallant, Duckie. Would you really have thrown him in the Bay?"

"Certainly," O'Connor said, friend of the working man.

A lot of people in that Bay, Morgan thought. Or threatened with it. Wilfred, the doorkeeper, opened the door and they went up to O'Connor's quarters. George Dunaway walked around, admiring what she saw. She stopped in front of one section of the bookshelves that Morgan hadn't looked at. "Oh, what lovely dirty books," she said, looking at the titles. "I do love dirty books."

O'Connor looked pained, then he smiled a better smile than most other people rated. "I have made a study of erotic literature," he said loftily. "As part of my work, you understand."

"Nothing else but," George Dunaway said, and winked at him.

O'Connor went out to the kitchen to see how lunch was coming along. Morgan was sitting in an armchair, but George Dunaway was still walking around when he came back. "We'll go into the dining room now. My man will serve us. By the way, that's a most becoming outfit you're wearing. Soon, I'm afraid, all the ladies will be copying you."

"Some are doing it now." George Dunaway was wearing a black silk shirt, green suede vest and flared trousers, high-heeled Spanish boots, a black flat-crowned hat. Morgan had never heard of a female bull fighter, but that's what she looked like.

"They'll never wear anything with such elegance," O'Connor said. "What do you think, Morgan?"

"Definitely not," Morgan said, and George Dunaway laughed at him. O'Connor did his best to laugh with her. Morgan smiled but he didn't laugh, wanting to hear what she had to say about Bullock. But she was not to be hurried and O'Connor went along with it, the old asskisser. In the dining room, when they were seated and the Chinaman was serving them, she discoursed on chop suey until Morgan wanted to choke her.

"Chop suey is a corruption of the Cantonese words, *shap sui*, meaning odds and ends. Bean sprouts, bamboo shoots, water chestnuts, onions, all important, but it's the soy sauce that really makes the meal. Don't you agree, John?"

The Chinaman was just about finished. "You got it light, rady," he said. Morgan caught the mean look he gave her before his face went blank again. It wasn't the chop suey he was mad at her about. There was more than that: John the Christian Chinaman was queer. Morgan looked at O'Connor and thought maybe so, maybe so, but it was none of his business.

"I haven't learned much more about Mr. Bullock," George Dunaway said. A minute before she had been blathering about soy sauce. Now she was all business. "I suppose Morgan's told you everything I've told him, Duckie?"

O'Connor said yes. "Then there's no need to repeat it." They waited while she tasted the chop suey. "Delicious. As you may know, real estate is in a slump right now and has been for nearly two years. Too many new buildings with too few tenants. Mr. Bullock bought extensive property in two areas to which he expected the street transportation to be extended. There was no real need for it, so the plan was shelved and finally abandoned, much to Mr. Bullock's dismay, I'm sure. So he's left with two big parcels of real estate that isn't worth nearly as much as he paid for it."

George Dunaway paused to dig into her chop suey. O'Connor had been eating a little while she talked. Morgan just drank coffee. "Really delicious," George Dunaway said. "Mr. Bullock seems to be one of those unfortunate people who turn gold into lead. Not only that, his own brother, who has a department store in Kansas City, is suing him for several outstanding loans. At least he's been in correspondence with an attorney here in San Francisco. My informant was unable to say how much these loans amount to, but it is said to be considerable. Oh yes, Mr. Bullock's department store seems to be doing well, but in recent months some of his suppliers, mainly in the East, have been complaining about increasingly late payment. My attorney, Rex Farnsworth, had to telephone some trade association to obtain that information. For the moment, that's all I can tell you."

Harriet Streeter came into the dining room as O'Connor was saying, "What you've told us is very helpful." Morgan wondered if she could have been listening in the hall. If she had, what she heard was not to her liking, unless something else was the reason for her bad mood. The way she looked, Morgan was afraid she was going to tip over the table and try to throw George Dunaway out the window.

"Ah, there you are, Harriet," O'Connor said. "We were just having a bit of lunch. I'd like you to meet Miss Dunaway. Miss Dunaway, this is Miss Streeter."

Harriet Streeter nodded stiffly and muttered something. George Dunaway said, "Let's not be so formal, Duckie. My name is George. May I call you Harriet?"

"If you like." Harriet Streeter was still standing, waiting to be invited to sit down.

O'Connor looked at her, not missing the mood she was in. "Sit down, Harriet, no need to stand on ceremony." Morgan noticed that he hadn't said *please.* "What about Hargis? You can speak freely in front of George."

"Can I now—?"

O'Connor silenced her with a look. "Get on with it—*please.*"

"Hargis escaped, just walked out of the ward," Harriet Streeter said. "Out of the hospital, no one stopped him. The policeman who was supposed to be guarding the ward was slacking off someplace. He was gone when I got there. Nobody seemed to think it was very important."

O'Connor started to say something, but George Dunaway interrupted with, "Excuse me, Duckie, thank you for the lovely lunch—my compliments to John—but I must be off. Rex has been trying to arrange bail for some of our ladies still in jail. The police have been making it difficult and I must see what I can do to help. I'll ring you if I have any more information. I'll see you soon, Morgan. So nice meeting you, Harriet."

Harriet Streeter grunted. O'Connor tore into her as soon as he came back from showing George Dunaway out. "There is no excuse for such rudeness. I won't stand for it. What in hell is the matter with you? George Dunaway has been of great service—"

Harriet Streeter didn't back down, even in the face of O'Connor's wrath. "Playing detective, is she, the spoiled little bitch?"

"That's enough."

"No, it's not enough. You trust her, you tell her everything, you tell me nothing. Go to the hospital, do this, do that, no explanation."

O'Connor's anger faded. "I didn't want you getting too deep into it. That's why. I'll explain now, if you're so dead set on it."

"It's about time."

"For pity's sake, will you let me talk?" And he told her all of it.

But it wasn't enough. "Why didn't you trust me from the beginning? But you trust her, don't you? How do you know she won't tell Bullock or some of her friends, thinking it's funny? How do you know *they* won't tell Bullock? These rich people are all alike, they stick together."

"Nonsense, you don't know what you're talking about." O'Connor was trying to be patient. "Bullock is a counter-jumper, a little Vermont grocery clerk in his bones, quick and sly and money grubbing. The Dunaways were wealthy people when they came here, brought class with them. Henry Dunaway and his daughter wouldn't be caught dead in the same room as a man like Bullock."

Duckie O'Connor, friend of the classy rich. Morgan had to fight to keep his face straight.

"I don't like her," Harriet Streeter said. "She's a rotten little dyke pervert. The way she dresses, my God! I've heard stories about her. Some of them must be true."

O'Connor's face clouded and Morgan wondered if Harriet Streeter knew about the queer Chinaman. Morgan decided it was probably so, not that he gave a fuck one way or another. But if she did know, it wasn't the place to be throwing around the word "pervert," even in anger. Morgan had to strain his imagination to see John and Duckie in bed together, but what the hell, all things were possible.

O'Connor had been staring at Harriet Streeter. "I don't care what stories you've heard, and how George dresses is her own business. And since you brought it up, you should be the last to talk about other people's sins."

Morgan thought she was going to storm out, but all she did was set her jaw in a stubborn line. "I still don't like her. She makes me sick. There's not a day the newspapers don't print something about her. Miss George Dunaway marching on city hall at the head of her bloomers brigade. Miss George Dunaway at the opera. Miss George Dunaway dining with Oscar Wilde at the Cliff House."

"Enough. Enough." O'Connor had to smile. "I read the papers too. You're a caution, Harriet,

211

that's what you are. Come on, let's be friends. I'm sorry for what I said just now, but your narrow-mindedness gets my goat. Eat some of John's delicious chop suey before it gets cold. If you don't want it reheated, then go to it." As Harriet Streeter reached for the dish, O'Connor winked at Morgan and said, "I'm sure you'll like it if you haven't eaten it before. All the basic ingredients are important, but never forget this: it's the soy sauce that makes the meal."

"You're crazy," Harriet Streeter said.

"Maybe so. Before it slips my mind, who the fuck is Oscar Wilde?"

"An English—" Morgan knew she'd stopped herself from saying "English queer." "He's a famous English writer, here on one of his lecture tours, a real show-off."

"I thought he was Irish," O'Connor said.

Nothing was said about Hargis until she finished eating. Harriet Streeter brought it up herself. "I know you'll be trying to find him. Why can't I help? I used to be a damn good private detective. I know more about finding people than you two do. Why can't I be of use? I'd be more use than that little bitch."

"Will you stop that? Quit it, I say. George isn't playing detective. She's making inquiries, and she's good at it. She's not going down the Coast to look for Hargis. Nobody's going to attack her in the Stock Exchange. But you want to go down where it's not safe for any woman."

"You took his money so that's where he'll go. Try to roll somebody or steal something he can turn into cash. You said so yourself. Listen, Duckie, let me look for the son of a bitch. Fucking pimp, I hate them."

O'Connor nodded his sympathy but said, "Morgan and I will look, and that's final."

"Is it?" Harriet Streeter was facing O'Connor and she turned to look at Morgan, who was on her side of the table. "The two of you will stand out like sore thumbs, especially you, Duckie. The cowboy and the preacher. What're you going to do, gum on false beards and mustaches?"

O'Connor didn't smile. "Very funny, Harriet. You're still not going down the Coast. Leave Hargis to us."

"You can't stop me. This isn't a whorehouse, where your word is law."

O'Connor's temper was simmering again. "That's where you're wrong, sister. As long as you live in this house—"

"Then I'll leave today, right now." Harriet Streeter got up from the table.

"Oh Jesus, who said you had to be rich to throw tantrums—"

Morgan cut in on this bullshit argument. "I have to telephone Bullock. It's nearly twelve-thirty. You can fill me in on the parts I miss."

"Smart-aleck," Harriet Streeter said. "Back-country smart-aleck."

O'Connor rubbed his forehead. "Be quiet so I can hear myself think."

Morgan went back to O'Connor's office and the operator put him through to Bullock's private number. "You're late," he snapped. "Never mind that. What have you got to tell me?"

"Not much, Mr. Bullock, but I'm working very hard."

"That's not good enough, Morgan." Going by the sound of his voice, Bullock was even more nervous than he had been during the first telephone call. "What *have* you been doing?"

"Asking questions. It's not easy with the rules you laid down." Morgan felt a twinge of guilt, thinking again that poking into Bullock's money troubles was not what he had been hired to do. He couldn't see where Bullock had lied to him—he could hardly be expected to discuss his business woes with a hired hand—yet there was something wrong. More than ever, Morgan was sure of that. If he could only talk to the man face-to-face.

Bullock was saying something that Morgan only half heard. "Mr. Bullock," he said, cutting into the string of complaints. "Would it be possible to meet with you?"

"What for?" Bullock was immediately suspicious.

"To talk. It's hard to talk on the telephone."

"I can't see why. What you're asking can't be done, out of the question, I'm far too busy. I don't want to hear any more about it. Find my securities and bring them to me. Earn what I paid you, for Christ's sake. Get some results or—"

Morgan took a chance. "You want me to quit, Mr. Bullock?"

Bullock didn't answer for a moment, then he came back mean as hell, his Yankee twang more pronounced. "You got another five hundred yesterday, so now you want to quit. Very convenient. Well sir, you can't quit, you hear that? You started this and you're going to finish it. You walk away with my money and I'll have the police on you."

Morgan smiled, thinking of a few answers to that. "I shouldn't have brought it up. If you still want me, I'll do my very best for you."

"Then stop this talking and do it. I can't wait much longer." Bullock's whiny voice went high on the last few words.

Morgan hung up the earpiece on the hook, still thinking there was more behind Bullock's jitters than bad real estate deals, store creditors, or his brother's threatened lawsuit. But why couldn't that be so? All that was enough to make any man think he was drowning in shit. Oh God, that Chinese puzzle again.

He went back in and found them still at it, the only difference being Harriet Streeter was back in her chair. If only they'd get this goddamn thing settled! If she wanted to go after Hargis, then let her go. But O'Connor was still against it. He was saying, "You haven't done any detective work in two years. Not just that, you're under some sort of strain all the time. I've tried to help you the best I can. You're not as wrought up as you were, but you're not ready to be taking on this Hargis business."

Harriet Streeter banged down her coffee cup, staining the tablecloth. "I don't have to get permission from you. What are you afraid of, that I won't be able to hold up, that I'll go back on the bottle and back on the streets? Think what you like, I don't care. I have a few dollars. I can get a room."

Even O'Connor knew when he was beaten. "You got nothing to say about this?" he said to Morgan.

"No." Morgan wanted no part of this argument.

"Very well then," O'Connor said, giving out a long sigh. "I give up. Go look for Hargis—but no fucking room. You will go out in the morning and come back at night before it gets dark. Are you listening, my dear willful young lady?"

"You can stop that right now!" Harriet Streeter shouted in sudden, raw rage. "I'm sick and tired of being called 'my dear young lady,' 'little sister, 'my dear this and my dear that.' I won't stand for it any longer. I'm no dear young lady. I'm a woman, an intelligent woman, and I can stand on my own two feet. So for Christ's sake, will you give it up? Call me Harriet and nothing else, do you hear? I wish you'd call me Streeter, but I know you won't."

"We're not in the frigging army here." O'Connor was exasperated.

"And you!" Now it was Morgan's turn. "You say my name like you were sucking fucking lemons, like you were talking to your aunt. Well, I'm not your aunt. Say my name plain and straight—think of me as *Harriet!*"

She shouted her name so loud that O'Connor pretended to be momentarily deafened.

"Go fuck yourself, *Harriet!*" Morgan shouted. The woman was crazy but maybe she had a point. For some reason, he did think of her as always having two names. If she kept on the way she was going a mean old aunt was what she would end up as. Fuck Harriet and her name bullshit. In his mind George would always have two names. It seemed to suit her chipper little nature. And you're crazy too, Morgan told himself.

He thought he'd get crazier if they didn't end this soon. But O'Connor was saying he didn't want her to go to the Coast fixed up to look like a streetwalker.

"How should I go, as a schoolteacher?"

"That's exactly right, *Harriet!* You'll go like you went to the hospital, as Hargis's worried schoolteacher wife. Maybe that'll get you some sympathy, some information, though I doubt it, knowing the rats that infest the place. You know it too, so be careful, don't take any chances. If you find Hargis, even get a smell of him, come right back here or use the telephone. If we're not here, John will be here. All right?"

Harriet was calmer now, for which Morgan was thankful. "I'll do what you say, Duckie. You worry too much, that's your trouble. I've gone after worse people than Hargis."

"I believe you, *Harriet!*" O'Connor's voice was patient except for the emphasis he placed on the last word. O'Connor didn't believe her and neither did Morgan. From what he knew of detective agencies, the work they gave women was chasing rubber-check artists, wayward wives, and con men. Yep, con men.

Harriet stood up. "I think I'll be going now." Morgan thought she looked more cheerful.

"Wait," O'Connor said. "Who's going to run the place while you're gone?"

Harriet gave a smile that wasn't quite as bleak as his own. "Maybe Morgan here can pitch in. Some of the ladies think he's very nice, isn't that right, Morgan?"

"I don't know what you're talking about, Harriet." No shouting. Peace on earth and all the rest of it.

"Dorothy can handle it." Harriet picked up her bag and went out.

O'Connor looked at Morgan. "I seem to have missed something. What do you think she meant about you and the ladies?"

"Beats me," Morgan said.

Chapter Fourteen

Morgan had trouble finding Bender.

Before he left the mission, he tried to get through to him on the telephone, but the operator at the Palace said he could be anywhere in the huge hotel. That's what she called it, this huge hotel, and she sounded pleased to be working in such a large place, but that didn't help Morgan. "I know who he is," she said, "and if you leave a message, I'll be sure he gets it. Where are you calling from, sir? Perhaps he can ring you there."

Morgan gave his name but not O'Connor's number, not wanting to involve Bender more than he had to. If he could find him, he'd show him the runt's picture, ask him for some more advice, and that's as far as it would go. Bender was a good man and he didn't want him tarred by even talking to O'Connor outside the convention.

There was no use trying to get him on the telephone. The operator was polite, but said it would be very difficult, meaning that the Palace was a madhouse for the hotel staff. Morgan had been there, and knew what she meant. All he could do was go over there and ask around.

It was one forty-five when he got there. Some late lunchers were in the dining room, but Bender wasn't among them. At the desk set aside for the conventioneers, all they could tell him was, "He's around here somewhere. Would you like to have him paged?"

Morgan didn't want that. Bender wouldn't mind, or if he did, he wouldn't show it. Morgan told the man behind the desk not to bother. He'd just wander around, hope to run into him. This was the first convention he'd seen up close, and it looked like the booze was flowing free even in the early afternoon. Going into one of the main convention rooms where somebody was making a speech, he found himself being bear-hugged by a down-home police chief who claimed him as a long-lost friend from another part of his state.

"Ain't you Chief J.J. Hines?" the drunk wanted to know. "Heard you made good, J.J. You was just a deputy back when I knew you." Then the drunk changed his mind after he turned Morgan loose and staggered back a few feet to take a better look. "Guess you ain't J.J. Hines after all. There's a likeness in the face, but you're too short."

Morgan wondered how tall J.J. Hines could be, seeing as how he was over six feet himself. He went into a room where they were showing slides, but Bender wasn't there when the lights came on. Finally he found him in one of the hotel's three bars, the one called the Gold Rush Room. Bender was no drinker, but he liked his beer, and that's what he was drinking now, at a table in the corner, with three men who were drinking something else. Morgan was turning away, thinking this was not a good time, when Bender spotted him and waved. Morgan waved back and would have kept going if Bender hadn't come after him.

"What's the hurry?" Bender said. "Afraid it'll ruin your reputation to be seen drinking with a flatfoot?"

"Don't want to bother you right now. When you have a minute I'd like to talk to you."

"No bother. You can talk to me soon as I have a few words with those fellows over there." Bender led Morgan to a table and came back a few minutes later. "Those fellows sell all kinds of police equipment, think the Kansas City Police Department ought to buy machine guns. When I said we already had them, which isn't true, they tried to sell me a later model. I hope you ordered me a beer."

"Here it comes," Morgan said.

The waiter set down two huge schooners of beer. This was the Gold Rush Room after all, a he-man place, no piddling little glasses here. "Can't beat Frisco for beer," Bender said with mock heartiness.

Morgan took a long drink. "San Franciscans don't like for their city to be called Frisco." That's what O'Connor said. It was news to him.

Bender smiled, liking this nonsense. "You've been keeping company with Miss Etiquette of the *Examiner*, is that it? What can I do for you, soldier?"

Before Morgan showed him the picture, he told him about the runt. "A man I showed it to said he looks like a lot of other strongarm robbers." Morgan put the photograph on the table and Bender put on the reading glasses he hated to wear. He studied the picture carefully.

"The man who told you that is right and wrong," he said. "This kid looks like a corner boy, but he's Wily Willy Goldshire's son." Bender took another look at the photograph. "This is him all right. Doesn't look one bit like his father. Wily Willy is a handsome man, this kid is a tall rat."

Morgan waited, but before Bender could go on, the salesmen he'd been drinking with stopped at the table on the way out. One of them, the most aggressive, said, "Hope we can do business, Chief. Nothing like the new Hotchkiss guns. Think what you could have done with them during the stockyards strike. Let me give you my card."

Bender took the card. Morgan got one too. Bender tore up the card after the salesmen went out. "I'd like to put that man to work in a slaughterhouse, twelve hours a day, six days a week, and see how he likes it. And without rubber boots or a rubber apron. See how he likes the stink that won't wash off, the bloody guts and the shit. Fucker uses toilet water, did you smell it?"

"You sound like a radical, Bender." Morgan wanted to tell him to get on with it.

"This kid," Bender said, tapping the envelope the photograph was in. "This kid, to understand what he's like you have to know about his father. William Pitt Goldshire, the name he's gone by for years, is probably the biggest crook in this country and the smartest. The scandal sheets call him the King of Crime, and maybe he is. The odd thing is—and maybe it's not so odd at that—everybody knows how big a crook he is, but he doesn't care what people say. He doesn't sue, he laughs. Goldshire bankrolls all kinds of dirty deals but always manages to stay at a safe distance. Never spent a day in jail, never been arrested, or if he was, it was long in the past and the records are missing. Comes from a highly respectable New York family—German Jews. Merchants and lawyers. Goldshire is the black sheep and glories in it. Are you getting a picture of what's involved here?"

"I guess so," Morgan said.

"Then listen good," Bender said. "Goldshire isn't just a black sheep, a ne'er-do-well who drifted into crime. He jumped in with both feet. For instance, it's known that he's the brains behind the Monk Eastman gang. Finances their operations and takes a sizable cut. There's nothing dirty he doesn't have a hand in. His family has long disowned him. The family name is Goldman, but he changed his to Goldshire, some kind of dig at the family, I guess. The Goldshire comes from his admiration of everything that's English, like Yorkshire Pudding, Worcestershire Sauce, that kind of thing. But it's also said he took the name because it sounds like 'gold shares'. That could be newspaper bullshit, but he does love the English. He even named the runt, and we're getting to him now, after Disraeli, the prime minister. People call him Dizzy or Runtshire, but that's behind his back. A good thing too, because he's a truly vicious little bastard. He likes to be called Dee, if he likes to be called anything, and most people settle for that. . . ."

Bender was laying out fact after fact, like he was reading from a police report. "Wait a minute," Morgan said, "how do you know all this?"

Bender signaled for two more beers. "Talking is dry work," he said. "All the credit for knowing has to go to Chief Inspector Byrnes of New York City. How else would I know some rat-faced kid? For some years now, Inspector Byrnes has been doing what others should have been doing all along: compiling a photographic record, as well as a written or printed record, of every criminal he can get his hands on. It's far from complete—how can it be?—but he's published an enormous book of his own called *Criminals of America*. In it are photographs, criminal records, aliases, how criminals work, who they prey on. And he doesn't just limit himself to New York, he corresponds with police chiefs and high-ranking officers all over the country. That's how I got to know him, by mail."

The waiter brought the beer. "Byrnes has made a small fortune selling his book to police departments, private agencies, interested civilians. Good luck to him. His book would be worth the money at twice the price. I bought two copies, one for the office, one for home reading."

Morgan picked up his schooner. "How did he get the kid's picture if his father has so much power?"

"I can't answer that. Just pulled him in off the

street, I guess. Byrnes is like that, but he's well protected. Hobnobs with the Wall Street crowd. In return for stock tips, he protects them from every kind of crook you can think of. God help the crook that Byrnes catches south of Fourteenth Street. So you see how well-fixed Byrnes is, and he's damn smart all the way, but he's never been able to pin anything on Goldshire, not even when he was prepared to cook the evidence."

The kid, Morgan thought, get to the kid.

"Like most policemen with any interest in their work, I knew of Goldshire and his above-the-law activities." Bender tapped the envelope again. "I didn't know he had a son till I bought Byrnes's book, and there he was, staring at me with a number plate on his chest. The first thing I looked for was a photograph of the father. It wasn't there and I couldn't understand why, so I wrote to Byrnes asking why he'd left out the biggest criminal in America. That was the start of our correspondence. He didn't have a picture of Wily Willy because he's never been arrested. Even so, Byrnes knows as much as any man can about Goldshire and his baby boy.

"The kid isn't quite twenty yet, but he's already a seasoned killer. Not a killer for hire; he works for nobody but his father, does only a few big jobs. Byrnes thinks he doesn't do any of the actual killing himself, though he may lend a hand just for the fun of it—that kind of lad."

Bender spoke casually, but Morgan got a cold feeling, thinking of the tight pasty face under the peak of the cloth cap.

"The killing he leaves to the big Russian he travels with," Bender continued. "They say this Russian used to be a political assassin in the old country. We get them all, don't we, as if we didn't have enough hard-working killers of our own. The Russian speaks little or no English, doesn't have to: the kid talks for him."

"There's no picture of the Russian?" Morgan asked.

"There's a picture but in it he's wearing a big bushy beard. Behind it he could be anybody. Shave it off and he could be any big man."

"You say they travel together."

"I meant it in the sense that they work together. According to Byrnes, the few select murders they do are done in the east, where most of Goldshire's interests lie. But they traveled all the way here, didn't they? But don't get me wrong. Goldshire, the father, is not murderously inclined. He's a businessman, an investor in big crimes, a money man. What I mean is, he resorts to murder only if somebody becomes a serious threat. He can call on Monk Eastman who has no end of killers on his payroll, but he doesn't, not for the few big jobs. His son, loyal lad that he is, is the only one he trusts not to get him hanged for murder. If a special murder has to be done, the son does it. A lot of closeness in that family, you almost have to admire it. The ugly, runty son always trying to please the tall, handsome father . . ."

Morgan was getting the picture now. Bender had been right to sketch it in the way he had.

"If Goldshire is so rich, why doesn't he quit?"

Bender's question wasn't for Morgan. "Why risk the hangman when you don't have to? Because he's a greedy son of a bitch, that's why. So he balances the risk against his greed and decides the risk is worth it. But only if the risk, he decides, is very small, and so far it has been, the way the son and the Russian work."

Morgan wished they were having this talk somewhere else. The bar was beginning to fill up with boozy police chiefs and their hangers-on, salesmen trying to sell something, freeloaders out for booze and women, all making a lot of noise. But it would have to do.

"They haven't killed me," Morgan said, "so they must be after the securities."

"They could be," Bender admitted. "They surely aren't after your boots and pocketknife. A hundred thousand is a lot of money, even to a man like Goldshire, but how would he even know about the securities? Well, yes, he could have heard on the crookvine that Bullock was a likely mark with all that valuable paper just there for the taking. That's more than possible, yes. But as I told you, Goldshire's operations are mainly in the east—New York, Boston, a few other big cities—so why would he send his son and the Russian all the way here to steal? I'm not saying he didn't—they're here, the kid never travels without the Russian—but why?"

"Could the kid be doing it on his own? Got word of the securities and decided to do the job himself?"

"Then why didn't he do it? Why is he following you around?"

"The first question, he got here after Lily took the securities and ran. The second, the securities are missing and he thinks I'll lead him to them."

Bender frowned at both answers. "How would he know they'd been taken? He didn't break in and wring that information out of Bullock, who is alive and well, I trust."

"I talked to him on the telephone at twelve-thirty today."

"And he said nothing about a visit from a runt and a Russian?"

"Come on, Bender, you know he didn't."

"Sorry, old man," Bender said. "Obviously they're not here to kill you or you'd be dead by now. They're not here to kill Bullock—why, I can't imagine—or he'd be just as dead. Which brings us back to why are they here? I can't see the kid starting up in the securities-stealing business without Daddy's blessing. It doesn't wash."

"Unless they had a falling out."

"I doubt it. Byrnes says the kid is devoted to his father, has no life except working for him. You'll have to come up with something better than a family quarrel. I'm a detective, or I was, and I have no quick answers, any kind of answers. Back home I'd shut myself off from people—anyway, as much as I could—and think about it. Here—" Bender nodded at the loudmouths at the bar, at the other tables "—I can't do that. I'm not saying I'm any great brain. Back home it would be easier to think."

"I don't want you to get into this," Morgan said. "You've done enough—more."

228

Bender smiled. "I'm not getting into it. I have this convention and besides, Flaherty wouldn't want me invading his territory. No police chief would. So you're on your own, I'm afraid. There are things you haven't told me and that's okay with me. Do it your own way. Let's just hope you don't get your dick caught in the wringer."

Morgan smiled back at him. "I'll try not to."

"All very well for you to say. It could happen. You know what you should do? You should take this story to Flaherty. They say he's all right, so he'll listen. You're dealing with the worst kind of people here. Worse they don't make 'em. Go to Flaherty and let him talk to Bullock. That way you're out of it, have no more responsibility. Having discharged your duty as a good citizen, you can go home."

"You think I should run?"

"If you don't want to run, try walking fast. But you won't take my advice, will you?"

"I'll think about it."

Bender said, "That means you won't do it. I wish to hell I'd never sent you to Bullock. I thought I was doing you a good turn. But it looks like I did you no favor. Now I'm telling you to clear out, go home. You're spoiling my vacation."

"I thought this was business."

"Every convention is a vacation." Bender nodded again at the back-slapping drinkers. "To have a good time there's only one rule: don't fuck so much you can't get it up for the little women when you get home. I broke the rule—I brought the little woman along. Go home, Morgan. Send a postcard to Kansas City so I'll know you're still

walking around. And now, my lad, I must cut this
short though it sorrows me to do it. We'll be leaving
in a day or two, and I don't have much time."

"Stay healthy" was the last thing Bender said
before they went their separate ways. Morgan
watched for a minute as his friend waded into
the crowd in the lobby. Bender was running for
vice president of the Police Chief's Association. A
man like Nathan Bender ought to be president, and
the hell with this vice shit.

Going out into Market Street with all its afternoon bustle, Morgan found it hard to believe that
the runt and his Russian sidekick might even now
be watching him as he pushed his way through the
revolving door. Everything looked so normal—the
cable cars moving along, pulled by cables set into
slots in the street, the policeman directing traffic at
the intersection, his whistle shrilling in his mouth,
the people waiting to cross. The sky was overcast
but it wasn't raining. It was a gray day but San Francisco was a perky, cheerful place in any season. Morgan would have been cheerful himself if not for the
thought of the two killers. He didn't think they were
out to kill him, not yet anyway. But what about
the others who'd been drawn into this? O'Connor
hadn't exactly stumbled in. He'd bulled his way in
under his own power, so let him take his chances.
George Dunaway was different. He had gone to
her, gotten her involved. To her it might seem
like an adventure, something out of a book, and
she'd feel no danger because she lived in a world
where money protected you from everything. It
could do a good job of that even if you knew the

danger was there. Even then, all the guards and guns were no guarantee against sudden death. He wondered how much the runt and his big shadow knew about George Dunaway. Maybe nothing. But if they'd seen her arrive at the mission, with all the fuss O'Connor made of her and Morgan himself standing by, the runt might try to check who she was. The Russian didn't count here, the runt did the figuring. If the runt left the Russian to watch the mission, he could go somewhere and get on the telephone, look her up in the city directory. All this was a lot of supposing. How was a big man like the Russian to watch the mission without being spotted by O'Connor's pimp-beating patrolmen? For that matter, how was the runt to do it, small though he was?

Already on his way to the feminist headquarters, Morgan had no answers. No doubt she'd protest like hell when he warned her and suggested that maybe she needed protection. Her answer would be that she was a modern woman and needed nobody to look after her. Hadn't he seen her lay out that big ox Effie with her French foot-fighting? The only trouble was, Effie was no killer, and foot-fighting wouldn't work. She could kick at the Russian till she got tired, but all she'd do was hurt her feet.

The office was locked—nobody answered his knock—and he went downstairs to the restaurant to ask Otto where George Dunaway might be. When she left the mission, she had said she was going to talk to her attorney about bailing out the women the police were trying to hold. She could

231

be at his office, at the jail, or on her way back to . . . where? That was another thing: she could even be in her apartment by now. That wouldn't be so bad; you couldn't just walk into a place like that. But there were ways to do it if you knew how. The New York kid would know how. Bribe the doorman, arrive with important legal papers she had to sign—something.

Otto, when he came out from the kitchen, wasn't pleased to see him; his spiky Prussian haircut practically bristled with resentment. His red face was redder from the heat of the kitchen and he was inclined to be difficult. No, he did not know where Miss Dunaway was or where she had gone. Miss Dunaway did not make a practice of informing him as to her whereabouts. If Mr. Morgan wanted to talk to Miss Dunaway so urgently, why had he not made use of the telephone—he had heard of the telephone, had he not? Then it would not be necessary to annoy busy people with his questions.

The restaurant wasn't that busy with the lunch crowd done and only a few drinkers left, but Otto wanted to make a fuss. "Many things I have to do that must be done," he growled. "Standing here to answer questions I do not have the answers to is not putting money in my pocket. In the kitchen the lazy bums are slacking off every minute I am not watching them."

Morgan apologized when what he really wanted to do was stuff one of Otto's strudels down his thick neck. "One last question if you don't mind, Otto, Mr. Otto—" Otto glowered at that. "Does

Miss Dunaway stop in here when she comes to the office? I thought maybe for coffee."

Otto was about the same height as Morgan, but he drew himself up, trying to appear taller, so he could look down. "Sometimes she does . . ." There was a pause. "And sometimes she does not."

"Then I'll wait over there by the window," Morgan said. "Can you bring me a roast beef sandwich and a cup of coffee?"

"I certainly can not." Otto was positive about that. "Calling a *waider* is what you must do. And now if you will excuse me, Mr. Morgen."

Morgan was eating the sandwich when George Dunaway came in. "For heaven's sake, what are you doing here, and eating a roast beef sandwich when there are so many splendid German specialties you could have. You're like the man who goes into a fine Parisian restaurant and orders New England baked beans, with corn pudding for dessert." The waiter was there as soon as she sat down, a lot better service than Morgan got. Not so young, like many waiters, this waiter couldn't do enough for her. "Today the roast goose is I can promise you very good, Miss Dunaway."

"I'm sure it is, Julius, but I'd like to have a roast beef sandwich and coffee." The waiter hurried away as fast as his old legs would carry him. "Don't expect me to be consistent," George Dunaway said to Morgan. "Was yours good?"

"I have to talk to you, George. It may be nothing, but we have to talk about it. It's about the securities."

George Dunaway was taking off her gloves.

"What's happened? Have they turned up? Is Mr. Bullock on his way to Australia?"

"Nothing like that," Morgan said. Right now he wanted her in her all-business mood. Right now she wasn't. There was mischief in her violet eyes, a teasing tone in her talk, and she was bubbling over by the time he told her about Wily Willy Goldshire and his son, the Russian assassin, and the danger she might be in.

"How exciting!" she cried, causing two grim-looking beer drinkers with enameled steins to look over in disapproval. "To think my life is in danger, actually in danger!"

"I said it might be in danger. If the kid finds out you're so interested in the stock market, making money out of it, there's a chance he'll come asking questions about Bullock's securities. He could have seen you at the mission, no way to be sure about that. If he thinks you're acting as Lily's go-between, that's where the danger comes in."

"I can take care of myself," she said defiantly, just as he expected. "I'm quite capable of defending myself against any assailant. Would you like to go upstairs and pretend to attack me—don't pretend, attack me—so I can show you what will happen?"

"No need for that." Morgan was thinking that the thumps on Otto's ceiling would bring him upstairs like a shot. He liked the idea of tangling with her, but not that way.

Arguing with her in a sensible way would do no good. "What if they catch you unawares and chloroform you, put you in a sack, sell you to the captain of a rotten ship who wants to keep his crew from mutiny? The sailors would have their way with you all the way to Hong Kong."

Her eyes grew bright and she said "um" to that. Then she laughed at him. "There wouldn't be any other women on board?"

Morgan told her not a one, and that got another laugh. "Such a ridiculous idea. You should write dirty books, but the plot you just made up has been used. All right, if you feel so strongly about it, I'll get Otto to protect me."

Morgan hadn't been expecting that. "You mean this Otto? Here?"

"Otto has seen the rough side of life. He was in the Prussian army."

"What was he? A cook?"

"No, no. He was something like a sergeant major. I forget the German name for it. I can get Julius to fetch him. He can tell you himself."

Morgan didn't want another go-round with Otto. "We'll talk to him later. But there's one thing. He hasn't been in the army for a long time. He's put on some pounds, had too much strudel."

"Not strudel, no. But he's an absolute fiend for roast pork and dumplings. What does it matter if he's a bit solid? Germans tend to get like that—weighty. I think he'll do very well as my bodyguard. He's a very good shot. In the army he won promotion because of his marksmanship. What do you think of that?"

"I think he can't follow you around San Francisco carrying a rifle."

"Now you're being silly. A rifle, indeed! Otto is just as skillful with a pistol. This past June he won

235

a medal for pistol shooting, some German picnic out on the Farallon Islands. It was in one of the newspaers. He showed me the clipping."

Morgan still wasn't sold on Otto. "How can he spend so much time away from the restaurant?"

"His younger brother works here as assistant manager and is quite capable of carrying on in his absence." George Dunaway smiled. "It will be like a vacation for everyone here. With Otto away, they can do their work without being yelled at all the time. Don't argue about it, Morgan, Otto is to be my protector."

"Let me give it some thought." He could hear Otto yelling back in the kitchen. The customers must be used to that by now. But it took more than yelling . . .

"You know what the trouble with you is," George Dunaway said. "You're jealous."

That stopped Morgan cold.

Chapter Fifteen

"Like hell I am!"

It was hardly the most tactful thing to say, and George Dunaway flushed with indignation. "Well, that's not very flattering to me, is it? After all—"

"I didn't mean it the way it sounded," Morgan said. Maybe he was jealous, hard to believe though it was. If he was, this was the first time it had happened since he was a kid. His way with women was to fuck them, for a night or a week, and then bid them a fond farewell. "It's just that you caught me by surprise. I—"

"Oh, can't you see I was joking? Surely you can't be jealous of Otto, even though some women might find him handsome in a Teutonic sort of way."

"Are you one of them?" Morgan realized he sounded sour.

"I will not be cross-examined. You are not my husband. Why, sir, I hardly know you." That brought on another fit of laughing. "Cool down, Morgan. It's so easy to get a rise out of you. You're so serious about this danger you think I'm in, I had to throw in a little levity. Forgive me."

"It's not funny. Listen, no more jokes for a while. Don't ask Otto to bodyguard you because you think it's funny. If you don't think he's the man for the job, I'll do it myself—"

Julius, the waiter, came to the table wanting to know what Miss Dunaway would have for dessert. "You know I shouldn't have strudel, Julius," she said to him. "It's so fattening, but that's what I'll have."

"On you a few pounds would look good," Julius said before he hurried off to the kitchen.

"I can't have you hovering over me like a mother hen. Cluck, cluck," George Dunaway said. "How will you ever find the securities?"

"I wish I'd never heard of the fucking things."

"Please, sir, we're in a respectable restaurant. You look for the securities and Otto will look after me. Let me tell you a story about Otto. One night last winter—a dark, rainy night, the neighborhood was deserted—I was working late, paying no attention to the time. Two men—they saw the light, I suppose, and knew who I was— broke in here and tried to rape me. Otto, who always works late on his books, heard my screams and came tearing up the stairs. One man he killed by breaking his neck, the other he threw through the plate glass window. But he didn't go all the way through—he hung there on the sharp, broken glass, bleeding to death. You know what Otto did?"

"He didn't call the ambulance."

"Oh, he called it all right. We went down to his

office, but his telephone wouldn't work. That's what he said. It took him ten minutes to get the operator on the line. When the ambulance arrived, the man was dead. So tell me, what do you think of Otto now?"

"I think he'll do fine," Morgan said.

"I say," George Dunaway said. "That looks like one of Duckie's Australians, the one that guards the door."

Morgan saw Wilfred looking around in the smoky light of the restaurant. He was breathing hard and looked like he was in a hurry. Morgan waved and called to him and he came over. "Beggin' yer pardon, Mr. Morgan, and lady, Duckie needs you to come over right away. Sent me 'cause I knows what ye look like. Urgent business. Most urgent." Wilfred wasn't sure if he should talk more in front of the woman. But the words came out anyway. "One of the boys spotted the runt. Come on, I got a cab waitin'."

Morgan got up. George Dunaway started to get up too, but he told her to finish her sandwich. "Talk to Otto, get that squared away. I'll let you know what happens."

Wilfred opened up once the cab was moving. "It's like this," he said after he yelled at the cabby to get a bleeding move on. "Philly Grimes was takin' a shortcut through this alley close by the mission when he spots this runty lookin' feller, see. Not a full hour ago this was. Philly has been told to keep a lookout for runts, see, like we all has. So Philly sees this runt and yells at him, tells him to stop. Only he doesn't stop, he runs into this old buildin' and vanishes like smoke. Now Philly is no coward and he goes in after him, but it's dark in there, see, and he thinks maybe he ought to get some help, search the place from top to bottom. Funny thing is, Duckie already had this place searched and a new padlock put on the door. Only now the padlock is hangin' loose, anybody can get in, and the runt goes in there with Philly watchin', but the runt disappears."

"Where is Duckie now?"

"Still searchin' around in there, I reckon. He was headin' that way with some of the boys while I was tryin' to catch a cab. They could be in there yet. A big old warehouse shut up a long time— they're goin' to tear it down. Dangerous in there, rotten floors, holes in places. You could get killed in there."

The cab stopped in front of the mission. Morgan paid the fare and stopped a fight between the cabby and Wilfred, who had been yelling at him all the way. "Down there, the space between the buildin's." Morgan looked where he was pointing, at an alley that wasn't much more than a slot dividing two commerical buildings. The man who was guarding the door in Wilfred's place came down the steps. "Duckie's still in there, that tall buildin' set back from the street. You see it, the one higher than the others?"

Morgan saw it. If the runt had been up that high, he had a clear view of the mission. Morgan headed for the alley, with Wilfred trying to keep up. Wilfred wanted to show him where the entrance door was, but there was no need of that. O'Connor and four of his men were coming out by the time they got there. He was slapping dust from his black coat and giving orders. "Two of you stay here by the door, grab him if he comes out. Try not to shoot him, but do it if you have to. The rest of you—"

O'Connor saw Morgan and waved his men away. "Search the neighborhood, keep at it." A short, wiry man was leaving with the others. O'Connor called him back. "This is Philly Grimes, the one that spotted him. I don't know if he's still in there. We went right up to the top floor, then back down to the cellars. We didn't find him. But we did find these—" O'Connor took a small pair of brass-framed binoculars from his pocket "—and the leavings of food on a window ledge, the top floor."

Morgan took the binoculars, looked through them, gave them back. "Good quality," he said. He took the rolled up envelope from his pocket and took out the runt's photograph.

"Look at it," O'Connor said to Grimes. "Take a good look. Is this the man you saw?" He turned to Morgan. "Did you find out who he is," he asked.

Morgan nodded. No use saying too much in front of Grimes, a crafty little man by the look of him. No telling who the runt was giving bribe money to.

"Later for that." O'Connor poked Grimes with a thick forefinger. "Is that him or isn't it?"

"It's him all right," Grimes said. "Only he wasn't wearin' clothes like in the pitcher."

"How so, Philly? What was he wearing? A top hat and an opera cloak?"

"Get away, you silly old man." Philly was past

sixty. "Little bloke was dressed more like a businessman. Nice little dark suit, light gray derby with a curly brim—real pop'lar right now—and I think eyeglasses."

"Was he wearing glasses? Make up your mind, you twit."

"Yarss, he was wearin' glasses, like the ones you stick on your nose with a clip. Looked like a reg'lar little gent, only his face was mean, like in the pitcher. Did I do good, Duckie?"

"Very good, Philly." O'Connor took the photograph and gave it back to Morgan. "Catch up to the others," O'Connor said to Grimes. "You know what the fucker looks like. You too, Wilfred, don't hang around."

Morgan and O'Connor walked back toward the mission. "The runt is the son of a big New York crook called Wily Willy Goldshire. You ever hear of him?"

"I've heard of him. Bender tell you that?"

"A lot more than that. He has good connections with the New York police. Bender says the kid kills people, maybe does other work, for his father. Important jobs, not penny ante killings. The kid works with a big Russian, a political killer back in the old country. The kid stalks the victim, picks the time and place, and the Russian does the rest. . . ."

They went up to O'Connor's quarters and Morgan filled in the rest of it while he drank a beer. The first thing O'Connor said when he finished was, "They're not here to kill you."

Morgan said the same thing he'd said to Bender: "Not yet anyway."

O'Connor wasn't about to offer any comfort. "They could change their minds, or the kid could. Decide he'd be better off with you out of the way."

"What good would I be to him dead?"

"I don't know. He might do it anyway, if he gets mad at you for not leading him to the treasure trove sooner than you do. Who knows how these fuckers think? I've known my share of professional killers, men who like to think they're in business, like a doctor or an undertaker, but there's none that isn't twisted and crazy inside. This kid, from what Bender said, fits right in with that."

Morgan wondered how George Dunaway and Otto were getting along. It was good to know a kindly madman like Otto was looking after her. It would be even better to get the news that he'd thrown the runt through another plate glass window.

"We may be on the wrong track," Morgan said. "We're thinking he's after the securities."

"Are we? I suppose we are, for want of something that makes better sense. There's so much we don't know."

They were sitting at a table in the kitchen and O'Connor was eating some cold leftover lamb. Morgan wondered where the Chinaman was. They had gone over it and over it and were back where they started. Morgan got up to get another bottle of beer.

"You said you knew who Goldshire was." Morgan sat down and filled his glass.

"He tried his luck here in the gold rush days.

Must have been pretty young then. I don't know how young."

"Bender says he's fifty-seven."

"San Francisco was the gold capital of the world then. What a time that was. Money everywhere, men spending it as fast as they could dig it out of the ground, wash it out of the creeks. Never caught the gold fever myself, did my prospecting right here in the city. Like I said, there was money everywhere. Land that wasn't worth shit a few years before now going for thousands of dollars per lot. Ramshackle saloons taking in so much money they hardly had time to count it. Whores coming up the coast from Chile, across Panama, round the Horn. Could charge what they liked, women were scarce. You could smell money in the air. Every tinhorn and stock fraud and cheat smelled it and came pouring in. Goldshire came too."

"Then you knew him?"

"No. I was in a different line of business, but I heard talk of him. He stood out from the other crooks, I guess, more of a gentleman than the others. What he was doing, if I remember it right, was selling stock in phony gold mines. Nothing unusual in that. A lot of other oily crooks were doing it. But the word was, Goldshire was doing it better. Then, alas, the Vigilance Committee— the decent people, some not so decent—started hanging some of the most needy cases, not a lot, and there was a sudden exodus of the unsavory. Goldshire was one of the first to go. I managed to avoid the greased rope, and here I am today."

"And doing good," Morgan said.

"Not for myself," O'Connor said. "I'll never starve, but the ladies come first."

Morgan was thinking. "Could Goldshire have known Bullock in those days?"

"Not too likely. What I know of Bullock, he ran a tent store at the diggings the short time Goldshire was here. Cheating the miners, getting his start. I can't see where their paths would cross. A frisky, thieving little chipmunk like Bullock and a smooth operator like Goldshire. I can't picture them together. Even then, Goldshire was heading for bigtime crookery, that was the talk, while Bullock was still selling overripe eggs and spoiled bacon and worrying about being robbed. You can't tie them together by going back that far."

O'Connor got up to put his plate in the sink. "And you can't tie them together now. Not unless the kid trying to find the securities ties them together. And we can't even be sure of that."

"I think we can be sure it's a big part of it. Nothing else makes sense."

"For what it's worth, it does." O'Connor turned when the Chinese came into the kitchen carrying a basket. "You took your own sweet time," he said peevishly.

The Chinaman took it the way he took all of O'Connor's other complaints. His bland face showed nothing. "I get the beer an' the hot sausages, boss, then I go down Chinatown, get the chop suey things the rady rike so good."

"Will you listen to this dolt." This was for Morgan. "Damn fool thinks George is going to be asking for chop suey every time she comes here."

"She likes it a lot."

"But not all the time. You went over to see her instead of coming back here. Well, I guess she's prettier than I am." O'Connor caught the Chinaman looking at him. "Make yourself useful, you. Go and dust the bookshelves, sweep the rug. Leave the basket. You can do it later."

O'Connor took four bottles of beer from the basket and put them on the table. "It made sense to warn her, things as they are. But what good is a warning? She's just a little woman."

Morgan told him about Otto. "Have you heard from Harriet?"

O'Connor pulled the corks from two bottles. "Not so far. I wish I knew what she was doing. I don't like her down the Coast. She's not ready to go back to that kind of work, if ever. Damn, I wish she'd find some decent man, get married, settle down."

Morgan looked up from his beer and caught O'Connor staring at him across the table. "What's that look for, Duckie?"

"I was thinking maybe you could use a wife, the long cold winter nights up in Idaho."

"You mean Harriet?"

"That's the one. You can't say she's bad looking. A bit on the glum side, needs cheering up—some good work between the sheets might do the trick. A harder worker you'll never find, believe me, I know. Smart too, can keep books, can typewrite to beat the band. And I'll bet you haven't missed the shape she's got on her. Would put your dumpy Idaho country women to shame, I'm thinking. Last but not least, she's a very good cook."

Morgan looked at the sly old villain across from him. "You're like an old woman, Duckie. 'You'll never taste heaven till you taste my granddaughter's sweet potato pie.' Save it if you don't mind."

"That's no way to carry on. Take a chance, man. Pop the question and see how she responds. What's the worst that can happen?"

Morgan said, "The least is she can pop me in the mouth. The worst, kick me in the balls."

O'Connor was not about to be put off. "You're only saying that because George has you by the balls. A most agreeable feeling that must be, but take some well meant advice: she's not for you."

"Whoever said she was? Did I say it?"

"You don't have to say it. It's as plain as the nose on my face. All she has to do is make an appearance and you get all sheepish. Like you're hiding a bunch of posies behind your back and don't have the nerve to present them to the lady."

Morgan didn't know what to say. Yes, he did. He said, "This is a bucket of shit."

"No, it's not," O'Connor said calmly. "You think I don't like George. Not so. I think she's a grand little creature, so feisty and full of spirit—and so rich. But I'll say it again, she's not for you."

"What's the matter with me?" Morgan felt compelled to ask. "Do I have a hump on my back?

"No hump but no money either. Not having money is as bad as having the hump. But let's go on. Suppose by some miracle, you won her heart and tied the knot, what on earth would she do in Idaho? Milk all the cows?"

"We have but one cow. The cook milks her." Morgan was trying to picture George Dunaway, mannish suit, fedora hat and cigar, walking down the street in Baxter, the one-horse town some miles from the ranch. Wouldn't that make them whisper.

"All right, no cow," O'Connor went on. "I can't see her feeding the chickens. Everybody must keep chickens up there."

Morgan said, "We don't. It's a horse ranch, not a chicken ranch. We get eggs from a farmer."

O'Connor threw up his hands. "Then what will she do?"

"Nothing, that's what she'll do. She won't be going there. I won't be asking her. And don't start up again with Harriet."

It was starting to get dark. O'Connor got up and put a match to the gas globe. "Damn, I wish she'd come home. I don't like to think of her out there. It's like she has to prove that she's as good as she ever was. Nobody ever is, you know."

Morgan didn't want to hear any more about Harriet. The woman was past thirty and took advice from nobody. Even George Dunaway, flighty though she was, had more sense. For all her joking, she was glad to have dangerous Otto to protect her from the runt, should he come acalling. He thought about the runt. The only one who'd seen him— said he'd seen him—was Philly Grimes. Well, he'd been there all right: O'Connor had the binoculars to prove that. But what about the clothes, the eyeglasses Grimes said he was wearing?

Morgan asked O'Connor how reliable Grimes was. "The way he described Goldshire's son, how much of that can be believed? I smelled whiskey on him."

"You mean did he dream up the gray derby, the business suit, the nose glasses?" O'Connor seemed mildly surprised. "Not on your tin-type. Philly drinks, sure he does, but not enough to start seeing things. Philly used to be a pickpocket back in the days when it was a dangerous thing to be. In the wild old days a man finding your hand in his pocket would shoot or stab you. No calling for the police. There were cases of pickpockets being lynched on the spot. So you see, a dip like Philly had to have a pair of sharp eyes, the ability to size up a man at a moment's notice. What Philly said he saw is what he saw."

"Goddamn!" Morgan said.

"Are you thinking what I'm thinking?"

"I think so. We've been keeping an eye open for a little man in a cheap suit and a hoodlum's cloth cap. All the time he's been walking around like a fussy little gent, pinch glasses and all. Like some up-and-coming guy in a lawyer's office, maybe an assistant head teller in a bank."

A long swallow of beer didn't make O'Connor look any happier. "He could be walking around like that. Or he could be dressed as a lot of things, probably not as a Chinese laundryman though. But why not? That chalky face under a skullcap, who'd give him much attention? If he's been doing all that, even some of it, he's one smart little rat."

"I should have tried harder to catch him that first night." Morgan was thinking about what he could have done. If he'd only waited right around the corner instead of hiding behind a stack of bricks, he might have been quick enough to grab the bastard.

"What you did would probably have worked with a less crafty cove. But the real killers, the ones who think and plan, can smell out a trap. It's some sort of sense they have, and maybe they're born with it, maybe it develops as they go along."

"You think there's a chance he's still holed up in there?"

"Not even worth a guess. There are tunnels below the street level, even down below the cellars. I don't even know what their purpose was. Some have been bricked up, but that was some time ago. I'd burn the place, but I'm afraid the whole district would go up. Old buildings burn like a forest fire."

O'Connor took the small brass-framed binoculars from his pocket and looked at them. "He's been up there looking down at us. If he had a scoped rifle he could kill somebody right on the steps of this building. A good thing that isn't his game. What galls my balls is he could be back up there. If he can get out, he can get back in. I thought a thorough search and a stout padlock would rule that building out. But he got the padlock off and made it look as if it hadn't been tampered with. When Philly yelled at him, he must have banged it loose, getting in there so fast."

The beer was starting to taste dead to Morgan.

Usually he could drink it till the cows came home, but tonight there was no enjoyment in this good brew. Every swallow seemed to remind him that he should be doing something instead of just sitting here jawboning to no purpose.

"I wonder where the Russian is," O'Connor said.

"Holed up someplace till the kid needs him, probably. Man that big can't just put on different clothes and lose himself like the kid. But in a room, the rent paid, making no trouble, he could lie up there as long as he likes."

"Yeah," O'Connor said wearily. "The city is full of furnished rooms and no-questions hotels. Asking around for a big foreigner would take the whole police department to do it. All I've got is a handful of getting-old reformed crooks. Good men, most of them, but where do they look? The Coast isn't the only place men lie low. Other districts provide them with hideouts. There's a small Russian district, maybe he's there. One advantage we have, the kid knows you spotted him but he doesn't know you followed up on it. That flash pan going off in his face, I doubt if he'd think as far as an actual photograph. He doesn't know we know who he is."

"No, he can't know that," Morgan said, "but I can't shake the feeling that he's always back of me somewhere. Like when I went to the telephone building, I walked down Front Street to Market. A long stretch of Front Street had no people on it. I looked back along that stretch and saw nobody. So how could he be following me there?"

251

"He doesn't have to be following you all the time." O'Connor was poking into the basket of groceries, more to be doing something than anything else. He came up with a string of red sausages wrapped in oiled paper and sniffed at them. "He knows he can pick up on you here. If he's up in that building, he can. Maybe I will burn that place after all."

"Burn what place?" Harriet said, coming into the kitchen. "Never mind, you probably won't tell me." She sat down at the table, reached for one of the beer bottles, found it empty, and muttered something under her breath. Morgan just looked at her, in no mood for any more of her bad-tempered bullshit.

"Good to see you again, Harriet," O'Connor said, elaborate politeness not quite hiding his annoyance. "For a while there, I thought you might not be coming at all. It's been dark for a long time and we've been waiting. You were supposed to be here hours ago."

Harriet still had the empty bottle in her hand and she banged it on the table. Morgan thought he might go to bed or sit in the bathtub, anything to get away from this pesky woman. "I have to be home before dark, is that it?" Harriet was working up to a full head of steam. "Like a child, like a fucking child. Well, let me tell you something—"

O'Connor had taken enough. "Shut your mouth or I'll shut it for you. Now take a deep breath and talk to us like a civilized human being. What did you find out about Hargis?"

Chapter Sixteen

"Not a lot," she said quietly, mindful of O'Connor's warning. But her voice rose a little in spite of herself. "I think I could have learned more if not for your curfew. Like a good little girl, I reminded myself it was long past my bedtime, so I dragged myself back here, God damn it to hell!"

"Now, now. Enough of that." O'Connor opened a bottle of beer and filled a glass for her. "If you had some scuttle on Hargis, you could have telephoned. We've been here all evening. We'd have come right over."

They waited while she drank greedily. "You'd come right over and send me right home, is that what you'd do?"

"We're getting nowhere here." O'Connor spoke calmly, keeping his temper. "What we would or wouldn't have done is not important now. You should have telephoned, but we'll forget about that. What about Hargis?"

"At first there was nothing, nobody even wanted

to listen to my dumb story. I started pitching my tale of woe to any woman I could find who wasn't drunk or doped to the eyeballs. You get nothing out of them except maybe *their* tale of woe. You know what they're like, Duckie. Most of the other street women gave me the fisheye, me in my schoolteacher's dowdy dress, trying to find a man who obviously didn't want to be found. They resented it and I don't blame them. They have a hard enough time without some mealymouth bothering them like the orphan of the storm. One poor woman was willing enough to talk—I guess she was lonely—but there was nothing she could tell me. 'I know what you're going through, honey,' she said. 'I went through it myself. Maybe you're better off without the lousy bum.' "

"So you got nothing out of the women," O'Connor said.

"Nothing much, nothing at all. One or two tried to work me for a few dollars, saying a friend or a friend of a friend might have some idea where he was. One little bitch made a joke out of it. Like how could I lose him if he was so big? Shit like that. The men were no better, most of them playing deaf and dumb when they weren't laughing at me. The regular Coast mugs wanted nothing to do with me. One recruiter for a house gave me his card and told me to come see him if I wanted to go to work as an entertainer. Another man, not a Coast mug by the way he talked, suggested that we discuss my problem in his hotel room. That's how it went for most of the day."

O'Connor was sympathetic, patient as a priest

hearing Confession. "Sounds like you had a bad time of it. What happened later?"

Harriet said, "The bad time was because of this damn dress, the dumb story I kept on repeating till I was ready to throw up. It's all wrong, the way I'm doing it. I should go in there like what I used to be—a whore. It wouldn't matter if they remembered me, maybe better if they did. I'd be talking their language, they wouldn't clam up like they do with the wandering husband story. If I had more than a few dollars in my bag—"

"We'll talk about it," O'Connor said. "What happened later? You were going to tell us."

Harriet said, "I was in a coffee joint thinking, this is a washout, better be heading back. I was paying the nickel check and the owner, some kind of a foreigner, was holding my nickel, paying no attention to me and kidding the clean-up guy, an American, a rummy, asking him if he'd heard about the other big-spending American who was looking all over for his wife. Offering a big reward, this guy, the owner was saying. He couldn't remembered the big guy's name, but he remembered the wife's name—Lily. He sang a few bits of "Lily of the Valley," thought the whole thing was funny. Why didn't the clean-up guy take a crack at finding her, he could get rich.

"The owner threw my nickel in the register. The clean-up guy said the big guy had talked to him and he thought he was a big phony. 'I got to be going home now,' he said to the owner, heading back to the kitchen. I went out and waited where I thought he'd come out, through the alley at the side. He tried to get past me, but stopped quick enough when I held up two dollar bills. I did the wife act for his benefit, saying this Lily was no wife, just a woman who my husband took up with. No interest in that, he wanted the money, booze money. Anyway, he said my husband had been in, asking about this Lily, and he heard in the saloon next door he'd been doing the same thing there. That's all he could tell me, so all I gave him was a dollar."

"What time was this?" O'Connor said.

"About eight-thirty, getting dark. I tried to follow it up, but I was dressed like this, had no money to spend. They've got cold-tea girls working the saloons, but a woman like me can't drink in them. All I could do was ask around at the other quick-eats. Had to lay out my other six dollars, big spender, but I did get a few answers. Hargis had been around earlier in the day, not all the time, he came and went. One man said he'd been drinking, another said he was staggering drunk. Nobody knew where he was putting up, had no idea, or wouldn't tell me. I came back here."

"Hargis must have robbed somebody," O'Connor said. "What about another beer?"

Harriet looked at her empty glass and made a face. "I could do with a real drink."

"All right. A drink might help you get some sound sleep." O'Connor didn't sound too enthusiastic, but he got a whiskey bottle and a glass from a cupboard. He did the pouring himself and put the glass in front of Harriet.

"A little more," she said.

She watched while O'Connor filled her glass to half full. "That should put you to sleep. In the morning, we'll all go looking for Hargis."

Harriet drank some of the whiskey, then all of it. "I don't like working with a brass band. You, Morgan, the whole shooting match. This has to be done quietly."

No one said anything to Morgan, so he said nothing. Maybe she was right about how it should be handled.

"There would be just the two of us," O'Connor said. "Me and Morgan, we could work the places you can't go."

The whiskey was getting to Harriet. "The places I can't go are the places I should go. Dressed right, I can blend in. Pick up again with some of my old pals—wonderful people, the sons of bitches. They'll talk to Harriet the Hoor a lot more readily than they will Mrs. Clem Hargis, the grass widow from Dog's Dinner, Arkansas."

Morgan had to smile at that. O'Connor didn't smile. "I said no to that this morning, I'm saying no tonight. It's too dangerous. If Hargis hears you're sniffing around asking questions, he could round on you and do you harm. The man is an imbecile in some things, a crafty bastard in others. Dumb or smart, he's dangerous."

Harriet said abruptly, "Can we talk about this in the morning? I'm tired and I'm hungry."

"I didn't think. You want me to get John up?"

"For God's sake, Duckie, I can fix it myself. Go to bed. You look as tired as I do."

"Good idea." O'Connor heaved himself out of his

chair. "Fix something for Morgan while you're at it. Show him what a good cook you are."

Morgan wanted to kick him in the ass. "Good-night, Duckie," he said.

O'Connor waved and headed for his room. "You want something to eat?" Harriet said to Morgan. She didn't ask with good grace, not that Morgan expected much else from her.

"I'll have what you're having if it isn't chop suey."

"What kind of stupid talk is that? I'm going to make an omelet with hot peppers. Want one?"

Morgan said sure and he watched her going at it the way she did everything else, irritably and efficiently. It was all done so fast, he thought maybe she could get a job as a short-order fry cook. She washed and dried the mixing bowl and slicing board while the omelets were cooking. Before Morgan could even think of saying grace, a steaming omelet was set down in front of him.

"This is good," he said, taking a bite.

"No need for compliments." Now that the omelet was cooked, she didn't seem to want to eat it. Typical of her contrary nature. Morgan didn't give a damn, it had been a long time since that roast beef sandwich at Otto's. "I think Duckie is wrong," she said. "I think my way of finding Hargis is better. What do you think?"

"I thought you wanted to talk about it in the morning."

"So I do—with Duckie. But you're here, I'm talking to you."

Morgan looked at her. "How did you ever get so charming?"

Her eyes blazed at him. "I'd like to throw this in your fucking face." One hand was gripping the edge of her plate. "You're such a fucking smart-aleck."

Morgan had no mind to get a faceful of eggs. "Better think before you throw that at me. I'm not Duckie and I won't put up with your shit. You won't break my balls like you're breaking his. If I ran this place, you'd be out in the street."

She smiled. Morgan was so surprised that he couldn't think of anything else to say. "You wouldn't throw me in the street," she said. "You might throw a man off the roof, but you'd never throw a woman in the street."

"I'd do it. Why wouldn't I do it?"

"Because you're a big old country Romeo, that's why."

"No need for compliments, sister." But Morgan smiled.

"It wasn't a compliment, brother. You think you're God's gift to women, that's what you think."

"How can I help it if women throw themselves at me? Crawl in the window, break down the door? All right, a joke is a joke. I'd just as soon not take sides in this. Duckie is the boss here. If we butt heads too hard, I'll leave, go it alone."

She was eating the omelet instead of throwing it. "But you know I'm right."

Morgan was reluctant to give an opinion. "I don't know if you are or not. Save it for morning."

That made her give up on the omelet, and she pushed the plate away. "I think I'll get another drink." Her face defied him to stop her. Morgan said nothing. It wasn't his place to stop her, not his liquor. He thought maybe she'd settled down a bit, but here she was, at it again, a wearisome woman. Difficult and quarrelsome, but still good looking. Good looking in spite of it.

She didn't just pour a drink and put the bottle away. She set the bottle down on the table with the cork out, as if she meant to make a night of it. Morgan decided she could only get worse as the liquor took hold, and he didn't want to sit there while she jabbed at him with her sharp tongue. Maybe O'Connor would come out and stop her. It wasn't up to him.

"I'm going to bed," he said.

"Why don't you?" she said, nasty as only she could be. "You can dream about sweet little Georgy-porgy with her sweet little fedora hat. 'Please call me George, won't you?'" Harriet's mimicry was pretty good, as it often is with mean-spirited people. Morgan didn't want to hear any more of it. He heard the clink of bottle and glass as he went to his room. No sound came from O'Connor's room. The walls were thick here, but not thick enough to seal in the big man's snoring. When O'Connor sawed wood, he sawed whole cords. There was no snoring tonight.

It was a relief to get away from Harriet. Usually, he liked to chew the fat with women, enjoyed the give and take of a lively argument as long as there was no hidden malice in it. Harriet didn't even smile as she slipped in the knife. Hell, she slipped in a no lady's handbag stiletto. She came stabbing at you with a rusty Bowie. Morgan hoped she'd have a hangover in the morning.

He was pulling off his pants when she came in the door. Morgan just looked at her. At least she didn't have the bottle, just the glass with an inch of whiskey in it. There was a key in the lock and she turned it and stood with her back against the door. Less than five minutes had passed since he'd left the kitchen, not enough time to drink that much whiskey unless she sloshed and drank as fast as she could do it. But she didn't look as if she'd been doing that. Still sharp-eyed and sharp-tongued, she said, "Keep on peeling, buster. Let's see what this poor female has been missing."

Morgan felt like an old prude for saying, "You know Duckie's right next door."

"Duckie's not in his room, he's in John's room. What do you think of them apples?"

"Where he is is his business. Not mine, not yours either." Morgan got his pants all the way off. "Why don't you go to bed?"

"That's what I came for. I can't promise you you'll get much sleep." And she started to take off her dress. It had a lot of buttons and hooks, but it fell to the floor quick enough. In a minute she stood naked.

"I'm to be raped, am I?" Morgan got the rest of his clothes off. Like her or not, she had a great body, a few reddish marks, maybe cigar burns from her whore days, otherwise smooth and rounded and white. He got into bed before his cock, coming up strong, drew her attention.

"I won't hurt you," she said, getting in beside

him. Then she began to laugh. The whiskey smell was not unpleasant. She kept on laughing and the rasp of it grated on his nerves, but at least it was better than the scolding voice that took so much away from her. Now she was feeling for his cock, the laughter fading, and he knew he was going to fuck her. A cock had no conscience, didn't know right from wrong, and a naked woman had no politics, as the other saying went, so what else would he be doing, with her pushing up against him?

"It's been a long time for me," she said. "It's never a long time for you, walking around with half a bone on. Did you fuck her? Did you fuck little Georgy-porgy, puddiny-pum, licked the girls and made them come?"

Morgan cut her short. "You want to get fucked or what?" It was rough talk, but she'd been asking for it.

"No, I'm going to fuck you." She was hurting his cock.

"Like how?" He thought he might slap her face if she squeezed too hard.

"Like I'm going to use your cock to fuck myself." She dug her nails into his cock and he slapped her face. A good thing she had short fingernails. All she got was a short slap. "You rotten son of a bitch!" she said, and started to cry.

Morgan pulled her close. "You got what you deserved. Nobody asked you to come in here and throw your weight around."

Her effort to pull away was half-hearted. "You want me to go?"

"Course not. If we can't be good friends, let's be good fucking friends. What do you say?"

Her quick nod said yes, but you wouldn't think they were any kind of friends, the way she went at him. The damnedest thing was the way she fought to keep his cock out of her. He had her on her back with her legs wide open, but when he tried to get between them and push his cock in she pulled them together. There was no clang of a gate, but that was the effect. He had to pry them apart and hold her steady before he could make the first thrust. He expected her to be tight and dry. What she was—his cock went in long and smooth—was sopping wet and fully able to take as many inches as he was able to give her. He was able to give her plenty, but she fought as much as she fucked, in the beginning. It started like that and got better as it went along.

He didn't think she was one of those women who had to be subdued before she could enjoy it. What he felt sure of was that here was a woman who didn't want to be fucked but at the same time needed it so bad that if she had to go without it any longer she'd go crazy. A good hosing would surely do her some good, and however she felt about it later, the good effects ought to last for a while. It was a relief when she finally eased back on the throttle and there was no longer any danger of a derailment and John Henry could do his work without any sudden alarms. Morgan knew he had to handle her a lot more gingerly than she'd handled his cock before he put it out of harm's way. And even as he fucked her with care, he knew all too well that she could jump the tracks and pile into him if at any moment she didn't like what he was doing to her. At first she just lay there and let him do it to her, but that changed when he started to suck her breasts. Even though her body remained sort of rigid, her crotch began to bump up into his and her fingers dug into his ass. A strange thing was that when she first livened up she made no sounds at all. Hissing through her teeth was the closest she came to expressing how she felt. But it was pretty fierce hissing, and though it wasn't the first time he'd come across it with a certain kind of woman, the sound Harriet was making put all others in the shade. He knew she was building up to a come when her body began to shudder as if an electric current had been switched on and there was nothing she could do to break loose from it. Then without any warning her head came up and she tried to bite his face and it was all he could do to keep her from inflicting real damage. He grabbed her mouth and held it shut and didn't release it until a whole string of comes subsided and it was safe to take his hand away. The fierceness of her come made him come and he gave a couple of long, hard strokes and shot his load into her. That started her coming again but this time there wasn't so much violence, and she clutched him and held him tight long after he was drained and she stopped shaking. Slowly she released him and he rolled off and lay beside her. They didn't say anything for a while. In the yellow gaslight he saw the shine of sweat on her fine, strong body, and she turned to face him. "Thank you," she said quietly, and it was the first time he'd heard her say anything nice, even close to nice. Usually she was wrangling about something, making some point that didn't need to be made, generally telling the world to go to hell. It caught him by surprise and he didn't know what to say. To say, "Shucks, twaren't nothin', ma'am" would probably get him a clout in the jaw and a couple of dozen dirty words to go with it. In the end all he said was, "You're pretty good yourself."

She had been waiting for him to say something and what he said seemed to please her. "I'm sorry I tried to bite you," she said, but offered no explanation for her behavior. Morgan could only wonder at her: inside of a minute she had come up with a thank-you and an apology. He knew her gentle mood wouldn't last, that it would be no time at all before she was her old cantankerous self again. Even so, it was good to see her as she was now, lying beside him, stroking his cock without hurting it. And after they rested and fucked again it was like being between the legs of a completely different woman. She murmured and kissed his face instead of trying to bite it. She even laughed when they rolled around on the bed and he put a pillow under her ass so he could shaft her in a way that made both of them gasp. "I'll squeeze your hand when I'm ready to come," she said. An instant later she squeezed his hand as if just saying it had excited her more than she could bear. Morgan drove his cock in all the way and gave her everything he had in him.

They rested again and talked. Mostly she did

all the talking, and as she did he sensed another change in her mood. It wasn't that she went right back to putting distance between them. It was more gradual than that, and there was no hostility that he could see. It was more to let him know that she had to be her own woman, that what had happened between them couldn't change that. She talked about getting back to detective work until he was tired of it.

"I must do something," she said.

"Why do you have to go back to being a detective? What's so satisfying about sneaking around after people, peeping through keyholes? Surely there's something else you can do."

"You mean settle down and get married. I'll bet Duckie's been talking to you. 'Fess up. Duckie the matchmaker talks to every more or less eligible man he runs in to. I'm not saying you're eligible— far from it, that ever-ready cock of yours—but he did talk to you."

"We had a few words."

"And what did you say?"

"I said I couldn't see a city girl like you milking cows and feeding chickens in the Idaho back-country. Or slopping hogs, for that matter."

Harriet laughed. "Goddamn right you couldn't. I don't know that I'll ever get married. The only man I'd even consider marrying is Duckie—he's a fine man, has been decent to me—but he's the way he is, no changing that. Back in Australia he was five years in prison. The prison did it to him."

Morgan had nothing to say to that. Duckie and

Harriet, what a pair they'd make. Talk about domestic disturbances!

"I've always wanted to be some kind of police," Harriet said, Duckie put aside for the moment. "But there's no such animal as a policewoman, and I didn't want to be a bull-dyke matron, searching women prisoners. So I did the next best thing, became a private detective. Did well at it too, until—"

She stopped and Morgan hoped she wouldn't tell the rest of the story. "But why do you have this hankering to police people? I can see when you were starting out, thinking it would be exciting, but why do you want to go on with it? Any kind of police work is dirty business."

"I knew you wouldn't understand, and, sure, I could probably do something else, but I don't want to."

"I guess you know what you want." Morgan wondered if she did. A bit late to be starting over after having had your life broken and scattered, but maybe she could do it.

"You'd understand if you had a thief for a father. That's what mine was, a petty thief, a small-time crook. Never a violent man, never carried a weapon, he just stole for a living, the way men deliver ice or milk. Sad to think of it, funny in a way, that was usually the time of morning when he came home from his kind of work."

"He doesn't sound so terrible," Morgan said.

Harriet said, "He wasn't. Compared to some other fathers in our neighborhood, he wasn't bad at all, was always a good provider when he wasn't in jail. Never served much time, in and out, small potatoes. It wasn't so good when he was inside, the coal and Christmas turkey from the district boss, if it happened to be Christmas and he wasn't there. And the canned food and the castoff clothes from the charities. But in or out, the whole neighborhood knew our father was a thief. It was like a stain on the whole family, my mother, my three brothers, and me. Going down the street, some errand, on the way to school, I'd see a policeman and I'd think, why can't my father be like that? Solid and respected."

Morgan didn't say that was the child talking. She wouldn't like it and he wanted no more arguments. He liked her better now, knowing something about her, but that didn't mean that he wanted to get tangled in what was driving her down what could turn out to be a dangerous road.

She got back to Duckie, something he'd hoped to avoid. "You'll stand up for me, won't you? When we talk in the morning, you'll make him see that my way of handling Hargis is the right way?"

"I won't go against you," he said. "You and Duckie have to thrash this out by yourselves. I'm the stranger here."

He felt her body stiffen beside him. "That won't do, Morgan."

Oh Lord! "All right. I'll say you should get a chance to try it out. That's the best I can do."

It wasn't what she wanted to hear, but she let it pass. And as a sign that she wasn't too disappointed in him, she reached for his cock. After that there was no more talking for the rest of the night. Finally they fell asleep and when Morgan woke up it was still dark outside and she was gone from the bed. Morgan looked at his watch: five minutes to five. Maybe she was in the lavatory or getting a drink of water. He hoped she wasn't drinking whiskey in the kitchen, getting up nerve to have it out with O'Connor. But maybe not: she seemed to have settled down before that last fuck.

Five minutes later, when she didn't come back, he got up and touched a match to the gaslight. Her clothes were gone. All he could think was that she had gone back to her own room downstairs. He turned off the light and went back to sleep.

Chapter Seventeen

"Harriet's gone, up and left. I can't find her anywhere."

O'Connor stood in the doorway of Morgan's room, wearing a dressing gown over undershirt and pants.

"Gone where?" Morgan sat up in bed, still tired from his exertions of last night.

"That's why I'm here, asking you. I heard her in this room last night. Had to get up to take a piss, heard her laughing—thought, why not, it'll be good for her—and went back to bed and back to sleep. When I got up just now, I found a drawer in my desk half-open, money and a gun missing. She's not downstairs, I looked."

Morgan buttoned his shirt and pulled on his boots.

O'Connor said, "What was the last time you saw her?"

"About four, around then. I woke up at five before five and she was gone. I thought she went to her room. I went back to sleep."

O'Connor tightened the cord of his dressing gown. "Well, she's gone, and it's a wet, miserable morning to be going anywhere."

Morgan looked at his watch before he put it in his pocket. It was just eight o'clock. He combed his hair back with his fingers.

"That goddamned gun! That's what I don't like. A Colt .32 double-action I took away from one of the ladies. Was she drinking much? I gave her that one drink. Did she drink after that? The bottle should tell us."

"I don't think she had that much. It didn't show on her if she did. One more after the one you gave her, a big one. She came in here not long after that, talking a lot as she usually does, but all right. I—"

"Wait till we get some coffee in us." O'Connor went down the hall, yelling for John. Morgan followed him into the dining room. O'Connor sat down heavily. He hadn't shaved and looked tired. "That damn gun bothers me more than anything else. The damn fool, she's going after Hargis the way she argued for, what else can she be doing? What did she say about that? Did you try to talk her out of it?"

"I said I wouldn't take sides, that it was between the two of you."

"You could have said more than that." O'Connor wasn't angry, but he wasn't pleased either. "You know I'm right."

"I don't know that you are. If she could be talked out of it, I would have gone along with you. I knew she was determined to go. I didn't think she'd take off before she talked to you. Maybe you should give her a chance."

John brought in the coffee and asked O'Connor what he wanted for breakfast. "What do I want? What do you think I want?" O'Connor pointed a finger at his Chinese bedmate. "I don't want chop suey, get it? I want the usual. You too, Morgan?"

Morgan said yes.

"What do you mean, give her a chance? Let her wander around the Coast with a gun and three hundred dollars in her bag? It's a daft idea, any way you look at it." O'Connor was twisting his napkin.

Morgan poured coffee for both of them. "She's not a kid and she used to be a private detective. You said she was doing all right till she met the con man. In her work she must have learned something about guns."

"I don't give a damn what she knows about guns. I don't want her carrying one around. I don't want her down there at all. *God damn it!* We'll have to go after the foolish bitch."

Morgan said, "Maybe you should give her a little time before you do that. I'm not saying you should give her a free hand down there. Give her till afternoon, is what I'm thinking. It's early yet. If she doesn't get on the telephone or come back here by afternoon, we'll go looking for her."

John brought in the steak and eggs and got out before O'Connor found something to complain about. He peppered and salted his eggs before he said anything. "A lot can happen between now and afternoon. It gets dark early and where will we be if we don't find her by then? I don't want to argue about it. You're as bad as Harriet. All the time she's going to get is how long it takes me to eat and then a short cab ride. I don't know if I'll find her right off, but I'll find her. It's better than wandering around in the dark."

"Whatever you say, Duckie. You know her better than I do."

"I wouldn't be making such a fuss if I didn't. We have here an over-wrought, high-strung woman, so miserable in her mind, I'm telling you, that there's no morning goes by that I don't fear to find her a suicide, hanging from a pipe or with the blue frothy mouth of prussic acid. So, you see, I *do* know her better than you do."

"She's that bad off?" Morgan didn't feel like eating anything else.

"Yes she is. Drinks at night in her room, thinking to dull the pain of misery, I suppose. Doesn't think I know about the drinking. I know it full well, and so does everybody else. Half the time, her bitching and arguing is the hangover coming out."

"Guess I should have caught on last night, but the way she talked wasn't so wild. For a while I thought she was settled down."

Harriet's waywardness wasn't enough to put O'Connor off his feed, and he ate as if he hadn't eaten in a week. "A good fuck can have that effect," he said solemnly, "especially if you haven't had one in a long time, but it's not enough for a woman like Harriet. Her moods swing up and down, you don't know what she's going to do next."

O'Connor threw down his napkin and stood up. "By God! I know what *I'm* going to do. Find her and drag her back here by the hair, if I have to. She can go back to bossing the ladies or I'll put her in the laundry—fuck the back talk."

Morgan got up from the table. "You want me to come along? Guess I'd better."

"No. You better go in my office and stay by the telephone, in case she decides to let us know what she's doing. I'll get dressed and be on my way. I'll turn that sinkhole upside down if I have to. No brass band, but I'll bring my little army. Trouble I don't want, surely, but pimp shit or any other kind of shit I won't take."

Morgan took his coffee into O'Connor's office and sat behind his desk. After a while he heard O'Connor going out. It was a gray, dripping day outside, not one to lift your spirits at the best of times. He didn't know the Coast—a few good nights was all he knew of it—and maybe finding Harriet wouldn't be so easy as O'Connor seemed to think. If he did find her there would be no dragging her through the streets by her hair. That was just O'Connor's way of talking when he got mad. What he'd do is bundle her into a cab, probably yelling her head off, and that could start a brawl down there. Or maybe not: O'Connor was well known to the tough mugs and they might think twice before tangling with his getting-old but still hard-as-nails Australians.

Morgan looked at the telephone, wanting it to ring. He jumped up when it did ring, but it was George Dunaway on the line. No mistaking her for anyone else, she was talking fast in that clipped voice before he had a chance to say more than his name. "Well, I must say you answer the telephone promptly enough—does Duckie have you employed as a secretary?—but you're very slow to call people who have been expecting to hear from you since sometime *yesterday*. Why is that, Morgan? I would have telephoned *you*, but I didn't want to make a nuisance of myself. Am I being a nuisance?"

"Lord no," Morgan said, then changed that to, "I'm always glad to hear from you." That wasn't right either, but he was glad to hear her voice. He should have telephoned her.

Her voice became sharper. "You're always glad to hear from me if I should *happen* to call. Like an old school chum calling between a change of trains. Unexpectedly, out of the blue, that sort of thing."

"Have mercy," Morgan said. "Let me talk."

"Of course I'll let you talk. Did you catch your little killer? Would you have called me if you *had* caught him? Of course you would have called me so I could get on with my work, and Otto with his."

"No, we didn't catch him, but he was here, watching the mission from the top floor of an old building. We know, because he left binoculars behind. The man who spotted him said he was wearing different clothes, eyeglasses."

"Oh, how exciting. But he got away. Do you think he could be lurking around here?"

"He could be, though I doubt it."

"I hope he is. Otto will tear his head off."

"Good. Here's what he looks like now. At least this is what he looked like yesterday." Morgan repeated Philly Grimes's description of the runt.

"He's quite up on the latest fashions, isn't he?" George Dunaway said. "All the men are wearing those hats. Rex wears one. So he won't stand out in a crowd, will he?"

"Afraid not," Morgan said. She didn't miss much, for all her prattle. "But that's the only description we have."

"And his companion, the Russian bear? What about him?"

"No sign of him—must be holed up somewhere, waiting for orders."

"How sinister!" George Dunaway put a shudder in her voice. "Like Frankenstein's monster, waiting to do his master's bidding."

Morgan didn't know who Frankenstein was, and he didn't ask. But he did say, "You don't have to be watching for a monster. He's just a very big man. May have a bushy beard, maybe not." Morgan was trying to think of a nice way to get her off the line. It was too early for Harriet to be calling. Just the same, he wanted to have the line clear.

"Is Duckie there?" she said.

That was the excuse he needed. "No, he's out looking for Harriet. You met her yesterday, when we were having lunch. She used to be a private detective before—she's down in the Barbary Coast trying to find Hargis. Duckie is afraid she'll get into trouble, so he's out beating the bushes."

"Well, she'll certainly get into trouble if she's as rude to people as she was to me. Though I must admit she's rather attractive in a grim sort of way. With the right clothes—" A giggle came over the line "—or no clothes at all, she could be *interesting*. How old is she, would you say?"

"About twenty-three or four." Morgan knew he shouldn't have said that.

It got her started again. "That's ridiculous. Are you blind? That woman can't be a day under forty. And not a very attractive forty. I must say, I'm astonished that you find her so very attractive."

"I don't. How is Otto?" Anything to change the subject.

"Otto is fine, guarding me like a great, fierce mastiff."

"Does he sleep at the foot of your bed?" Another dumb thing to say, and it got the response it deserved.

She gave a merry, satisfied laugh. "Ah, you are jealous. But if it will set your mind at ease, you poor man, Otto slept in the room next to Effie's last night—oh yes, she's here, can't have too much protection, can I?—and the dear fellow will be sleeping there until further notice, which, of course, must come from you."

Otto, the pork and dumplings son of a bitch! "Maybe Otto and Effie can get together. They're both Germans, aren't they?"

"Effie's family are Dutch. There's quite a difference. By the way, Otto's becoming quite the feminist. The three of us are going to a feminist lecture tonight."

Morgan could see bull-necked Otto sitting on a folding chair, in a damp, badly lit rented hall,

Kit Dalton

trying to look interested. The ass-kissing kraut would dress up as a Scotch Highlander, bagpipes and all, if the lovely lady asked him to.

"Listen," he said, trying to get back to the real world. "Duckie will be calling in any minute."

"I can take a hint." George Dunaway was annoyed again. "Yes, I'll get off the line. I certainly can do that. And if you want to talk to me again, you will have to telephone me. I hope you find your so very attractive Harriet. Goodbye."

Women! How could you figure them? Morgan went back and sat behind O'Connor's desk. Rain was running down the windowpanes and it was quiet except for small noises coming from the kitchen. A typewriter stood on a stand beside the desk, a stack of paper next to it, ready to be used. He rolled a sheet of paper into the machine—at least he knew how to do that—and tried to type 'George.' It came out as 'Georg$,' and that made him smile. The dollar sign was right above the E. He tried typing 'Lily' and got 'likky.' There must be something queer in his head to make him typewrite it like that, though what it was he couldn't imagine.

He went to the kitchen to get a bottle of beer. John was there, cleaning the gas stove, and he gave Morgan a sideways look that could only be read as: *I'm trying to get my housework done, you big bastard.* But there was more in it than that, and what it seemed to say was: *Don't get any ideas about Duckie—he's mine.* Morgan got out of there fast.

Back behind the desk, drinking beer from the

bottle, he knew it was going to be a long day unless they brought Harriet back, at least got some news of her. But the telephone remained silent and he yawned. He tried to read that morning's *Examiner*, and found nothing that interested him. The British and the Germans had their eye on the Hawaiian Islands, and Uncle Sam didn't like it. Some engineer was trying to drum up support for his plan to build a bridge to Oakland. It could be done, he said, in spite of the tides. Another crazy man wanted to revive interest in an idea that had come up during the Civil War: California should secede from the United States and declare itself "The Republic of the Pacific." Morgan knew Uncle Sam wouldn't like *that*.

He let himself go to sleep, knowing the bell would wake him if it rang. He woke up once in the afternoon, then slept on till dark. Lord, how he needed that sleep. Harriet had been as fierce in bed as any woman he'd ever met. Making up for lost time, all credit to her for that. He wondered if they'd have another night between the sheets. Maybe not. He wondered if she even liked him. There were a few moments when she seemed to have let her hair down and buried the hatchet, but that could be his imagination seeing things that weren't there. Harriet's moods swung high and low and maybe he caught her when the fucking was good and the world didn't seem so bad—then came the gray morning and she was back on the warpath.

He went out to meet O'Connor when he heard him coming in. O'Connor was pulling his raincoat off and the Chinaman was waiting to take it. "Fetch me a beer, chop-chop. Looked high and low," he said to Morgan. "Not a sign of her. Goddamn! Where can she be? God, I've got to rest my feet."

Behind the desk and looking tired, Morgan seated across from him, O'Connor said, "Holy Christ! It wasn't that we didn't look. I don't think there's a rathole we missed, starting right after we left here this morning. And it's not like we just asked questions and believed what we were told, took the word of those cocksuckers down there. No sir, we went into places and we *looked*. Oh, I made some new enemies amongst the pimps this day. One dago cunt tried to get on his high horse. 'I gotta police a-pertection, Duckie, you canta do-a dis to me, I'm a-gonna call Cap'n Gruner, I gotta warn a-you.' Spaghetti bender was lucky I didn't tear off his fucking waxed mustache, put him in a leaky barrel and float him back to Naples." O'Connor sighed. "But he didn't have Harriet. We didn't find Hargis either. He was there, showing money, but not today."

O'Connor took off his clergyman's collar and put it on the desk. There was a round red mark on his neck and Morgan thought it looked like what you might see on the neck of a man who had been half-hanged and then cut down while he was still breathing. Rubbing at the mark, O'Connor had the look of a man who'd been through something as bad as that. Well, maybe not as bad as that, but close enough to make no difference.

"I guess nothing happened here today," O'Connor said.

"Not a thing," Morgan said. "George called not long after you left."

"Nice little gal, such a sweet disposition, sensible too." O'Connor was coming out of the doldrums. He had a soft spot for George Dunaway, Morgan knew, and it wasn't altogether because she was rich. "If only Harriet could be as sensible," O'Connor added. "That little woman has a head on her shoulders, you can take that from me. Did she have anything more to say about Bullock?"

"No. She just wanted to know what happened yesterday."

"Did you tell her about Harriet?"

"No reason not to."

"Did she think Harriet was rude to her?"

"If she did, she didn't bring it up."

Now O'Connor was taking off his elastic-sided shoes. "That's a real lady for you. Harriet could learn a lot from her, take a few tips on how to behave."

"They're both nice ladies," Morgan said gallantly.

O'Connor picked up a shoe and smelled it. "Foot powder is what I need. You know damn well Harriet is no lady, or if she ever was, she doesn't act like one now. I don't know why I take so much trouble with that woman."

"I feel bad about Harriet," Morgan said, and he did. He'd been thinking about her since he woke up and saw it was dark—dark out there in the dirty streets of the Barbary Coast—a woman alone asking questions. The people she asked might or might not believe the wandering husband story.

Not everybody there would be out to kill or beat or rob her. One or two would be enough. Harriet had grown up learning to be tough, and it had worked all right when she was a detective. What she showed now wasn't much more than tough talk. Mix that with hysterics brought on by drinking, the drinking itself, self-hate, and loneliness and it wasn't toughness at all, just a flailing out at the world. . . .

O'Connor looked up from his own gloomy thoughts. "I don't see why you have to feel bad. What did you do to her? I heard her laughing, something you never hear with her."

"She told you about her father?"

"That miserable cocksucker, I'd like to break his bones. I'll bet she told you. Merciful Christ! How many a long hour I listened to it when she first came here. Thought it would do her some good for me to listen. It didn't, not that I could see. Did she tell you what a good provider the thieving father was? And did she tell you about walking down the street and seeing some harness bull and thinking to herself: why can't my dad be like him, so full of the law's majesty, so respected? If the one she's talking about was respected, then he must have been the only copper in the whole city of Chicago to be so described."

"No need to sneer at her, Duckie."

"Nobody's sneering at her, boyo. You only had to suffer her last night. I had to listen to her for a month before I decided it was time to call a halt. I'm not her father once removed, and I don't want to be. What I try here with these women is to give them a chance. Some can be helped, some can't. I can't say Harriet hasn't made some progress—as for her work, it couldn't be better—but she wallows in self-pity, as if it's something to sustain her. Her burgling father be damned! She should have had *my* father, the exact opposite of hers, with his praying and his rosary beads, and never a kind word for his family."

"Some people take things harder than others," Morgan said.

"I can do without the potted wisdom," O'Connor said. He got up, went to the telephone, and talked to the operator. "Thank you, dear, I wanted to be sure it was working." He got back in his chair. "Harriet thinks—is convinced of it—that her life is worse than anybody else's, and when you're in that frame of mind, there's not much that can be done to help you. Harriet's little secret, not so secret, is she loves to be miserable, sucks on it like a baby blanket. Take little George there, spoiled as all get-out, nothing she can't have, yet at the same time, I think, she'd never break down and feel sorry for herself if something really bad happened to her. . . ."

Morgan thought that was probably true. There was a toughness there, even a meanness, that would carry her through bad times. Hard to think what they might be. Even so, he knew she'd face up to them without bitching about it. Well, she'd bitch plenty, but she wouldn't go under.

"I think I'd better go down there," he said. "What harm can it do to take another look?"

"At this time of night?" O'Connor shook his head.

"It's late, and can't you hear the rain? And besides, where can you look that we haven't looked? We didn't poke into every building in the Coast—how could we?—but we looked in every likely place. I threatened, laid out money, called in favors—still we couldn't find her. If she's there, wherever she is, she's not out in the streets at this hour, in the rain. If you have to go, leave it till morning."

"Will you be going back in the morning?"

"A few of the boys can go, just in case. The rest of us will be looking and asking questions in the districts that border on the Coast. If she's not in the Coast, damn her, I have an idea where she might be. All we can do is keep looking. But for you to go down the Coast, this late, makes no sense."

Morgan stood up. The rain was coming down hard, beating on the windows. "I'll just take a look around, then come back."

"Dowd was down there today," O'Connor said. "I spotted the cunt watching us near the Bluebird Hotel, a place we'd been in. That was in the early afternoon. Didn't see him again for the rest of the day, which suited me fine. Any day I don't see that cunt is a good day. These days there's not much chance of seeing him at all, not like when he had white-slaving on the brain."

"You think somebody you roughed up could have called him?"

"You mean somebody that's paying him protection? Not a chance. Dowd is the only honest copper in this city. I can swear to that. Many a time in the old days I prayed for him to turn crook so I could pay him to stop bothering me. One time—

284

no witnesses—I did offer him money. You should have seen the look on his face. I guess he hates me all right."

"Maybe there are people down there he doesn't hate."

"Dowd is not on the take, I'm telling you. He's head man of the Hotel Squad, such as it is, and that's what he does. A few of the hotels in the Coast are all right. Bigtime gamblers put up in them, like the atmosphere. Cunt men with money do the same because they're safer than most places. If somebody gets rolled or murdered, Dowd has to respond to it. With the fleabags he drags his feet, but he does go if the trouble is bad enough."

Morgan was at the door. "Whatever he was doing, he must have gone home by now."

O'Connor was still in his chair, waiting for the telephone to ring. "I don't think you have to worry about Dowd," he said. "I did talk to Joe Seligman and that's settled. At least I hope it is. It's the civilians down there you have to look out for."

Chapter Eighteen

Morgan stood on the steps of the mission, buttoning the raincoat, thinking that this was a night to be following people, not finding them. Rain was coming down hard and once he was away from the mission door, with its two lights, it was dark except for streetlights spaced far apart on Front Street. This was a commercial district, ship stores mostly, some warehouses, and everything had been closed for many hours. If the runt was watching somewhere, sheltered from the rain, he could follow along with little chance of being spotted.

On a night like this, he could even bring the Russian. The Coast wasn't that far away, a patch of streets between Sansome and Grant, with a few blocks of Pacific Avenue as the main drag. It straggled away on all sides, but the city fathers tried to keep it bottled up where it was. Morgan's hotel, the Pacific, was down a few blocks from the Coast, and he thought of the Colt .45 single-action locked away in the hotel safe. It was the gun he'd rather be carrying than the one in his pocket. But maybe the Bulldog Webley was better for close work.

No "civilians" tried to rob him by the time he reached the corner of Pacific, where the bright lights started. After that, there wasn't much danger of being strongarmed, and from here on in, he'd only have to deal with the pimps and the pickpockets and the "enticers," as O'Connor called them: men who tried to steer you into dope parlors, dirty shows, whorehouses that catered to queers, anything you could name or think of. Already, barely on the outskirts of the Coast, they were dodging along beside him, calling and smirking, telling him what they had to offer. Some were touting free tryouts, others guaranteeing money back if he wasn't satisfied. He did his best to shake them off without getting too tough about it. That could be a mistake if they had tough mugs trailing along behind to back them up. But no matter how you handled it, there was always some danger of getting into a scrape that could leave you bleeding in the street, your money gone like your attackers.

He had a hundred dollars on him, enough for just about anything, but he had no plan, not even a place to start from. All around him were bright lights, the racket of shooting galleries with chained .22 caliber rifles, barkers shouting outside flea circuses and freak shows, saloons going full blast, player pianos and live musicians rattling and blaring inside. The Coast never closed. It stayed open night and day. The reformers couldn't close it, and the earthquake tremors that shook the city now and then were just a minor annoyance; maybe a tidal wave would be noticed.

Morgan went into a saloon to get away from the street rats. Noise was as thick as the smoke and he had to fight his way to the bar. There were drinkers with cloth caps and top hats, young hoodlums and young sports. In the back, on a platform raised above a dance floor, a band was adding to the din. Morgan got a bottle and a glass, paid fifty cents, and drank from the bottle. In a place like this, no telling what you'd pick up from a glass. All he was going to do was look around. Asking questions at this desperate hour would get him nowhere. The idea—the only one he had—was to drift along through the Coast, stopping into saloons, gambling halls, and other places and then move on. He wasn't bothered by the question that if O'Connor hadn't caught up with Harriet in the daytime, what chance did he have now? Sometimes things did happen by chance. George Dunaway had taken the runt's picture by chance. Coming through an alley half-drunk, Philly Grimes had spotted the runt. So maybe he'd stumble over Harriet in his nighttime tour. Fat chance, he had to admit.

But he'd come out in the rain to look for her, so he kept on doing it. The next saloon he drank a beer in wasn't much different from the one before. It was smaller and smokier, that's all, and there was no band. Cold-tea girls were working the drunks at the tables along the side and in back. Some doubled as whores, which meant that the saloon had fuck rooms upstairs; the place was not a regular whorehouse. A few street whores were drifting around trying to sell it. Some of the saloons allowed them to come in off the street when it got late. The bartenders got a cut if the whore took a customer to her room. A room was where Harriet might be; the women who didn't work in a house usually had some kind of room, and however small and roach-ridden it might be, it was better than no place at all. Some of the far-gone whores fucked their hard-up customers in doorways and alleys, but that was known as The Pox Trade, and most whores kept away from it until they were at the bottom of the bottom.

He thought he saw Harriet hanging over a drunk at a table in another place. And she still looked a little like Harriet when he got closer. Under the caked powder, the blotchy rouge, the frozen face had some good looks left, the body was nearly as shapely. But she was shorter and older and suddenly she didn't look anything like Harriet—the fire had gone out in this woman. Looking up from the mumbling drunk, thinking this big rube was more like it, she smiled like a skull and said, "Hello there, big fella," and drove Morgan out of there before she could close in for the kill.

Breathing in what passed for fresh air, he knew he could have asked her about Harriet. He could have done the same with all the whores he'd seen. But this was the desperate time of night when the johns were thinning out, too drunk for fucking, or had gone to sleep it off. All he'd get now was bullshit not very different from what Harriet got when she tried it as a schoolteacher. Only with him it would be somewhat different and probably dangerous. They wouldn't all have a choker waiting to rob him, but they might. It would be step this way, sir, I know where she is and just follow me, I'll take you to her. Then, whack!—his money would be gone and he'd wake up in an alley or not wake up at all, depending on whether they used a lead pipe or a knife.

It looked like finding Harriet by chance wasn't going to happen. He had been drifting around for an hour and all he had to show for it was a bellyful of beer. One saloon and gambling hall after another hadn't turned her up. Down the street was yet another gambling place and he thought he'd give it one more try, then head back to the mission. It was on the second floor and he went up the stairs without much hope. It was a long, narrow room that ran through the building like a railroad flat. No music here, but plenty of noise and smoke. It was cheaper looking than the other places he'd been in, but you couldn't hang around if you didn't gamble. The way he felt, sitting in on a game was the last thing he wanted to do, so he went to one of the roulette tables. A few women were in the place. Anybody could gamble in the Coast as long as they had money. At the table where he stopped, an elderly woman in an elegant silk dress was placing bets, taking ten dollar bills from a handbag that seemed to be choked with them. Standing behind her with folded arms were two big colored men with dark suits and resolute faces.

"Watch yourself, sonny," she said to Morgan in a loud voice. "These games are rigged." No one took any notice. After that she ignored him and went on laying down the tens. Morgan didn't ask her why she played at a rigged game. He didn't want to talk to her at all if he could help it. Besides, the bodyguards might take offense on her behalf. After losing the small bets he made, he left.

He was heading back to Front Street, still on Pacific Avenue, when a gun jabbed into his back and Dowd's voice said, "We'll take the gun. You just walk along, not too fast; we'll be right behind you." A hand reached into Morgan's coat, found the Webley and took it. Dowd said 'we,' so there were two of them, but the other man wasn't the big plainclothes man from the hotel. Dowd called him Dutch. "Try no tricks," Dowd said. "Dutch here has a special reason for not liking you." Dutch—Dutch Hoff, that was the name Packy mentioned back at the Brian Boru. Morgan wondered if Packy had dumped the bucket of shit on him after all.

There were a few people on the street but they didn't notice or didn't care if they did. "Where are we going?" Morgan said. "The station house? What do you want with me?"

"Just walk along," Dowd said, a shake of anger in his voice. "You'll know when you get there."

Morgan felt a push, but it wasn't Dowd doing it. "You don't have O'Connor to back you now," Hoff said.

"Quit that, shut up," Dowd said. "You'll get your chance."

Unless there was a station house on Front Street, that wasn't where they were going. The mission was down about five blocks, but they turned him the other way—still on Front, but a lot darker here. The closest street light was out and the next one still working was a good distance away. Morgan didn't think he had much of a chance of making a break for it. The avenue, with people around, would have been the place to try that. But even there they could have shot him in the back and gotten away with it. Resisting arrest, a suspect attempting to escape—anything they chose to say wouldn't be questioned.

They stopped him at the end of an alley. It was darker there than in the street. "This is the only station house you're going to get," Dowd said. "Walk in there, run if you like, no way out the other end, no need to shoot you. But if Dutch has to look for you, he'll get madder. You and your limey gun!" Dowd threw the Webley to the end of the alley.

Hoff shoved Morgan again, this time a lot harder, and he stumbled over a broken box. All Dowd said was, "Can't you wait? Mr. Blaney of Lugwig, Oregon, is going to tell us every single thing I want to know."

Morgan didn't like the sound of that. Damn O'Connor and his Ludwig, Oregon, bullshit! Dowd had checked.

"This is far enough," Dowd said when they were nearly at the end of the rubbish-strewn alley. "Back against the wall." Dowd was trying to be calm, but Morgan could hear the angry shake in his voice.

"Let me soften him up a bit before you start, Lieutenant." Hoff was swinging a leather-covered sap with his free hand. "Face the wall, mug."

That meant the kidneys. They'd have to kill him before he held still for that. Beat a man in the kidneys hard enough and he never recovered from it.

Dowd was smaller than Hoff, but he pushed him away. "I told you to quit it. You may have to beat him, but not yet. Just stand by and let me talk. You," he said to Morgan. "Your name isn't Blaney and you don't come from Lugwig, Oregon. If you don't know Ludwig, it's a tiny place and there's nobody there called Blaney. Don't deny it. Deny it and I'll give you to Dutch. What's your real name?"

Morgan answered promptly. "John Masters, Eugene, Oregon."

"You hear that, Dutch?" Dowd said. "He still lives in Oregon, but has a different name. A smart-aleck, a country joker, is that what you are? Never mind answering. I'll find out soon enough. What I want to hear about is O'Connor. Why were you with him in that hotel? Why your—his—interest in Hargis? Hargis escaped from the hospital, as if you didn't know. A woman came there claiming to be his wife. O'Connor sent her and we'll catch up to her too. You can talk now."

"I'm just staying at the mission," Morgan said.

"I said wait," Dowd said to Hoff. "Get the fuck out of my way. You—Masters, Blaney, whatever the hell your name is—you don't seem to know what you're getting into here. O'Connor and his sheeny friend Seligman are trying to ram it up my ass, but this time it's not going to work. This time I'm going to get the goods on O'Connor and you're going to help me do it. He's working a white-slave racket out of that mission, and I'm going to prove it. You're going to talk and then I'll take you into court—the D.A. will—and you're going to talk for the jury. Then we'll see how much pull he has in this town. Talk now. Last time you'll be asked nice."

"I know nothing about O'Connor," Morgan said, thinking of the beating he was going to get. He might not be able to make them kill him. "As far as—"

Hoff hit him high on the arm with the sap. Dowd must have nodded. "Hit him again," Dowd said. "Don't mark him in the face." Hoff hit him again in the same place and his arm went numb. "Suck my cock," he said to Dowd. "I won't tell you shit."

Hoff swung the sap at his mouth, but Dowd grabbed his arm and made him stop. "I told you not in the face. You," he said to Morgan, trying to control himself. "There's something wrong about you. You don't look like you fit. What're you doing, putting money into this? You're dumber than you look, if that's what you're doing. O'Connor will cheat you and throw you in the street. Listen to me, you country clown. O'Connor takes in plenty and keeps most of it for himself. What money does he spend on those whores? Fuck all. I don't know where he keeps all he steals, but he's got it. And you want to protect a cocksucker like that. Cocksucker is right! He's as queer as a three-dollar bill."

Morgan remained silent, but Dowd demanded an answer. "You don't mind doing business with a cocksucking queer?"

"I don't know anything about it," Morgan said.

"I'll tell you something else you don't know," Dowd said. "Something you should think about. I'm going to hang a white-slaving charge on O'Connor, get him ten years if it's the last thing I do. Sure this town is full of whorehouses, but most of the women are in there of their own free will. White-slaving is different. They sell white women to Mexes and chinks. They dope them and sell them, chain them to the bed. Nobody likes a white-slaver."

Dowd spoke to Hoff without turning his head. "Get ready to wake him up, Dutch. He's not paying attention."

"Like this, huh?" Hoff hit the wall beside Morgan's head. The sap was covered with leather, but the lead inside it made a clunking sound.

"You want to go to Folsom with O'Connor?" Dowd said. "I'm tired of talking to you. I'll make one last effort. You think I can't send him away if you don't talk. The catch is, you will talk, and not because of how hard Dutch beats you—show him the glove, Dutch."

"With pleasure," Hoff said. He reached into his raincoat pocket and slipped what looked like a bulky black-leather glove over his right hand. Dowd was now holding Hoff's pistol and his own. Hoff raised the gloved hand and flexed his fingers. "The salesmen at the convention call that a Persuader," Dowd said, not angry now, his voice sounding dead.

"It persuades you to talk before your balls get crushed," Hoff said. "See, it's got a kind of a hinge in it, locks onto your nuts, gives that extra grip, if you get my meaning."

Morgan knew Hoff wanted to get started, but he was waiting for Dowd to give the order. Dowd was a fanatic, but there was some decency left in him, maybe not a lot. To the fanatic any cruelty was justified in the war against the evildoer.

"You'd use a thing like that?" Morgan said.

"Yes, I would," Dowd said, getting angry again, maybe angry at himself. "If there's no other way. You've had your chance—"

Dowd stood back holding the two guns. Hoff reached at Morgan and got kicked in the stomach and staggered back yelling. He tried to grab one of the guns from Dowd, but Dowd moved away from him, saying, "Use the sap, you stupid bastard. Put him down and then use the glove." Morgan moved away as Hoff crowded in with the sap swinging in the gloved hand. "Stand still or I'll shoot you," Dowd told him, trying not to shout. Morgan, still trying to dodge the sap, shouted as loud as he could: "Shoot me, you dirty fucking pervert! You like crushing men's balls, don't—"

Morgan fell back into a pile of trash as the sap hit him in the chest. Broken bottles cut his hands, but he rolled and was out of the way when the sap swung down at his face. Then he was up on his feet, a broken bottle in his bleeding hand. He didn't have much more than the neck of the bottle, but Hoff could see it and didn't come in so fast. Dowd had his gun and wouldn't give it to him. Morgan knew Hoff wanted to kill him and not having the gun was all that was stopping him. But he had the sap and he had his big hands. He was bigger than Morgan, a lot bigger than Dowd. Dowd went around with big men to make up for the weight and muscles he lacked. Morgan wanted to get at Dowd more than the man who wanted to kill him.

"Break his arm," Dowd called.

Morgan called Dowd every dirty name he could think off. He didn't know if all his shouting would make any difference. They were in a dead end alley off a dark street and if somebody did come along, what could they do? The mission was fairly close, but not close enough for anything to be heard.

"You're queer yourself," he shouted at Dowd. "You rotten fucking cocksucking queer—"

"Break the fucking arm!" Dowd shouted, then stopped.

Morgan was still backing away from the sap, thinking if he could duck a swing he could get Hoff under the arm with the jagged glass. Hoff swung and Morgan stabbed him in the side, missing the armpit where it would have done the most damage. Morgan didn't know how bad Hoff was hurt, but he screamed as the broken bottle penetrated several layers of clothing. The scream rose up through the high, narrow walls of the alley. Morgan screamed himself, screamed and screamed, until Hoff rushed straight at him with the limp-handled sap swung back over his shoulder. It came down with tremendous force and Morgan threw himself to one side, hitting the wall with his head, sliding down until his ass hit the ground. Hoff jumped in and tried to smash his skull while he was down. The sap hit the wall and Morgan stabbed Hoff below the kneecap. Hoff backed off, hopping on one leg, shouting at Dowd, "Shoot the fucker! Shoot him! I'm wounded!"

Dowd still had Hoff's gun in his left hand. He aimed his own gun at Morgan, but didn't fire. Hoff was behind him now, pushing at him, telling him to shoot. One push was too hard and he came staggering forward. Morgan hit Dowd a glancing blow to the face that knocked him down. The guns flew out of his hands and he went scrambling after them in the rubbish. Hoff tried to rush Morgan, but his wounded leg gave way and he started to fall. Morgan slashed at his throat with the broken bottle. Instead of slashing open his jugular, all it did was make a long gash in his coat collar. But it was enough to back him off after he managed to get up on his feet. Dowd reached up to grab at Morgan and got a kick in the stomach that doubled him up, and he lay there grunting with pain. Hoff had better balance now and was moving in again. His bad knee was giving him trouble and he tried to hold it stiff so it wouldn't collapse again. He swung the sap at the hand Morgan was holding the bottle with. The sap slammed down on the jagged edges and stuck there until it tore loose. The bottle split and Morgan threw it away. His hand wasn't injured, but the force of the blow sent pain shooting all the way up his arm. Moving in again, Hoff was cursing Dowd for losing the guns. Dowd yelled back, "Get hold of him! Bring him down! Grab him! Knock him down!" Dowd yelled something and Morgan thought he'd found one of the guns. Dowd was closer than Hoff and Morgan kicked at him and missed. Strong fingers grabbed his ankle and twisted and he crashed back against the wall. Hoff staggered in and hit him a sliding blow on the side of the face before he could get up. He shook his head, trying to clear it, taking blows on both arms as he raised them to protect his face. Hoff was wielding the sap and kicking at the same time. Morgan jerked back his legs and shot them out with full force. Hoff screamed and went down on both knees and stayed there swaying until Morgan lurched to his feet and kicked him in the chest. But there was no real force behind the kick and it didn't topple him. Not yet able to get up, Hoff swung the sap at Morgan without hurting him. Morgan screamed like a madman and jumped with both feet up the way he'd seen George Dunaway do it. Both bootheels struck Hoff in the chest and flung him back and he cried out in agony as the bad knee bent the wrong way. Falling back at the same time, Morgan hit the ground with such force that the breath blew out of him like a blast of steam and inside his head it was darker than the alley. But his head cleared and when he could see again in the half-dark, Hoff was still tangled in a mess of rusty wire where he'd fallen, flailing with both legs, trying to keep him away. A kick in the balls might send him into a screaming fit and Morgan tried for it. Hoff jerked up both legs to block the blow and there was a squelching sound as the pointed boot toe dug into the bleeding knee. More sobbing than screaming, Hoff went bumping backward on his ass until he was stopped by the wall. Morgan went at him with another two-footed heel-kick that slammed his head against the bricks and threw him sideways.

Morgan dived in to grab the sap, but Hoff's thick, heavy body was on top of it. He was still grabbing when Dowd landed on his back and started to choke him. Strong fingers dug into his throat and his chest heaved as his air was cut off. Close to blacking out, he jerked his head back and smashed Dowd in the face, felt bones break and was suddenly able to breathe again. With blood spattering from his smashed nose, Dowd still managed to get up. Morgan knew there wasn't much strength left in him. He knew there wasn't much left in himself. But they tangled and fell and rolled in the dirt, and when Morgan was on top and thought he had Dowd finally pinned, he drew back his fist for a blow that would finish it. But before he could deliver it, Dowd clawed up a handful of dirt and threw it in his eyes and tried to get at his throat. Morgan slammed his fist at what he could no longer see. The shit in his eyes was sharp and gritty and burned like lye. Some of the blows took effect and he heard Dowd grunt. One slam hit nothing but hard-packed dirt and he grunted himself. Under him, Dowd was like a goddamn eel trying to get out. He did, and Morgan couldn't even see what he was clawing at. Dowd was on his feet, but Morgan shot out a leg and tripped him and he fell. About ten feet away Hoff was groaning and trying to get up. Morgan couldn't see, but he knew he was between Hoff and Dowd. The way his eyes were, what difference did it make . . .

Suddenly, Dowd cried out, "I've got you now!"

A gun went off and Hoff screamed and a body fell. In the dark Dowd was yelling and the gun fired four times, the bullets ricocheting off the brick walls. Something hit Morgan in the head and he fell on his face. There wasn't a sound except for Dowd coming close, his feet scraping through the rubbish. Morgan tried to move, but his muscles wouldn't work. He could hear all right, though. Dowd was bending over him. He heard the hammer being cocked for the killing shot. . . .

There was a sudden scuffle in the dark and Dowd cried out. Morgan smelled perfume, and he felt Dowd being lifted away and something like a small-caliber-pistol shot cracked in the dark. But it wasn't a pistol shot, the sound was different. Like a neck being snapped.

Then Morgan didn't hear anything else.

Chapter Nineteen

The stink of ammonia jerked his eyes open.

O'Connor was standing beside the bed, a cotton ball in his hand. "Sorry, no smelling salts," O'Connor said. The door was closed and no one else was in the room. It took a while for Morgan to realize that he was in his own room.

"I can see," he said. He raised his hand to the side of his head, where a patch of hair had been shaved off and a folded gauze bandage was taped in place. His head throbbed with pain.

"John washed out your eyes with a weak solution of boric acid. He's good at that sort of thing. Sand, dirt, maybe iron filings—rusty. You'll have red eyes for a few days, but John says you'll be all right. The head wound isn't much more than a burn. You want me to call a doctor?"

"Dowd shot at me. After that it was all hazy." Morgan was trying to remember.

"Dowd? You say Dowd shot you?" O'Connor was

startled out of his usual calm. "Slow now, tell it to me slow."

"First you tell me how I got here."

"Night guard found you on the steps. No telling how long you'd been there. He says he didn't hear a thing. Opened the door for no special reason and there you were. Whoever brought you here was quiet about it. Your good samaritan wanted no credit. Once again, do you want a doctor?"

"I'll stick with John for now. Say thanks. I'll do it myself. It's an awful thing to think you might be blind for good. You think I could have crawled here?" Nothing came back except the few last moments in the alley.

"The shape you were in, I doubt it," O'Connor said. "I suppose you could have. Your coat wasn't scraped though—good and dirty, but not scraped like it would be. Get on with it, will you? What happened?"

Morgan told him. Piecing it together after the fight started wasn't so easy. "Dowd fired off five rounds," he repeated. "I think the first one killed or wounded Hoff. I got hit in the head and went down. I couldn't move, but I could hear. Dowd came up close and—"

O'Connor said, "You don't have to go over it again. You got hit by a ricochet, it looks like. Spent bullet bounced off your skull, not enough to kill you. You want a headache powder?"

"No. I want a beer."

While O'Connor was gone for the beer, he felt himself up and down. Plenty of sore spots, cuts on the back of one hand, otherwise not too bad except for his head. And his eyes. Christ! he didn't want to think about his eyes.

O'Connor gave him the beer and helped him to sit up so he could drink it. "One bottle," he said firmly. "It's not good to drink with a head injury. Any injury. You look awful. I think maybe I should get a doctor."

Morgan thought it was the best beer he'd ever tasted. "You don't want a doctor getting into this."

"A discreet doctor," O'Connor said.

Morgan shifted his head on the plumped up pillows. "If I start dying you can get a doctor. Somebody should go down there and take a look."

"Nobody's going near that place, especially you. If Hoff is dead in there—and maybe Dowd, from what you think you heard—it's the last place to go looking. Whatever happened to them, the police could have found them by now. They could be watching. You think there's nothing to tie you in?"

"No. They did it nice and smooth. A few people down the street. It was wet, raining. They were walking fast, going the other way."

O'Connor pulled a chair close to the bed and sat on it. "Looks like somebody helped you, if we can go by your story. Dowd was all set to kill you and somebody grabbed him, maybe broke his neck. You're sure of that? All right, you're not sure."

"All I can tell you is what I remember."

O'Connor took the empty glass and put it on the table. "It could be somebody from the Coast, spotted them snatching you, followed along—I don't know. It could be. It could be. Everybody down there hates the police. But to butt in on two mean detectives? That's stretching it too far."

It hurt even to think. "I heard Dowd thumbing the hammer back, then suddenly he wasn't there. I heard—felt—him being lifted, then the snapping sound. Like—I can't be sure what the sound was. But just before I heard it, I smelled, like, perfume, toilet water, hair oil, something like that."

"You must have a strong sense of smell," O'Connor said. "That alley stinks like the town dump. It has to be the place I'm thinking of, right down from the corner. Even the bums don't sleep in there, it's so bad. Dowd must be crazy, pulling a stunt like that. Put me in Folsom, the crazy cunt? Well sir, that's been tried, and as I told you, I'm still here."

"I'm damn glad you're here."

"Don't go sentimental on me," O'Connor said. "I told you not to go down there. What did you accomplish, for Christ's sake?"

"Not a thing." Morgan was too tired to care.

"Hey, maybe Dowd is dead. Wouldn't that be Christmas in September! Hoff would be no great loss to humanity, but Dowd! The man who swore to put me in Folsom! I suppose I should shed a tear, but it seems the waterworks have gone dry. But I can offer up a prayer: Please Lord, let the cunt be dead!"

Morgan hadn't seen O'Connor in such a good mood since Burke got burned. "Doctors be damned," he said. "I'll get you another bottle of beer." But when he came back with it, his mood was back to gloomy. "I hate a mystery. I hate something I can't get my hands on. Maybe they'll have something in the papers. Too early yet, but I'll let you know. Drink your beer now, lie back and rest. I'll look in on you."

The second beer put Morgan to sleep. At first it was uneasy, then he sank down to where there were no bad dreams.

"You look a little better," O'Connor said when Morgan woke up. He didn't know what time it was, maybe the afternoon. It wasn't night because there was light at the window. The throbbing pain in his head had eased off some.

"We still haven't been able to find Harriet," O'Connor said. "The boys have been out all day— I was out for a while—but she's still missing. It's three o'clock now, some daylight left. I'd like to get in a few hours search. Better to do it in the daytime. You think you'll be all right? I'll leave the door open and you can call John if you need anything. He'll be by the telephone."

Morgan propped himself up. "You're not going back to the Coast?"

"No. Just a few of the boys are down there now. Just in case. The rest of us will be searching through the other districts. Some close to the Coast but not in it. A few a bit removed. Just a few blocks can make a difference in a neighborhood. What the hell do you think you're doing?"

Morgan had his legs over the side of the bed. "I think maybe I'll come along with you."

"Get back in the bed. You don't look like you

could walk to the corner. John will play nurse to you and the telephone. John will bring a bedpan if you need it."

"Jesus Christ! Duckie, I can get up to shit and piss."

"Good man. You're on the high road to recovery, I can see. In the meantime, stay in the frigging bed. Nothing in the papers, by the way."

"You think there will be?"

"Plenty, if they're found dead. I'll buy the late editions, see if there's anything. I've got to be off. Stay in bed."

Morgan got out of bed right after O'Connor left. Reaching for his pants he knocked over a chair and John came in and protested. "Duckie say you stay in bed, you stay in bed. Get up now you are one damn fool. You stay in bed I rub your back, good alcohol rub."

Morgan didn't want a rub, least of all from this guy. Then he thought, why don't you think like a human being? The man is just trying to help. Just the same, he didn't want a queer Chinaman looking at his cock.

"I'll be all right. Just sling my pants over here and—"

John was already at the door. "I fix you nice hot bath."

"And that's all you'll do," Morgan, the country bigot, said to himself. He knew George Dunaway would laugh at him.

But all John wanted to do was draw a bath. He didn't want to *give him* a bath. Right now he didn't want anybody in the tub except himself, not

307

even George Dunaway, who gave him more than a backrub in *her* tub. He decided the bullet that didn't kill him must have rattled his brain pretty good for him to be thinking along those lines. There were very few times when the thought of a woman didn't appeal to him, and this was one of them.

Chest deep in hot, soapy water, he began to feel better. Goddamn! there was nothing like a hot bath for soothing aches and pains, and he had plenty of both. His eyes burned, but, thank God, he could see. He guessed he'd shoot himself if he ever went blind. Quit the grandstanding, he told himself, you're getting as bad as Harriet.

The soap he was using had a faint lemon scent, nothing like the strong yellow soap back home. It made him think again of the sweetish smell just before Dowd went to kingdom come. Went somewhere. The smell was strong and sweet, something you'd expect to smell on a woman who laid it on too thick. But there were men who went around smelling something like that. In Missoula, Montana, there was a gambler they called Smelly Nelly because his name was Nelligan and he smelled like a whorehouse. He used pomade on his thinning locks, slapped toilet water on his face after he shaved, and carried a scented handkerchief in his sleeve.

John knocked on the bathroom door, but didn't open it. "Miss Dunaway call on the teraphone, boss. I say you in the tub and she say she go downstair to eat an' you teraphone her in thirty minute or she teraphone you. You got that, boss?

"I got it, thanks." Morgan heaved himself out of

the tub and dried off. He could have used a shave, but what the hell, all he'd be doing is talking to her on the telephone. Any other time he would have been glad to see her, but not today. She'd ask what the hell happened to him, and what the hell would he say? That he was strongarmed on a dark street? Why not? O'Connor said it happened all the time. But he'd just as soon tell her nothing till he had to. He had no intention of telling her about Dowd. Trusting her with Bullock's secrets was one thing, but putting himself in an alley with Dowd and Hoff, if they were dead, could mean a murder charge. Trust didn't stretch as far as his neck might.

He dressed and went to O'Connor's office and gave it more than half an hour before the operator put him through to her office. Nobody answered and he sat down to wait. Ten minutes later the telephone rang and she was saying, "Lolling in a bath in the middle of the day, who do you think you are? Oscar Wilde?"

That name again. "It's not the middle of the day and I wasn't lolling." The word was new to Morgan. "Whatever lolling means."

"It can mean lots of things, you naughty man. Haven't you ever lolled in the hayloft when you were a boy?"

"I guess so," Morgan said. "But I quit it when I was old enough for girls."

"Um," George Dunaway said. "Listening to your voice, I feel like doing a little lolling right this instant. I've been told they do that in Paris. Two lovers, unable to be together for some reason, stimulate each other over the telephone." George Dunaway laughed and put on a French accent. " 'Allo Central, Hi want to loll.' "

Morgan smiled. "There must be some law against this kind of conversation."

"There's a law against everything. Why don't you come over so I won't be forced to loll by myself? I'd come over there except I'm expecting a very important telephone call and can't leave the office."

"Neither can I," Morgan said. "Harriet still hasn't come back and Duckie's still looking for her. I have to stay by the telephone."

"Why aren't you—" Morgan could tell she was annoyed. Like a kid who always wanted to get her own way. "Excuse me, will you? Otto and Effie are *fighting!*" Morgan listened to her bawling them out, something about leaving the fucking furniture where it always was. It took a while.

"I tell you, they wear me out," she said when she got back to him. "Now about this ridiculous woman—Harriet, is it?—why aren't you out looking for her instead of lounging in the bathtub? Since you're so very interested in her, I should think you'd be out leading the pack."

Lord! How she carried on. "Duckie doesn't need me."

"I know just what you mean. It's terrible not to be needed."

One thing you had to say for her, she always made you smile. It was hard to think of her being left out of anything. "She'll probably turn up," he said.

"I think she's just looking for attention. Oh, I almost forgot. Have you heard about the two policemen—detectives—who were murdered on your street? I don't know where exactly. The newspaper says their bodies were found in an alley off Front Street. You mean you haven't heard?"

There it was, Morgan thought. "It wasn't in the early paper."

"Wait. I'll read it to you." Morgan heard a chair scraping the floor. Then he heard her telling off Otto, it sounded like. Then she got back on the telephone. "I can't read it," she said. "Otto spilled paint on it."

"Tell me about it," Morgan said, thinking about Dowd. He was sure he'd never mentioned Dowd. He had to be careful not to sound too interested.

"Oh, it's a very big story, as you can imagine. Two detectives! I forget their names. One was shot, but they don't know how the other one died or they're not saying. Pending an inquest, et cetera. The one they're not sure about is a lieutenant. Dowling? Dundy? It was Dowd. Lieutenant Aloysius P. Dowd."

"They have any idea who did it?" Morgan said cautiously.

"No. But the commissioner said he's confident that the case will be solved within twenty-four hours. Of course, that's what they always say, isn't it? But two detectives, one of them a lieutenant— they'll have to do something. There was something about the Black Hand's possible involvement, but I'm sure that was thrown in for dramatic effect. The Black Hand sells newspapers, so foreign, so deadly.

Whenever there's a crime like this, they always blame the anarchists or the Italians. Or both."

Morgan wanted to get off the subject. "Nothing new on Bullock?"

"Shouldn't I be the one asking that?"

"Harriet got some information about Hargis, but then she disappeared." Morgan wanted to keep it as simple as he could. "It looks like she's gone after Hargis on her own, and that's what Duckie is afraid of."

"I'm sure no harm will come to her," George Dunaway said, yawning or pretending to yawn. "A woman like that makes trouble for others, never, never for herself. Let's forget her, shall we? I've just had a very good idea, and I'm surprised I didn't think of it sooner. Why don't you leave that sweet Chinese boy in charge of the telephone? You can leave my number with him and he can ring you here if there's an emergency. All you have to do is jump into a cab and you'll be here in ten minutes."

Morgan didn't feel like jumping anywhere. "What about Otto and Effie?"

"What about them? I'll send them downstairs to eat strudel."

"I can't do it," Morgan said. "I promised Duckie I'd stay here."

"Very well then." Morgan could feel her bristling at the other end of the line. "You must attend to your business and I must attend to mine. And I can't do that, can I, while you're being such a telephone hog. Why don't you get back in the bathtub and loll over a picture of Harriet? Good-fucking-bye!"

Now there was a woman with a temper, but it came and went, didn't mark her like it did Harriet. He was still in the office trying to limber up, when John came in and said it was time for his glycerin eyedrops. So he sat in the swivel chair and John tilted it back and examined his eyes. "Red, boss," John said. "Like poach egg an' ketchup. Hol' still."

Morgan sat up with drops of glycerin running down his face. "Good, boss," John said. "I get you smoke grasses, then you don' scare the radies."

What ladies? But Morgan tried out the smoked glasses when John came back with them. They made everything look grayer than he was feeling. John was back in the kitchen, so it was safe to put them in his pocket. Back in his room he tried more exercises. The arm where Hoff had sapped him was sore and bruised. This was his pitching arm, his shooting arm, and he hoped he wouldn't have to play baseball or shoot anybody for a few days. But he'd come out of it pretty well. He could have been in the morgue with Dowd and Hoff.

He sat down to pull on his socks and boots. No Barbary Coast hoodlum had killed Dowd. O'Connor wasn't buying it, and neither was he. But if they wanted to blame it on the Black Handers, it was all right with him. Doubtful if they'd come snooping around the mission. To the police, the bad feeling between Dowd and O'Connor would be well known, but it was long in the past and O'Connor would hardly wait till now to kill his old enemy. There was a long chance that Dowd had said something to somebody before he started out

313

to perform his brand of fanatical goodness. Not too likely. If Seligman was greasing the skids for him, he'd be careful. Dowd was gambling that if he could bring a solid case of white-slaving to the district attorney, they'd have to send O'Connor to jail, even in a city like San Francisco where a political boss could make a judge shine his shoes if he felt like it. It hadn't worked out.

Morgan finished dressing and went back to the office, where he looked at a framed map of the city fixed to the wall. It was a detailed street map and he was able to find the mission building on it, but not the alley, not that it mattered. He knew where it was, would never forget it. The Barbary Coast wasn't named as such, but he knew the streets. O'Connor and his Australians were moving out from the edges of the Coast. Morgan wondered if they'd go into Chinatown, which bordered on the Coast but wasn't a part of it. The Chinamen tolerated foreigners, meaning whites—what else could they do?—but didn't encourage them. If they wanted to come in to smoke dope—the few Chinese women there were jealously guarded—that was all right as long as they paid for it. But anything else you wanted from them, no dice.

But that wasn't quite right. American money talked, even in Chinatown, so it was possible that Hargis had a safe hiding place in there. But why would he want a hidey-hole if he spent so much time showing money in the Coast? Simple enough answer: he didn't want to risk getting robbed and killed when he was too drunk to defend himself. Wherever he was, he was gone from the

Coast, O'Connor said. And so, it looked like, was Harriet.

What was he going to do for a gun if he needed it in a hurry? The Webley was somewhere at the end of the alley, or the police had found it by now. The gunsmith stores would still be open, but he didn't want to go out and sending John to buy a gun was not a good idea. Dowd was dead, so there was no reason why he couldn't get his gun from the safe at the hotel. John came in when he called.

"You know where the Pacific Hotel is?" John said no, and Morgan showed him where it was on the map. "Take a cab over there, pay my rent—here's some money—and get my gun and money from the safe. You got that?"

John nodded. "But no cab, boss, I run. You teraphone them I am coming."

Morgan knew he was right: they gave the Chinese a bad time in San Francisco. He got through to the hotel and explained the situation to the desk clerk, whose voice he recognized. "I'll give your China boy a receipt for the rent," the clerk said. "Thank you for stopping with us, Mr. Morgan. We hope you'll come back soon."

Morgan got a bottle of beer and was still drinking it in the office when John came back with his gun, his money, a spare pair of pants, and a few shirts he'd left to be washed. He put the money in a drawer in the desk and checked the Colt for rust spots. He always kept it cleaned and oiled, but San Francisco was a damp place right now. Even so, there was nothing wrong with it and he put it in the drawer with the money. Back home, he carried it in a holster; traveling, he just stuck it in his waistband and covered it with his coat. It was good to have his regular gun back. He'd owned it for a long time and liked the feel and the balance. Too bad about the Webley, a fine gun in its way, but now gone for good.

He sat there looking out the windows, watching it get dark. John came in to light the gaslamps and asked if he wanted some 'nice-good' chicken soup. "Boss say you eat chicken soup."

"What else have you got?" What did O'Connor think he was? A Mexican War veteran on his last legs?

"I got con beef," John said. "Cook real slow the way Duckie like."

Morgan ate corned beef and cabbage and drank beer with it. John brought seconds and he cleared the plate. It was after seven, the time Bullock said he went home from the store, and Morgan asked the operator to ring the house number.

"Bullock residence," the English butler said.

"This is Mr. Morgan. I'd like to speak to Mr. Bullock."

"I'm afraid Mr. Bullock isn't available at the moment, sir."

"By that do you mean he's in the house but can't talk to me? Or that he hasn't come home yet? Or that he's been home and has gone out again?"

"I'm not at liberty to say, sir. But I will tell him you called."

Pain in the ass limey. Morgan tried again, keeping his temper. "Are there nights he works late at the store?"

"I'm afraid I can't help you, sir," the butler said, and hung up.

No wonder the Irish hate you people, Morgan thought. It looked like things were taking a new turn. Bullock had said to call him anytime, made no difference how late or early it was. Call him on the shitter if need be. Well, he didn't go that far, but he got the point across. Now, all of a sudden, he was harder to find than the Hermit of Snake River.

Morgan was in the kitchen getting another beer, when the telephone rang. He got to it as fast as he could without running. It was Harriet and she sounded drunk or close to it. "Is that you, Morgan?" she asked vaguely, after Morgan had told her twice. "Where's Duckie? I want to talk to Duckie."

"Duckie's out looking for you. Where are you?"

"You'd like to know, wouldn't you?"

Oh Christ! A guessing game. "Duckie is worried about you," Morgan said. "Come on, where are you?"

"You mean Duckie's worried, but you're not?"

"Everybody's worried, including me. Don't keep me hanging here. Tell me where you are." It sounded like she could be upstairs over a saloon or in a room in back of it. Saloon sounds—a brassy band horn, a rattling drum—came over the wire, but they were muted.

Harriet was not to be budged. "All right," she said. "Duckie's worried and you're worried. What I want to know is, is Georgy-porgy worried?"

Morgan tried to get away from that. "I don't know what she is. She hasn't been here since." He wondered how far gone with drink she was. If she drank the way O'Connor said, she could probably hold a lot. Whatever condition she was in, it was like talking to a child. A drunken child.

Harriet was mumbling and Morgan said, "Tell me where you are and I'll come right over. I can't do a thing till you tell me where you are."

She might have been laughing, it was hard to tell. "You mean, be a pal and tell you where I am?"

Morgan wanted to throttle her. "That's right."

"That's right all right. Only I won't do it, see. I'm too busy to tell you. I been working. I haven't slept, see. Maybe I did sleep for a—"

"Harriet, I have to tell Duckie something when he comes back. Or if he calls I want to be able to tell him you're all right. Then he can come in from the lousy streets. This is the second day he's been trudging around in the rain."

"But *you* haven't. *You* been talking to Georgy-porgy on the telephone, you son of a bitch! Smart-aleck shitkicking son of a bitch!"

The saloon sounds were still going on. "What about Hargis? If you've been working so hard, what about Hargis?"

"Hargis is where the dogs won't bite him," she said.

"You mean he's dead?"

"That's what it usually means, Elmer. Ol' Clem has knocked around his last woman. Yes siree."

Morgan didn't know if he could believe her. Drunks said anything. He thought of O'Connor's gun. "Did you kill him? He attacked you and you killed him?"

"Wouldn't you like to know?"

"Harriet—"

"I didn't kill him, Lily killed him—" She stopped to think, or maybe she was just needling him. He wanted to reach out and grab her by the neck. "She stabbed him. He was dead when I found him. A few minutes sooner, I could have nabbed her."

"How do you know Lily did it?" If Hargis had money on him, it didn't have to be Lily.

"Lily did it. She stabbed him in the back and then cut his throat. You want more information, ask the lady herself. I'm going after her. I don't have time to talk to you. You think you're going to get into this—take the credit—after I've done all the work. Not a chance, buster."

Morgan thought she was going to hang up. "Please, Harriet, stay where you are. Where are you?"

"All right, you poor bastard. I'm at the New Hope Saloon across the street from where Hargis is—a hotel. Room 24. But I won't be here when you get here."

Harriet hung up.

Chapter Twenty

A cab took him to the New Hope Saloon. It was on a corner and the hotel, called the Carlton Arms, was across the street from it. The saloon looked and sounded tough and the hotel was plain seedy, with a few broken windows and a general air of neglect. Hargis couldn't have pulled a big job if he was here.

Morgan put on the lightly smoked glasses, thinking to change his face, but he didn't go into the saloon to ask about Harriet. There was a limit to how far he'd stick his neck out. She said Lily had stabbed Hargis to death, but he wasn't ready to take her word for it. Not yet, anyway. If she'd killed Hargis, or even if she hadn't, it was a mistake calling from a saloon so close. Saloons didn't have telephone booths, so she must have paid the owner or the manager to let her use his private line. Whoever she'd talked to would remember her and he didn't want to be remembered too. Which wouldn't be hard to do, with his red eyes and gray glasses, with the taped patch above his ear that his hat didn't quite cover.

He knew he was on the edge of Chinatown—had seen it from the cab—but there were no Chinamen around. Nobody was around except an occasional man going in or coming out of the saloon. The hotel was at the corner of Stockton and Jackson, with a side entrance on a narrow street called Marshall Place. There was a sign over the door but no light, no desk at the top of the steps that went up from the street. Morgan tried the door and found it wasn't locked in spite of the lateness of the hour. Maybe the desk clerk had forgotten to do it or maybe they weren't fussy. He eased up the steps and saw the desk right across from where he was. All he could see of the night clerk was the side of his head. It looked like he was sitting upright on a chair, not doing much of anything. Then his head moved and Morgan knew he wasn't asleep. Or maybe he was asleep and his head just moved. It was hard to tell in the dull yellow light of the lobby. Back stairs started up from where Morgan was and the clerk, if he looked that way, could see anybody coming in or going out.

He wasn't looking now and Morgan went up, keeping to the side of the bare wooden steps so they wouldn't creak. One of them creaked anyway and he stayed where he was, waiting for the clerk to come and look. Nothing happened and he got up to the second floor without being challenged. The hall was long and the only light came from a single gaslight. The other one wasn't working. Going toward Room 24 he heard loud snoring in one room, a man sobbing or coughing in another.

Harriet hadn't closed the door to Room 24 when she left. It was open a few inches and the room was silent, but not completely dark. A gaslight still glimmered in spite of a torn mantle, and he hoped it wouldn't quit altogether before he had a chance to look around. It didn't take much light to see Hargis lying dead on the blood-soaked bed. There were no signs of a struggle in the room and it looked like the first stab wound had killed him. Maybe so. He could have been dead drunk when the stabbing began. One way or the other, he hadn't put up a fight.

Morgan stood looking at the dead man. The body was dressed in a shirt and pants. There was plenty of blood on the shirt and the bed, but not as much as there would have been if he'd bled to death. Bodies bleed very little after they're dead. Once the heart stops pumping, the bleeding slows and then stops. Morgan knew that and not much else. What difference did it make how he died? Still, he found himself thinking of the way Hargis had been killed, the awful hate that must have led up to it. That would have to be Lily—a sneak thief usually didn't kill—and the stabbing and throat cutting let Harriet off the hook. She had a gun and would have used it.

He heard coughing in the hall, but the man doing it passed the door and kept on going. A quick search of the dresser turned up nothing but a few items of clothing. A new cheap shirt still had the tag on it. No suitcase, no extra boots. Hargis had left whatever he owned, which couldn't be much, back at the Fremont Hotel.

There was nothing under the bed but a chamberpot with piss in it. Anyway, what had Hargis to hide? O'Connor had taken his money and his papers. Morgan knew he should get out of there. Looking at a dead man wasn't going to get him any further along. Maybe he should try to telephone O'Connor and see if he'd returned to the mission. But John knew where Morgan was heading and besides, he'd left a note for O'Connor. The telephoning could wait. What could O'Connor do?

The only place he hadn't looked was in Hargis's pants pockets. What the hell did he expect to find there? The body stank of blood and shit and there was a taste of sour bile in Morgan's throat as he forced himself to go through the pockets. Nothing but a few coins, a few dollar bills. To get at the hip pockets he had to turn the body face-down on the bed. Turning the body pulled on the bedclothes and he saw what looked like a bunched up piece of pale blue silk. Then he saw it was a pair of women's wispy underpants and he had to hold them up to the flickering light before he was able to read what was embroidered or machine-stitched above the crotch: GANG'S ALL HERE AT LIDO PIER, in two lines of lettering. Lido Pier, wherever the hell that was.

Lido Pier sounded like one of those amusement piers that stuck out into the sea or sometimes a lake; they had one in Chicago, which he'd seen. The most famous was in Coney Island. Now and then they had naughty stories about Coney Island in the *Police Gazette:* bullshit stories about the naughty women there and what you could get other than winning a prize at a coconut pitch—very popular reading with the barbershop crowd. Country rubes liked to read about what city rubes did on the amusement piers.

Morgan took another look at the silk underpants before he put them in his pocket and got out the side door without being seen. This time the clerk was asleep, his chair tilted back, a cushion behind his head. It wasn't raining now, just dark as hell except for a few streetlights. This wasn't the Coast and it was quiet here except for the rackety saloon. No clusters of bright lights, no barkers drumming up business. Morgan stood on the corner, wondering what he should do. A party of drunks came out of the saloon, and he walked away along Jackson Street. One street was as good as another if you had no destination in mind. Maybe, he thought, he should go back to the mission and talk to O'Connor, or wait for him if he hadn't come back yet.

O'Connor knew everything there was to know about San Francisco. There was a good chance he'd know what Lido Pier was and where it was located. The hell of it was, this amusement pier—if that's what it was—could be a long way from San Francisco, maybe not even in the state of California. Lily had worked in Galveston, or so Bullock thought, so it could be there. He felt like a dirty old man, carrying a pair of lady's underpants in his pocket. What if they had nothing to do with Lily? What if Hargis used them for sniffing and

324

meat-beating? Some men used ladies underwear the way other men used dirty pictures. It was stretching it to see Hargis trying to get into them.

Walking along he thought it was just as hard to see Lily wearing something with a slogan on the crotch. A dumb slogan it was and it didn't fit with the elegant, haughty Lily he'd been told about. Bullock said it, and so did Angelique. A cold fish, Angelique said, like butter wouldn't melt in her cunt. Everybody had a hidden side to them. Maybe part of Lily's was to go around wearing joke underpants underneath her elegant clothes; Morgan had no way of knowing. He'd never seen Lily except in a small photograph that showed only her head and shoulders, and for all he'd listened to, he could get no clear picture of the woman. Was she as cold a fish as Angelique said, or did she have a sense of humor hidden behind her refined lady's manner?

It was like beating his already-sore head with a stick. But for all the questions that hurt his head, somehow he knew that Lily had been wearing the damned things when she came to kill Hargis. The poor bastard must have been awake or at least not dead-drunk asleep when she got there. And even if he'd wanted to kill her or beat her for running out on him, she had talked him out of it. But nothing had been disturbed in the room, so they must have talked—Lily telling Hargis, her husband, how good things were going to be for both of them. Then it seemed sure enough that she'd stripped down to her underpants as a gesture of good faith. Morgan knew he was just guessing, but one thing was sure.

Hargis hadn't fucked her unless he did it with his pants on. Maybe she hadn't stripped off at all. Maybe she just took off the underpants and threw them at him as a joke. A joke from their past life together, seven years before? That could be. But whatever she did, she had put him at his ease and then she had killed him.

Morgan came to a cab stand at the end of a Chinatown street. Only three cabs were in line, two drivers sitting up on their respective seats, one drinking coffee at a little open fronted hut with a tin roof. What could he lose by asking about Harriet and Lido Beach? The first driver stopped him before he finished describing Harriet.

"You want to hire a cab?" the man said.

"Maybe," Morgan said. "Not yet. Is it worth a dollar to you to answer a few questions?"

"First the dollar, mister."

Morgan handed up the dollar. "Fire away," the driver said.

Morgan asked both questions, taking some pains to describe Harriet. "You might have seen her earlier tonight."

"Only I didn't. This amusement pier, never heard of it. Mister, they don't have amusement piers in this city. If they ever did, it was before my time."

The driver was in his early twenties, and before his time didn't take in many years. Morgan got much the same answer from the second man. He was sure he hadn't seen Harriet, and as for Lido Pier, there could be such a place, but if it did exist he'd never heard of it. "But I'm in town only two years," he said. "Thanks for the buck."

The man drinking coffee was too far away to have heard any of this. But he knew Morgan was asking questions and he gave him a suspicious look before he said a word. This man was middle-aged and sour, wearing an old slicker with tears in it.

"You want a cab?" he said.

"No. I'm trying to find a woman—"

The man gave a bitter laugh. "Do I look like a pimp, mister? All right, it's too miserable out for jokes. This woman you're trying to find, she wouldn't be your wife, would she?" Morgan hesitated and the man said, "She's your wife all right. I can tell. Makes no difference. I haven't seen her."

Morgan held up another dollar bill, thinking this sour bastard was holding something back. The man eyed the dollar, but he said, "I still haven't seen her."

"Do you know where Lido Beach is?"

The man gave Morgan a crafty smile. "If you know where she's gone, why are you asking me?"

"Then you took her there?"

Before the man answered, he reached for the dollar. "I took her part way there, about halfway there, but she changed her mind and told me never mind, she had something else to do. But Lido Pier was where she wanted to go when she got in. I tried telling her as I'm telling you, there's no Lido Pier any more. Was popular five, six, ten years back, but it burned down, the whole pier, end to end."

Morgan gave the man another dollar to keep him talking. "Could it have been rebuilt?"

"I'm telling you it's gone for good. Took many a fare out there when it was a going business. Not these days. It's gone. Never that great an attraction, but the sailors at the station liked it."

"What sailors?"

"Coast Guard sailors. Used to be a training station out there. Coast Guard took over most of the area after the pier burned. Some houses on the land caught fire and burned, but not the whorehouse. That was still there after the fire. I used to take men out to it, them not caring about the pier. But that trade fell off too. Only fare I got to go there since then was tonight. Your wife. I tried to tell her it was all deserted out there now, nothing but marshes and sand dunes. I'm afraid your wife had been drinking, mister. She told me to mind my own fucking business. That was the word she used. I've always said women shouldn't drink."

A whorehouse that might still be there. "What about the sailors?" It was hard to see Lily in a two-dollar sailor whorehouse. But then Lily hadn't always been as fancy as she was now.

"Maybe there's a few still there," the driver said. "Seems to me I read something about them moving the training station down to San Diego. But don't quote me on that."

Morgan gave the driver the dollar bill he'd been holding. "I'd like to go out there, where you put my wife off."

"I didn't put her off, she got off herself. Say, mister, is there something wrong with your eyes? The glasses—"

"Caught a whiff of vapor off a tub of lye soap."

"Country fella, eh?"

"Farmer. Should have been more careful. Let's get moving, all right?"

"Just let me finish my coffee," the driver said. "The reason I asked about your eyes is, I don't see so good myself."

Bad for you, good for me, Morgan thought. But maybe he was lying. He'd seen the money plain enough. Then again, he could probably smell it.

The cab was moving at a good clip when he remembered that he should have called O'Connor. But they were moving away from the Coast by the time he thought of it, and the rest of the town was closed down for the night. He could tell the driver to turn around and go to the mission, but that would waste too much time. There might be nothing where he was going, nothing but sand and sea smell—Harriet herself hadn't gone all the way—but it was worth a look.

The streets were deserted, but it was taking a long time to get there. He saw a sign that said Judah Street, but there were more empty lots than houses on it. After a while, the street petered out and there was nothing but a few shacks and the smell of the salt air. The driver was slowing his horse. "This is where she got off," he called down when he stopped. "Right here. See that barrel with the paint on it?"

"What about it?"

"This is where she told me to pull up. I remember the barrel. Funny place to be getting off."

The driver was right. There was nothing around, no houses, no people. Off to the side of the road he saw the sheen of water in the dark. It smelled like a salt marsh. He could smell the sea somewhere up ahead, but couldn't hear it.

"I didn't like the look of it," the driver said. "A woman alone getting off in such a place. But what was I to do? Forgive me, mister, your wife is no kid. It wasn't my place to stop her. Mind your own business, she told me, so I did."

"How far to the pier from here?"

"I would say close to a mile. A good walk on this road, in the dark, if that's where she was headed. But if so, why get off here?"

"I don't know. She's a bit mixed up." Morgan got out of the cab and closed the door. "You go on back. I'd better look for her."

The driver took the money. "It would be better if you waited till daylight. Get help."

"I'll just look around. Daylight's not far off now."

"I got to get back," the driver said. "Should have been in bed hours ago. Hope you find your woman safe and sound. Good night now."

After the cab vanished into the darkness, the only sound was the wind coming from the sea. It was wet and blowing hard and cold. Morgan took the Colt from inside his belt and put it in the pocket of the raincoat. The road was rutted under his feet, and he wondered where in hell Harriet could be. It looked like she had misjudged and gotten out of the cab too soon. That would be about right, if she didn't know how far she had to go. He didn't know either and all he could do was walk along.

After a while, he could hear the sea crashing on the beach. Past a straggle of Australian pines bending in the wind, he could make out the bulk of a large house standing by itself. A glimmer of light showed in one of the upstairs windows. Either it was a weak light or the window was heavily curtained. No other lights showed anywhere, in the house or along the edge of the sea. The sky was starting to fade to gray, but it was still a long time till daylight. Rain was carried on the wind, making it hard to see, and when a big gust came he couldn't see the light at all until the wind died a little. The light remained steady but faint and when he got closer he saw where it was coming from, a second floor window in a three-story house.

Getting close was easy because of the Australian pines planted as a windbreak in years past when there were more houses here. He passed a fire-gutted house with nothing left of it but the chimney. Now he could see the twisted iron supports of the old pier, still jutting up out of the sea. Everything was gone now, but it must have been a lively place when it was in full swing. The loud music, the beer parlors, the women parading in pairs in bright clothes, and the sailors prowling after them.

He watched the house from the last line of trees. To one side of it was a marsh pond that might not have been there when this place was alive. At one time an iron fence had gone around the house. Now parts of it had fallen or had been carted away. In what once was a garden, weeds grew as tall as small trees, all bent by the wind. Weeds grew right up to the broken brick steps, came up through the rotting porch, blocked the path that went from the gate to the steps. If not for the light, the house might have been dead and abandoned for a hundred years. But the light was there and he looked up at it, faint behind cracked shutters.

Staying outside the fence, he circled the house to see if any lights showed in the back. No telling who might be in there with her. The back of the house was dark, but that didn't mean that Lily was alone. If she had confederates, they might be asleep. Somebody had to own this place—still, that somebody wasn't necessarily here. After all this time, the house could be owned by the city or the county. But he wasn't taking any chances. Lily wasn't going anyplace right now, it looked like.

He tried the back door and it wasn't locked, but the hinges squeaked when he opened it. It was a small sound made smaller by the wind, but it was enough to stop him before he opened the door the rest of the way and went on into the kitchen. An old wood burning stove stood against the wall, the back of it protected by sheet iron. The fire was out in the box, but the stove was still warm. Turning away from the stove, he nearly knocked over a table with dishes on it. The door to the hall was open and he went down a hall into a big room that must have been the parlor. If the empty house had been cared for, Morgan would have found sheeted furniture. Instead, he saw a smashed up piano tipped over on its back and a few chairs with the legs torn off. Pieces of half burned furniture were stuck in the fireplace. The toe of his boot tapped against an empty bottle and it rolled a few inches in the thick dust. He stopped and then moved on toward the stairs, stepping over other bottles. Tramps had been in here.

There wasn't a sound except the creaking of an old house hit by gusts of wind. More light was coming in now, but it was still hard to see, and when he got to the top of the stairs he heard someone walking. A faint sound, but it was there. He figured the room with the light would be about halfway down the hall. The doors of the rooms he passed were open, but he didn't check inside. He'd done enough checking. Only one door in the hall was closed and he was edging toward it when it opened and a woman came out carrying a bag. She left the door open and turned toward the stairs.

"Who are you?" was all she said when she saw him.

There was no panic in her voice, only a trace of fear, and she got it under control before he could answer.

"I'm here for the securities," he said. Then he added, "Your husband hired me to find them and bring them back. My name is Morgan."

She saw him looking at the leather bag still in her hand. "You think I have them in this? The securities you expected to find? I don't have any securities, in this house or outside it. I left my husband but I took nothing of his. How could I? Is this his way of trying to get me back?"

Morgan found himself staring at her. After all the talk, this was Lily. The golden hair was dyed dark brown and the black dress and short traveling coat were ordinary, nothing to look at twice, but nothing could disguise the arrogance and, yes, the elegance of this woman. Her face under a wide-brimmed brown hat was beautiful and somehow that was the only ordinary thing about her. On Market Street, any time the fancy stores were open you could see a dozen like her. It was the arrogance that made her beauty shine.

"I am leaving now and you are not going to stop me," she said.

"I'll stop you," Morgan said. "Throw the bag over here."

"You have no right. But if you want to look in my bag, I suppose you will."

The bag landed in the dust with a soft thud. If she had a knife in her pocket, she was too far away to use it. Morgan reached down and snapped open the bag. There was nothing in the bag but neatly folded clothes, nothing underneath.

"Well?" she said.

"We'll go in the room," Morgan said, "and then you'll tell me where they are." He left the bag where it was and followed her inside.

"I can't tell you what I don't know." She was facing him again. "What kind of trickery is Derry up to now? Tell me that if you can. Of course you can't. He's hoodwinked you as he has so many others. What did Derry say exactly?"

Bullock's first name was Derwent, yet it was funny to hear her call him Derry. It didn't suit him at all, the cranky little Yankee. A better name for him would be Silas or Ebenezer. Try as he might, Morgan couldn't see him in bed with this woman.

"Your husband said you walked off with his securities," he said. "Valued at a hundred thousand dollars. The butler says you left with two bags. He remembers offering to get a cab for you."

"Yes, he did offer to get a cab. But all he saw was one bag, the one out in the hall, and you've already looked in that."

That seemed to settle it for her. Morgan knew he'd have to search the house. It was an awful big house. "The butler is sure he saw two bags. Where's the other one?"

"Hammond never liked me," she said, thinking about it. "I suspect he stole the securities and is trying to blame it on me. Or Derry still has the securities and is paying Hammond to say what he's saying. Hammond has worked for Derry for eighteen years and there's nothing—"

Morgan felt a great weariness and knew it was only the start of it. "If Hammond stole the securities, why is he still there? You know he didn't steal them. You stole them."

The room was very big and must have been very fancy at one time. Under the dust and cobwebs was flocked wallpaper, faded and peeling now. A four-poster bed without the canopy was all that remained of the furniture. The mattress was intact, but it was mildewed and dirty. Tramps had been in here too.

She hiked herself up on the edge of the high bed. "Suppose I did take them, how would that be stealing? After all, Derry and I are married."

Morgan wasn't sure how to play this. He could hit her hard with Hargis's murder and see how she

335

took it. He thought she'd probably do what she did
with the securities: deny it absolutely, then try to
blame it on somebody else. That seemed to be her
way, and if it worked, got things confused, why not
try it again?

For now he'd soft-pedal it. "I'm not up on the
law of husbands and wives," he said. "All I know
is your husband wants the securities back. That's
why he hired me, and I mean to get them."

"Oh, do you, now?" She talked classy enough, but
it wasn't the real thing, not like George Dunaway's
clipped voice. But it was pretty good for a woman
who'd started life in an orphanage. Even that might
not be true. A good chance nothing she said was
the truth.

"You might as well give them up," he said. "If
you want to take legal action against your husband,
that's between the two of you. If you think you have
a claim on them, go to court. My job is to return
them to where they came from."

She moved back on the bed, displaying a little
more shapely leg than she had to. "You really are
working for my husband, I suppose? You didn't
just hear about the securities and decide to make
up this story?"

"Your husband's private telephone number at the
store is 867. Your maiden name was Lily Sears.
The first house you worked in was in Fort Smith,
Arkansas. You want me to go on?"

"No," she said. "I have something to tell you and
I want you to listen."

Chapter Twenty-one

"I have to be honest," she began. "I took the securities and I have no intention of giving them back. Please don't interrupt. When I married Derry, I hoped to bring him some of the things he lacked in his life. Youth, honesty, love, and what was most important, understanding. I hoped to crack that hard old Yankee shell of his. Yes, I know he's much older than I am, yet that didn't seem to matter. You see, my father was killed in a duel when I was quite young and, loving my father so much, I've always been more comfortable with older men. Do you see what I mean?"

Morgan just nodded. A coal miner fighting a duel! That's what Bullock said her father was, but that didn't have to be true either. Getting the truth out of this one would be like pulling your own teeth.

"To be brief," she went on. "Derry turned out to be a bitter disappointment. Hard as I tried, I found it impossible for him to change the habits of a lifetime. If you've been to our house, then you'll know what a shabby old place it is, yet Derry resisted every effort I made to give it some life and color. Decorating cost too much, out of the question, what was the matter with the place the way it was? Derry was just plain stingy, no other word for it. Getting the household money out of him was a nightmare, can you believe that?"

Maybe that part was true, Morgan thought. If she kept dragging this out, he'd have to light a fire under her. But he had to admit that she told it well, a fine performance all round. A lot of work had gone into making her a copy of an honest-to-goodness lady. His experience with real ladies was limited, but he'd known a few—fucked a few. In that department they were no different from other women.

"I had to make a break," she was saying. "Derry watched me like a hawk, made me account for every penny I spent. I think he suspected what was in my mind and more and more he tried to keep me in a cage. . . ."

Morgan thought of the popular song that started, "She was only a bird in a silver . . ."

"But I tricked him," Lily said. "I had to do it, he forced me. I took the securities and ran away and I'll never give them back. I feel I am entitled to a life of my own and the securities are my only chance. I'm sure you can see that."

"I can see it," Morgan said. "But where does it leave me? You think I should go back to Bullock and tell him I tried and failed?"

She was showing more of her lovely legs, but

there was nothing bawdy about it. A lady being informal with a friend. His raincoat hid the hard-on he was getting, as if she didn't know it was there. But he could keep his cock in his pants the way a cool-headed soldier keeps his sword in its sheath even when he's lusting for battle.

"That would be too much to ask, wouldn't it?" Lily said.

"It would. I won't do it." Morgan wanted to make that clear. "I'd never collect the second five hundred if I did that."

"Is that what he's paying you? A thousand dollars to recover a hundred thousand! Typical of Derry."

Morgan didn't think what Bullock was paying was so bad. Everybody he'd run into lately seemed to think a thousand dollars was chickenfeed. "It does seem kind of small," he said. "But it's money in the hand."

"If he ever pays you." Lily must have decided that she was showing too much of herself because she pulled down her dress a little, but not before Morgan saw she wasn't wearing underpants. GANG'S ALL HERE AT LIDO PIER, he thought. That could wait for a while.

"Why wouldn't he pay me?" he said.

"Because he's a miser, that's why. Once he had the securities back in his hands you could whistle for your money."

"You think I'm that much of a fool?"

"Oh no," she hastened to assure him. "I think you're very intelligent. But you see, Derry is so devious he'd look for a way to cheat you."

"But you'd never do that?" It must be light

out, Morgan thought, but you'd never know it in this musty room with the sagging old curtains pulled tight.

"I always keep my word," Lily said firmly, an echo of O'Connor. "It's always the best policy with people who can help you."

"Ah yes," Morgan. "Help you how?"

"We could share the securities, seventy-five percent for me, twenty-five for you. I think that's fair, the risk has been all mine."

"Not enough. Fifty-fifty or nothing." A crook would be greedy. Morgan knew he had to act greedy or she wouldn't believe him.

Lily pretended to think about it. "All right. If that's the only way. I think you're being unfair, but I'll agree to your terms."

"Good," Morgan said. "Where are they?"

"Not here. You'd hardly expect me to keep them here."

"Why not?"

"Because it's too great a risk. Anybody could break in and find them. They wouldn't even have to force the locks. There are none. Tramps, drifters—"

"I think they're here. If we're going to be partners—"

"They're not here, I tell you. They're in a very safe place. That's where I was going when you surprised me. You saw me. I was leaving. I had one bag. Why can't you believe me?"

What she said made some kind of sense, but he didn't believe her. This one would never let a hundred thousand dollars out of her hands. "I still think they're here."

Her sudden flash of anger was well done. "They're not here. If you don't believe me, why don't you search the house. Go on. I can't stop you."

"That's true," Morgan said, not making it a threat. Threats could wait, not that they'd do much good. Lily was an iron lady. "But that could take all day, more than that, and where would I start?"

Her phony anger was still simmering. "You can search till you're black in the face and you won't find them—they're not here!"

Morgan gave one of O'Connor's windy sighs. "I can see it's going to be a long day. Here's the way it is. I say they're here, you say they're not. I won't let you leave. Scream and holler all you like, there's no one to hear you."

"You're not going to beat me, are you?" She asked the question without fear. "You can do it, but what will it get you? The securities are in a safe-deposit box and how will it look if I'm battered and bruised when we go there? That's finally where we'll have to go."

"You wouldn't want to go alone? The way I look wouldn't scare the safe-deposit keeper? You wouldn't want me to wait on the corner, down the street?"

"That would be better, of course." Then she gave him a look. "But you'd never agree to that, would you?"

"Never," Morgan said. "Never in a million years. You could lose yourself in a crowd, or try to. You could start to scream, 'This man is bothering me, please help me!' Or you could smile and ask the manager, somebody, to let you out the back door. And there I'd be, alone at the altar."

You could learn a lot about scheming from Lily. The way she changed course was as smooth as sailing on a glassy sea. "I wish you knew me better," she said. "If you did you'd know how nice I can be. You think me hard and conniving, but the fact is I'm nothing like that. Life can be hard and one must learn to survive, but that doesn't mean that one must lose all feeling. . . ."

This one was putting too much honey in the liar's stew. Morgan thought he'd give her another five minutes before he pulled Hargis out of the hat. Not a word had been said about Hargis and she hadn't asked him how he'd tracked her to Lido Pier. Of course, throwing Hargis at her might not work. There was nothing to tie her to the killing of her husband. He had gone in and out of the hotel without being seen. Likely she had managed to do the same.

"What I'm thinking," she said, "is not so much dividing the securities as sharing them. I know nothing about you. If you're married, for example. Or if you're a regular private detective. And I certainly don't know how you came to be injured—"

"I fell down the stairs," Morgan said. "No, I'm not married. I only work as a detective when it's worthwhile." Maybe he shouldn't have said the last part. It sounded dumb.

If Lily seemed to think so, she didn't show it. "Do you get much business?"

"Not much. Mostly I work for a horse rancher. Not much money in that."

"I should think not," Lily said. "You seem to lead a rather aimless life, I'm afraid. With me, all that could change. I like you, Morgan. I like you very much. Another man would have threatened and bullied me. You are not a very young man, and I like that too. Together we could do many things. . . ."

Talk about shotgun marriages! "You think it could work?"

Lily was sure it could work, but they had to be practical about it. He could hardly expect her to fall head over heels on such short acquaintance. First, friendship and trust, and love would follow. "I have to tell you I can be difficult," she said.

He didn't doubt that for a minute. "That's all right. I'm not so easy to live with myself."

"That makes two of us," she said lightly. "But I'm sure we'll get along." From her tone you'd never know that she'd murdered her husband not many hours before. And what about Harriet? Was she lying dead somewhere in the house? Or was she dead drunk in a ditch?

"I think we should be leaving," Lily said.

"No," Morgan said. "The securities are here."

"Oh for God's sake, what can I do to convince you?" She got off the bed and moved close to him. Thinking of the knife, he grabbed her hand before she could put it in her pocket. That made her laugh. "Do you think I have a gun? I was looking for my handkerchief. See for yourself. See, I'm putting my hands above my head."

"Turn around," Morgan said. He felt the pockets of her coat, but there was nothing in them except the handkerchief. She pressed her backside against his hard-on while he was doing it. He moved back from her as she turned. "I had to be sure. I'm sorry."

His coat was open and she could see his cock pressing against his pants. "I forgive you," she said, coming close again. "And you don't have to be sorry for wanting me."

"I'm not sorry for that." Morgan pulled her close and she came to him eagerly. "Let me get this wet coat off," he said. Their eyes met. She knew he had the Colt in the pocket of the raincoat. He pulled off the coat and threw it under the bed. She didn't miss that either. He wondered where the knife was. She unbuttoned his fly and took out his cock. Her coat was on the floor by then. She unbuckled his belt and his pants dropped around his ankles. He reached around her and unfastened her dress and it fell. She got the slip off herself and now she was naked—no underpants.

There was an old blanket on the bed and they got under it. A far cry from Madame D's to this place. But Lily might have been back there, and her face said she was queen of the whores wherever she went. Morgan had a crazy thought: after all he'd been through, he was about to get the finest fuck in San Francisco. And they way she went at it, he could see how well she deserved the title. She wasn't merry and girlish like Angelique, and she wasn't hard-assed professional like the whore at Burke's place. He knew she'd kill him in a minute, but right now what she showed was a kind of loving concern, as if she really cared about him. It was a new experience for him and he liked it. He would have enjoyed it even more if not for thinking about the knife. It had to be somewhere. He didn't think she'd got rid of it. A knife seemed to suit her, silent and deadly like herself. Was it under the mattress? Was it close enough so she could reach it? It had to be somewhere. Where he didn't want it to be was in his back.

"You must relax," Lily said, showing some more of that loving concern. "You're so tense and there's no need to be. No one ever comes here, we're quite alone. Relax now and let me love you."

Let me love you. Great stuff! Knife or no knife, Morgan was more than ready to let her love him. And the odd thing was, what she was doing to his cock and balls wasn't so very different from what other whores did. But with her it was *different*. She fondled it and stoked it in the most loving way, treating it like the most precious thing in the world. It was precious to him, especially when it was in the hands of a woman who might have a knife hidden. A quick slash and that would be the end of him even if he didn't die. He'd heard of men who lost their cocks to the knife or the razor. Some died and some didn't. But what good was life without a cock?

"You're not relaxing," Lily said. "You're tense and you're tired and you must relax." She moved down smoothly between his legs and started to suck his cock. It was done gracefully, the way she did everything else. Angelique made a joke of it, the whore at Burke's did it like a chore, not a specially hard chore, just a chore that had to be gotten out of the way. Lily wasn't like that at all. You'd think she'd never sucked a cock in her life. She even managed to seem a little puzzled about how it should be done. The shy virgin bride so eager to please her new husband on the first night. Cunt hounds would like that—all ages would—but the old boys would like it best of all. No wonder she had been so much in demand. Old Bullock must have thought he was in heaven the first time she sucked his withered dick. . . .

Morgan came in her mouth, but instead of spitting it out or swallowing it, she let it run back down over his cock. "Oh dear," she said. "Let me wipe you."

She wiped his cock with a corner of the dirty blanket. So delicately, so daintily, it made him think of lace handkerchiefs. Now that his cock was relaxed, if not himself, he expected her to start again with the trip to the safe-deposit and how happy they were going to be in their new life together. But she showed no inclination to talk about anything, and that seemed like it could be another one of her ruses.

"How did you find this place?" he asked her.

"I used to work here," she said. "It was the first place I worked when I came to San Francisco. I didn't know a soul. I met a girl who worked here and she told me about it. It wasn't like the other houses," she said. "So much fun with the sailors on the pier. There was an amusement pier here then. She was a silly girl, but I liked her. We'd go out on the pier on our day off. It was summer then and the pier was always crowded. It was noisy and vulgar, but I hadn't been many places, so it was all new to me. We drank beer with the sailors, we won prizes at the booths. I'd never done anything like that before. Winning prizes. One prize I liked more than any of the others—a silly thing, but I did win it."

GANG'S ALL HERE AT LIDO PIER. Morgan thought she must be telling the truth about the underpants. That meant she didn't know that he had been to Hargis's room. Or she thought she knew, but it didn't matter if she meant to kill him.

She talked on and he didn't try to stop her. "That was six years ago, a little more," she said. "This wasn't the worst place I'd ever been in. I was just a raw country girl and it was a start in the city, but I knew I wanted more than sailors and sports with straw hats. The madam here must have seen something special in me. She'd been some kind of actress or player in her younger days and she began to nag me about how I should try to appear more ladylike. 'Gents love a lady,' she used to tell me. 'Some don't but most do.' She wasn't trying to improve me out of the goodness of her heart. If she could fix me up to look and talk like a lady it would mean that she could charge more for me. But it got me thinking. See this room? This was the fanciest room in the house, the Queen's Room, she called it. The last queen had run away and she needed a replacement. This bed was new then, so was the wallpaper. There was a carpet, pictures on the walls. . . ."

Morgan looked around. The lamp was guttering

out for want of oil, and when it did it would be dark in the room, the curtains drawn as they were. There was dust everywhere, the dank smell of an abandoned house.

"You came back here to hide," he said.

"Yes. I knew nothing about the fire on the pier. I thought this place would be as I'd left it. It's off the beaten path and I thought I could hide here for a while. Instead, I found this. I thought it would do for a few days."

"It's awful all right," Morgan said.

"I thought I'd never see it again after I left." Lily made a show of giving Morgan more of the blanket. "I had some money saved by then, so I could be choosy about the next house I worked in. If you go to them looking desperate they think you'll take anything they want to pay you. That wasn't for me. I worked in one place, but the owner was a vile foreigner, so I moved on to another which was better but not much better. The last house I worked in before I married Derry was the best of all. I suppose Derry told you about Madame De Mornay's?"

"He did."

"And did he tell you I was such a lady? She always said I was."

"He told me. You did get to be a lady." Anyway, a lady in her own mind, Morgan thought.

"It wasn't so easy," Lily said. "When I wasn't working I read books on self-improvement. No one objected, though some of the girls laughed at me. On my night off I went to the theater to listen to how the actresses talked. And I had a special friend, a professor at St. Ignatius College who helped me with my grammar . . ."

The lamp went out and Morgan thought of the knife. But all she did was press up against him, caressing him, as if she didn't want to go on talking. That was all right with him because he was hard again and wanted to fuck her. After that he'd have to get tough with her if she refused to hand over the securities. In a way he felt sorry for her, but the way she'd killed Hargis canceled that out. Not that he gave a damn about Hargis, it was just that all the stabbing and throat-cutting turned his stomach. How she got to Hargis he'd never know unless she told him. It wasn't likely that she would, even if he hit her with it point-blank. If she'd killed Harriet there was no proof of it downstairs, and he'd looked around pretty good.

"Come into me," she said. It was so sweetly said, such a gentle invitation. He slid his cock into her and she responded to his thrusts, not with violent spasms but with warm appreciation of what he was doing to her. But she quickened her pace when he did, grinding her crotch into his, and her cunt tightened around his cock and then released it. No showing off here, she knew what she could do and she did it perfectly. It went on like that and when she came with a cry he couldn't be sure if she was faking or if it was the real thing. After six months with Old Man Bullock maybe she needed it. Morgan shot his load into her and lay on top of her until she gently eased him off.

"It was very good for me," she said quietly. "I don't like to talk about things like that, but I felt

Kit Dalton

so close to you. And it's only the beginning, you must think of that. We'll go away where we can be safe, no one to disturb us." She paused and Morgan thought here it comes. "But first we must go and get the securities. We can't think of doing anything until that's done. I've been thinking. We can take a coastal steamer to Seattle, maybe to Vancouver, and from there—"

"You're lying," Morgan cut in. "You have the securities here."

"Oh God!" she said wearily. "You're starting that again."

"You killed your husband and I can prove it," Morgan said. "You knifed him in his bed, cut his throat, and you left your underpants behind. 'Gang's all here on Lido Pier.'"

Her body was rigid but her voice was calm. "I don't know what you're talking about. I don't believe a word you're saying."

"What about the police? You think they'll believe me? But the police don't have to get into this. Just show me the securities. We can still split them fifty-fifty. This is the last time we're going to argue—"

"God damn you!" she shrieked, pushing at him. "On the floor! Behind the curtains!"

It happened so fast. Morgan was getting off the bed. The door slammed open and three shots blasted at the bed. Lily screamed and Morgan jerked his head around and saw her dying with a knife in her hand. Three more shots came, then three more. Now there were two shooters cutting loose. Morgan crashed down on the floor and rolled toward his coat. Bullets tore up the floor but didn't hit him. He rolled again and got off two rounds from the single-action Colt. A face and a hand showed around the side of the door and two more bullets splintered the floor. The face pulled back just before Morgan fired at it. One of them was yelling in a high voice. The face showed again and Morgan shot a hole in it and a big body thumped down on the floor. One last shot came from the doorway and then he heard somebody running for the stairs. Morgan ran out and a small man turned at the head of the stairs and fired at him. The bullet broke a window at the end of the hall. The small man ran down the stairs and Morgan fired after him and missed. Morgan had only one round left. Running down the long hall he saw the small man grab up a bag from the floor and dive through the open front door. Morgan ran over a woman's body and out onto the porch and shot the small man in the back while he was trying to get to his feet at the bottom of the steps. Morgan went down the steps and turned the body over with his foot. The runt looked at him and died.

Morgan picked up the leather bag but didn't look inside. He didn't have to. He knew what was in it. A horse and buggy stood outside the iron fence. The reins were tied to the fence and the horse was tearing at the weeds—a city horse, used to noise. Morgan checked the reins and went back inside to look at Harriet's body. She lay on her back just inside the door. If he'd come in the front door he would have seen her. Her face had been slashed, so had her throat. It hadn't been cut like Hargis's.

A single slash had severed the big vein and her life's blood had rushed out of her, making a dark red pool on the floor. He tried to patch things together in his mind but it was all guesswork. Lily had surprised Harriet and killed her, then she'd gone upstairs to pack. She came down carrying the bag of securities, then suddenly remembered that she'd left the bag with the clothing in it behind in the room. She put the bag of securities inside the door and went back upstairs to get the other bag. She was leaving for the last time when she saw him in the hall. It was close enough. It didn't much matter.

Upstairs he looked at the body of the man he knew only as the Russian. A shaggy, matted beard masked the face so completely that it was nearly impossible to tell how old he'd been. A pungent smell came from the dead man. No mistaking it, he'd smelled it during the last moments before he blacked out in the alley. The Russian had used it to perfume his beard. It was greasy and it stank. He went through the Russian's pockets and found no identification of any kind.

Lily lay dead on the bed, a bullet hole on the left side of her chest, a double-edged pointed knife still in her hand. He got dressed and carried the bag of securities downstairs and went down the front steps. The dead runt lay on his back, his canvas rainhat knocked off by the fall. The runt sure wore a lot of hats. Morgan searched his pockets and found a wallet containing about two thousand dollars, made up of fifties, twenties, and smaller bills, all held together with a rubber band. He put the money in his pocket and looked through the papers and cards in the wallet. Three cards stated that the runt was a member of the Broadway Athletic Club, an honorary fire marshal, an out-patient at Bellevue Hospital. The runt's full name was Disraeli Gladstone Goldshire. Some handle. Morgan put the cards and the wallet back in the runt's inside pocket. Whoever found him would know who he was.

Morgan turned toward the house, thinking of Harriet. She had been an unhappy, difficult woman who was generally a pain in the ass, but she'd shared his bed and he hated to leave her like that. He could telephone the police, tell them where she was, leave no name. Or he could get O'Connor to do it.

The horse was still tearing at the weeds. A rented horse, the name of the stable that owned him was painted on the side of the buggy. Morgan climbed into the buggy and flicked the reins, but took his time getting back to where the city began. He had a lot to think about.

The runt and the Russian? How had they done it?

Chapter Twenty-two

"These securities are counterfeit," George Dunaway said.

That was nearly an hour after he'd come in carrying the bag, and while he talked it stood unopened on the dining room table. He told them about Harriet before anything else. George Dunaway said nothing. O'Connor waited to hear more.

"There was nothing I could do to stop her from going out there," Morgan said. "You knew how she was."

O'Connor nodded. "Indeed, I do." He got up. "I'll be back in a few minutes."

"Where are you going?" Morgan said.

"To make some arrangements," O'Connor said. "Before it gets too late in the day. May be too late now. But it's a lonely place out there and the weather is bad. It may be as you left it. We'll see."

George Dunaway poured more coffee for Morgan. "Do you want more brandy in it?"

354

"No more," Morgan said. "I don't want to get sleepy."

George Dunaway added brandy to her own coffee. "What was she like? I mean Lily."

Morgan didn't tell her much. "She killed two people for those securities. That should tell you what she was like."

"Not really. She must have been a very daring woman."

Morgan thought of Lily dying with the knife in her hand. If the bullets hadn't started flying he'd be lying dead out there. But he said nothing about that. It had no bearing on the overall story. "She was very determined," he said.

O'Connor came in and sat down. "My men are on their way. If the police aren't there, she'll get a decent burial. We don't want the police to trace her back to here. If my men get there in time—" O'Connor nodded toward the bag on the table. "They can't connect her to *that*."

"Open it," Morgan said. "It's all there."

"You do it," O'Connor said to George Dunaway.

They watched while she spread the securities on the table. She rubbed the edge of one of them between her fingers, then she unfolded the stiff paper and held it up to the light. She inspected the signatures carefully. "They look all right," she said. "But—Do you have a magnifying glass?"

"In the bottom drawer of my desk," O'Connor said. "Is there something wrong?"

"I don't know, I have to look." She took some of the securities into the office.

"Smart woman, that," O'Connor said.

"They were one step behind me all the time," Morgan said. "How could the kid have managed to do that? It keeps eating at me."

"The kid must have had a lot of practice. But even that doesn't explain it. But I suppose it does. It's possible the kid had some help, somebody local. But that goes against what Bender told you, the two of them always working alone."

"Bender gave me the best information he had. It wasn't fresh off the telegraph. They could have changed their way of working for this job. It wasn't just a straight killing."

"These securities are counterfeit," George Dunaway said, stopping in the doorway to shake the paper in her hand. "They're very good but they're counterfeit." She came to the table and pushed the other securities aside. "Pick up any one of them and compare the signature to the one I just brought in. Take the glass and look carefully. You'll see the two signatures are exactly alike."

O'Connor studied the signatures. "Aren't they supposed to look alike?"

"Not exactly alike, that's what's wrong with them. Instead of being signed by an expert forger they were signed by some kind of mechanical device. The paper is fed into it and it signs mechanically. The paper is perfect, so is the printing, the numbers are just numbers. After securities are printed and signed they go to the ends of the earth. The numbers are just numbers unless the legitimacy of the securities is questioned."

"Then they can be traced?" O'Connor said, putting the spread-out securities in a neat stack.

"They could be traced if securities with certain numbers are reported missing. It could be done, but it would take an enormous amount of work. Securities circulate in the same way as paper money—well, not quite so freely—but they can be found anywhere. Or, I should say, they can't be found if someone keeps them out of circulation—Holds them until they cool off, as they say. That can mean years. A problem can arise if the forger or the buyer, supposing there is one and there usually is, doesn't hold them long enough."

O'Connor picked up one of the securities, then threw it back. "By God, that's it. Bullock bought them, meant to hold them, but Lily put a crimp in his plan. That's why he kept them at the house instead of in a bank. No bank would have caught on—how could they?—but he knew they were phonies so he kept them at the house. With Lily running around with a bag of counterfeits his neck was on the block. No wonder he didn't want to confide in the police or the private agencies. You've been dealing with a desperate man, my friend."

"He didn't look so desperate to me," Morgan said. "Worried, yes. Desperate, no. He wanted it kept quiet, but he wasn't sweating about it. He seemed to think Lily could be found and the securities brought back. He asked me to bring Lily back if I could. That doesn't sound so desperate to me."

"The runt and his killer hadn't showed up yet," O'Connor said. "That could have happened the same night you were there. Early the next morning maybe. Bullock bought the dud securities from Goldshire but now he wanted them back, so he sent the kid and the Russian to get them. Bullock was to be killed to tie up the loose ends. Except the securities weren't there—Lily had them—and that's the only reason they let Bullock go on living. Suddenly getting Lily back wasn't so important any more. The best he could do to save himself was to tell them you were out there looking for Lily. So they followed along."

"I did tell him the hotel I was at," Morgan said. "The kid started following me that first day. Followed me to the Palace, all the time after that. Not knowing what to expect, Bullock's nerves started to go on him. I knew there was something wrong when I heard him on the telephone. Forget about Lily, just find the securities, he said. It fits. A few holes in it, but mostly it fits."

"Yes," George Dunaway said. "It fits well enough, but the question is, why is this batch of securities so important? These are dated two years ago, so they're not so very hot. Others not much older are in circulation. If Willy is as wily as you say that policeman says, why is he so concerned about having them traced back to him? There has to be— I'm sure of it—a more compelling reason than the counterfeiting itself."

"I don't see why," O'Connor said. "Possessing counterfeit paper, buying and selling it, can get you a long sentence. Why wouldn't Goldshire be nervous?"

"Yes. But what came up to make him nervous?" George Dunaway sipped the laced coffee. "So nervous that he sent his son and the assassin all the way here. He'd already taken a risk when he sold the counterfeits to Bullock—we're assuming he did—but such risks are a part of his business. And there would hardly be any risk at all if Bullock held the securities long enough. But he didn't, he couldn't—Lily took them. And here's my point: Goldshire couldn't have known that when he sent his son and the assassin on their deadly errand."

O'Connor nodded. "You're right, he couldn't have known. And you can be sure Bullock didn't send him a telegram informing him of the good news. He must have done a distressing thing in his pants when those two showed up on his doorstep. We came for the securities, they say. And he says, well, er, they seem to be missing. So they can't kill him now, they have to hear what he has to say. I've got this very determined man named Morgan out there looking for them he says. If anybody can find them, he can. Yes, that has to be it."

Morgan said, "That's some of it. George is right. Why is Goldshire so worried? He has to be or he wouldn't send the kid all the way here. Bender says—"

"Maybe Bender could do some checking. I know what he told you, but that's not new. We need some up-to-date information. Bender could—"

"Leave Bender out of it," Morgan said. "He's going home if he hasn't already gone. I don't want him getting mixed up in this."

Morgan must have sounded angry because O'Connor held up his hand. "All right. All right. It can be done without Bender. I'll send a telegram to New York, but I don't know how long it'll take to get a reply."

"Can you trust your man?" George Dunaway said.

"Absolutely. I could lose him his job if he talked. Soft job, a police inspector. We go back some years. Man used to be a sergeant here before it got too hot for him."

George Dunaway was delighted at the crookedness of it all. "You're wonderful, Duckie. You think of everything. But won't the telegraph operators read your message?"

O'Connor shrugged that off. "What do they care what they send? They send in their sleep. Anyway, the way I write it no telegrapher will be able to make it out. Crook lingo, police lingo, much the same."

Morgan watched George Dunaway as she watched O'Connor write out the message with a gold-nibbed fountain pen. Now and then she darted a look at the securities, as if to make sure they were still there. Funny girl, getting mixed up in something like this. The killings out at Lido Pier didn't seem to mean much to her, but why should they? O'Connor took his time with the message, crossing out words, putting new words in their places. Then he wrote the whole thing over in block letters.

"That ought to do it," he said.

John came in when he was called. O'Connor gave him the message and the money to send it. "Wait there for the reply," he said. "Don't you move from that telegraph office, get it?"

"Why are you so strict with him?" George Dunaway asked after John went out."

"It's all he understands," O'Connor said.

"I think he's rather sweet. If you ever want to get rid of him I'll be glad to take him."

Morgan wondered what she knew about O'Connor and the Chinaman. Maybe nothing. He hoped the reply from New York wouldn't take all day. He wanted to sleep. The killing of Harriet had taken something out of him, and he was tired. George Dunaway was drinking more spiked coffee. O'Connor sat with his hands folded across his belly.

"I tried to get through to Bullock last night," Morgan said. "It was after seven so I figured he'd gone home. The butler said he wasn't there. No, he said he was unavailable. Tried asking him more, but he hung up on me. Maybe I better try him again."

O'Connor got up. "Stay where you are. You'll get nothing out of him, but by Christ, I will. Hammond took money from me and he'll never get another job if I let that out."

O'Connor came back a few minutes later. "Bullock's gone over the hill," he said. "Ducked out yesterday. Went to the store the usual time, came back in the afternoon in an awful hurry, packed a couple of bags and told Hammond he had to go away on business. Said Kansas City, so we know that's not where he's heading. Could be anywhere. The strain got to be too much and he lit out."

"You don't think the butler could be lying," George Dunaway said. "Could he be hiding in the house?"

"No, he's gone. Hammond sounded like he was

ready to abandon ship himself. No pay packet forthcoming, he'll take off before the creditors start coming through the windows and doors. But I think he's more afraid of our absent friends. They came to the house a few hours after you left. Beat on the door till he had to get out of bed to answer it. Two men—our New York friends—were in the library with Bullock half the night. A lot of loud, threatening talk before they left about five o'clock. The kid must have waited till you started out for the Palace. What time was that?"

"Before six," Morgan said.

"It fits," O'Connor said. "I'm afraid you won't be collecting any more money from Bullock, now or later. Now the question we have to ask ourselves at this point: what are we going to do with the securities?"

Morgan thought he caught a look—more like a glance—between O'Connor and George Dunaway. She had been there when he finally got back from the house at the pier. O'Connor said she came over after he telephoned her. Maybe so. He knew he could be wrong about the look, but he said, "Bullock won't stay away for long. If he can scratch up some money he'll be back."

"Not a chance. Whatever happens with Harriet, it'll have to come out that Goldshire's son is dead. It will surely get into the newspapers. You say he had cards with his name in his wallet?"

"Three cards. Disraeli Gladstone Goldshire. Other papers, some money. I put the wallet back in his pocket."

"You should have taken the money, but I *know*

you're too honest for that. The police will take it if somebody doesn't beat them to it. You can take it from me, Bullock won't be back. He'll run twice as fast, bury himself twice as deep when Goldshire hears his son is dead. Wouldn't you say so, George?

"Definitely," George Dunaway said. "I don't have the slightest doubt that we've heard the last of Mr. Bullock."

O'Connor began to put the securities back in the bag. "Which brings us back to—who gets possession of these crisp little darlings? The police? The State of California? New York State? The Government of the United States? It's hard to decide who has a claim. They're forgeries so do they belong to the forger? No, he sold them, as is usual. Well, then, do they belong to the crook who bought them? Or do they belong to Willy Goldshire, who seems to think he has a claim. What do you think, George."

"I think it will be difficult to establish ownership, Duckie."

"Exactly." For some reason, O'Connor took the securities out of the bag and put them back on the table.

Morgan said, "Nobody owns them, they're phonies. We can't give them to the Treasury Department, they'd ask too many questions. But we could send them back in the mail, by express, no sender's name."

O'Connor said, "They could fall into the wrong hands."

"Then we should destroy them," Morgan said.

"Burn them up in the fireplace. Case closed."

O'Connor and George Dunaway were staring at him. "It would get them off our hands," he said.

John came in with the telegram. O'Connor tore it out of his hands and ripped it open. A slow smile spread across his wide face. "Good," he said. "Very good." He looked at them. "I'll have to translate. 'W.P. Goldshire leading suspect in murder of J. B. Villard, factor and money lender, January this year. PD believes two men hired by Goldshire killed Villard during robbery at his house. Cash, securities, jade objects stolen. No evidence against Goldshire, but the two safecrackers have since disappeared. J.B. Villard Junior, a lawyer, has been keeping case alive in the newspapers. Has hired private detectives, written to senators and congressmen, will give the NYC district attorney no peace. An attempt was made on J.B. Villard Junior's life May of this year. Has hired private bodyguards. Vows to hang W.P. Goldshire if it takes every penny he has. That is all. Love to Maggie Moran.'"

O'Connor tore up the telegram and put the pieces in a coffee cup. "There you have it, why Goldshire is so rattled. The Hound of Heaven is after him in the shape of J.B. Villard Junior. That was his mistake. He sent his thugs after the wrong man. I should say the wrong man's father. I doubt if this fellow will ever get anything on Goldshire, but he'll keep trying. So Goldshire is frightened and will stay frightened. But he will take time to think about Bullock. Not Bullock's fault, of course, but Goldshire won't take that into consideration.

When he hears of his son's death he must decide whether to pursue the matter further or let it drop. I think he will decide to let it drop. What do you think, George?"

"Why don't you ask me what I think?" Morgan said.

O'Connor looked at him with a deadpan face. "All right, what do you think?"

"I think he'll let it drop," Morgan said. "That's what I'd do in his shoes. But I guess Bullock will have to keep looking over his shoulder in case he doesn't. He won't be back, not soon anyway. So now, what about the securities? There's a good chance Villard Senior knew they were counterfeits when he bought them."

O'Connor showed some impatience. "Of course he did, he was a factor and a money lender. Or he put up the money for the forgeries. Whatever, he knew what they were. I say we keep them, let them get cold, put them to some use. We can all use money, even George here."

That made her laugh. "What do you mean even George? I have expenses you don't even know about. My feminists, other things. But in the end, if you need money, you need it. Money may be the root of all evil, but it can be used to do good."

"A truer word was never spoken," O'Connor said, sounding more Irish than Australian. "It's putting money to work that does it, no use leaving it to molder in a tin box."

"Or in a fruit jar." George Dunaway was getting into the spirit of the thing. "Or in a hollow oak tree."

"I think you're a couple of crooks," Morgan said.

They turned to stare at him. "You can keep it if you like. Just count me out. And I don't want to get any letters from Leavenworth."

"You're insane," George Dunaway said, getting very angry.

"Shush, dear," O'Connor said. "Listen to me, Morgan, there's no danger of Leavenworth if we do it right. Hold onto the securities, don't even think about them, let them cool off. A year or two from now we'll ease them into the great cash river that flows along to the bank. George can help us with that, I'm thinking."

"Yes, I could do that."

"There you see," O'Connor said to Morgan. "We'll divide them three ways and then we wait. It's only a hundred thousand and it'll never be missed. You'll have your fine ranch, I'll have my much improved mission, and George will be fighting for the rights of women. A lousy hundred thousand, but think what we can do with it. We won't waste it like the government, that's for sure. Be sensible, man, come in with us."

"How do you think the Astors and the Vanderbilts got their start?" George Dunaway wanted to know. "My own great-grandfather for that matter. That old man was a smuggler in South Carolina. You know something, Morgan, I never thought you'd turn out to be such a religious fanatic."

"Oh, leave him be," O'Connor said. "Don't try to turn the man against his principles."

"I'm very angry at you," George Dunaway said.

Her lovely violet eyes showed how angry she was. "How can I respect or feel affection for a man who shows so little regard for money? You know what you are? You're a goddamned chump!" And she stomped her foot.

Morgan tried to grab her, but she dodged away from him. "Duckie, help me!" she cried. "This man is attacking me!"

O'Connor waved his hand, didn't get up from the table. "Ah, he doesn't mean it. Settle down, the both of you."

"You tell *her* to settle down. She's driving me crazy and so are you. Listen to me. If you're trying to rope me in because you think I'll talk, put it out of your mind. I'm up to my neck in this shit, so how can I talk? If that isn't good enough for you, I don't know what is. I don't want to hear one more word about securities. Stick them up your ass for all I care."

"Such language!" George Dunaway jumped up so fast she knocked over her chair. "I refuse to remain here and be insulted by this Bible thumper." She divided the securities and put her share into the bag. "Duckie I wish you'd come over later. This man here has made me lose my temper and I *hate* that! Come over later and we'll get gay together. There may be a sweet young lady I met just yesterday. I'm sure you'll like her. We'll get gay."

"Get gay how?" O'Connor asked warily.

"Laugh! Sing! Dance! You're down in the dumps, Duckie, you need to get gay."

"I'm gay enough," O'Connor said.

367

George Dunaway turned at the door and gave Morgan a look. "I'm still very angry at you, but you can come over if you like. Perhaps I can talk some sense into you. Or if you want to be surly about it, perhaps I'll see you in Idaho one of these days."

"You can nag the flowers," Morgan said.

"Such a spirited little thing," O'Connor said, gathering up his half of the securities. "You think you'll be coming over?"

"Let me think about it," Morgan said.